"Holly James shows her impressive versatility in her third novel, *Name Your Price*. It bursts with chemistry so hot, it threatened to burn my brain while also [being] full of emotions that pulled on my heartstrings. There is so much more to Olivia and Chuck's love story than their intense physical attraction and James masterfully peels back their layers one at a time to reveal the sweet and supportive love story at the center. All set against the glamorous and fast-paced backdrop of Hollywood, *Name Your Price* is such a delicious treat for your summer reading and all year round!"

—Meredith Schorr, author of *Someone Just Like You*

"Holly James has flown to the top of my auto-buy author list! *Name Your Price* is sexy and smart with top-notch tension and laugh-out-loud humor. This is the kind of book you can devour in one sitting, and yet, these characters will be living rent-free in my mind! I absolutely adored this book from start to finish!"

—Falon Ballard, author of *Right on Cue*

"*Name Your Price* starts with a cinematic bang and never loses steam. Olivia and Chuck are the feisty, sexy, adversarial duo of readers' dreams. The way James expertly unravels these characters and explores their psychology on the page is pure magic. This is romance catnip through and through."

—Livy Hart, author of *The Great Dating Fake-Off*

"In this clever spin on the reality dating show trope, Holly James poses the question: How much money would it take to reunite with your ex? The result is a riotous good time that's perfect for readers who want to laugh and swoon in equal measure. An absolute delight from start to finish!"

—Lindsay Hameroff, author of *Till There Was You*

NAME YOUR PRICE

A NOVEL

HOLLY JAMES

DUTTON

DUTTON

An imprint of Penguin Random House LLC
penguinrandomhouse.com

Library of Congress Cataloging-in-Publication Data

Names: James, Holly (Novelist) author.
Title: Name your price: a novel / Holly James.
Description: New York: Dutton, 2024.
Identifiers: LCCN 2023050406 (print) | LCCN 2023050407 (ebook) |
ISBN 9780593473931 (trade paperback) | ISBN 9780593473948 (ebook)
Subjects: LCGFT: Romance fiction. | Novels.
Classification: LCC PS3610.A5663 N36 2024 (print) |
LCC PS3610.A5663 (ebook) | DDC 813/.6—dc23/eng/20231106
LC record available at https://lccn.loc.gov/2023050406
LC ebook record available at https://lccn.loc.gov/2023050407

Printed in the United States of America
1st Printing

BOOK DESIGN BY DANIEL BROUNT

This is a work of fiction. Names, characters, places, and incidents either are the product of the author's imagination or are used fictitiously, and any resemblance to actual persons, living or dead, businesses, companies, events, or locales is entirely coincidental.

For my husband, who is priceless
. . . and always leaves on every light in the house

NAME
YOUR
PRICE

OLIVIA MARTIN COULD NOT pinpoint the moment she became the type of woman who wanted to throw dishes, but it might have been when she met Chuck Walsh. Together, they had only two speeds: tearing each other's clothes off or tearing each other's heads off. And that morning, someone was going to get decapitated.

"Well, that's just *fine*!" Chuck bellowed, arms out as he danced his bare feet away like she might actually let loose the coffee mug in her lifted hand. He'd hardly had time to pull on his pants before they began shouting. She was scantly better in her underwear and his tee shirt she'd grabbed from the floor as they had, in fact, just finished tearing each other's clothes off.

"*Fine*? It's *fine*?" Olivia yelled, and set the mug down before she did anything else she'd regret, given she was already roiling in self-directed rage for sleeping with him. The mere thought of smashing the mug into his kitchen floor filled her with a satisfying rush, but she let it go. If only she had the same willpower to resist when it came to him.

The dishes were utilitarian at best anyway—something to stock Chuck's cabinets in an illusion of domesticity when the man lived off fancy restaurant menus and set catering. She could smash up his whole West Hollywood apartment with a bat, and he wouldn't care. If she really wanted to hurt him, she needed to go for the miniature city skyline of skincare products lining his bathroom sink. Creams and balms and serums made to preserve his gorgeous face in a state of tempting perfection. Or his closet. As much as she loved tearing his clothes off, Chuck loved putting them on, and who could blame him; he looked hot as hell in anything he wore.

They hadn't even made it to his bedroom that time. They'd done it right there on the kitchen floor in a heated makeup session that turned Olivia's messy world right side up for all of ten minutes. Ten minutes of Chuck's hands and mouth, his obscenely flawless body, his knowledge of her body like a cartographer tracing his favorite map. It had been perfect, like it always was, and she'd expressed her appreciation for his skill by digging her nails into his back and kicking the floor in repeated thuds the downstairs neighbors could surely hear.

And then Chuck opened his mouth and reminded her what they had been making up over in the first place.

"*Yes*, it's *fine* if you never want to talk to me again because, quite frankly, I can't take this anymore!" he said, and threw out his arms in a dramatic show. His wingspan took up half the granite and chrome kitchen. He lived in an apartment well above his means, something truly better suited for an A-lister, which was part of the reason he was so broke.

But Olivia was hardly one to talk. She was broke too.

Olivia grumbled again, feeling cheated that *she* was the one who'd come over to break up with *him*, and not only had they just slept together, but now he was turning himself into the victim.

He was a magnetic, irresistible, but ruinous force, and she knew what had to be done. Even the *Titanic* sank, after all. And something as big as what they had together, something electric but fraught with arrogance and egocentrism—belief that their problems would resolve on their own without any work—was always destined to sink anyway.

But she couldn't deny that the spark was still there, would probably always be there. Standing there in his kitchen, Chuck looking so good barefoot and shirtless in jeans that it should have been illegal, she felt her body aching for him. She sensed the urge in him too. She saw it in the way his tongue flashed over his lips while he stared at her, chest heaving from all the shouting. Even though they'd just had each other, they could never get enough. Even if it killed them both.

They were fire and gasoline—or they had become as much. Back when they'd met, when Olivia had come to interview him for an actor spotlight feature in *Mix*, the entertainment magazine she wrote for, there'd been an instant spark. She'd found herself agreeing to a date that same night and immediately passed the interview assignment to someone else because she knew after one afternoon with him that they had no shot at a professional relationship. The spark quickly exploded into an all-consuming addiction of fighting and making up that she'd tried and failed to kick multiple times over the past six months, but Chuck was so loyal that extracting him from her life left Olivia considering calling an exorcist.

If she was honest, though, it was as much him not leaving as it was her not letting him go.

Until now.

"I can't *believe* you didn't show up!" she shouted, her renewed anger back to boiling now that her blood had stopped speeding from being tangled up on the floor with him.

"*I was busy*," he said, repeating his useless defense from earlier.

Olivia scoffed and folded her arms. "You knew about the party for *weeks*, Chuck. You had plenty of time to plan." Memory of the disappointed look on her beloved grandmother's face from the night before stabbed her in the heart all over again. "I reserved a special room at her favorite restaurant. I even got permission to invite her best friend from the care home. *You* were supposed to be there but instead left me alone with two octogenarians wearing their best pearls and wondering why they'd been stood up!"

He flinched at each truth she volleyed at him.

Instead of listening to his excuses last night when he finally called *hours* later, she showed up at his apartment bright and early this morning to give him a piece of her mind.

She ended up giving him her body too, but that was neither here nor there. What *mattered* was that it was the final straw, and they were done. Over. No more Olivia and Chuck.

"What was *so important* that you skipped my grandmother's birthday party?" she asked, knowing his response would not measure up. Not unless he'd been rescuing kittens from a burning building and donating AB negative blood to save lives at the same time.

"I had a last-minute audition," Chuck said. He lifted his arms and let them fall at his sides.

Olivia glared at him. It was plausible since they'd gone to dinner while the sun was still high in the sky to suit the guest of honor's meal schedule. And she knew Chuck had been struggling to find work lately because of the recent incident that had given him the reputation of being difficult on set, so he was likely to jump on any opportunity he had.

A moment of weakness got the best of her.

"Did you get the part?"

Chuck chewed his lip and silently stared at the floor in response.

Olivia instantly regretted her sympathy and went back to fury. *"Argh!"* she growled, and snatched her denim shorts off the floor to step back into them.

"Where are you going?" Chuck called after her when she marched for the front door.

"Away from you, once and for all!" she said, and wrenched open the door.

He followed her and took their argument into the hallway. "Liv, I said *I'm sorry* for missing the party. I'll write Grandma Ruby an apology letter. I'll send her flowers. I'll—"

She whirled on him and shouted, "You can't fix this, Chuck!" She turned and jammed her finger into the elevator button. Thoughts of taking the stairs to get away from him faster tempted her, but ten stories seemed like nine too many in that moment. "You always do this! You're so obsessed with your career that you can't see beyond your own nose. You forget there are *other people* in the world—namely, *me!*" She reached out and pressed her palm to his bare chest to prevent him from following her as he was wont to do. The brief contact was regrettably pleasant, and she told herself it would be the last time she ever touched Chuck Walsh.

Chuck had different ideas because he followed her into the

elevator when it arrived anyway. "That's not fair, Olivia. You know I'm killing myself to make it in this industry, and I have to take opportunities when they come up."

"Well, they always seem to *come up* at the worst times, Chuck."

"You know I can't control that. Not all of us have the industry dangling at our fingertips like you do."

She turned to him with a sharp glare. "Do *not* go there."

He flinched for the slightest second, knowing he'd toed a line that was off-limits. Then his eyes narrowed into a cool glare. "Why am I always the bad guy? You think you've done everything right in this relationship?"

She folded her arms and stared up at the ceiling, not wanting to hear it. She watched the floors light up as they sank lower to the ground.

Chuck faced her with his hands on his hips, seemingly unperturbed that he was about to arrive half naked in the building lobby. "What about how you never let anyone help you with anything? Or how you turn everything into a competition that you have to *win* all the time? Or the way you leave toothpaste in the sink and use the last of the coffee and have horrible taste in music?"

She gasped, most offended by the final remark. The other things were half true, but her taste in music? Line. Crossed.

"Now you're just being mean," she said as they arrived in the lobby with a *ding*.

Chuck spilled out into the room behind her, a modern tile and stone space, with his arms out and still arguing. Her flip-flops smacked against the shiny floor. Heads turned from the few other building occupants who happened to be coming and going. They were so wrapped up in arguing with each other, the staring hardly registered. "I'm not being mean, I'm being honest!" Chuck said.

Olivia stopped near the round table in the lobby's center and caught a whiff of the freesias billowing from a vase there. She turned and Chuck almost ran into her from following so closely. Already breaking her no-more-touching promise, she jabbed her finger at his chest. "You want *honest*, Chuck? Okay, let's play this game. How about how you leave the toilet seat up and I fall in, in the middle of the night. Or how you never do the dishes. Or how you bend over backward trying to keep everyone happy all the time—"

"Yet it somehow never seems to work with you."

"—or the way you sleep through every movie I want to watch—"

"Stop picking boring movies, and I won't fall asleep."

"—or how when you chew, it sounds like rocks in a dryer—"

"You know I have a mandibular disorder."

"—or how you take up the whole bed lying diagonally—"

"Sorry I'm six foot three."

"—or how you leave on *every light in the house*. My electricity bill is higher on the nights you stay over."

"Well, that won't be a problem anymore either because—"

"WE'RE DONE!" they said at the same time.

They'd reached the lobby doors. Olivia pushed through them onto the sidewalk bathed in morning L.A. sun, the gauzy bluish kind that made one acutely aware of the city's air quality.

"You know what your real problem is, Olivia?" Chuck said, having followed her yet again.

This man. She swore.

"You never finish a fight. Look, you're even running away from this one right now. How is anything ever supposed to get better if you don't stick around to see it through?"

His honesty was too bright in the morning light. Taking a microscope to herself was not on the day's agenda, which had already fallen so far off course she'd need a crane to get it back on track. She was supposed to be broken up with him, a clean cut. Goodbye. Not whatever this dramatic drag out into the street was. Though she should have known that what had started with a spark would end with a blast.

Had she not been so caught up in arguing with him, she might have noticed the young man across the street filming them with his phone.

She turned to Chuck for what she swore to herself would be the last time. She was used to him digging in when they fought, but by the look on his face, he was finally at the end of his rope too. "Well, I guess I'm running one last time because this is over!"

"Oh, it's *so far over* it's like it never even started!" he seethed.

Olivia's blood boiled again. She hated seeing the satisfaction he was getting out of the demise of their relationship. She'd wanted the upper, righteous hand. She'd come to do the dumping, and to her horror, the dumping was mutual.

"It's so far over, *you couldn't pay me to get back together with you!*" she retaliated. Her voice bounced off the high-rise apartments and echoed across the street.

Chuck scoffed like she'd wounded him. They were both strapped for cash—for very different reasons—so the insult carried an extra punch.

"At least give me my shirt back!" he shouted.

In a fit of rage and honest indifference—her dignity was

shredded by now—Olivia stopped and peeled his tee shirt over her bra. She wadded it up and threw it at him.

"I wouldn't get back together with you *for a million dollars!*" she added for good measure. She poked him in the chest again, also for good measure, and stomped off toward her car.

Chuck pulled his tee shirt back on. "Baby, there's *no price* high enough!" he said as Olivia sank into her seat and cranked the engine.

She lowered her window and threw her middle finger in the air as she drove away, flipping off the whole scene in part as a final act of solidarity with Chuck Walsh because for once he was right: there was no price high enough.

O N SUNDAY, OLIVIA FAITHFULLY made her way to Willow Grove to visit Grandma Ruby. Anger from her fight with Chuck from the day before still swam in her blood like angry piranha. Spending Saturday cleansing her apartment of all his belongings had helped take the edge off, but the sting lingered.

At least she had severed the tie. Goodbye, Chuck.

The Willow Grove care facility nestled at the base of the Hollywood Hills in an as-advertised copse of willow trees. Olivia paid their eye-wateringly steep premium because Grandma Ruby deserved the best care. She had, after all, stepped in when Olivia's parents lost themselves to the wiles of fame.

Olivia had never known either of them. Rebecca Martin and Bradley Harris had died in a car accident when they were run off the road by a frenzied mob of paparazzi on their way home from a party. She had only been a year old and at home with a babysitter. The only memories she had of them came from two sources: her mother's old films and the vicious tabloid coverage of her parents' affair that had resulted in her birth.

See, her father, a successful Hollywood talent manager, had been married when she was born—but not to her mother. To a very famous actress. It was a scandal of such epic proportion that Grandma Ruby stepped in after their deaths to shield Olivia from the spotlight and raise her as her own.

That was why Olivia had no qualms about forking out money to allow her grandmother a comfortable life after the sacrifices she'd made. It was as if Ruby had reached the finish line with her own daughter and circled back to the start for another lap with her granddaughter. The sense of familial duty wasn't something Olivia could have swayed one way or the other as a child, but her gratitude that her grandmother hadn't shipped her off to an orphanage was immeasurable.

The problem now was that money could, unfortunately, be measured, and Olivia was running out of it. Her mother's estate had lasted most of her life. She'd used good portions of it to pay for college and graduate school and then her grandmother's care when she needed more support than Olivia could offer with a full-time career. But the funds were drying up.

Some Sundays Olivia visited later in the day and had dinner with her grandmother, but she knew that midmorning she'd find her in the community room with her best friend Violet.

She parked and crossed the parking lot to the entrance. Willow Grove boasted a sparkling fountain and neat palms lining the main stucco building. Residents were housed in quaint cottages with around-the-clock access to whatever care they needed. The nursing staff were angelic in their patience and kindness. They knew everyone by name.

She walked up the front steps and entered the tiled reception area smooth with airy, arched walkways and serene oil paintings.

"Good morning, Ms. Martin," the woman behind the reception desk greeted her. She automatically pushed a clipboard in her direction.

"Hi, Caroline," Olivia said with a soft smile. "How is she today?"

"Oh, she's lovely. She's in the community room with Violet."

"I figured," Olivia said, and returned the clipboard after signing in.

Caroline replaced it on her desk. "She'll be happy to see you," she said, in what Olivia knew was an effort to soften what she said next. "Dr. Park wants to speak with you when you have a moment."

Olivia gave her a dutiful smile, knowing that Dr. Marilyn Park, Willow Grove's director, wanted to talk to her about money. "Of course."

She'd hoped she could slip into the community room and enjoy her visit undetected, but she should have known better. She took care not to have any financial conversations within earshot of her grandmother so as not to worry her, and as soon as she turned the corner in the right direction, there was Dr. Park stepping out of her office as if she'd been waiting.

"Olivia!" she called with a pleasant smile. A striking woman with jet black hair neatly pulled back but still falling past her shoulders, Dr. Marilyn Park wore a smart pantsuit under her white coat. She clicked toward Olivia in her shiny heels and met her gaze with her sharp, dark eyes. She was easily twenty years older than Olivia and intimidating in a shrewdly intelligent way while at the same time exuding the comfort of a lifelong caregiver. "How are you?" she asked.

Olivia gripped the strap of the purse she'd slung over her

shoulder. She'd brought a bigger bag to carry in the box of raspberry tart cookies from Grandma Ruby's favorite bakery. "I'm good, thanks. And thanks again for letting me take Violet out to dinner with us the other night. I know my grandma really appreciated it." Dr. Park likely saw through Olivia's attempt to butter her up with praise, but she politely smiled, nonetheless.

"Of course. A little out and about is good for everyone once in a while." She let a silence pass as if in hope Olivia would fill it with a promise to pay her bills on time.

"We had a great time," she said instead, which wasn't entirely true since she'd spent a chunk of that time annoyed with Chuck and plotting their impending breakup. She shook the thought and tried to make an escape. "It was nice to see you, Dr. Park." She moved to step around her, but Dr. Park took a mirroring step and blocked her path.

"Olivia, Accounting tells me you're over two months behind on payment. Now, we love Ruby and want to do everything we can to help continue her time here, but we're reaching the point where we can't extend without payment anymore. Our facility is in high demand. I hate to deny space to those in need."

You mean other paying customers, Olivia thought. Willow Grove might have been filled with compassionate caregivers, but it was a business at its core. A sudden vision of finding another, inferior care home or, worst case, squishing Grandma Ruby into her tiny apartment with her swam through Olivia's mind.

"I understand, Dr. Park. And I'm sorry. I'm doing everything I can."

She nodded like she didn't fully believe her. Sympathy folded her dark brow. "Like I said, we'd hate to lose Ruby, but we can suggest alternatives for care if it would help."

Olivia clenched her jaw in fear. Dr. Park was saying everything short of *Pay or get out*. She steeled herself with a confidence she didn't have. "That won't be necessary. I'll catch up on payment soon. Please excuse me." She successfully stepped around her this time and continued down the hall.

She had no idea where she would get the money to continue paying for Willow Grove, but she'd figure it out. She *had* to figure it out. For Grandma Ruby.

Quiet sounds of chatter welcomed her closer to the community room. The sunny oval space offered a view of a courtyard with benches and a koi pond. Inside, a TV was mounted on one wall with a couch and two armchairs below it. Behind the setup were clusters of tables and chairs for gathering to chat or play a card game. Sunday was the busiest day for families visiting. Groups of similar-looking people collected around their respective elders. Great-grandchildren bobbled about. Olivia spotted her own elder sitting on the couch beneath the TV. Violet sat beside her sipping tea and chatting as if they were the only two people in the world.

Olivia joined them with a smile. "Hi, Grandma," she said with a gentle hand on her shoulder. She felt her sharp bones beneath her sweater.

Ruby turned and her face lit up like the Fourth of July. "Oh, my darling girl!" Ruby pushed herself up from the couch, the knitted blanket on her lap falling to the floor, and folded Olivia into a soft hug.

As was custom, Olivia held her breath while they embraced because hugging her now eighty-five-year-old grandmother felt like hugging a glass doll.

Ruby pulled back and held a smooth palm to Olivia's cheek. She gazed at her with watery blue eyes and a smile soft with crinkles. "I know it's only been two days, but I'm happy to see you again, dear."

"I'm happy to see you too, Grandma. Hi, Violet."

"Hello, honey," the friendly woman on the couch said. Violet wore a lavender sweater and had her wispy white hair still curled from the party. It looked like little clouds resting on her dark skin. She leaned forward to set her teacup on the coffee table.

"I brought you some treats," Olivia said, and pulled the box of cookies out of her bag.

Ruby gasped and reached for it as she sat back down. "Oh, my favorite! Vi, these are my favorite."

"I know, dear," Violet lovingly said.

Violet was just as healthy as Ruby, Olivia knew from being friendly with her son, who she sometimes ran into on visits. Randall was old enough to be Olivia's father given the generation gap between most of Willow Grove's residents and herself. She was one of the few adult grandchildren in charge of a family member. Most caregivers footing the bill were married, middle-aged people also balancing mortgages and college tuitions, not freshly thirtysomethings barely making rent and breaking up with their boyfriends.

The thought that she was in a financially disadvantaged category gave her an ounce of comfort about being behind on payments.

"Well, if you play your cards right, I might share," Ruby said, and pulled at the box's lid. Her knobby hands laced with purple veins struggled to get a grip.

Olivia gently took it from her and broke the seal to pop it open.

"Thank you, sweetheart," Ruby said, and squeezed her arm. She pulled out a golden cookie with a gooey raspberry center peeking through the cutout top and took a bite. "*Oh,* my absolute *favorite.*"

Sounds of her grandmother's happiness filled Olivia's heart with a warmth unlike anything else.

"Do you want one?" Ruby offered the box.

"Only if you're willing to part with one."

"For you, of course," Ruby said with a smile. Tiny crumbs dotted her lip. Olivia reached out to wipe a smudge of raspberry from the corner of her mouth. She took a cookie from the box and bit it. They were indeed delicious.

"So, how's your beau?" Ruby asked. "I was so sorry he couldn't make it to dinner on Friday."

Olivia reflexively rolled her eyes. She swallowed the expletive trying to slip out of her mouth. "He's sorry too. And we broke up."

Ruby gasped and Violet clucked her tongue.

She'd brought Chuck along on a few visits, and he'd been the talk of the town for days after, she'd been told. A minor celebrity with a killer smile who reminded the men of their youth and the women of feelings they hadn't had for years, sure, Olivia could see it. She knew both her grandmother and Violet had a crush on him.

Too bad he'd stomped on her last nerve.

"That's a shame," Violet said at the same time Ruby gasped again. Her inhale was so sharp, a beat of panic struck Olivia's heart like a drum.

"What is it?" she asked.

Ruby had sucked in a cookie crumb and began coughing. She held a hand to her mouth, eyes watering, and pointed at the TV. "It's my Rebecca!"

Olivia flinched at the sound of her mother's name. She and

Violet turned to the giant flat-screen, and Olivia's mouth fell open.

She expected to see one of her mom's old movies playing on TV, but instead, she saw herself. And Chuck. Both of them half dressed and shouting at each other on the sidewalk.

"What the . . . ?" She trailed off in shock.

Someone had caught them on camera from across the street. They stomped and flailed their arms, clearly arguing. She could not believe her eyes. There was Chuck looking like a six-pack snack in his jeans and nothing else, and there she was in her cutoffs, his shirt, and looking like . . . her mother. Her dark hair tumbled down her back, loose and still mussed from the scene on the kitchen floor. Her legs were bare and bronzed in her shorts. She could not fault her grandmother's confusion.

Olivia dove on the remote and turned up the volume.

"You couldn't pay me to get back together with you!" she heard herself shout.

And then she pulled off her shirt and threw it at Chuck.

Her whole body flushed with embarrassment. She had the urge to change the channel or at least jump up and stand in front of the TV to block her grandmother's view, but she was too shocked to do either.

"Honey, that's not Rebecca," Violet said, her own mouth hanging open. "That's . . . Olivia? Where's your shirt?"

"Oh my god," Olivia said, and threw her hand to her face. She went to change the channel, but Violet held out an arm to stop her.

The video froze, and the view zoomed out to a studio scene. It was one of those mindless TV shows where they played clips of videos from the internet and a comedian host made jokes about them. The host stood on a small stage beside the image from the street projected on a green screen. His lips bent into an open-mouthed grin. "If they get any royalties off this video that's blowing up the internet, she won't have to worry about getting paid for anything ever again."

A cold sweat broke out over Olivia's body at the words *blowing up the internet* at the same time Grandma Ruby gasped.

"Olivia, why are you on TV?"

Olivia grumbled, frustrated for multiple reasons. "I have no idea. I don't even know how they got this!" The video played again, and the urge to hide hit her like a lightning bolt. "I have to go."

She didn't want to leave, but she needed to get to the bottom of whatever had landed her half naked on TV. She had a sneaking suspicion it somehow had to do with a certain ex-boyfriend, and Willow Grove was not an ideal location for a shouting match over the phone with Chuck Walsh.

"You just got here!" Ruby protested.

Olivia stood and kissed her cheek. "I know, and I'm sorry. I'll visit again soon."

Violet gave her a sympathetic look and then reached for Ruby's hand. "Ruby, how about we go for a walk, hmm? Get some fresh air?"

Olivia only hoped she still had a friend like Violet when she was their age.

She stepped back into the hall and caught a glimpse of Dr. Park having a conversation with a nurse outside her office. Olivia couldn't shake the feeling it was on purpose and they intended to keep an eye on her. She thought she heard her call her name as she hurried toward the exit, and she chose to ignore it. Her concern over the video was rattling her brain too loudly to think of anything else anyway.

• • • • •

OLIVIA DROVE HOME, AND BEFORE SHE GOT THE CHANCE TO call Chuck, someone called her.

"Hello?" She answered the unknown number as she unlocked her apartment door and stepped inside. The small space still smelled like the coffee she'd made before she left to see her grandmother. She dropped her keys in a dish by the door and kicked off her shoes.

"Ms. Martin?" the man on the phone asked.

"Yes?"

"Hi. My name is Parker Stone, and I'm the executive producer on *Name Your Price*."

"The TV show?" she blurted in surprise.

"Yes. I'm calling to—"

"How did you get this number?" Olivia cut him off, still stunned and with her mind jumping to catastrophic conclusions over how far the video of her and Chuck had spread if an executive producer was calling her. She walked farther into her apartment and pulled the shades on the windows in her living room, suddenly feeling the need to hide.

"Mr. Walsh gave us your contact information."

Olivia stopped yanking her curtain halfway and rolled her eyes so hard, she thought she might pull a muscle. "Of course he did."

"What's that?"

"I said, *of course he did*. And how did you track him down, put out an ad for most insufferable actor in Hollywood?"

She thought she heard him stifle a laugh.

He came back with the sound of a hidden smile in his voice. "No. We actually found him through his agent once the video of the two of you went viral. He graciously shared your contact information with us."

Olivia felt betrayed and wanted to punch a pillow. She walked into her bedroom and sat on the foot of her bed with a huff. "*Gracious* is too generous. I'm sure there was an ulterior motive, which I have to assume is why you are calling me. So, what do you want?"

He softly chuckled. "I appreciate your candor, Ms. Martin. Mr. Walsh mentioned we might encounter it when reaching out to you."

"Yes, I'm sure that was the *exact* description he used. So, what is it?"

He cleared his throat and came back sounding rather serious. "The clip of the two of you online has reached massive viewership in record time and is still growing. We see it as an opportunity. We'd like to meet with you to discuss doing a segment on our show. We are prepared to make an attractive offer."

Olivia's blood cooled as she let his words sink in. She had zero desire to be on TV; her mother's charisma and penchant for fame did not live in her veins. But she couldn't ignore her money issue. She needed more cash than she had, and a brief stint on TV might be worth it.

"How attractive?" she asked.

"That's what we'd like to discuss with you. In person. To-morrow."

She popped up from her bed, annoyed he was being vague and that she'd considered taking the bait. "Why can't you tell me now? I've seen your show, you know. You guys offer money to people to do awful things like work at a sewage plant for a month or live in a cabin with no phone or TV. My situation is a little different."

She wandered into her kitchen and opened the pantry. This conversation—her whole morning, actually—was making her want to stress-eat. She found a hidden box of strawberry Pop-Tarts she'd missed in her sweep of Chuck's junk, his one guilty pleasure, and tore open a wrapper.

"We understand, Ms. Martin. And that's why we are prepared to make a substantial offer. We want to film a segment like we've never done before, and we think you and Mr. Walsh are the perfect opportunity."

"Hmm. Well, the only problem there is that we can't stand each other. If you want to film people fighting, there are about a hundred franchises that beat you to the punch."

He went quiet again and came back with the sound of another sly smile in his voice. "Sure, but none of those shows had the perfect setup fall into their laps like we have here."

The Pop-Tart had gone stale. She threw it in the trash.

"What does that mean?"

"It means that we want to give you an opportunity."

"To do what?"

"What you said on the street yesterday."

She burst out laughing. "You must be out of your mind. Like I said, no price high enough."

"With all due respect, Ms. Martin, Mr. Walsh said no price high enough. You said a million dollars."

Olivia stopped laughing. The weight of what he said slammed into her like a wrecking ball and left her breathless. "Are you serious?"

"Yes. If you come to the studio office tomorrow, we can discuss in more detail. I'll have my team email you the meeting information. I hope to see you there." He hung up and left her blinking at her phone in shock.

He couldn't be serious. No way. Right?

Her head was spinning, and the stale Pop-Tart had dried out her mouth. She opened the fridge and found a hard seltzer, telling herself Sunday morning booze was permissible since on any given Sunday after a visit with Grandma Ruby, there was a chance she'd be out brunching and three mimosas deep with her best friend Mansi anyway.

Calling her best friend suddenly seemed like the best idea since Mansi never failed to talk sense into her and she was a lawyer who could probably explain her rights regarding everything that had just happened.

She took her seltzer to her couch and put her phone on speaker.

"Hey," Mansi answered, out of breath and surely on her Peloton.

"Hi. So, you know that show *Name Your Price*?" she said with no further preamble.

"The one where they pay people to do shitty things? Yeah," Mansi said, her breath tight. How she could bike and talk at the same time, Olivia didn't know. She imagined her in her home gym in her Westwood high-rise. Mansi made gobs of cash in the corporate law sphere and was one of the most intelligent people Olivia had ever met. "Also, what's with that clip of you and Chuck online?"

Olivia sat up and sloshed her seltzer. "You've seen it?"

"Yeah. It's all over the web. I assumed you knew."

Olivia thumbed her phone to find that the clip was indeed trending. "Oh god."

"What's the matter? You guys look hot."

That fact was, admittedly, hard to deny. But that didn't mean

Olivia wanted hundreds of thousands of people gawking at her in her underwear.

"Thank you, but regardless, I don't know who posted it, and *Name Your Price* just called me about being on their show. So, can I sue someone or something?"

The whir of Mansi's bike slowed in the background. She took a deep breath, and her words began coming in a more fluid stream instead of staccato bursts. "Maybe. What happened?"

Olivia sighed out a big breath, exhausted by it all. "Long story, but Chuck and I broke up yesterday morning and that argument was the culmination of it. I guess someone caught it on camera from across the street. Now it's online, and the executive producer of *Name Your Price* just called and offered me a million dollars, I think, to come on the show. They want to meet tomorrow."

The whirring stopped altogether. She heard a thump like Mansi had hopped off her bike. "Um, *what*?"

"It can't be real, right? I mean, it sounds ridiculous."

"Wait, wait, hold on. First, you broke up with Chuck?"

"Yes."

"That's big news."

Olivia silently agreed. It was big news. And despite her having shouted it to the masses in the video, Mansi knew her well enough to confirm because her dating history with Chuck had been erratic.

"Are you okay?" Mansi asked.

Olivia paused, tripped up by her friend taking a moment to ask because she realized that she hadn't taken a moment yet herself to think about it. The truth was, she'd been avoiding thinking too deeply about it for the knowledge that doing so would put a needling anxiety in her gut. Her hardwired fear of being alone would reach up and grip her around the throat if she wasn't careful. So instead, she thought about how angry she'd been on Saturday morning and how angry she was now that their fight had been broadcast all over the internet.

"I'm fine," she told Mansi.

Mansi was quiet for long enough that Olivia wondered what she was thinking. There was a strong possibility that she didn't believe her, but she didn't press. "Okay," she eventually said. "And second, the EP called you?"

"Yes. Like five minutes ago."

"What did you say?"

"He didn't give me much chance to say anything. He said they'd email me the meeting invite and then hung up on me."

"Um . . ."

Mansi was never at a loss. Olivia relied on her keen mind to guide her through the more confusing aspects of life. Her silence left her floundering.

"Well, do you want to do it?" she finally said.

"Do what?"

"Be on their show."

"God no! I don't even know what they want us to do, but I can't imagine it's worth it."

Mansi was quiet again for a few beats. Olivia could almost feel the cogs of her brain working.

"Liv, that's a lot of money, and I know you could use it."

A lot of money. What an understatement. She could forgive Mansi, though. She lived in a world of obscene wealth and dealt with clients who made a million dollars a month.

"Of course I could, but I don't believe this offer is real, and even if it is, the stipulation involves Chuck, and we both know that's a bad idea."

Mansi did not immediately agree that it was a bad idea. "Maybe you should hear them out? I mean, it can't be *that* bad. It's not like they can force you to get married or anything."

A dark laugh burst from Olivia's lips. "*Definitely* no price high enough for that."

Mansi responded with a decisive tone in her voice. "I think you should hear them out."

Olivia was normally one to take her best friend's advice— that was why she'd called, after all—so she let herself consider it.

Regardless of what the show wanted her to do, a payday like that would change everything. She suddenly saw her money problems disappear. Grandma Ruby could stay at Willow Grove for years on that budget. She could move into a bigger apartment. Get the mysterious whistling sound her car made fixed. The possibilities stretched far.

"Hmm," she said, noncommittal.

"You'd want to take a close look at whatever contract they throw at you to know exactly what you're getting into, but I'd say you should consider it," Mansi said.

Olivia mulled it over, chewing her lip. She sipped her seltzer. "Will you come with me? To the meeting tomorrow?"

"As your lawyer or your friend?" Olivia heard the smile in her voice.

"Both?"

"Yeah, sure. Send me the info when you have it."

"You're the best, Mansi. Thank you."

"Of course. Now, tell me about your breakup."

Olivia flopped back on the couch and spent the next half hour dissecting the end of her relationship.

When she sat up, she noticed that Chelsea, Chuck's younger sister, had sent her a message.

What is this video of you
and Chuck?

A pang of guilt hit her right in the heart. With no siblings of her own, she'd grown fond of Chelsea, an artsy college kid ten years younger than her who routinely changed her hair color and walked around with smudges of paint on her forearms. She lived at home in Ohio with their parents during the summer but spent the rest of the year in L.A., where she went to school. Olivia hadn't seen her since the farewell dinner they'd had back in the spring at the end of her sophomore year at UCLA. She and Chelsea had gorged on heaps of pasta, and Chuck had a single giant meatball at a classy Italian place in Brentwood that night. Chelsea *worshipped* her older brother, which meant she had spent enough time around him and Olivia to know that their relationship was volatile at best.

Exactly what it looks like.
We broke up.

For real? She included a crying cat face emoji.

Olivia hated to break her heart, but there was no sense in lying to her.

Yes. Sorry, Chels. Xo

She waited for a response, and when she didn't get one, she decided to brave finding the viral clip online. Given the spread, she had her choice of major social media accounts to view from. She picked one on Instagram and through one squinted eye watched herself peel off her shirt and throw it at Chuck.

"Don't read the comments. Don't read the comments. Don't read the comments," she muttered as she navigated to the comments.

An abundance of fire emojis, heart eyes, and sweating faces filled the comment section, along with a few fruits and vegetables that had been repurposed into innuendos.

Hot.

I'd get with him for $1

You'd have to pay me NOT to get with him.

That's @ChuckWalsh. Dude's an a-hole.

Umm, how about some love for the hottie in the cutoffs?

They owe it to the world to make beautiful babies.

Isn't she, like, some dead movie star's kid?

Someone tell @AstridLarsson_Official that the love child that killed her marriage is rampaging in L.A.

The last comment made her regret looking. She closed the app and took a deep breath. The spotlight, any form of it, was not something she wanted. She'd had qualms over dating a celebrity for that exact reason, but Chuck had nullified those qualms the first time he'd looked at her and pulled her in so deep that she couldn't bring herself to worry about him being semifamous. But spotlight by proxy aside, the main reason she didn't want to be in the public's eye was that she knew it would rekindle interest in her parents. She did not need to be the reason complete strangers started slandering them online again some thirty years later. She *especially* did not need Astrid Larsson to be made aware of her modern existence. She'd gone her whole life without ever crossing paths with the woman her parents had wronged, and she wasn't about to start now.

This had *TERRIBLE IDEA* written across it in bold shouty caps.

But.

Liv, that's a lot of money. She heard Mansi's words again and could not deny them. With a sigh, she decided to get a better idea of what she might be getting herself into with *Name Your Price.* She'd seen the show a few times but only in passing and had never really paid close attention. On her phone, she navigated her way to the show's website and clicked the video link to a clip from a recent episode.

The show's host, TJ Price, a tall, confident man who fit the Game Show Host mold so well that Olivia could see the veneers in his mouth, narrated the overview. This episode followed a woman from Manhattan who'd agreed to work on a farm in rural Idaho for six weeks. Olivia had to admit, seeing her swap stilettos for Muck boots was rather entertaining.

She clicked to another episode preview and saw a businessman trade in his suit and tie for a trash collector jumpsuit.

A third preview strayed from the society-type-getting-their-hands-dirty theme and followed a young man so painfully shy that he couldn't even look at the camera on his journey to auditioning for a part in a live musical.

In all cases, TJ met with them on occasion for interviews to check in on how they were surviving their newfound misery. Each contestant had a significant chunk of money on the line if they lasted in their new environment, didn't quit their job, and made it through a live show. The whole trajectory of their experience was condensed into a single hour-long episode.

Olivia considered and realized that not everything the contestants were challenged to do was objectively terrible, though most of it was, but the point was that it was terrible *to them* and that was what made it entertaining to watch.

The list of things involving Chuck that were terrible *to her* was not short, and before she even started making it in her head, wondering what the show might want to put them through, she got a text from a number that she should have blocked.

Hey. I know you're mad at me, but
please show up tomorrow.

She read Chuck's message and didn't respond. He was right: she was mad at him. And she planned to show up tomorrow, but leaving him wondering if she would gave her enough satisfaction to peacefully enjoy the rest of her Sunday.

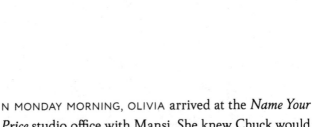

O N MONDAY MORNING, OLIVIA arrived at the *Name Your Price* studio office with Mansi. She knew Chuck would bring his agent, and having Mansi at her side made her feel both more confident and like they were heading into a divorce mediation.

She'd worn heels and high-waisted pants with a fitted blouse because she knew Chuck would show up looking irresistible in whatever he wore, and she wanted to be on the same level. Sure enough, as she and Mansi marched up one end of the walkway leading to the office, Chuck and his agent came up the other, and the sight of Chuck made her heart bungee-jump through her torso the way it did every time she saw him, even when she was mad. It was as reflexive as blinking. Something in him called out to something in her, and it was hard to ignore.

He was effortless in dark jeans and a tight tee. His sandy hair fell in a perpetually disheveled mop that needed an occasional hand through it to keep it in check. Sunglasses hid his hazel eyes, but Olivia could feel his gaze raking over her with a look like he wanted to bite her lip. He tucked his own bottom lip between his perfect teeth and let it slowly release like rising dough.

"Good morning," Mansi said when the four of them met at the path's intersection. She shot out her hand to Chuck's agent. "Mansi Patel."

"Cameron Smith," the agent said. He looked as slick as Mansi in a suit and shiny shoes, but Olivia knew Mansi could eat him for breakfast.

"You brought a lawyer?" Chuck asked, directing his question at Olivia.

"Charles," Mansi said to him with a curt nod as if they'd just met and they hadn't taken tequila shots and sung karaoke together on multiple occasions. "You can direct any questions you have for my client to me."

Olivia bit away the grin trying to bend her lips.

Chuck frowned at her. "Nice to see you too, Manse."

"Same goes for my client," Cameron the agent said.

Mansi lifted a brow.

He awkwardly nodded at Olivia. "If she has anything to say to him, I mean."

Mansi left her perfectly manicured brow arched as if she were not impressed until Cameron cast his eyes down in defeat and headed toward the door. Chuck followed.

"Thank you for coming," Olivia whispered to Mansi, stifling a laugh as they fell in step behind them.

Mansi gave her a knowing wink.

The studio office was nothing to write home about. A slice of corporate America housed in a standard mirrored building with palms out front and a marble lobby. They followed a receptionist down a hall to a conference room with a glass wall and leather chairs around a long table. Olivia recognized one of the men sitting at the table as TJ Price, the show's host. One of the others, a dark-haired man with graying flecks at his temples and glasses, must be Parker Stone, the EP who called her. She couldn't be sure who the other two people were: one woman, one man, in prim suits. Maybe they brought lawyers too.

A round of introductions was made, and Olivia ended up sitting as far from Chuck as possible, with Mansi and Cameron in between them and on the opposite side from the *Name Your Price* team.

"We'll cut right to it," Parker the executive producer said. He used a remote to click on the TV mounted at the end of the room.

The video of Olivia and Chuck's fight played for everyone to see. Even though she knew countless strangers had viewed it, being forced to watch it in a room full of people made her want to hide under the table. It got to the part where she whipped off her shirt, and she noticed Chuck's hand that was resting on the table slowly close into a tight fist. The sight stirred something inside her. Perhaps he felt defensive that everyone could see her exposed. Perhaps he just felt turned on.

Parker hit pause on the video and turned to their side of the table with a smile. "You can't buy passion like that. You two are a ratings gold mine. We want to bring you on the show and take it further."

"It's been taken plenty far already," Olivia muttered.

The woman on the other side of the table, who had in fact been introduced as a lawyer, leaned forward. "Ms. Martin, we are prepared to pay for the rights to the video, which will effectively cease its spread online outside our control."

"The rights to the footage will most certainly be covered in any agreements made today," Mansi said like it wasn't even up for discussion.

"Of course," the other lawyer said.

"So, what exactly are you asking them to do?" Mansi asked.

Parker cleared his throat and nodded toward the lawyer. She produced a stack of papers that she split in two and slid across the table. Mansi and Cameron each grabbed one. "We're asking them to agree to come on the show together."

Olivia fought not to scoff or roll her eyes. She wondered what Chuck was thinking down at the end of the table. She watched Mansi's eyes scan the document. She didn't make much effort to try to read it, though she was curious, because reviewing the contract was the whole reason that she'd brought her lawyer friend with her.

"This seems a little out of scope for your show, doesn't it?" Cameron asked. "I mean, you guys usually do dirty jobs and entertaining relocations. You want them to live together? For a month?"

"*What?*" Olivia blurted. She rocked forward and reached for the contract. Mansi held out a hand to calm her and stop her from tearing it by accident.

Chuck didn't seem fazed, which made Olivia think he already knew this minor detail.

"No one said anything about living together!" Olivia hissed to Mansi. When she'd decided to come to the meeting and at least hear them out about the offer, she expected maybe a date or two. Certainly not *moving in together.*

"Mr. Stone," Mansi said, "I agree with Mr. Smith that this proposal is beyond the scope of your normal show. What makes you think this will be successful, and what's in it for my client's benefit?"

"How about a million bucks?" TJ spoke up for the first time. He casually leaned back in his chair with an ankle on his knee and clicked a pen in one hand. He wore a black blazer over a gray tee shirt and smugly smiled like he owned the room.

Olivia blinked in shock. They were actually offering a million dollars? Mansi hadn't mentioned that, or perhaps it wasn't on the front page of the contract, and she hadn't gotten to it yet. Or perhaps she did know and was protecting her friend from having to regret agreeing to spend a month in the same house with her ex because even a million dollars wasn't enough to say yes.

"Yes, well, that is something to consider," Mansi quietly said, and flipped the first page of the contract. Her eyes continued to scan.

TJ popped up out of his seat. "Think about it," he said, and spread his hands like one did when asking others to envision something. "A new direction for *Name Your Price*. I mean, I love seeing a city girl shovel pig shit, or a shy gamer dragged from his basement to join the dating race, but *this*. I saw the chemistry you guys had on the street—I *felt* it, and our viewers will too! We've never had a couples segment before. What could be better than a pair of combustible exes trying to live together? The sponsors will be *begging* for airtime on this episode."

"You're actually serious," Olivia heard herself say. The words slipped out. She was in too much shock to control her mouth.

TJ skipped around the table to her side. He spun her chair and leaned down to her eye level. His were brown but bright. His musky cologne hit her in a rush. "Yes, Olivia." He stood and kept one hand on her chair and used the other to point down the table. "Why deny the facts? You and Chuck are a beautiful couple, and people *love* beautiful couples. Putting the two of you on TV is a ratings guarantee." He clapped his hands together and smiled around the room.

Olivia frowned up at him. "You left out the part where we can't stand each other."

He dropped his gaze back to her and leaned in with a rush that made her lean back in surprise. "That's the point, Olivia! That's what people will come to see." He stood back up, and Olivia tried not to get dizzy from all his movement. He looked over at Chuck and winked. "And if the two of you maybe find a little spark of magic, a little *temptation* to rekindle that flame we saw on the sidewalk, then we'll tune in for that too."

Olivia's face heated. Her brain was screaming *disaster* at her with the enthusiasm of a drunk football fan. She scrambled for an excuse to escape what was clearly a terrible idea. "I have a full-time job. I can't just—" she started to say, but stopped when she felt Mansi's hand gently land on her arm and squeeze.

"Your description of the living arrangements and filming location is vague. Can you elaborate?" she asked.

TJ gestured at Parker to respond. "The house is in Pacific Palisades. We just confirmed it today, after the contracts were printed. It will have all necessary accommodations for a temporary but continuous stay—pool, gym, grocery delivery. You'll be set up for the full month. The camera crew will come and go, but you'll have no reason to need to leave."

"Wait," Olivia said, gaping at them. "We can't *leave*?"

The *Name Your Price* team exchanged looks with one another. TJ was the one to finally speak, and he did it with a grin that put an uneasy feeling in Olivia's gut.

"That's the object of the game, Olivia. If you and Chuck can figure out how to stand each other in close quarters for one month after that fantastic breakup we witnessed in all its glory, you win the money."

His words landed, and an invisible bomb exploded in Olivia's brain. She unstuck her tongue from her dry mouth. "And if we don't make it?"

TJ casually sat on the table's edge and grinned. "Game over."

Game over. She honestly didn't know if she had it in her.

"And, of course, you'll be presented with a set of challenges while you're in the house," TJ added.

"Challenges?" Olivia asked as Mansi flipped another page of the contract, surely looking for this part.

"Yes," TJ said. "We're not going to film you doing nothing all day. This isn't *Keeping Up with the Kardashians.*"

Olivia could only imagine what horrors they had in store for them.

It occurred to her that Chuck hadn't said anything this whole time, which led her to realize that he had already agreed. This whole meeting was happening to convince one person to say yes.

Her.

She leaned forward so that he could see her from the other end of the table. "Can I talk to you outside, please?"

He met her eyes with a flash of guilt and nodded.

They both rose from the table, and he opened the door for her to leave first. She walked out of the conference room and then kept going all the way outside. Not only did she need fresh air, but she also needed to make sure no one in that room could hear them.

They stopped under a shady tree back on the pathway where they'd earlier met. Olivia couldn't help but notice the flecks of green the backdrop brought out when she looked up into Chuck's eyes.

"Did you already agree to this?" she asked him.

"No. I can't without you."

"But you knew what they were offering."

He paused and raked a hand through his hair. "Yes."

She threw her head back and groaned. "*Chuck!* How did you let me walk into that? I wouldn't have even considered it if I'd known they had some elaborate *Big Brother–Love Island* knock-off planned. Why didn't you tell me?"

He moved like he was going to squeeze her arms but dropped his hands at the last second. She hated herself for wishing he had touched her. "Listen, Olivia, I'm sorry. I know you don't want to hear me say that, but I had to take this opportunity. They hunted me down through Cameron, and Parker called me. Before I knew it, they were making me an offer. All I had to do was get you on board."

"Well, you failed because I am not doing this. You shouldn't have agreed either."

"It's a *million dollars*, Liv. A million dollars! You try saying no to that."

Her blood was boiling again. "I don't have to try because I'm saying *no* right now! It's not that hard! No!"

He made a strangled sound of frustration and squeezed his hands in his hair. He dropped his arms with a slap against his thighs. "This doesn't have to be so hard. I need the money; you need the money. All we have to do is stick it out for one month together."

Olivia folded her arms and looked away. She hated to admit that he was right. They both needed money: her, for her grandmother's care, and him, to afford to live in a world with more and more jobs drying up. And a million dollars would do the trick, even if it was split in half and heavily taxed. When she really considered it, she realized she couldn't say no.

But it was going to be one hell of a challenge.

"Fine," she said. "But we need rules."

"Rules?"

"Yes, Chuck." She stepped closer to him and lowered her voice to a hiss. "We both know that we are basically a lit stick of dynamite together, so we're going to have to . . . keep our distance in the house. Otherwise, we'll just blow up and lose."

His eyes narrowed as he looked down at her. They were standing close enough that she could smell a hint of mint on his breath. Without her needing to fully spell it out, he knew precisely why they needed to keep their distance. The reason tangibly filled the air between them. "That's a good point. We can't risk that. So, what will the rules be?"

Olivia scoffed with a roll of her eyes. "Not *now*. We have to go back in there and finish this nightmarishly ill-informed decision we are making first. We can talk about it later."

"Okay!" he agreed at the harsh bite in her voice. "Can I at least get a shake on it so that I know you're not going to turn on me when we get back in there?"

Olivia let out a mighty sigh, hoping she wasn't making the biggest mistake of her life. She stuck out her hand. "I can't believe I'm doing this."

A smile twitched his lips upward as he slipped his hand into hers. "Thank you."

"Well, this looks promising," Cameron said as he materialized. Mansi was right on his heels.

Olivia dropped her hand with a flush in her cheeks.

"Good news," Mansi said. She nodded at Cameron. "Inside

source says the show is desperate for a ratings boost. That's why they want a new direction."

Cameron proudly grinned. The source must have been his.

"What does that mean?" Olivia asked.

"It means we've got some leverage," Mansi answered. "They want you two badly, and they're probably holding back with their offer."

"We've got room to negotiate," Cameron added.

Mansi shot him a smile.

"Did you two become a team while we were out here?" Chuck asked.

Cameron clapped him on the shoulder and turned them back toward the building. "We're all in this together if you say yes, so we should start acting like it."

Olivia realized she'd asked Mansi to come as a favor, and Cameron was there for his job. She wondered if she should cut in Mansi for a percentage once they reached an agreement. Knowing her, she'd probably refuse the money.

Mansi held Olivia back and gave her a serious look. She spoke with her voice lowered. "Olivia, are you sure you want to do this?"

Olivia looked at her in surprise. "You were the one who encouraged it!"

"I know! I just . . . Sorry." Mansi bit her bottom lip, which was painted dark red. "I'm only doing my best-friend duty by giving you one last out."

"I appreciate that, Manse. But I think I can handle it."

Mansi nodded.

As they walked back inside, Olivia chewed her lip in thought, wondering if they really could pull it off. She thought of what was riding on it, of Grandma Ruby happily laughing with Violet at Willow Grove. She thought of how absolutely mad Chuck drove her and how she'd wanted to shove him out the window on Saturday morning. She wondered if she could keep one in check for the greater good of the other.

When they returned to the conference table ready to negotiate, she took Cameron's inside intel to heart and opened the discussion with a bold move.

"I want to make two things clear if we are going to agree to this," she said. All eyes turned to her. "I want an advance . . ." She trailed off and glanced at Mansi to make sure she wasn't out of line. Mansi subtly, if not curiously, nodded.

The female *Name Your Price* lawyer glanced at Parker, who bobbed his head a fraction. "We can accommodate that, Ms. Martin," the lawyer said.

"Good," Olivia said with a rush of relief. She could use the money up front to pay off her Willow Grove debt and keep Grandma Ruby comfortably in her home while she did the show.

"And the other thing?" TJ asked, sounding genuinely intrigued.

Olivia sat up straighter and looked at Parker. "Mr. Walsh and I have agreed on new terms."

Chuck leaned forward in his chair to cast her a curious look.

She kept her gaze straight ahead on Parker. "We want a million dollars. Each."

Parker blinked hard once. TJ's lip curled up. The lawyers remained neutral. Olivia felt Chuck's gaze bore into her for a hot second before he straightened himself in his seat and calmly looked across the table.

He nodded once and then said, "Each."

OLIVIA WALKED OUT OF the meeting in a daze. After an hour of negotiation and a few phone calls, they'd settled on a final agreement—including the stipulations of a fifty-thousand-dollar advance and a million dollars as the prize money. Each. She couldn't believe it. Her heat-of-the-moment declaration on the street had the potential to change her life. All she had to do was live in a house with her ex for a month and not kill him. Which may be easier said than done, but she'd figure it out. She had a million dollars on the line.

"You're sure?" Mansi had whispered to her one last time before she inked her name into the contract. Olivia wasn't sure about Chuck, but she was sure she needed the money, so she'd nodded and scrawled her signature.

They all shook hands, and Parker told them they would be in touch soon about a schedule since they didn't want to lose any momentum with the video having gone viral.

When they parted to carry on with their days, Olivia gave

Chuck a frosty glare and climbed back into Mansi's Mercedes. They were paying her to live with him, not be nice to him.

"Well, this is gonna be fun," Mansi said. "A month of Chuck Walsh just when you thought you were done with him."

"It will be painful but necessary," Olivia said. "Thanks again for coming."

"Of course. I just don't want to have to say I told you so when you want to kill him after one day."

"Oh, I already know I'll want to kill him. The next four weeks will be a test of restraint and summoning the acting skills buried in my heritage."

Mansi gave her a small smile. "Well, let's hope you've got your mom's chops."

Olivia smiled back. As a kid, she used to put on her mother's movies and pretend she was the one having a conversation with her instead of her scene partner. She'd memorized lines of dialogue from her romantic comedies and the few more mature dramas that her grandmother had let her watch. No such opportunity existed for her father, seeing that he was never in a movie, and that had left the fragile bond tying her to her parents at all a hair thicker for her mother. Now this bizarre opportunity had given her a chance to explore a side of herself rooted in the defining characteristic of the woman she'd never known, because if she was going to survive living with Chuck in front of cameras, there would be a fair amount of pretending going on. The thought of it put a warm, if not slightly intimidated, sensation in her chest.

Mansi drove Olivia back home, where she got in her own car to head to work. Most everyone at the magazine worked remotely these days, but Olivia enjoyed coming into the office when she needed an escape from the four walls of her tiny apartment. She thought breaking the news to her boss that she needed time off to be on a TV show was something better done in person anyway.

When she arrived at the building that housed *Mix*, she took the elevator up to the fourth floor. A few coworkers sat in their cubicles, but the grid of mostly empty desks looked like the final moments of a chess game with only a few pieces left on the board.

In a turn that she herself still to this day didn't fully understand, she'd made a career out of writing about celebrity culture. It was a strange addiction of sorts. Media coverage was all she had to remember her parents by, and while she abhorred what she saw there, steeping herself in that world helped fill the ugly, misshapen hole in her heart over what the media had done to their family. It was a scab she couldn't stop picking. Perhaps some subconscious drive to infuse more integrity into reporting on celebrities as artists, to spare the world the type of headlines she'd seen about her parents and the tragedy that befell them, kept her around too.

She walked to her desk, dropped her bag, and woke her computer. The screen fizzled to life, and her eyes went straight to the number in a round, red dot informing her how full her inbox was. She grimaced at it and scanned the first few messages at the top. One stuck out, a reminder from Willow Grove that her payment was past due, although that problem now at least had a short-term fix. She decided that rather than diving into the rest of the messages sure to overwhelm her, she would go tell her boss her news.

Stephanie had an office in the row of small suites around

the floor's perimeter. She never worked from home because she had two small children who made it near impossible. Olivia found her at her desk wearing her customary look of simultaneous focus and frazzle. Her blond bob was pulled half back in a clip, and her sleeveless blouse had a smudge near the collar that looked suspiciously like Magic Marker. Stephanie always reminded Olivia of the eye of a hurricane. Chaos swirled around her—her children, her job as a senior editor—but she herself was remarkably calm.

Olivia knocked on her doorframe.

Stephanie's head popped up from where she had been staring at her computer. Her messy desk splayed out before her like someone had overturned all the drawers on top of it. Stacks of papers teetered, and Post-its fluttered like rainbow eyelashes. A coffee mug that had likely held coffee earlier that morning had become a pen holder. "Olivia," she said with a serene smile. "How can I help you?"

"Good morning, Stephanie. I wanted a quick word if you've got a few minutes."

She looked around at her desk like something there would inform her of her schedule and looked back up. "Sure. Come in."

Olivia got right to the point because she knew Stephanie's time was limited. "So, I'm going to be on a TV show?" She wasn't sure why she said it like a question. Perhaps because she was still in shock.

"Oh? Which one?"

"*Name Your Price.*"

Stephanie arched a knowing brow. "Would this have anything to do with the video of you online?"

A hot flush curled into Olivia's cheeks. She grimaced. "You've seen it?"

"I think everyone's seen it," Stephanie said with a gentle smile. "I'm sorry to hear that you and Chuck broke up."

Of course Stephanie knew about Chuck. She had been the one to send Olivia on assignment to interview him, and she'd been the one Olivia had to tell that she couldn't keep the assignment because their relationship had crossed from professional to personal faster than a lightning strike.

"Right. Thanks," Olivia said awkwardly and unsure how else to respond. "Anyway, *Name Your Price* wants us to live locked in a house together for a month. If we make it without leaving the house, we win." The *if* in her statement came out with a bit more emphasis than she meant.

Stephanie narrowed her eyes. "Interesting. Do you need time off?"

"Oh, um, well, I was thinking I could work remotely because I'll need *something* to keep me sane in there, but—"

"I know you have plenty stored up, Olivia. You never take time off." She said it almost as if scolding her. It was true. Olivia hoarded her time off in case she needed to use it to care for Grandma Ruby. "And the timing is rather perfect what with you submitting your Power Couples piece last week—which is excellent by the way. Your interview with Jack and Gemma Lincoln was the cherry on top." Stephanie lifted her hand into the OK symbol.

"Thank you," Olivia said with a proud smile. She'd spent months tracking down meetings with six Hollywood couples for a feature piece in *Mix*. Turned out, getting two busy, powerful people in the same place at the same time for an interview was a tall order. For the final couple, she'd spent last Monday chatting with the daughter of a famous music producer who had her own radio show and her Emmy-winning screenwriter husband in their home. Stephanie was right: with that project wrapped up, right now was fitting for taking time off.

"Take the time, Olivia. You deserve a break," Stephanie said.

Olivia involuntarily huffed a laugh. "You make it sound like a vacation. I'm going to be locked in a house with my ex-boyfriend and a bunch of cameras."

Stephanie laughed. "Well, when you put it that way, maybe not. But I'm serious. I know you're under a lot of pressure caring for your grandmother, and maybe a little change in routine will do you some good."

Olivia had confided in Stephanie on more than one occasion. She knew about her family history, of course she did. And even with the potential to bust her career wide open by leveraging it, Stephanie never pushed her to. Olivia had always respected her for that.

"Thanks," Olivia said.

"Of course. And maybe when you get back, we can talk about writing one of the harder-hitting pieces you've had your eye on."

She never pushed her on her parents, but she always pushed her in other ways.

Olivia had written profiles on actors, musicians, famous directors. Her dream was to one day be a best-selling biographer, but she was still cultivating relationships and earning enough clout for anyone to trust her with their life story. Stephanie was always passing her opportunities to earn that clout and encouraging her to take a risk on writing a splashy breakout piece.

"Sure," Olivia said, grateful but not exactly committing. "That would be great. Thanks, Stephanie."

"Good luck with your TV show," Stephanie said.

Olivia left her office in another daze. Everything was falling into place. All she had left to do was tell Grandma Ruby she'd be gone for a month.

When she returned to her desk, she found a new email waiting at the top of her inbox. One from Parker Stone.

SUBJECT: Move-in Schedule for NYP

Hey, gang. We're excited to get going. See attached for details.

See you soon!

—P

Olivia opened the attachment and felt her heart lurch up into her throat. Apparently, she'd be seeing them very soon because they were moving in the day after tomorrow.

Not a minute after she finished Parker's email, she got a text from Chuck.

Hey roomie. Did you get that email?

Olivia rolled her eyes.

Yes. And don't call me roomie.

What should I call you?

How about cellmate.

Could you at least try for optimism?
This isn't going to be that bad.

                              Chuck, this is literally a
                              nightmare scenario.

Yes, and that's the point. At least we
know what we're getting into.

Olivia realized he made an excellent point. It wasn't like they were walking into the situation ignorant. She sighed and remembered what they had talked about that morning outside the studio.

                              So, about these rules . . .

Yes. Agreed. Necessary. Let's meet
tonight at Mel's. 8.

Chuck's pushy little text messages irked her something special, and it dawned on her that one benefit of living with him for a month would be a significant reduction in text communication.

Unless they locked themselves on either end of the house and only communicated electronically, which might be a solid idea, now that she thought about it.

Either way, she agreed that they needed to lay some ground rules, off camera, before they got into this mess they'd signed up for. And seeing that she had one day to get her affairs in order before *Name Your Price* locked them in and threw away the key, a prompt meeting with Chuck was necessary.

See you there, she responded, and wondered if she should read into the fact that he'd picked the diner where he'd turned her world upside down with a kiss on their first date.

• • • • •

MEL'S WAS A GREASY SPOON OFF SUNSET BOULEVARD. THE PER-fect late-night hideaway after seeing a show or drinking too much and needing something battered and fried to sop it up. Or, as was happening at the moment, the perfect place to discuss boundaries for avoiding homicide while locked in a house with your ex for the sake of a reality TV show. Olivia ordered a milkshake with extra whipped cream to help the conversation go down easier. Chuck got decaf coffee. Night had fallen outside, and the summer sky glowed a shade of dusty purple above the city lights. Not a single star was visible.

At their booth, a cushy cove with worn, red leather seats and a laminate table, Olivia watched Chuck watch her pluck the cherry from her shake's fluffy top and suck the cream from it. His Adam's apple bobbed, and he wet his lips. He lifted his coffee for a sip, and Olivia couldn't tell if his reaction was jealousy that she was indulging in a treat or tempered arousal from watching her do things with her mouth.

"You can have some if you want," she said, and pushed the shake to the table's midpoint. She dipped her long spoon into the whipped cream and ate the white puff it returned with.

Chuck smirked at her. "You know I can't."

"Sure you can," she said, and sucked on her spoon. It popped from her mouth with a slick sound that made Chuck lick his lips again.

"No, I can't. Do you know what it takes to look like this?"

he said, and gestured at himself, specifically the middle part of his body.

The face hadn't been up to him. That was a blessing from whatever Grecian god statue his parents had prayed to. The height was genetic too, and sure, the abs, lats, delts, and whatever else made up a torso and arms fit for an action hero probably had roots in a fortunate gene pool, but Olivia was well aware how much work Chuck put into his body. The gym and the diet and all the routines had dictated their life. Like when she was hormonal and craving salty grease, but he was having a keto week. Or when she wanted to see a matinee at the theater, but he had to get in a workout during an afternoon window. Or when he left a pile of sweaty, squishy clothes on the bedroom floor because he came over after a run and she stepped on it with a bare foot.

"Yes, I do know. I used to date you, remember?"

He gave her another smirk, and she pushed the milkshake closer.

"That's why I know one milkshake isn't going to kill you. Half a milkshake, actually."

His eyes widened at the sweating glass of frozen chocolate, but he pressed his lips together and ultimately resisted.

She pulled the glass back to her side of the table. "Suit yourself. Your restraint is remarkable when you want it to be."

"What's that supposed to mean?"

She found the straw buried in the cream and took a long, brain-freezing pull. "It means we should talk about what we came here to talk about."

Chuck sat up straighter and leaned his elbow on the table. "Right."

The elephant between them was that neither of them

showed restraint when it came to the other person. Not emotionally. Not physically. They were explosive magnets, and they both knew it. And an explosion would not lead to the million-dollar paycheck they both needed.

"Ground rules," Chuck said.

Olivia nodded. "Ground rules."

They stared at each other, neither of them sure where to start.

"No sex?" Olivia said, jumping straight into the deep end.

Chuck sputtered into the coffee he'd been about to take a sip of. She handed him a napkin. "Sorry," he said, and dabbed his lips. "Going right for the big one there."

Olivia shrugged. "I mean, it's the most obvious and problematic one, right?"

He gave her a look that positively melted her to the booth. "Olivia, the sex was never a problem."

Heat curled up from low in her belly and spread into her every extremity. She pressed her thighs and her lips together. The urge to throw her milkshake aside and climb across the table into his lap was the exact reason she knew this was the most important rule.

"No, it wasn't a problem," she agreed. "It was what came after." She took another pull of her shake in an effort to lower her body temperature. "And before, honestly."

Chuck sighed, as he too was well aware of the cyclical nature of their problems. Fight, make up, fight, make up. Rinse and repeat. On and on for all eternity. There was no beginning and no end, but part of what kept pulling them back to each other, part of what made them put up with the fighting, was their physical connection. If they cut off that life source, they just might be able to really call it quits and survive living together.

"No sex," he agreed.

"And if there's only one bed in the house, I get it."

A laugh popped from his lips. "Liv, it's a house in the Palisades. It probably has like five bedrooms."

"Oh, I seriously doubt that, Chuck. It's probably a condo, and the pool and gym they mentioned belong to the property complex. They know we can't stand each other. I'm sure they are planning a hundred ways to sabotage us—remember the cryptic *challenges* they've got lined up? You really think they'd put us in a house large enough that we could avoid each other?"

"That . . . is an excellent point." He stroked his jaw again. "What else do you think they might do?"

Olivia sighed. "I don't know. Forcing us to eat, sleep, and exist in the same space is bad enough, isn't it?"

Chuck gave her a look that she couldn't fully interpret. "You're right. So, I guess we just keep our distance?"

"As best we can, yes."

A silence settled between them aside from Olivia's straw hitting an air pocket in her milkshake and making a rude sucking sound. Chuck's phone pinged with a message.

He reached for it, and Olivia noticed his lips twitch up at the corners when he looked at the screen. He started tapping out a response.

"Who's that?" she asked, rotely and not even thinking she didn't have the right to inquire about his personal business anymore.

"My sister," he answered just as automatically as if the idea of new boundaries hadn't registered to him either. "She's pretty pissed at me right now."

"Why?"

He stopped typing and looked up as his phone let out the

whoosh sound of a sent message. "Because of this whole situation," he said, and waved his hand over the table.

She knew he didn't mean Chelsea was upset that they were having an evening chat at a diner.

"She's mad that we broke up?"

He quietly laughed in the form of a little huff out his nose. "Liv, she adores you. As far as she's concerned, I've ruined everything and taken away the big sister she never had—which, ouch. I think she likes you more than me."

The warmth that filled Olivia's chest felt like the sun on a crisp fall day. At the same time, a wave of guilt washed over her for feeling like she'd somehow let Chelsea down. She tried to drown it with another pull of her milkshake. "I think you will forever hold idol status for her, don't worry."

He shook his head with a soft smile and shoved his phone back in his pocket. "Unlikely. She's threatening to fly out here and stab me with the blunt end of a paintbrush."

Olivia grinned at the thought of Chelsea hopping a flight and showing up in paint-stained overalls to harangue her brother. "What's she doing this summer?"

"Art camp. She's a counselor for a bunch of tweens trying to find their inner Monet."

"That suits her."

"Yeah, it's kind of perfect. She'll be back for school in September. We should take her—" He cut himself off midsentence as if he'd tripped. His brow furrowed. "Sorry. Never mind."

His interrupted suggestion that the three of them spend time together—because clearly that was what he had been about to say—left Olivia with a sense of sadness she wasn't sure where to place. Those days were obviously over.

She returned to her milkshake for solace. "How are your parents? How's your dad doing after his surgery?"

Chuck lit up with the usual sunbeam shine that mention of Barbara and Sam Walsh summoned from him. Olivia had been lucky enough to bask in the source of that light on the occasions she'd met his parents, and while it was golden and beautiful, it always left her wrung out and drained like a long day in the real sun. The presence of something so wholesome and unconditionally absolute served to remind her that she'd never had the same. No doting from the two parents who'd given her life, at least.

"They're good. My dad's doing really well, apparently. I was thinking of flying out to help around the house for a while, but my mom said he's already up and about. His doctors are impressed he's recovering so well."

"Your dad's a sturdy man."

"He is. Took a new hip like a champ. He says thanks for the get-well card."

Olivia had sent him one two weeks ago when he'd had his hip replacement. Little did she know her relationship with his son would be over by the time he'd recovered. The thought made her ache the same way discussing Chelsea had. His whole family had been over-the-moon happy when their relationship had turned serious. They'd welcomed Olivia with an enthusiasm she'd at first found intimidating but had grown a fond affection for. Losing them felt like more than just a casualty of their breakup.

"Tell them hi from me," she said with a weak smile.

A sad look washed over Chuck's face, twinged with something Olivia couldn't identify. He nodded. "I will."

Another silence filled the space between them. Chuck drummed his fingers on the tabletop.

"Nice job getting them to double the prize money, by the way. That was a bold move," he said in a shift of topic.

A smile bent Olivia's frozen mouth. "I figured we had nothing to lose."

He smirked and raised his coffee mug as if toasting to her. "Well, now we have double the amount to lose."

"You say that like it's a bad thing."

"It is if we can't pull this off."

Olivia took a final slurp of her shake. "Then let's do our best to stack the odds in our favor."

"Agreed. So, what do you think they're going to make us do?"

"Hopefully nothing too terrible. I won't even have work to distract me while we're in there."

A look of surprise crossed his face. "You took time off?"

"Stephanie gave it to me when I told her about the show. Why do you sound so surprised?"

He tilted his head and gave her a knowing look. "Because you never take a break, Liv. I was sure you'd find a way to multitask, even while trying to win a million dollars." He was scolding her just like her boss had, and she didn't like it.

She found one last bit of frozen chocolate to suck through her straw with another gurgling sound. "Not this time. What about you?" she probed, knowing Chuck did not currently have a job to take time off from and unable to resist provoking him.

Where she thought she might see an icy glare or a snarky smirk, Chuck actually sighed. He ran a hand through his disheveled hair, and she tried to ignore the flash of his biceps that peeked out from his tee shirt's sleeve. He had a small tattoo on the inside of his right arm that was the perfect size for pressing her lips into, which she had done many, *many* times. "Nothing to take time off from right now, unfortunately." The note of dismay in his voice stirred something inside her. She knew he'd been struggling to find work—they'd argued about it plenty— but broaching the topic when they weren't screaming at each other let her see the sincere distress he was trying to hide. It made her want to probe deeper.

She set her glass aside and placed her hands on the table. "Chuck, does this still have to do with whatever happened with Richard Sykes?"

He quickly turned to her, and the look on his face told her the answer was yes.

It was no secret that Chuck Walsh was difficult—perhaps the worst label an actor could earn—but the reason why had never been fully disclosed. The clickbait headlines had planted seeds in the Hollywood rumor mill soil and left Chuck's repu- tation decaying without going into any real detail.

Up-and-Comer Chuck Walsh Fired from
Star-Studded Blockbuster

A-list Director Richard Sykes Drops Walsh Midshoot

Chuck Walsh Loses the Bet on Safe Gamble:
Rising Star Loses Breakout Role in Next Summer's Hit

When it had all happened a month ago, Olivia only wit- nessed what she saw in the tabloids plus Chuck in a mopey, drunken stupor for a few days claiming he didn't want to talk about it.

She'd let it go.

"I'd rather not talk about that," he said now. The sharp edge to his tone told her not to push, and she knew if she did push, they'd end up fighting and someone would storm out.

Olivia of yesterday might have demanded he tell her, but Olivia of today—the one with a million dollars on the line if she could figure out how to coexist for a month with the man sitting across from her—impressed herself by dropping it.

Instead, she sighed and turned to look at the counter. She and Chuck had sat there the night of their first date. They'd seen a show at Whisky a Go Go and wandered down the street once they left the sweaty little red box. They'd been plenty close to each other during the show, smashed together with the crowd near the stage for some punk band she'd never heard of that Chuck knew, but sitting knee-to-knee at the diner counter after had somehow felt more intimate. At least that was how Olivia remembered it. She also remembered the basket of fries they'd shared, though she ate ninety-five percent of it, and how Chuck had wiped a dribble of ketchup off her lip and then sucked it from his own thumb in a way that had nearly made her combust.

Then, of course, there was the way he'd slipped his hand into hers when they walked back outside, and she'd felt at once like her body was an enormous swarm of butterflies and a bomb that was about to detonate. And how when he'd leaned her up against the cool stone wall of the building and kissed her like no one else had ever kissed her before, she thought every star in the sky had aligned for them.

"Liv? *Hellooo?*" Chuck said now, and waved his hand at her. "What?"

"I said dibs on the TV whenever there's a game on that I want to watch."

The shimmering, nostalgic fantasy that had been replaying in her mind disappeared in a puff of smoke. Whatever sweet memories had been trying to convince her that Charles Michael Walsh was some kind of romantic hero had almost succeeded. Alas, the man sitting across from her claiming rights to the televised snooze fests that were professional sports was none other than her ex-boyfriend.

She pushed her way out of the booth. "Whatever, Chuck."

He sipped the rest of his coffee and watched her stand. "Are you going to make me pay for this?" He gestured at their table.

Olivia looped her purse over her head. "Yes. Consider it compensation for landing us on a TV show that I don't want to be a part of."

Chuck turned around in the booth as she began to walk away. "A TV show that could make you a millionaire!" he called after her.

"Only if I manage not to kill you!" she called back, and shoved open the diner's door.

No one raised a head at their dramatic exchange. Given the crowd that hung out around Sunset after dark, they were not even close to being strange.

Olivia passed back into the summer evening and wondered, sincerely, if she had it in her to win this game.

HAVING TWENTY-FOUR HOURS TO get her affairs in order before essentially going off-grid for a month made for an exceptionally busy day.

Olivia woke early and planned a visit to Willow Grove both to pay her debts and to break the news to Grandma Ruby that their next four visits would be by phone only. She also had other errands to run like finally shipping the online purchase returns that had been piling up by her front door for weeks, picking up a prescription, and retrieving her dry cleaning. Of course, it was also the last time she would get to see Mansi for a month, so they'd planned to go to dinner that night.

But the first thing she had to do was pack. She didn't really know what type of wardrobe being locked in a house for a month required, but she planned on piles of athleisure and a few swimsuits, maybe a dress or two. She dug her big suitcase out of her closet and left it open like a gaping mouth on her bed.

Starting from the bottom up, she packed underwear and socks, sweatpants, leggings, tees, shorts, maxis and sundresses, her favorite bathrobe, and three sets of pajamas. When she pulled open the drawer where she kept her swimwear, the sight of a yellow bikini stopped her efficiency in its tracks.

The last time she had worn it was a long weekend in Cabo with Chuck. He'd gotten a room at some mega resort through a friend, and they'd spent three days mostly in bed and occasionally on the beach. And then there was the afternoon in the ocean when they stood in the swelling waves and he put his hand beneath her bikini bottoms. *Nobody can see*, he'd whispered when she halfheartedly tried to protest for fear of getting caught by the swarms of beachgoers on the shore. Her worry and will to resist evaporated when he moved his skilled hand under the water until she was shuddering and clinging to him to stay afloat.

The memory broke a sweat out over her skin. As if someone had bumped her thermostat up to ninety degrees. Her conversation with Chuck from the night before—their rules—suddenly felt irrelevant. *No sex* was pointless if four triangles of fabric and a memory had her wanting to call him to come over.

She took a steadying breath and decided to call someone else.

"Hey." Mansi answered on the second ring. Olivia heard sounds of Mansi's morning routine in the background: a sink running, soft music playing, a coffee brewer gurgling.

"Hi. I'm having second thoughts," Olivia admitted.

"What? No. Too late for that. The only thoughts you should be having are of a million dollars, Liv."

"I know, but—"

"Did something happen?"

"No! Yes, I mean—*ugh*. I don't know."

Mansi paused. "*Olivia*," she said slowly, drawing out her

name. "I know that tone. You're only this flustered after an encounter with Chuck." She suddenly gasped. "Did you sleep with him last night?"

"No!" she said, but could not fault Mansi for asking given her track record.

Another silence passed.

"I'm sensing a 'but' here," Mansi said.

She was right: there was a *but*. And Olivia didn't know what to make of it.

Olivia released a breath and confided in her friend. "I don't know, Manse. I'm packing right now, and I grabbed this bikini I wore on that trip to Mexico, and it made me think of . . . *things* we did there, and now I'm worried about what might happen in the house."

Sounds of dishes clinking filtered through the phone. "First of all, that's hot that an article of clothing can make you think of him and actually says a lot. And second, what are you so worried about? So what if something happens between you in the house? I'm sure they'd turn off the cameras for the actual act, Liv."

Heat flooded her body at the thought of what might get caught on camera. "Ew. There better not be one of those creepy night vision cameras in the bedroom."

"I will sue them into oblivion on your behalf if there is."

"Thank you. But getting caught on camera is less of a concern than wanting to *do something* worthy of suing them over catching on camera."

"I don't follow."

"*Ugh*, Mansi! You know Chuck and I can't keep our hands off each other, even when we're fighting—*especially* when we're fighting."

"You are saying this to someone who has seen your face

flushed and clothes rumpled in enough inappropriate venues to have lost count, Olivia. I am well aware of this fact."

She flushed again and silently thanked Mansi for all the times she'd tucked her tag back in or straightened her earring or offered her fresh lipstick when she and Chuck returned from the bathroom at a party or the dark corner of a bar.

"Right. Sorry. I mean that I'm worried we'll lose control and do something we regret and end up losing the money—even though we've discussed it and agreed no sex."

"Wait, you guys did like a pre-show pact?"

"Something like that, sure. We thought it would be a good idea to lay some ground rules."

"That was an excellent idea," Mansi said, and Olivia could picture her nodding in approval. "Going in prepared will give you the best chance of success. But now you don't think it's enough because of a bikini?"

Olivia held up the tangled yellow strings and frowned. Just looking at it, she could feel the pressure of his hands on her body. She began to sweat again. "I don't think it's enough because it's Chuck."

"That is a valid concern," Mansi astutely agreed, like she knew full well Olivia was powerless over her desire for him. "Well, what do we need to do to fix it? Cold showers? Chastity belt? You know what, I've heard cheese kills sex drive, so maybe have them stock the house with it."

Olivia quietly laughed. Mansi had never met a problem she couldn't solve. "I think we'll have bigger issues on our hands if I move to a steady diet of cheese, no matter how tempting that sounds."

Mansi hummed again like she was thinking. "Well, what

then? Do we need to get you laid tonight, so you go into the house with someone else on your mind?"

"No!" she blurted before she really thought about it. But when she did think about it, she realized that she hadn't slept with anyone except Chuck for months, and those months had ruined her for wanting anything different because no one else would ever measure up.

"I am so screwed, Mansi," she said with a sigh.

"Quite the opposite, actually."

Olivia glared at her suitcase in place of her friend. "Thanks."

Mansi laughed. "Sorry. Maybe just don't pack the incriminating bikini, then?"

She looked around at the piles of clothes she'd laid out and realized nearly all of them had some kind of history. Perhaps she'd have to fit buying a whole new wardrobe into her busy day too. But she knew that no matter what she was wearing, ratty bathrobe or ball gown, Chuck would find a way to strip it off her in one fell swoop like a magician or peel it off piece by piece like the delicate wrapping on a very expensive gift. Both tactics drove her wild, as it did when they found creative ways to leave all their clothes on.

"Maybe I should just wear a trash bag," she said, knowing Chuck would find a way to make her feel sexy even in a pouch of sticky black plastic too.

"How about this," Mansi offered. "We have a code word, and you can text me when you need to, when you're in the house and feeling *tempted*, and I'll send you pictures of objectively unsexy things, no questions asked."

A laugh bounced Olivia's shoulders. "That . . . might actually be helpful."

"Perfect. I'll start screenshotting random stuff to have it ready. What's our code word going to be?"

Olivia thought about how desperate it was to need a code word and unsexy text messages from her best friend in order to control her desires, but she was willing to do whatever it took to win the money. "How about 'yellow bikini'?" she said, and tossed the swimsuit in question aside.

"I love it. Now all you have to do is keep it in your pants for a month."

Olivia groaned.

"You can do it, girl. I'll see you for dinner later."

"Bye, Manse. Thank you."

●   ●   ●   ●   ●

ONCE SHE WAS SATISFIED WITH HER PACKING, OLIVIA TOOK A trip to Willow Grove. For once, she did not enter the serene and sterile care home like a timid bunny darting through the woods but rather marched up to the director's open door and knocked.

"Olivia," Dr. Park said, surprised. She sat at her neatly appointed desk reading her computer screen. "How can I help you?"

"Hi. Sorry to barge in on you like this, but I wanted to let you know that I have the money. Part of it, anyway." She entered the office and extended the check she'd written. It probably would have been more appropriate to send it through the accounting department, but handing it directly to Dr. Park felt like it earned her a few points back for her delinquency.

"You— What?" Dr. Park started and stopped as if she'd

been prepared to roll out her customary lecture on overdue bills at the mere sight of Olivia.

"I can pay you now. It's a long story, but I signed a contract to be on this reality TV show and negotiated an advance as part of the deal. I don't technically have the money yet, but I will in a few days. So maybe don't cash this for like a week? But it'll be there, I swear." She found herself both smiling and blushing over spilling her life story to someone as esteemed as Dr. Park. She probably needed to get back to work running Willow Grove, not listen to Olivia ramble.

"I see," she said with a hint of doubt as she took the check. "Well, this is great. I was actually going to call you today to let you know that our financial hardship grace period will expire at the end of this month. At that time, we'd have to move Ruby—"

"That won't be a problem," she said, cutting her off. "I promise."

"Oh. Okay, then, Olivia. Please let me know if anything changes."

"I will, Dr. Park. Thank you. And also, I won't be able to visit in person for the next month. I'm going to go let my grandmother know right now, but I wanted you to know too since you won't see me. I'll still call every week, and you can still contact me for any reason. I just won't be able to come here in person unless there's an emergency."

Dr. Park eyed her suspiciously but didn't press. "Okay, Olivia. We'll be in touch if anything comes up."

"Great. Thanks. I'm going to go see my grandma now." She skipped out the door before the intimidating woman could make her feel any more inadequate by simply existing in her esteemed white coat with her degrees mounted on her office wall, or before she could ask Olivia any more questions about the strange update that she'd just given her.

Willow Grove was quiet on a Tuesday midday. Olivia passed through the calm, airy halls and out onto the property. Grandma Ruby's cottage stood third to the left down a short pathway.

When she arrived, she knocked and then stepped inside. Her grandmother's small home was decorated in soft earth tones and smelled like fresh lemons and sugar. Ruby sat in her favorite living room chair facing out her front window. She held a pencil and worked a Sudoku puzzle from the thick book that Olivia had stuffed in her birthday gift basket.

"Hi, Grandma," Olivia gently said as she came around into view.

Ruby looked up with a welcoming smile. "Olivia, sweetheart. What a pleasant surprise." Her eyes crinkled at the corners.

Olivia sat on the sofa adjacent to her. "Yes, sorry for just dropping in, but I needed to visit today."

Ruby used her pencil to mark her page in the book. She gave her granddaughter her full attention. She wore the soft pink sweater from a shop in Venice Beach that Olivia had also stuffed into her birthday gift basket. "Well, to what do I owe the pleasure?"

Seeing that she had taken great pains to keep her grandmother in the dark about her money problems, Olivia had thought carefully about how to tell her about the TV show and why she had to say yes to it.

"Remember when I was here on Sunday, and I told you Chuck and I broke up?"

"Oh yes. I was so sorry to hear that. Have you two made up yet?" Hope danced in her voice with as much spirit as the shine in her eyes.

"No, we haven't," Olivia said, and knew it would disappoint her grandmother. "But we did get invited to be part of this TV game show."

"Oh! How exciting. What are you going to do?"

Olivia braced herself to navigate explaining the strange premise. "Well, that's what I'm here to tell you. To be on the show, we have to go away for a month, so I won't be able to visit you each weekend—but I'll still call! And you can call me for anything, like always."

Ruby blinked at her. "Where are they sending you?"

"Not far, Grandma. And I can come see you if anything urgent happens. Dr. Park knows she can call me for anything important."

Ruby reached across the table and lovingly cupped Olivia's cheek with her soft hand. "I'll be fine, my dear. You and Chuck go off and do what you need to do to repair your relationship, hmm?" She gave her a little pat.

"Oh no. Grandma, that's not what we're—"

Ruby pushed herself up out of her chair with a soft grunt. "You know, the first time I met that boy, I knew there was something special about him, and something special between the two of you. I could see it on both your faces."

The comment landed oddly on Olivia. There might have been some truth to it, but the time for granting it any importance had passed.

Ruby motioned for Olivia to stand with a wave of her hands. Olivia obeyed, and she folded her into a hug. "Listen, you go take care of your business, and I'll be here. Don't worry about me."

"Okay, Grandma," Olivia said once she had her breath back from being squeezed.

Ruby cupped her cheek again. "I'd rather see you work things out with Chuck than waste your time with this old lady."

A cynical laugh burst from Olivia's lips. "The first of those things is impossible and the second isn't even true. You aren't old."

Ruby echoed a laugh. "You never were a good liar, my dear. Don't try to flatter yourself out of your guilt for abandoning me for a month," she said with a wink.

"Grandma, you just said not to worry about you—"

"I'm kidding! Now, go on," Ruby said. "I'm sure you've got a busy day you need to get back to." She kissed Olivia's cheek and motioned her toward the door. "Send Chuck my love."

Olivia waited until she'd turned away to roll her eyes.

●　●　●　●　●

AT LONG LAST, OLIVIA FINISHED ALL HER CHORES AND ENDED UP out to dinner with Mansi. They landed at a trendy bistro on the Westside with an outdoor patio strung up with twinkling lights and an abundance of ferns. It felt like an enchanted jungle.

"So, how does it feel? Your last night of freedom," Mansi asked as she sipped a glass of red wine the same color as her lipstick. Olivia had always been envious of the bold colors she could pull off. Where Olivia opted for pale pinks, peaches, and roses, Mansi stocked up on colors called Crimson Lust and Deep Merlot and those with vague though somehow still apt labels like Goddess.

Olivia sipped her own wine and felt it go down like a smooth tonic. One of her favorite parts of dining with Mansi was her impeccable taste. "Like I'm being sent upstate to a penitentiary tomorrow."

"Yes, but instead of being locked up with all women, it will be only one hot guy you can't stand."

"Not helping, Mansi."

"Sorry. But I did bring something to help!" She bent and reached for the gift bag nestled by her feet. Olivia had seen her carry it in and could only imagine what was inside. Mansi extended the white bag sprouting with pink tissue paper. "Some survival supplies."

Olivia took it with a curious smile. "You didn't have to get me anything, Manse." She shoved her hand into the puffy present and pulled out a wad of tissue.

"Of course I did. I'm not going to see you for a month, and I know you will need more help than code 'yellow bikini' texts while you're in there."

"Well, I don't think it was necessary, but thank you anyway," she said, and grabbed the first solid object she felt. A small plastic box filled with two rows of round balls of wax. "Earplugs?"

"Indeed," Mansi said, and sipped her wine. "I did extensive research. Those block out snoring, traffic, and problematic ex-boyfriends."

Olivia snorted a laugh, not having expected her gift to contain anything so pragmatic, though she was dealing with Mansi, so perhaps she should not have been surprised. She stuck her hand farther into the bag and felt two more objects: one, a smooth box taking up the whole side of the bag, and the other, smaller with a sharp plastic edge that she wrapped her fingers around. She pulled it out with another laugh.

"A padlock?" she said at the sight of the little metal box with a U-shaped hook inside plastic packaging she'd surely need scissors to open.

"You might need it!" Mansi blurted with a grin. "There's nothing in the contract saying that creating restricted access zones inside the house is against the rules, I checked."

Olivia chuckled and set it on the table next to the earplugs. Installing it would require tools and hardware, but honestly, she might be up for it, especially if it meant locking Chuck in some small portion of the house while she had access to the rest of it. Perhaps there was a cellar.

"You are nothing if not practical, Mansi," she said, and reached for the final item in the bag.

Mansi winked at her and coyly sipped her wine as she watched her lift the narrow box.

Olivia got it halfway out of the bag before she dropped it with a gasp. Her face flooded with heat. "*Mansi*," she hissed in embarrassment at the sight of a label in metallic pink script. She recognized it from a high-end adult toy store.

Her friend cackled like a delighted witch. "What? You have *needs*, Olivia. And if we're running Operation Yellow Bikini while you're in there, you are going to get lonely, not to mention frustrated and all pent-up. This is meant to help keep you from doing anything with Chuck you'll regret. Plus, it's rechargeable, so you won't have to keep replacing batteries when you inevitably kill it."

"Mansi!" Olivia scolded again. She glanced over her shoulder to make sure no one was witnessing their wildly inappropriate exchange. She stuffed all her gifts back in the bag and buried them in tissue paper. "You couldn't have given me this *at home*? Or even *in the parking lot*? This isn't exactly a dinner table gift."

"You know, for someone who has made out with Chuck, if not done more, in public all over this city, you're being awfully prudish about this," Mansi said with a laugh.

Olivia glared at her.

"Oh, don't give me that look. You'll thank me when you're not wound tighter than a guitar string for having had no physical contact for weeks—I know how you get. Who cares if the contact comes from a piece of robotic silicone."

Olivia realized that Mansi, in her endless wisdom, made an excellent point.

Until she met Chuck, Olivia had never been a voraciously sexual person. Her appetite had been moderate at best, but she had realized after their first night together that that was because she hadn't known the full extent of what existed. That someone could make her feel so desired with a single look that satisfying that desire took precedence over everything else. That her own desires, her wants and needs and indulgent fantasies, could be put front and center with no expectation for reciprocation. But that she would *want* to reciprocate so badly, to unravel him the way he did her, that the satisfaction of it was greater than what he made her feel. That all of that would add up to the need for his presence becoming physical and his absence intolerable.

Sometimes she hated him for how much she wanted him. For what he'd done to her by showing her what was possible. For the fire he'd lit in her blood that made her ache.

She pulled Mansi's gift bag into her lap and gently hugged it with a repentant smile. "Thank you for the gift, Mansi," she shyly said.

Her friend laughed, and they enjoyed the rest of their dinner.

When they left the restaurant, they'd just hugged goodbye on the sidewalk when Olivia heard someone shout her name.

"Olivia!"

She turned just in time to see a bright flash pop in her face.

It left her reeling and blinking stars, and she didn't realize what had happened until she heard Mansi bark.

"Hey! Leave her alone!"

"Just trying to get a few shots of the infamous *love child*, sweetheart. Don't worry about it," the voice behind the flash said. It was a man Olivia didn't recognize, but she knew in a heartbeat that he was a photographer who'd sell pictures of her to the tabloids. And hearing the name he'd called her bottomed out her stomach at the thought of what story they'd print with them.

Another flash went off, and Olivia held up her hand to block it.

"I said, leave her alone, asshole!" Mansi shouted. She wrapped a protective arm around Olivia and turned them the other way.

"Come on! I'm not hurting anybody," the man said, and followed them. His flash continued throwing sparks into the dim night as he spoke. "Olivia, want to pop off your top again like you did in the video?"

Her body went rigid, and she froze for half a step.

Mansi squeezed her arm around her. "Ignore him. Just keep walking."

"*Olivia*," the man taunted. "Come on, honey. Turn around for me."

Her chest had grown tight, and each breath came with more effort. It took everything in her power not to take off running down the sidewalk, but that was what he wanted. A scene.

"Fine. You're not nearly as friendly as your mother. Didn't she sleep with like half of Hollywood back in the day? We all know she hooked up with at least *one* person's husband."

At this, both Olivia and Mansi stopped walking. Before

Olivia could react, Mansi whipped around and stabbed a finger in his face.

"Listen, motherfucker. If you say *one more word*, I will throw a harassment suit at you faster than you can blink. I will bury you in charges so deep, there is no amount of trashy tabloid photos you could sell to dig yourself out. I said: Leave. Her. Alone. Hear me?" She said it with such malice, Olivia shivered in the warm night.

She could see the fright on the photographer's face. He'd gone pale and his eyes were as wide as the full moon. Olivia was surprised he managed not to pee his pants.

"I hear you," he nearly whispered.

"Good," Mansi said just as quietly, which was somehow ten times scarier than her screaming at him.

Olivia still stood like a statue on the other side of them, and just as Mansi turned back around to her, the man lifted his camera and snapped one last photo of her surely looking like a deer in headlights.

Mansi froze, and a look like she wanted to turn around, smash his camera, and beat him with her Prada bag flitted across her face, but he'd taken off running. She returned to Olivia's side and gave her a tight smile. "Well, congrats on surviving your first paparazzi," she said in a breezy but sarcastic tone.

"Thank you," Olivia quietly murmured, still stunned. She tossed a final glance over her shoulder at the man retreating down the street. She got a sinking feeling in her gut that those photos would end up online, and nothing good could come out of that.

A S IT TURNED OUT, both Olivia and Chuck had been wrong about the house where they were set to spend the next month together. It was neither a cramped condo nor a sprawling mansion, but rather a semimodest, single-story house with a nice yard tucked away behind a gate. Olivia reasoned the privacy would be useful given the paparazzi incident on the sidewalk the night before.

She also reasoned that Chuck had brought an unreasonable amount of luggage.

He'd shown up wearing a loose, billowy button-down with rolled sleeves and a pair of brick red shorts like he was going on vacation. His sunglasses perched in his messy hair and his phone stuck from his shirt like a pocket square. He leaned on one suitcase's extended handle and crossed his ankles. His boat shoes made him look ready for a yacht. It reminded her of the yellow bikini trip to Mexico, and she imagined him smelling like sunscreen and a hint of sweat. The idea made her lick her lips. The way his eyes widened at the sight of her in her curve-hugging red maxi dress gave her an admittedly large swell of satisfaction.

The romantic notion that it was just the two of them battling their perennial attraction in a gated driveway in Pacific Palisades dissolved when Olivia took note of the whole motley *Name Your Price* crew unloading equipment from a van as she approached from the rideshare that had dropped her off.

"What's all this?" she asked Chuck, and gestured to his six—*six*—suitcases. He stood among them like a Roman sculpture in a boxy little garden.

"My stuff."

"Your *stuff*? Chuck, how could you possibly need this much stuff for a month-long stay in a house with laundry and where you'll surely be lounging by the pool in swim trunks each day anyway?"

He smirked at her and her reasonable set of a single large suitcase, a computer tote, and a toiletries bag.

She smirked back, sure that one of his medium suitcases was taken up solely by his daily ten-step skincare routine.

"Let's save the drama for the cameras, shall we?" Parker Stone interrupted them. He approached and clapped his hands together with a smile. He looked more casual than he had at their meeting at the studio, wearing an untucked button-down and jeans. He was midfifties and wore a wedding band on his left hand. "Welcome to your new digs, kids," he said, and squeezed each of their shoulders. He guided them toward the front door. "Now, the plan is to shoot your arrival and first impressions of the house. Then we'll give you a little tour inside and let you get settled before we set up for an interview with TJ this afternoon." He sharply cut off and whipped his head around. "Where even is TJ?" he asked no one. "Mark! Have you seen TJ?" he shouted at a burly man lugging camera equipment up the driveway.

Mark shook his head. "Nah. That asshole is late for everything."

Parker sighed. "Host of the show and thinks he's the goddamned king . . ." he muttered. "Anyway, just hang for a few minutes and we'll get rolling." He left them as quickly as he'd come, and it made Olivia dizzy.

She and Chuck awkwardly stood between their pile of belongings and the house's entrance. Like many homes in affluent pockets of Los Angeles, it was beautiful. It might not have had towering privacy hedges, an ocean view, and a tennis court, but it was made of glass and stone, with lush, manicured landscaping and plenty of natural light. At least Olivia got that impression from where she stood in the front yard.

"Is all filming this chaotic?" she asked, and gestured at the swarm of people burying the prim front lawn in crates, cases, and duffel bags. A frenetic energy hung over them all while they hurried about and shouted to one another.

"Pretty much," Chuck said with a snort. "You'll get used to it, don't worry. Soon you won't even notice they're there."

Olivia swallowed a nervous lump in her throat because in truth, she *was* worried about being on camera. She knew she didn't have to remember any lines or hit any marks, but she'd never done anything on film before, and she wasn't sure she'd be able to overcome the nerves racking her body like live wires at the mere thought of it.

"Hey. You'll be fine, Liv," Chuck said as if he'd read her like a book. The fact that he had annoyed her. As did the fact that he reached out and gently touched her arm with an assuring squeeze that admittedly accomplished the job and made her relax. What was more, that simple, genuine gesture reminded her how much she already missed the feel of his hands on her.

She shook him off and side-eyed him. "Don't."

He looked wounded for a brief second. His lips pursed and he nodded. "Sorry. You seemed worried, so I thought— Never mind."

A new car pulling into the driveway interrupted their conversation. Where Olivia half expected TJ Price to have finally shown up and climb out of the zippy Prius—though she had to admit, she would have expected him to arrive in something a little flashier—she instead saw an eager young man pop out from the driver's seat and begin unloading grocery bags from the trunk.

"Who's that?" Olivia asked.

"Probably our runner," Chuck said.

"Our what?"

"An assistant who runs errands for the production."

The young man, who could not have been a day over twenty-one, bounded up the driveway with grocery bags swinging from his elbows and a case of seltzer in his arms. He was tall and skinny with brown skin and a pair of smudged glasses that had begun to slip down his nose. He smiled so brightly at them Olivia could see all his perfectly white teeth.

"Hi! I'm Tyler," he chirped. "I'd shake your hands, but mine are a little full." He awkwardly laughed, and Olivia instantly liked him.

"Hi, Tyler. I'm Olivia. Do you need a hand?"

"Oh no. I got it, Ms. Martin," he said, and juggled his load. "I'm just stocking the house with groceries for you. I started with some basic staples but let me know if there's anything specific you want. I'll be happy to get it. Hi, Mr. Walsh," he said with a smile at Chuck.

"Hey," Chuck said in a disinterested tone that sounded dismissive.

"I loved your last movie," Tyler gushed. "That scene with the car and the thing." He mimicked an explosion sound and happily laughed. "It was so cool."

"Thanks," Chuck offered with a smile that didn't reach his eyes.

Olivia was about to whack him in the arm and tell him to stop being rude to someone who was clearly a fan, when another car came screeching into the driveway. The front gate had been held open for all the traffic. This car was much more what she'd expected TJ Price to crawl out of. A modern Batmobile in jet black that was so low to the ground, he really did have to hoist himself up out of it.

"Sorry I'm late!" he hollered, and trotted up the driveway. "Traffic on the 1, you know how it goes. So, who's ready to party?" He grinned at them, and a whiff of his cologne hit Olivia in a rush when he stopped on the front porch and punched his fists into his hips. He was close to her in age and exuded the confidence of someone used to commanding the room.

"Nice of you to join us," Parker said with an annoyed bend to his lips. He rejoined their crowd on the porch, this time with a cameraman on his heels. "Okay, gang. We're set up to roll, now let's— Tyler, move. You're in the shot."

"Oh! Sorry, Mr. Stone," Tyler blurted. He tore his starry-eyed gaze from Chuck and walked backward from the porch. "Where should I put these—?"

"Just leave them in the car for now," Parker tersely instructed. "I'll let you know when you can come inside."

"Okay, but some of this stuff is frozen, and it's pretty warm out—"

"Tyler! You're a smart kid. Figure it out!" Parker called over his shoulder. He turned back to Olivia and Chuck with a tight smile stretching his lips. "Sorry. He's my daughter's boyfriend. My husband made me hire him this summer. I swear, nepotism is going to be the death of me in this town. *Anyway*, let's get going."

Olivia tried to keep up. Chuck looked unfazed and maybe a bit bored.

They walked right up to the front door before Parker turned around.

"As a reminder before we go in," he said, "you've consented to be filmed around the clock inside the house and on the property. All the common areas and backyard are equipped with cameras and microphones. In addition, the film crew will be here daily except for Sundays. And"—he paused for dramatic effect—"one final reminder: if you leave the house other than to go into the backyard, you lose." He grinned at them like he was entirely too pleased with himself. "So, what do you say, Olivia and Chuck, are you ready?"

The desire to turn around and run hit Olivia so hard, she would have done it if Chuck hadn't surreptitiously pressed his hand into her lower back. He held it there like a guardrail, and in that moment, she was thankful he'd touched her because otherwise, she would have lost them the game before they even started.

"Yes," Chuck said.

"Mm-hmm," Olivia echoed in a breathy murmur that didn't even sound convincing to her.

"All right, then! Here we go!" Parker sang. "TJ, take it away."

He opened the front door, and Olivia got the distinct sense that she needed to take a final deep breath before plunging into the sea. Parker stepped back, behind the camera, and TJ stepped forward, in front of it with Olivia and Chuck.

The house welcomed them with a tiled entryway flooded with natural light coming in from a skylight. The décor included a stash of natural artifacts—driftwood tables, succulents, tasteful art—and modern amenities. Given that the house was shaped like a U, the pool glittered straight through the back wall, with each wing stretching into the shady backyard on either side of it.

"Welcome to your home for the next month, Olivia and Chuck. Kitchen and living area to the left; bedroom, gym, and office to the right; bathrooms on both sides," TJ said.

Olivia gazed around at the truly lovely setting in a daze, doing her best to ignore the cameras pointed at her face. Her apartment could have fit in it four times over, and even if it was modest by L.A. standards, it probably still cost five million dollars given the location.

"This is beautiful," she said at the same time Chuck said, "Sorry, did you say bed*room*? As in singular?"

TJ grinned and beckoned them to the left wing. "Sure did, Chuck."

"Does that mean there's—"

"Only one bed? Indeed. We thought it would keep things interesting."

Olivia threw Chuck an annoyed look that said *I told you so* as they rounded into the living room, which was, to her surprise, completely empty aside from a flat-screen TV sitting on a low stand. The camera crew followed on their heels.

"Where's all the furniture?" she asked.

TJ gave them another sly grin. "Being delivered tomorrow. Teamwork and assembly required."

Olivia's heart sank. Not only at the prospect that they had nothing to sit on, but also that they'd been sentenced to flat-box furniture they'd have to assemble to remedy the situation.

"Wait, we have to put it together?" Chuck said, eyes wide.

"Yes," TJ confirmed with a nod that managed to look smug.

Olivia gave Chuck a desperate look that she felt one of the cameras zoom in on. She could imagine the show overlaying a comedic sad trombone over it when the scene aired. They'd never assembled furniture together before, but seeing that they managed to get in a fight over the littlest things, the activity that notoriously sent couples spiraling into outrage did not hold promise for them.

"Something else we thought would keep things interesting," TJ said. "This way." He breezily waved them toward the kitchen on the other side of the dining room, where they at least had a table and chairs. The left wing of the house was essentially one continuous, open room. The kitchen held a large granite island with barstools, a stainless steel pillar of a fridge, and an impressive range. "Fridge will be stocked daily with ingredients for a meal that you both have to agree on eating together for dinner."

"Or what, we starve?" Chuck said with a dark laugh.

TJ gave him a look over his shoulder that said he was serious. "Precisely."

Olivia tried to stifle her groan. Agreeing on what to have for dinner was one of their biggest challenges. They'd waste *hours* arguing over where to go, what to order to dine in, what to cook at home. The mental labor was exhausting, thanks in no small part to Chuck's particular diet habits. She'd name every restaurant in WeHo, and he'd shoot them down one by one for some reason or another: *too far, too greasy, too loud, too small, too slow, exclusive use of paper straws.* Most nights when they ate together, she'd end up eating a bowl of cereal and he'd have a protein shake and they'd sit in silence staring at the TV, annoyed with each other. Coming up with a communal meal choice every day for the next month might be enough to send her packing on its own.

"Why is there a lock on the dishwasher?" Chuck said. He pointed to the strange contraption that looked part child-safety device, part industrial clamp holding the shiny silver door shut.

"Because, dear Chuck, a clean kitchen is key to a happy couple."

"Oh my god," Olivia muttered, seeing their intention.

Dishes.

They would inevitably pile up because Chuck never did them, even though sticking them in a dishwasher took all of a few minutes and made life much easier. If they had to wash them all by hand, Olivia would be hurling dinnerware again in no time.

They passed into a hallway with a set of glass doors that led out onto the pool deck, all the while Olivia acutely aware of the lenses pointed at her increasingly distressed face. Second thoughts roiled inside her like a spirited pep rally. Chuck tried to open the door on the opposite interior wall, but like the dishwasher, it was locked.

"What's in here?" he asked.

The grin on TJ's face was sinister and satisfied. "The second bathroom. Access to it waits behind one of your challenges. You'll learn more about it later."

Olivia closed her eyes and scrubbed her face with a hand. Sharing a bathroom with Chuck was a recipe for disaster. He'd take up ninety percent of the real estate with his trunk of products and leave the other ten percent a mess with towels and dirty clothes. Just the thought of it already made her want to scream.

And she realized that was the whole point.

After they'd left that negotiations meeting feeling high and mighty over their victories in the contract, the *Name Your Price* crew truly had sat around thinking up inventive ways to torture them.

They passed into the backyard, and a cool breeze coming in off the distant ocean ruffled Olivia's skirt. Palm trees rustled a scratchy hiss. Ivy crawled the stone wall surrounding the yard and the outside of the pool house in the corner, which looked like it had sprouted from the green oasis itself. The pool sparkled like a giant sapphire gemstone in the center of it all. Two cushioned lounge chairs and a table with an umbrella and chairs were scattered on the deck. The camera crew pivoted around in front of them to capture their reactions.

"Let me guess," Chuck said in a dry tone, "the pool is rigged with alarms, and we can't actually get in it."

TJ burst a laugh. "No, but that would have been a good idea. The backyard is fair game. Except for the pool house, obviously. The film crew will be using it on occasion."

Of course they couldn't go into the pool house. An escape on the property would have been too easy. At least they could spend time outside if they needed to. Like a prison yard. Olivia silently hoped TJ wasn't about to tell them they were only allotted one hour of sunlight per day.

They reached the other side of the house and entered a sliding glass door into the bedroom. The bed was a queen size at most, and Olivia was glad she'd have it to herself, though she didn't know what Chuck was going to do without a couch that night until their furniture arrived the next day. She'd leave it to him to figure out.

"Bathroom through there," TJ said, and pointed to what was obvious given the en suite nature of it.

Olivia saw a glimpse of a sunken whirlpool tub and a glass-stall shower. She sincerely hoped there was more than one sink.

"And this way," TJ said, waving them through the door into a hallway, "leads to your office and gym."

The generic, utilitarian office had a desk, chair, and bookshelf. The gym, on the other hand, was impressively large—larger than the bedroom. Someone must have knocked out a wall at some point to expand. The floor was a bouncy type of rubbery wood and one whole wall had been replaced with a mirror. It held a treadmill, rower, stationary bike, and all sorts of weight equipment.

Chuck waltzed right in, brazenly confident and feeling at home, and reached for the top bar on a squat rack that resembled a cage. He did an effortless pull-up that Olivia had to avert her gaze from. "All this fair game too?" he said when he landed back on the floor.

"All yours," TJ said. "Use it as you see fit."

Chuck was smiling, and Olivia was suddenly aware of something.

It was another form of sabotage, this one more stealth than

locking doors and forcing communal meals. They'd given them free access to parts of the house that involved partial nudity (the pool) and physical exertion (the gym) because both of those things would make for good TV and render the other person precariously horny if either of them engaged within view.

It was like they'd studied the Manual of Olivia and Chuck and knew all the buttons to push.

"This is a nightmare," Olivia whispered, and noted a camera zooming in on her face again.

TJ must have heard her because he smiled as he waved them onward. They passed back through the entryway, where their luggage had been brought inside. When they returned to the empty living room and kitchen area, they found Tyler shoving groceries into the fridge.

"Oh! Sorry," he said in a dramatic whisper and ducked out of sight of the cameras. He kicked the freezer drawer closed on his way around the corner.

Olivia wondered if the frozen items he'd mentioned were perhaps desserts, maybe chocolate ice cream, because she could certainly go for a stress treat.

TJ called for their attention with a clap of his hands. His booming game show host voice was in full effect. "All right. So now you've got the lay of the land. And remember, you can't leave the house other than to go into the backyard until your time is up. Otherwise, game over." He looked at each of them for signs of confirmation.

"Yep," Chuck said.

"Got it," Olivia echoed while she silently said *a million dollars a million dollars a million dollars* over and over in her head.

"Excellent. Now, one more thing before I leave you to unpack." He held out his hand like he expected someone to place something in it. When nothing happened, he closed his eyes and sighed. "Tyler!"

Tyler poked his head back around the corner. "Yes, Mr. Price?"

TJ shot him an impatient glare. "The first challenge. I need the first challenge!" He snapped his fingers and held his palm out again.

"Oh! Sorry," Tyler blurted again. He scurried over to the dining table, where he grabbed a large, flat envelope and brought it over to TJ's waiting hand.

"Thank you," TJ said through a tight jaw. Then he robotically blinked and turned back to face Olivia and Chuck and the cameras. "Excellent. Now, one more thing before I leave you to unpack." He repeated his line from before like nothing had interrupted him. "Your first challenge."

Olivia and Chuck glanced at each other, unsure what to expect. Chuck was the one to finally grab the envelope and open it. He slid out a sheet of paper with the *Name Your Price* logo at the top and scanned the short paragraph of text. Olivia leaned in to read it, but only got past the first few words before TJ cleared his throat.

"Out loud, please?" he said, and nodded at the cameras.

"Sorry," Chuck muttered like he should have realized. He too cleared his throat and began to read.

"'Olivia and Chuck, welcome to your new home. To make your stay more interesting, your first challenge, beginning now and lasting the duration of your time here, is no physical contact. This includes but is not limited to holding hands, hugging, cuddling, kissing, and any more intimate sexual acts.'" TJ bounced his head and smiled at each word like they were notes in a song. Chuck glanced up at him while Olivia felt her insides shrivel in dread. Chuck continued to read. "'Should you engage in any of the aforementioned acts, your prize money will be reduced by an amount deemed suitable by the production crew based on the severity of the infraction'—wait, is this for real?" Chuck blurted. "We can't touch each other, or we get docked money?"

Olivia snatched the piece of paper out of his hand and read it for herself. It was all right there in black and white.

"Indeed, it is for real, Chuck," TJ said with another sly grin. "We thought this would keep things interesting. Like I said in our meeting: your chemistry is incredible. Now!" He paused and reset with a breath. "I'll leave you two to unpack and get settled before we do our first interview. We want to get it out of the way today in case you don't last the night." He said it like they were cast members in a slasher film whose fate was in the hands of a deranged madman—which, when Olivia thought about it, felt appropriate seeing they were locked in a house of horrors that had just gotten a hundred times worse.

Chuck snorted. "Thanks for your faith."

TJ simply smiled. He checked his smartwatch. "Let's meet in an hour for the interview. We'll set up out back since there's no furniture to sit on in here to easily get you in the same shot." He gave them a mocking wink and stepped away.

"Perfect," Parker said as he reappeared. "Let's cut there for a second." The cameramen who had been following them the whole time lowered their cameras. "Do you guys have any questions?" he asked.

Olivia was in too much shock to speak. *No touching?* Yes, of course they'd agreed to *no sex*, but no touching? At all?

She glanced at Chuck to see him smooth his hand over his

stubbly jaw as if he knew how much she enjoyed the soft scratch of it against her face, her chest, her thighs, and was thinking the same thing about how high they'd just raised the stakes on them.

"Um, yeah," Chuck said to Parker. "This no-touching thing. What kind of money are we talking here?"

Parker grinned. "As the challenge said, that depends on the severity of the infraction. So, let's just say, if you're going to do it, make sure it's worth it."

Olivia flushed at the word *it* and everything it implied. They should have seen this coming. She felt like a contestant on a dating show who'd been duped into flying to a private island fully stocked with eligible, chiseled bachelors only to be told they were all off-limits. There were at least five shows with the same premise, all hinging on forced proximity but no hanky-panky.

Not that she wanted to touch Chuck. Because she didn't. They were broken up. But that didn't mean it wasn't going to happen. And now her prize money was at risk if it did happen, and she suddenly wanted to turn around and run out the front door because all of this was a terrible idea.

She turned to Chuck with a glare. "You better behave yourself."

He flinched. "*Me* behave myself? The rule applies to us equally, Liv."

"Yeah, well, you're the one more likely to break it."

A smug, playful little grin curled his mouth, which she admittedly wanted to kiss right off his face. "Am I?"

She grumbled and turned away from him to see Parker waving over Tyler.

"Tyler is going to be your gofer," Parker said. "He'll be in charge of delivering your groceries each day for whatever you decide to eat together. I had him put some basics in the pantry and fridge for breakfast and whatnot, but dinner has to be together, at the table or bar. No exceptions."

"Yes, Mr. Stone?" Tyler asked when he reappeared from the hall.

"Come here and give Olivia and Chuck your number so they can tell you what to shop for."

"Oh sure!" he said with the adorable eagerness of a puppy. He recited it, and they both added it to their phones.

"Thank you," Olivia said.

"Of course, Ms. Martin."

"You can call me Olivia."

"Okay," he said with a faint flush to his cheeks. He glanced at Chuck like he might make the same offer, but Chuck ignored him and headed for the entryway.

"Do you need help with your luggage, Mr. Walsh?" Tyler called after him.

Before Chuck could respond, Parker stepped in. "Let's let them do that on their own, Tyler. Benny!" Parker called to the nearest cameraman and made a circular motion with his finger pointing upward. "Let's keep rolling."

If Olivia thought they'd be left in peace to unpack, she'd been sorely mistaken.

Benny the cameraman lifted his equipment, and when she returned to the entryway to find her luggage, she saw another member of the film crew step in the front door.

Olivia hurried after Chuck, hoping to talk to him before they were on camera again. "Why are you being so rude to Tyler?" she whispered, and reached for her suitcase.

"What? I'm not being rude," Chuck said, and slung one of

his bags over his shoulder. He gripped another by the handle and turned toward the bedroom. He would have to make multiple trips to get them all.

"Uh, yes you are. He's just being nice, and you're blowing him off at every turn—" She cut herself off with a gasp. "Wait! Is *this* why people think you're difficult on set? Because you're mean to production assistants?"

Chuck stopped walking so fast that she ran into his back. She hoped that didn't already count as a no-touching infraction because there was nothing that she could have done to prevent it. He turned around and gave her a serious look. "I'm not mean to anyone on set. Especially not assistants."

She recoiled from the look on his face. "Okay, sorry."

He softened and shook his head. "Sorry. I guess he reminds me of someone, and it's something I'd rather not think about." He sighed. "It's just hard to be around all this when I haven't worked in a while. Kind of a slap in the face, you know?"

Olivia honestly had not thought of that. That it might be difficult for Chuck to be on what was for all intents and purposes a film set when he'd been struggling to find work.

"Sorry, Chuck. I didn't think—"

He cut her off with a shake of his head. "It's fine." He looked over his shoulder toward the hall and then back at her. "Time to make some TV, I guess."

CHAPTER

7

THEY SPENT ABOUT TEN minutes unpacking together in the bedroom, mostly arguing over how to divvy up the hangers—Chuck relinquished five to her. *Five!*—before Olivia walked away, at the risk of snapping one and using it as a shiv. She decided to give him space with his precious clothes; she'd finish unpacking later. She didn't have much time to kill anyway before a makeup team arrived to prepare her for the interview.

They set up in the bathroom—which did have two sinks, thank goodness—and attacked her with brushes and powders and sprays that left her glowing but wearing enough product to clear out an Ulta. When they finished, she blinked her false lashes at her reflection in the mirror. All made up, she bore an uncanny resemblance to her mother. One that settled an odd layer of discomfort over her like an itchy blanket.

The person who rigged her up with a microphone told her she had five minutes before she was needed out back. Though she'd interviewed her fair share of actors and visited plenty of sets, she felt completely out of her element being on the other end of the deal. She planned to spend those five minutes taking deep breaths and figuring out how to stop fidgeting.

So far, she was failing at both.

"Hey. You okay?" She heard a familiar voice from behind her.

She turned to see Chuck in the doorway. With the crew out in the backyard setting up, they were alone for the time being. She didn't know where Chuck had been while she was pampered and prepped, but he looked good enough to taste. He'd changed into a cream button-down that complemented the short, silky blue dress she'd put on, and he'd left the top two buttons open and rolled the sleeves. Chuck was well aware of how to highlight his features.

In truth, Chuck was one giant feature. Head to toe, he didn't have a bad angle.

Olivia felt her knees give for an embarrassing second. She swallowed the carnal urge she always got at the sight of him and remembered she was preparing to film an interview for a TV show largely because of him, and she was not entirely happy about it. Also, she wasn't allowed to touch him.

She turned back to the mirror and tugged at her dress, letting her annoyance back in. "I'm fine. This just isn't exactly my comfort zone."

He stepped into the bathroom, and she became very aware of his presence behind her. No one had spritzed her with perfume, and they probably should have since she was nervously sweating, but Chuck smelled divine. Something spicy and fresh at the same time, layered over the smell she'd come to know as just *him*. She had to fight the urge to turn around and shove her nose into the familiar contours of his chest. "Ah, well, it's mine, so I'm happy to give you some tips," he said with a smug smile.

She watched her eyes roll a full loop in their reflection. "That won't be necessary."

A pause passed, and Olivia could feel every inch between her back and his front buzzing like an electrical storm. She could also feel his eyes taking in her appearance with a hunger that she hated to admit burned in her own belly.

"You look great," he said, shyly, which was out of character for him. His compliment came off polite and like something one would say to someone they'd only recently met and had not yet crossed any boundaries with, and she and Chuck had crossed every boundary that existed.

She shot him a half glare in an effort to shield both her appreciation and reciprocal opinion and to remind him they'd laid ground rules.

"What?" he said with a sly grin. "There were no rules about compliments."

"Well, maybe we should add some," she said with a tilt of her chin.

His eyes took another indulgent tour of her curves. "Good idea. Especially if you're going to walk around looking like this."

Her cheeks burned. She turned around to face him. "Chuck, you can't—"

He cut her off by gently cupping his hand over her mouth. His palm was warm and soft. He raised one finger to his own lips, pushing them out into a shushing shape, and shook his head. He took his hand off her mouth and pressed it over the tiny microphone clipped to her dress. Given its position and the cut of her dress, his hand rested right over her heart and halfway on her bare skin. She felt it blistering there. "Lesson number one: don't say anything you don't want people hearing when you're wearing one of these. You never know who might be listening."

She glanced down at his hand splayed against her chest, trying to gather her bearings, and reeling at the feel of his skin on hers. *Of course*, she thought, feeling foolish. Hot mics were the source of earth-shattering scandals. She didn't even think that someone might have been listening.

She looked back up at Chuck and found a guarded earnestness in his eyes. "Got it. You better move your hand before they write us up for an infraction."

He gave her a sly smile and dropped his palm.

Her chest felt as if it had been scorched, inside and out. She shook the feeling and moved for the doorway. "Let's get this show on the road."

Chuck followed her. "Lesson number two: don't say clichéd things like that."

She glared over her shoulder and stepped into the bedroom. "Sorry I'm not up on the lingo with you and all the other C-list actors."

"It's B, and don't say 'lingo' either."

"Your narcissism is still intact, I see."

"As is your self-righteousness."

"Still leaving the seat up too?"

"Now more than ever."

"Of course you are, because being inconsiderate is an intrinsic part of your personality."

"I'm also still tall, and I know how you love to take offense to things I can't change."

"Olivia! Chuck! Right on schedule," Parker greeted them when they came through the back door. He held his arms out like he planned to hug them, and they both blew right past him.

"I only want you to change the things that make me want to scream," Olivia snapped back.

"Well, by my count that's everything," Chuck retorted.

Olivia ignored him and crossed to the pool deck's shaded corner, which had clearly been set up for filming. They'd moved three of the patio chairs into a small cluster with a garden table between them with a vase of flowers on it. Olivia plopped down in a chair without direction, assuming she'd end up there anyway. Chuck sat in another chair and straightened his collar.

"And I see we're having a great afternoon," Parker mumbled, following them as they bickered.

A crew of techs swarmed them. The makeup artist from earlier swiped a brush down Olivia's nose and across her forehead. The sound tech reached behind her and clicked on her microphone's pack. Olivia noted out of the corner of her eye when he did the same thing to Chuck, and she realized their mics were never on.

Heat pooled into her lower belly and pushed up into her face at the thought that Chuck had used the hot mics as an excuse to touch her off camera.

She glanced sideways at him, still feeling the heat of his hand on her chest, but he wouldn't look at her. His eyes stayed forward as the makeup artist gave him a final brushing too.

"So!" Parker said, drawing their attention with a clap of his hands. "We're eager to keep things rolling."

TJ Price chose that moment to join them. He entered from the kitchen wing's back doors wearing a blazer and jeans. A makeup bib fluttered around his neck like a doily, and he shoved the end of a sandwich into his mouth. He took a hard swallow and removed the bib. "Let's do this, huh!" he said with a beaming grin, and joined them in the makeshift studio. He sat in the chair adjacent to them. The techs pounced on him like a pack of wolves.

"Right," Parker carried on, sounding exasperated. "We'll be starting with a couples interview. We want to give the viewers a chance to get to know you both. They've all seen the video from the street—and Chuck's backlog of work—by now, I'm sure." He gave Chuck a wink, and Olivia tried not to scoff when Chuck beamed like he had just been patted on the head. "But we want to give them *more*. We want them invested. Sound good?"

"Yes," Chuck said with a nod at the same time Olivia said, "That depends on what you're going to ask us."

TJ chuckled. "I like her," he said as if everyone there were his personal audience. "I like you," he said again, directed at Olivia. "I knew you were something special from the moment you demanded we double the prize money. Actually, from the moment you flipped off everyone in the street." He chuckled, and Olivia winced in chagrin.

"That was aimed at me," Chuck butted in.

The panel lights they'd set up blinked on, and Olivia flinched in the high beams despite already being outside in the daylight.

"Quiet, please!" someone called from off set where she could no longer see.

TJ chuckled again, darker this time. "Sure, Chuck. But I still enjoyed it."

"It wasn't yours to enjoy . . ." Olivia thought she heard Chuck mutter as if he wanted full possession of her ire.

Her lip twitched the tiniest bit upward at the thought.

"Okay, here we go, folks," Parker said from somewhere behind the camera that was suddenly aimed at Olivia like a gaping eyeball.

A cold sweat broke out over her skin, and her breath lodged high in her chest.

A new person stepped forward, a man with a shaved head and glasses at the end of his nose. "Olivia, Chuck, I'm Dan, your director for this interview. Pleasure to meet you. TJ is going to lead you through some questions. Just answer them naturally and honestly, and we'll see where we end up. Okay?"

Olivia found something about this new person calming. She didn't know what, but she was thankful for it because the lights, the camera, a half-dozen people staring at her, and her ex sitting three feet away in front of them all—the one person she might have turned to for comfort if she could only stand him—had her ready to burst with nerves.

"Sounds good. Thanks, Dan," Chuck calmly said.

Olivia found a surprising ounce of relief in the sound of his voice and nodded.

"Great. Here we go!" Dan said. He disappeared behind the camera and called action.

TJ leaned forward, ready. Olivia noted that he didn't have a script or any notes. "Olivia, Chuck: America's new favorite couple. Thank you for joining us."

"Hi, TJ," Chuck said, and Olivia took the cue from him.

"Hello," she added.

"So, by now everyone has seen your public breakup in all its glory. In that clip, you both state you would not get back together. Olivia even put a dollar amount on the likelihood. And now here you are on *Name Your Price* in an attempt to live together for the next month. By the time this interview airs, that video will be news to no one, so we want to give viewers the chance to get to know you better. Who are Olivia and Chuck? What's *your* story?"

He blinked at them with a wide, expectant smile, and Olivia found herself too aware of the camera to speak.

The warm rumble of Chuck's voice caught her off guard and once again eased her discomfort. "Well, I'm an actor, and Olivia is a writer for *Mix*. They were doing a spotlight on me, and we met when she came to interview me. Of course, as the consummate professional she is, she immediately dropped the assignment when our relationship turned personal." He said it fondly. As if the memory was one that he held special.

In truth, Olivia remembered it fondly too. Despite having cursed his name and wishing she'd gone through with the assignment and never agreed to a date in moments she was most frustrated with him, the memory of the first time she saw him up close still set a swarm of traitorous butterflies loose in her belly.

"Was it love at first sight?" TJ said with a bounce of his eyebrows.

Chuck laughed a funny sound. "It was something at first sight, that's for sure."

TJ sat forward in his chair. His elbows pressed into his knees. "Tell us more about that. You two have incredible chemistry; I can feel it right now. I mean, anyone who saw the video can see it plain as day. Is that what drew you together?"

Heat blossomed on Olivia's cheeks. She hoped it wasn't visible on camera.

"Olivia? What are you thinking?" TJ asked, and she felt her face grow even hotter.

She was thinking about how after she'd told her boss she couldn't keep the assignment, she and Chuck went out that night they met and made out outside Mel's diner, a blur of lips and loose clothes and wandering hands. She was thinking about how they slept together the next night and the next and the next and the next. She was thinking about how every time they were together it felt simultaneously like stars aligning and the worst idea she'd ever had. She was thinking that her feelings for him were a complicated mess, and she'd made it even messier by agreeing to let a TV show tape them for the whole country to watch.

But she wasn't about to say any of that.

"I guess you could say our chemistry drew us together."

"Mm-hmm. And what tore you apart?" TJ asked, startling her like he'd thrown a bucket of ice water on warm embers.

Olivia and Chuck swapped a glance, and she realized there wasn't an easy answer to that question.

"How long is this interview?" Chuck said with an awkward laugh. He smoothed his palms over his knees, and Olivia wondered if he was nervous too and simply better than her at hiding it.

"As long as it takes!" TJ said with a guffaw. "I sense this story goes many layers deep. Why don't we start with that day in the street? What led to that argument and Olivia's now viral declaration?"

Olivia snorted, feeling the rage of it all come rushing back. "He stood me up for my grandmother's eighty-fifth birthday party."

TJ flinched, and Chuck took a sudden interest in looking at his fingernails. "*Ouch*, Chuckie," TJ said. "That stings."

Chuck rolled his eyes. "Don't call me that, and I didn't *stand her up*. I had an important audition to go to."

"For which you didn't get the part," Olivia added. "So it

turned out leaving an innocent old lady wondering why her party guest ghosted her was all in vain."

"I won't get any parts if I don't go to auditions!" Chuck snapped.

"Well, you're not getting them even when you do go, so what's the difference?" Olivia snapped back. "It was *one night*, Chuck!"

"One night that could have changed everything!"

"Okay!" TJ interjected. "I see the fuse here is short. No wonder that scene in the street was so explosive."

"You should have seen what you missed upstairs . . ." Chuck muttered.

"What's that?" TJ asked.

Olivia shot Chuck a death glare, daring him to elaborate.

"Nothing," he said, backing off.

TJ looked back and forth between them like he was watching a tennis match. "I sense there's more to the story here, but I also sense we aren't going to get very far in this interview with the two of you together."

"Can't say we didn't warn you," Olivia said with an annoyed arch of her brow. She leaned her elbow on the chair's arm and sighed.

TJ looked back at her like it was a challenge. "How about this?" he said after a beat. He looked over his shoulder at the camera crew and Parker and waved his hand to cut. "Why don't we start with some one-on-one footage for this segment?"

"Sounds great," Chuck said, and stood up. "I volunteer to go second." He stepped away and left Olivia sitting there in the spotlight.

"I—" she started to say, and stopped when she felt all eyes on her.

"Olivia? Is this okay with you?" Dan the director asked.

She felt trapped, but storming off set might ruin her chances of getting paid, and that was, after all, the whole point.

"Sure," she said, defeated.

"Excellent," Dan said. "TJ?" He gestured at him to carry on, and Olivia didn't like the sly grin on TJ's mouth.

"Let's do it," TJ said.

Dan called action again, and Olivia felt the camera boring into her like a drill. She'd lost sight of Chuck behind all the equipment.

"So, Olivia," TJ resumed. "You're a writer for *Mix*. What draws you to that line of work?"

She felt herself settle into a much easier interview. "I like learning about people. I like telling their stories."

"That makes two of us," he said with a grin. "You have an interesting story, don't you?"

An uncomfortable feeling separate from the one due to the lights and camera took root at the base of her spine and began to climb. "What do you mean?"

TJ settled back in his chair. "Well, you're the daughter of a rather famous—or should I say, *infamous*—couple, aren't you? Rebecca Martin and Bradley Harris?"

Olivia startled at the abrupt shift in direction. "Um, yes. They were my parents."

"Your mother was a brilliant actress. Such a tragedy. How well do you remember them?" He gazed at her with an expectation that said this had been part of his plan all along, to get her to talk about everyone's favorite secret scandal, and she was not equipped.

Her mouth went dry. She had to unstick her tongue from her teeth. "I don't remember them at all. They died when I was a baby."

"And your grandmother raised you, is that right?"

Olivia expected someone to yell cut. This had nothing to do with her and Chuck, and frankly, she was uncomfortable talking about it.

But the camera was still pointed at her, and the lights were bright. She didn't know the rules of interrupting filming.

"Yes. My grandmother raised me." Her voice nearly shook.

"Mm-hmm. And what about Astrid Larsson?"

Olivia felt as if she'd been punched in the stomach. She even rocked forward slightly. She didn't know how to respond. She didn't know what TJ wanted from her. She was beginning to sweat. A bead rolled down her cheek. Or maybe that was a tear, she couldn't tell. "What about her?" she managed to say.

TJ casually held out his hand palm up. "Have you ever talked to her about it all? I mean, your parents' affair ruined her marriage."

The statement knifed into her. Olivia had never spoken to Astrid. She imagined the woman loathed her simply for existing, but she'd always been thankful that Astrid had never sold her side of the story either. She had been notoriously tight-lipped for nearly thirty years despite the public's pleas for dirt. If she ever changed her mind, the enormity of her broken silence would send shock waves through the entertainment world and surely upend Olivia's quiet life, and she did not want to be thrust into the spotlight as the living, breathing reason that everyone's favorite actress was heartbroken.

She was suddenly angry with herself for not seeing the trap she'd walked into. *Of course* they were going to ask. She was an idiot for not realizing it.

"Do you feel guilty about the role *you* played in it all, Olivia?" TJ asked.

Her lips began to tremble. She felt cornered. Tears hot with anger and embarrassment washed her eyes. She blinked them away as best she could. "I . . . um . . ."

"Okay, I think that's enough." Chuck reappeared from behind the cameras. He put himself between Olivia and the crew. She didn't even know he was still in the yard.

"Hey, man. No one called cut," TJ protested.

"Yeah, well, these questions are out of line. They have nothing to do with us, and that's what we signed on for," Chuck said with an edge to his voice. He turned to face Olivia. The soft look on his face caught her off guard. "Are you okay?" he asked.

"Yeah," she said weakly.

He held out a hand like he was going to pull her up but remembered the rules and beckoned her instead. "Come on."

"Um, we're not done," TJ said, annoyed.

"I think we are, though," Chuck said without turning around. He flipped up the back of his shirt and unhooked his mic pack. He unthreaded it through the front of his shirt and wadded the tangle in a ball.

A reluctant smile lifted Olivia's lips that he was coming to her defense. She followed suit and unclipped her mic before disentangling it from her dress.

"You guys can't leave," TJ whined as they tossed their gear onto the table.

Chuck ignored him and spoke directly to the executive producer. "Parker, you can call my agent about the direction of the show. I'm sure he'll have concerns after he hears about this." He stepped around the crew and nodded at Olivia to follow him.

They walked off toward the house and left the crew gaping after them.

Olivia waited until they were back in the bedroom to speak. "Chuck, what are you doing? We can't leave! We need the money!" she said in a harsh whisper.

Chuck stopped to face her. "Don't worry. They need us. We have to show them they can't push us around."

The way he said *us* shot a pang of . . . something through her.

"You don't think they're going to get mad?"

He casually shrugged. "Probably, but that's their problem. He shouldn't have gone after you like that. It was out of line, and they need to know it."

Discomfort from TJ's questions left a bitter taste in her mouth. At the same time, she felt a swell of affection toward Chuck. "I should have known they were going to ask about my parents. I feel like an idiot. But thank you," she said. "For stepping in like that."

He gave her a soft, sympathetic smile. "No problem."

An ease settled between them, and Olivia nipped it in the bud before it could blossom into something that would lead to trouble. "Is *this* the kind of behavior that gets you fired from sets?"

He rolled his eyes with a sigh. "No."

"Sorry! If you're not going to tell me, then I'll just keep making assumptions."

"You and everyone else . . ." he muttered.

Olivia let it go, knowing he wouldn't surrender. "So, are you actually going to call your agent?"

Chuck glanced out at the pool deck. The film crew milled about looking bored and like they were used to such drama. Parker and TJ were having a heated conversation under the umbrella.

"No," Chuck said. "Not now anyway. Let's give them a few minutes. They'll come around."

"You sound remarkably confident about that."

He shrugged. "They've invested a lot in this show. They aren't going to let us walk that easily. And besides, we haven't broken any rules, so it's not like they can kick us out."

She realized he was right. She chewed her lip, hearing her heart still beating too fast in her ears, and watched Parker and TJ's conversation. Her eyes drifted over to the camera crew on the lawn. One of them had slipped off his shoes and stood ankle-deep on the pool's first step. A dip in the water didn't sound half bad; she considered taking one later that night.

She turned back when she felt Chuck's fingertips graze against her shoulder. She looked down at his hand hovering with his thumb tracing out a little circle, and then up at his face.

He guiltily bit his bottom lip. "You had a . . . um . . . fuzz on your sleeve." He brushed the backs of his fingers against the crown of her shoulder again.

Olivia arched one brow at him, not believing him for a second and feeling the same fiery ache she'd felt when he'd put his hand over her chest an hour earlier. "A fuzz? Just like I had a hot mic before the interview? I *knew* you'd be the one to break the rules, Chuck."

He opened his mouth to respond when Parker appeared at the door. He knocked on the glass and slid it open.

"Hey, guys. Sorry about that. We're ready to get things back on track now." He gave them an apologetic smile and beckoned them with a hand before turning around.

Olivia glanced at Chuck.

He'd stowed his guilty gaze and put on a smug smile. He

held out a hand and nodded at the door. "Told you they'd come around."

● ● ● ● ●

THE INTERVIEW TOOK UP MOST OF THE AFTERNOON. ONCE THEY were done and Olivia had peeled off her fake eyelashes, Chuck left her alone in the bedroom to finish unpacking.

She made use of her allotted five hangers and took the liberty to steal a few of his. He certainly didn't *need* ten different pressed shirts, nor the blazer he'd hung in the walk-in's far corner like it was some kind of precious artifact. He'd packed a small mint of clothing—one of his button-downs alone was worth half of everything Olivia had packed combined—and she couldn't deny that the soft, rich fabrics felt heavenly between her fingers when she removed them from their hangers and folded them on the dresser in the closet's center. She gave herself credit for not simply throwing them on the floor.

She was unloading her socks into a drawer when an otherworldly screech that she'd never known the likes of tore through the house.

"*OLIVIA!*" Chuck screamed like a banshee.

She jumped so hard, she stubbed her toe on the dresser and dropped the little nugget of folded socks she held.

"*OLIVIA, COME HERE NOW!*"

In a panic—because he had to be in grave danger to be making such sounds—she took off running toward his voice. Her heart slammed into her ribs. The cameraman who'd been in the closet with her followed right on her heels. A pain in her toe from catching it on the dresser throbbed up through her shin like a hammer stroke with each step as she ran down the hall. He'd called from the other wing of the house, and by the time she found him in the living room, she was ready to dial 911 on the phone clutched in her hand, slick with panicked sweat.

Except Chuck was not floundering amid a bloody murder scene like she'd expected. He was standing in the middle of their furniture-less living room pointing a remote at the TV.

"What?" she demanded, out of breath and hopping on one foot while her toe turned purple. "What happened?" A second cameraman stood in the corner, aiming his equipment at them.

Chuck turned to her with an ill, stricken look on his face. "There's no internet," he said as gravely as if they'd been sentenced to death.

Olivia exhaled a breath big enough to make her head hurt. "*Chuck!* I thought you were dying out here!"

"I might as well be!" he nearly shrieked. He clicked the remote at the TV, which Olivia then noticed was a gray screen with *No Signal* scrawled across it. "Nothing works. There's no cable, no streaming. I hadn't checked my phone before now because we've been busy since we got here, but look for yourself!" He nodded at her phone clutched in her hand.

Her speeding heart had begun to slow. She took a breath as another kind of panic set in. "There can't be no internet," she muttered as she thumbed her phone. When she saw that her Wi-Fi signal had been reduced to none, she realized that she hadn't checked her phone since they'd arrived either. She had an unread *How's it going?* text from Mansi, so at least the cell service worked. But no internet . . .

"No," she said plainly. "This can't be."

"I know. It's like they jammed the signal," Chuck said. "Did you guys know about this?" he asked the two cameramen in the room with them. Parker and TJ had long since left.

Neither of them responded.

Olivia hobbled over to the kitchen island where she'd left her tote, her toe still aching, and scrambled for her laptop. "No, no, no," she said in a rush. She pulled it out and pried it open to see the Wi-Fi signal completely empty. "*No!*" She slammed it shut and held her face in her hands. "There can't be no internet."

How was she supposed to check her email? How was she supposed to know what was going on in the world? How the hell was she supposed to distract herself from being locked in a house with Chuck Walsh for a month?

"Maybe it's like the second bathroom," Chuck offered. "Maybe we can win it in a challenge or something."

Olivia groaned. Even one day without a connection to the outside world would be torture. She was tempted to call it quits right then and walk out the front door with her hands up in surrender.

"This is just another way they are trying to break us," she said.

"What?" Chuck looked up from where he'd squatted by the TV. He'd found a basket full of DVDs. "I will sleep through literally all of these . . ." he muttered as he ran a hand over the cases.

Olivia rejoined him in the empty living room. "They've set this whole house up to test us, to make it harder for us to be here together, Chuck." She flung her arm at the kitchen. "The dishwasher, the dinner plans, only one bathroom, only one bed. No touching. It's all designed to make us break. And now this." She sighed in dismay. "No internet means we're going to have to . . . spend time together. Talk to each other."

Chuck looked up at her and swallowed like he wasn't sure what to make of the prospect. He looked back down at the basket of DVDs and plucked one out of the ten options. "Or just watch *Finding Nemo* on repeat for a month."

"Don't hate on the fish."

A genuine whine spilled from his mouth. He flopped back on the carpet like a cranky kid, and Olivia half expected him to throw a tantrum.

She felt the same way, but instead of melting down, she took a breath. "This is fine. It's fine," she said with a shrug and a false sense of confidence. "We can do this."

In response, Chuck groaned and smacked the *Finding Nemo* case against his forehead.

● ● ● ● ●

THEY'D MADE IT TWELVE HOURS IN THE HOUSE TOGETHER BY the time Olivia was ready for bed, which, all things considered, was impressive. Exhausted from the move-in and interview and still cranky about their new accommodations, they opted for eating what Tyler had already supplied rather than requesting ingredients for a full dinner they would've had to muster the strength to agree on. Olivia had an ice cream sandwich and a piece of toast, and Chuck was defeated enough to microwave a frozen burrito.

The camera crew had left for the night, but the glowing red dots from the lenses mounted in the corner of each room made Olivia feel like they were being watched by tiny vampires. She'd left Chuck to his own devices to carry out his ten-step bedtime skincare routine because she knew she would have thrown an elbow trying to share the same bathroom space he'd commandeered ninety percent of, just as expected. She'd changed into her pajamas, shorts and a stretchy camisole, and taken her toothbrush and facial cleanser to the kitchen sink. When she returned to the bedroom to find him nestled into one side of the bed with a book in his lap, she froze in her tracks.

He was shirtless and under the covers from his waist down. Her eyes went to his cut arms and naked torso like magnets. She hadn't seen him shirtless other than in her imagination since that day on the sidewalk. She knew he slept in his underwear, if not naked, and she sincerely hoped he hadn't stripped down before staging this coup. But perhaps most problematic was that he was wearing her ultimate kryptonite: his glasses. His vision needed only slight correction, and he wore contacts during the day, but the pair of black frames he put on at night easily took him from already gorgeous to hot professor fantasy status. She bit her lip at the sight, and then remembered they'd had a deal.

"What are you doing?" she asked, annoyed.

"Reading," he said without looking up. "I found this on the shelf in the office. I'll take classic sci-fi over *Finding Nemo*. And besides, this will probably take me a month to finish anyway." He lifted the thick paperback from his lap, and Olivia saw he was a few pages into *Dune*.

She walked into the bathroom to deposit her toiletries and returned to the bedside with her hands on her hips. "I meant, what are you doing in the bed? We agreed that I get it."

He put the book down and gave her a serious look. Or perhaps it was the glasses making him look serious. She hated to admit they gave him an air of authority. "No, *you* said you get the bed. I never agreed."

"I—" She realized he was right. She'd claimed the bed, but the only thing they'd actually agreed on was no sex. And sharing a bed, well, it didn't need to be stated that one thing would lead to another. And now they had an official hands-off rule to contend with. "Chuck, no," she said. She waved her arms in a chopping motion like an X.

"Liv, it's fine. Look, I'll build a pillow wall." He grabbed one of the spare pillows and shoved it up against his hip. "I'll stay on my side; you'll stay on yours."

Olivia rolled her eyes. They'd never stayed on separate sides of the bed in all their time together. They slept in a tangle of sweaty limbs or spooning or, most commonly, didn't sleep at all.

She knew it would be impossible, and after the day she'd had, she didn't want to deal with it. Not to mention, a slip-up would cost them money.

"Chuck, please. My foot hurts from when I came running over your little meltdown in the living room earlier, I essentially got harassed in our interview today, this house sucks, and I'm really, really tired!" Her voice rose into an exasperated whine. She clenched her fists at her sides and stamped her good foot.

Chuck gave her a weary look. "And you think all those things don't apply to me too?"

She arched a brow at him. "None of those things apply to you!"

"*Ugh*, you know what I mean, Liv! I know you had a rough day, but so did I! I'd sleep on the couch if we had one, but we don't. This feels fair." He patted the pillow he'd squished into the bed's center, then held up his hands. "Hands off. Promise. I won't lose us any money."

He could make all the promises he wanted, but she was worried about herself. Inevitably, that pillow would end up on the floor, and she'd roll over into his warm chest and nuzzle her face into her favorite crook between his shoulder and neck. Then he'd pull her close, and his hands would find their way to her thigh, her back, under her shirt—

"Chuck! Get out!" she snapped.

He didn't move but instead set his jaw and cast her a defiant look. Those damned glasses only worked in his favor. "No."

They silently stared each other down. The test of wills left Olivia's pulse quickening. She felt it fluttering in her wrists, her throat. Her breathing picked up, and when she saw Chuck's tongue flash over his lips, a little pink dart like a dare to give in, she steeled herself.

"Fine," she said.

A smile bent his mouth as if he'd won, but instead of climbing into the bed with him, Olivia turned on her heel and left the room. She left him staring after her and walked back to the kitchen.

She knew she could get him out of the bed. He just needed the right incentive.

The kitchen lights automatically flicked on when she entered the glossy space. She yanked open a few drawers, muttering to herself until she found what she was looking for.

"*Yes*," she hissed victoriously, and clutched the small metal object in her palm.

Chuck had resumed reading by the time she returned to the bedroom. She felt his eyes follow her as she walked into the closet with purpose.

She ran her fingers over the luscious sleeves dangling on his side and picked out a baby blue shirt with a mononymous Italian label. Chuck looked great in it, of course, but he looked great in anything, so the loss wouldn't be too bad. She pulled it from its hanger and marched back into the bedroom holding it up by the collar like a stray cat.

He sat straight up as if he'd been electrocuted. "What are you doing?"

Olivia wickedly smiled and snapped open the lighter she'd found in the kitchen. "Get out or I'll burn it."

Chuck's face drained of color as he visibly fought not to leap out of the bed and save his precious clothing. "You wouldn't *dare*."

She flicked on the flame and held it dangerously close to the shirt's elegant cuff. "Try me. And I'm honestly surprised we've made it this far together without me having lit anything of yours on fire before."

"*Olivia*," he warned.

She held the lighter closer and grinned in the flame's flickering light. "There's a simple solution here, Chuck. Get out, and I will spare the shirt."

His throat bobbed as he swallowed. She could see his jaw working from across the room. She'd upped the stakes in the battle of wills by adding a victim.

"What's it going to be, Chuck: the bed or the shirt?"

He stared at her with both panic and fury in his eyes. His struggle was as tangible as the fabric between her fingers. He silently shook his head.

"Fine," Olivia said, and moved the flame closer to the sleeve.

"No!" he shouted, and flung himself from the bed, revealing that he was wearing boxer briefs under the covers. In one swift move, he lunged at her, grabbed the shirt, and threw open the sliding door. He dashed out onto the patio, swearing and moving like he was going to plunge the whole thing into the pool and maybe even jump in with it, when he pulled up short and realized nothing was on fire.

A victorious cackle tore from Olivia's mouth as she snapped the lighter shut. "Good to know where your priorities are."

He turned to face her, his miles of bare skin bathed in moonlight, and scowled at her with a murderous look.

They stared at each other, and it took them the same amount of time to realize that not only had she successfully gotten him out of the bed, but she'd also gotten him out of the house.

They both blinked in what felt like slow motion before lunging at the door. Olivia was standing closer to it, so by the time Chuck reached for it, she'd slammed it shut and flipped the lock.

"Olivia!" he yelled at her, standing on the other side of the glass.

She could not stop the sinister smile that spread her lips. Her plan had worked out far better than anticipated.

"Good night, Chuck," she said with a flirtatious little wave.

"Are you kidding me?" He pressed his hands against the door, fingers splayed wide. "You can't leave me out here!"

She only laughed harder. She nodded at the cushioned lounge chairs. "By my count, there's more furniture out there than there is in here, so you're better off."

He glanced at the chairs and in his sweep, his eyes landed on the doors on the opposite side of the house leading to the kitchen. He cast her a determined grin before he took off toward them.

Olivia took off at the same second, knowing he was much

closer to them given the house's layout and praying they were already locked. She ran through the halls, her injured toe throbbing, and got there just in time to see him trying to yank them open against the lock.

"Olivia! Let me in!"

Her laughter returned. "You'll be fine. It's summertime in L.A. You might as well be sleeping on a tropical beach. And don't even think of hopping the fence into the front yard and losing us this game on the first night. I'll lock the door before you get there anyway."

He gave her a look worthy of treason and stomped off.

"Good night, Chuck!" she sang.

She returned to the bedroom and climbed into the plush bed. Through the door she could see that he'd settled on one of the lounge chairs with his back to her. She peacefully drifted off, thinking that surviving a month might not be so bad after all, but also that she might have just started a war.

OLIVIA WOKE IN THE morning at first confused about where she was. The sheets were softer than hers at home, and the silence was punctuated only by gentle bird chirps—not the rush of traffic and occasional clang of a dumpster lid being dropped. It was almost jarring. She quickly remembered she was in a secluded house in the Palisades and not her apartment.

She sat up when she also remembered that Chuck had spent the night outside.

Through the back door, she caught sight of him still in the lounge chair, one arm dangling off the edge. His broad shoulders eclipsed the sides of the frame. He'd put the shirt on at some point and left it unbuttoned.

A pang of guilt hit her at the thought that he might have truly gotten cold.

She took the silence within the house to mean that the camera crew hadn't returned yet and figured she should use the opportunity to let Chuck back in before they made a scene, although the blinking red dots in the ceiling corners reminded her everything was already being recorded. She cringed at the thought as she climbed out of the bed and did her best not to look directly at any of the lenses aimed at her.

It was barely after seven a.m., the morning fresh and dewy outside. A marine layer had settled over the house while they slept, turning everything muted and gray, and she remembered they were much closer to the ocean than where either she or Chuck lived. The washed-out sky would burn off later and return to California blue, but for the time being, it felt like there was a dull dome over the top of them. As if they were in a snow globe filled with gauzy fog.

Chuck didn't stir at the sound of her sliding open the door; he was notoriously difficult to wake. He'd made her late to so many events. On the occasions they'd had to get up early for anything during their relationship, Olivia had resorted to yanking off the sheets, swatting him on the butt, threatening to pour cold water on him just to drag him out of bed. In all her trials and errors, she'd found the most effective tactic to be simply announcing she was getting in the shower and walking through the room naked.

There would be no nudity this morning, at least not on her part.

A blast of air fresher than anything she breathed just a few miles inland hit her when she opened the door. The rustling palms and chirping birds greeted her like a garden lullaby. From beneath her bare feet, the chilly concrete pool deck sent a wave of goose bumps raising her skin. She wrapped her arms over her chest.

Chuck's glasses sat on the ground below his dangling arm, as if he'd dropped them when he fell asleep. Olivia picked them up and safely set them on the small table for fear anything might happen to her favorite accessory of his in the impending storm she was about to incite when she woke him.

"Chuck," she said. "Time to wake up. The camera crew will be here soon." She didn't know if the last part was true, but she'd rather not get caught red-handed for having made him sleep outside by any in-person witnesses.

He stirred at the sound of her voice and took a deep inhale. He mumbled something and turned on his side.

Olivia rolled her eyes, knowing it would be easier to drag a bear out of hibernation. "Chuck!" she called, and clapped her hands with a sharp smack. "Wake up!"

He growled at her and sat up with a stretch. "I'm awake. Stop yelling at me."

Like the traitorous magnets they were, her eyes went straight to his bare chest. Her ogling was cut short when Chuck let out a sharp breath with a wince.

"What?" she asked with a jump, startled.

He reached for his glasses on the table and threw a hand to his lower back. "Ouch."

"Ouch, what?"

His face screwed up into a knot and his breath grew shallow. "What do you mean, *ouch what*? I slept on a lounge chair. What do you think I'm *ouching* about?"

She stepped back as he climbed off the chair in slow, painful motion. She thought he was only being dramatic until he froze halfway hunched over and groaned like his body was splitting in half.

"Oh!" Olivia blurted, and threw out her hands like she might need to catch him. "Are you okay?"

He tried to straighten up but didn't get far before he let out another pained gasp. "I strained my back in the gym the other day, and this— Nope! Nope, this did *not* help." He crunched over into a crescent shape and hissed through his teeth. "I need to go inside and lie down." He hobbled like a brittle old man with Olivia trailing on his heels.

"You hurt your back?"

He cast her a glare as best he could without fully turning his head. "What does it look like?"

"No, I mean before last night. Why didn't you say so?"

"Would that have made any difference? *Oh god.* Can you please open the door?" His words came out in a rush like even breathing hurt.

They'd reached the bedroom's back door and Olivia hurried around him to open it so that they could pass inside. "Of course it would have made a difference. If I'd known you were hurt, I wouldn't have—"

"*Ow.*" He cut her off with another guttural groan. He took tiny little steps to the foot of the bed, where he turned around and stiffly fell back onto it like a tree going down in the forest.

"What do you need?" Olivia said from where she hovered over him as she tried to gather her bearings. She'd been asleep not five minutes before.

Chuck reached up for a pillow and shoved it under his head. "You didn't happen to pack a massage gun, did you?" His voice was pinched and tight.

Olivia's mind flitted to the inappropriate dinner table gift Mansi had bestowed on her as the closest possible thing— which she had in fact packed—but she was not about to offer it up on camera, and it certainly wasn't strong enough for his needs anyway.

"No."

"Damn." He lifted into an arch that looked like it did more harm than good and winced again. "Nope. Bad idea."

"Chuck, I'm so sorry," she said, truly feeling it.

"It's fine," he said through gritted teeth. "I just need to lie here for a little bit. It'll loosen up."

She gazed down at him having gone rigid in pain. "It doesn't look fine. And isn't lying still only going to make it stiffer?"

"Well, I can't move, so it's the best option right now. Just give me like ten minutes. I'll be fine."

"Okay, but what if I—"

"Liv, I'm fine." He turned his head to look at her where she stood wringing her hands at the bedside. He gave her a soft smile that landed closer to a grimace. "I mean, I'd give up a million dollars to have you give me a back rub right now, but since that's not on the table, I'll work with what I've got, which is over-the-counter anti-inflammatories. Could you actually get them for me? In my toiletries bag in the bathroom."

"Yes. Definitely." She hurried off and left him there flat on his back. In the bathroom, she pawed through his neat case of balms and creams and hair products until she found a rattling bottle of blue gel pills. She filled a glass at the sink and carried it all back to him.

"Thank you," he muttered when he did his best to sit up and swallow the pills. "One day in and you've already taken me down," he said with a smirk.

"Chuck, I'm—"

"I'm kidding. Don't worry about it. It's been tight for days and was basically a bomb waiting to go off. I'll be better in a little bit."

Olivia chewed her lip, feeling truly awful for him. "Is there anything else I can get you?"

"Nope, I'm good," he said on another tight breath.

"Okay." At a loss and still feeling guilty, she wandered through the hallway and out into the kitchen area. She was certainly wide awake now, but a cup of coffee was still in order. When she opened the pantry to find the coffee, she saw a bag of potato chips. The sight of junk food inspired a thought that eased some of her guilt, and if she was lucky, it might make the man in the other room feel a tiny bit better.

She grabbed her phone and pinched it between her ear and shoulder to call Tyler while she set about making coffee. To her surprise, he answered right away.

"Good morning, Ms. Martin," he said.

"Oh, hey, Tyler. I wasn't sure you'd be up. Sorry it's so early."

"Of course I'm up. What can I do for you?" he asked without a hint of bother.

Olivia lowered her voice; she wasn't sure why. Perhaps because she still felt bad about what had happened and speaking it softly would lessen her guilt. "I need you to pick something up at the store."

"Oh sure! That's what I'm here for. What is it?" His eagerness made her imagine him clicking a pen, ready to jot a note.

"Strawberry Pop-Tarts, please."

● ● ● ● ●

NOT TEN MINUTES HAD PASSED BEFORE THE DOORBELL RANG. Olivia was going to give Tyler a tip if he'd delivered on her request so quickly, but she was instead greeted by Parker and a camera crew when she opened the front door.

"Morning!" Parker sang with as much pep as Tyler had when she'd called.

Olivia wondered if everyone on the production was a morning person.

"Hi, Parker." She hardly managed a greeting before he pushed inside the door with the crew on his heels. Thankfully, they weren't rolling yet because the look of surprise on her face would not have been flattering on TV.

He surveyed the entryway and welcomed himself into the living room. The intrusion reminded Olivia that she'd signed away her privacy for the chance at the prize money, so there wasn't much point in being annoyed with it.

"Where's Chuck?" Parker asked. A sly grin lifted one side of his mouth. "You didn't kill him last night, did you?"

Olivia huffed a dark laugh. "No, fortunately. But he's not feeling well this morning. He . . . um, hurt his back."

Parker arched a curious brow at her. "Intriguing. I hope he's okay because it should be only a minute until—"

"Parker, where do you want this?" someone called from the entryway.

Parker smiled. "Until that."

Olivia did not like the mischievously pleased look on his face. A feeling of dread over what *that* meant settled in her belly on top of the very strong coffee she'd had. The mix was not pleasant.

Parker breezed past her back out into the entryway with his hands up like he was conducting an orchestra and ready to give instructions. Olivia hurriedly followed.

They arrived to see a team of delivery men hoisting large, flat boxes through the front door, and the pieces clicked.

Their furniture had arrived.

Their furniture that would have to be assembled.

Parker looked to Olivia to answer the question of where to put the boxes.

She tried to keep the dread out of her voice when she managed to say, "The living room is fine."

The crew wrangled the trio of boxes—a couch, a chair, and a coffee table, she saw on the labels as they went by—into the living room and left them without any ceremony.

"So, everything go okay last night? The house is all good?" Parker asked from beside her as she surveyed the pile of oversized boxes dirty from being shipped.

She turned to him with a sour look. "Yes, Parker. The house with no internet, no food, one bed, one bathroom, and my ex who I can't touch is lovely."

He gave her another self-satisfied grin. "Excellent. Well, I was just popping in to make sure things were on track and you guys didn't already bail. Oh, and to give you this." He produced another large, flat envelope like the one that had decreed no touching, and Olivia winced. "TJ will be here soon for what comes next."

"What comes next?" she hesitantly asked, and took the envelope.

"You'll see," he said in a cheery tone.

Olivia tapped the envelope against her palm. The crew hadn't lifted their cameras yet, and she assumed they'd want her to read the message with Chuck, so she left it sealed for the time being. "I can't wait," she said flatly.

He winked at her. "I'm needed back at the studio. Crew will be here all day; TJ should show up around eight. You should have plenty to keep you occupied." He nodded at the furniture. "Tell Chuck I hope he feels better. Benny." He pointed at the cameraman nearest them and spun his finger in the air, the move Olivia now knew was his way of saying *let's roll*.

He left nearly as quickly as he'd come, and Olivia was

suddenly alone in a room full of deconstructed furniture with two cameramen expectantly watching her.

She sighed and silently repeated her refrain of *a million dollars a million dollars a million dollars*. The envelope weighed heavily in her hands. She could only imagine what was in it and was sure it had to do with the furniture situation. Looking at the largest box, she could see that they would have a navy blue couch with black wooden feet if they could manage to put it together.

A memory suddenly invaded her mind swiftly and aggressively enough that she could do nothing to stop it.

The first night she'd gone back to Chuck's place with him—which was the night after she'd met him, she was slightly embarrassed to admit—they'd sat on his couch. As they'd kissed again, she knew even then that his lips against hers changed everything. They'd gone to dinner before, and when he invited her back to his place after, they both knew her coming was a given without him needing to ask, the same way they knew the couch was just a charade, a pit stop formality, to ease their guilt over jumping into bed after knowing each other hardly twenty-four hours.

His kisses that night were different than the ones outside Mel's diner had been the night before. In the privacy of his home, he kissed her with more hunger, more desperation. Like she was a deep well he needed to reach the bottom of to find the water that would keep him alive. He'd laid her back on the couch; she'd wrapped her legs around his hips. They were halfway undressed, hearts pounding, when he'd mumbled "Bedroom?" against her throat, and all she could do was nod in response.

He'd carried her to his room simply because he could, and perhaps also because he didn't want to break contact with her.

She remembered drawing this conclusion at the time amid swooning hard enough to pass out because *she was being carried to bed* by a man so desperate to have her that he couldn't bear the thought of setting her down. Whatever his reason, she'd clung to him with the same desperation, the same need to seal her body to his, until he'd laid her down on his mattress. Then he'd—

"Olivia?"

The sound of her name jarred her out of the fantasy with the force of a fishhook.

She blinked several times and looked up to see Tyler standing in the living room entryway with a shopping bag looped over his arm. "The door was open, so I came in. I got what you asked for." He held out the bag with a smile.

Pulling her brain from the lurid memory took an embarrassing amount of effort. She blinked several times more, her face surely flushed, and remembered she was on camera. Benny had set up in the corner already.

"Um, thank you," she said to Tyler. Her head was still spinning.

"Of course." He beamed at her. "Need anything else?"

"Not right now, I don't think. I'm going to take this to Chuck. I'll be right back." She headed for the hall and worked to fully pull her mind out of her memory. *Damn it, Chuck.* His hooks were so deep into her, clothing *and* furniture could make her fall victim to memory. She shook it away and entered the bedroom.

"Chuck?" she called. "Good news, I got you something to help you feel better—" She rounded the doorway to find the room empty. "Chuck?"

"I'm in here," he said from the bathroom.

She turned in that direction, expecting to find him at the sink. "What are you—" She cut off with a gasp.

"I'm taking a bath. The heat helps."

Olivia dropped the bag and threw her hand over her eyes. "You're naked!"

"Yes," he said flatly as if in a trance. "That is generally required for taking a bath."

Her heart started pounding. She'd seen it all before, of course, but wasn't expecting to walk in on it unannounced. He sat in the tub up to his chin, and the water only made everything look . . . enlarged. Forget the couch memory; this was ten thousand times more powerful. "Okay, well, um, here are some Pop-Tarts. I thought you might like a treat. I'll just leave them here for you." She scooted the bag with her foot, hand still over her eyes.

"Thank you."

She couldn't tell if the thick slowness to his voice was from being in pain or the spell the bath had him under, but he sounded ready to go back to sleep.

"Also, the furniture is here, and they gave us another challenge in an envelope. TJ is set to show up in ten minutes."

"Oh. Okay. I'll get out, then."

The sound of sloshing water made her do an about-face and dash into the bedroom. It took several deep breaths for her to shake the image of him naked in the tub, which was only made harder by the memory she'd been indulging in moments before. She was tempted to fire off her first *yellow bikini* text to Mansi for help but instead decided to head back into the living room.

There, she found that TJ had arrived early.

"Olivia!" he sang in his booming voice. He threw out his

arms and sent a waft of his thick cologne billowing from his blazer. "Good morning. Where's your other half?"

She made a mental note to start setting an alarm so that she was actually *awake* if the crew was going to show up crowing like roosters every morning.

"He's getting out of the bath. He'll be out in a minute."

"Ah. And what were you doing back there with him, hmmm? I hope nothing *scandalous*." He waggled his brows and shimmied his shoulders with a wink. "Actually, who am I kidding— I hope it was scandalous!" He let out a loud guffaw, and Olivia wanted to go back to bed and start the day over. Scratch that. She wanted to go back to the day she and Chuck broke up and keep their argument inside his apartment so that they'd never land in this ridiculous situation in the first place.

"No scandals, TJ. Sorry," she said with her best smile for the camera.

TJ eyed her like he didn't believe her.

Chuck emerged from the hall wearing a black tee shirt and a pair of loose shorts. His skin was rosy from the hot water.

"Ah, good *morning*, Chuck!" TJ boomed.

"Hey, TJ," Chuck responded with a fraction of the enthusiasm. He was upright and moving and sounding less miserable, so Olivia had to assume he was already in better shape.

When TJ headed into the living room with the crew, she nudged Chuck with her elbow and quietly murmured, "You okay?"

He shot her a half smile. "Yeah. Pop-Tarts are a universal remedy." His eyes snagged hers for a tender second before she looked down and followed TJ.

They found him standing among the furniture boxes holding

an iPad with *1:00* glowing in enormous red digits, and it served as a distraction. "Are you ready for your next challenge?" He gestured at the envelope in Olivia's hands.

"That depends on what it is," she muttered, and slipped her finger under the seal. Chuck stood behind her smelling like soap and still radiating heat from his bath. Olivia cleared her throat and began to read the letter inside.

"'Olivia and Chuck, we hope you are enjoying your stay. In an effort to make it more comfortable, we have provided you with new furniture. You will have one hour to assemble as much of it as you can. Anything left incomplete at that time will be removed from the house. Remember, teamwork makes the dream work. Good luck!'"

Chuck reached for the letter and nodded. "Okay, an hour is plenty of time. Three pieces of furniture, two of us. This should be easy."

Olivia was less optimistic about their ability to handle Slot A and Part B without issue, but she agreed that an hour should be enough time.

And, like he was dousing their newly stoked flame of hope with water, TJ grinned and reached into his back pocket. "There's more."

They both looked up at him.

"More?" Chuck said.

With his most self-satisfied sinister grin to date, he held up a pair of handcuffs. "Indeed."

Olivia's belly bottomed out at the sight of the shiny silver rings. In the right context, handcuffs and Chuck were a delicious combination—she knew from experience. But this was *not* that context. Not even close.

"You're both right-handed, right?" TJ asked, and approached them with one of the rings open like a hooked jaw.

"Yeah . . . ?" Chuck said. The trepidation in his voice stirred every nerve in Olivia's body. Whatever was about to happen was not good.

"Excellent," TJ said. "Olivia, would you please turn around?"

She did as she was asked, now standing shoulder to shoulder with Chuck and facing the opposite direction, and felt TJ take her right wrist. The metallic click of the icy cuff closing around it made her heart skip in an unpleasant way. She looked over at Chuck as TJ took his right wrist and shackled it to hers. The tiny chain links between the cuffs were hardly two inches long. When TJ finished, they faced opposite directions with their dominant hands bound together at their sides.

TJ stood back and clapped his hands. Olivia looked over her shoulder to see him reach for the iPad and jab it with a finger. "Your hour starts now."

They stood there frozen, both blinking in disbelief.

"Are you joking right now?" Chuck said.

"Nope! *Go*," TJ cheered. "You're already losing time!"

They both took a step forward—in opposite directions—and the sheer mass of Chuck's body versus hers pulled Olivia backward to the floor.

"Ow!" she cried when she fell on her butt.

"Oh! Liv, I'm sorry," he said, and helped her up.

"Take it easy, Chuck. You're way bigger than me!" she scolded, and soothed her bottom with her hand.

"I'm sorry. Let's just—" He started to turn around.

"No, that won't—" Olivia said, and spun the other way.

"Let me go this way—"

"That's not going to—"

"Ouch!"

"Sorry."

"Put your arm over here—"

"It doesn't bend that way!"

They spent a few minutes twisting and turning, trying to find a position that would allow them to function, but it was no use. They were stuck.

"We're just wasting time!" Olivia finally blurted when he tried to spin her in another useless dance move. "Stop!"

Chuck held still and huffed a tight breath, already frustrated. "We need a plan."

"You're right." She twisted around in front of him, her back to his front, and her arm yanked around backward, so that she could see the boxes. "Which of these do we want the most because we're probably only going to have time for one: couch, chair, or table?"

"Couch. Definitely couch."

"Agreed. Let's do the couch."

"Great. Where do we start?"

"Well, I assume we need to open the box," she said drolly.

"An attitude isn't going to help anything right now," he said, and set off for the kitchen to find a sharp object.

Olivia stumbled backward in his wake. "No, and neither is you yanking me around like a rag doll! Stop it!" She yanked on his arm with a sharp pull. "We are *attached*, Chuck!"

"Sorry. I'm not used to having to account for *someone else*," he said, and yanked back. He pulled open a kitchen drawer to a useless pile of tea towels.

She scoffed. "That's symbolic."

"What does that mean?"

"It *means* that you often forget there are *other people* in the world beside yourself. Like ones who invite you to birthday parties for their grandmothers that you don't show up for."

"Oh, are you *ever* going to let that go?" He pulled open another drawer and found pot holders and oven mitts. He moved to the drawers in the island and dragged Olivia behind him.

"I'll let it go when you apologize and *mean it.*"

"I *did* mean it! I apologized a hundred different ways, and you still refuse to forgive me. I swear, Olivia, sometimes I think you don't *want* to forgive me."

She gasped, offended. "What does *that* mean?"

He reached for yet another drawer, this one full of rubber bands and an array of plastic takeout silverware and chopsticks. Olivia wondered who'd put it all there and what this house had previously been used for. "It means that sometimes I think you *like* to be mad at me. It gives you an excuse to push me away—and to run away from our problems."

Growing tired of his search and their conversation, she tugged him back over near the fridge to the drawer where she'd found the lighter the night before. She pulled out the box cutter she'd seen and flipped up the blade. The overhead lights glinted off the sharp razor where she held it up between them. "Well, a lot of good running did me this time because look where we ended up."

His eyes bounced from the blade to her. His chest pumped from shouting, and his nostrils flared. She could see the vein in his forehead that throbbed when they fought. She could have painted a portrait of him from memory. *Angry Man during Fight with Girlfriend.* Except this time, as he stared at her fuming, something soft cracked open in his eyes. Something fragile that looked almost . . . hopeful. "Yeah," he said quietly. "Look where we ended up. Nowhere to go this time."

Olivia wasn't sure what he meant by it, but she saw the clock in the living room. They were down to fifty minutes. "Come on," she said, and spun around to pull him in that direction.

She handed over the box cutter and let Chuck do the honors. When he cut open the couch's box, dragging her hand along with his, the longest side of the cardboard fell forward like a drawbridge and set a flurry of Styrofoam beads broken off from the inner padding fluttering. The parts were efficiently packed inside like a jigsaw puzzle. They both stared at it, him facing forward, her from over her shoulder.

"This is going to take forever," Chuck said.

"Forty-nine minutes!" TJ sang out from where he was gleefully watching the whole scene unfold.

Olivia spun around and dug the instruction manual out of the box. Of course, it was a dozen pages of uninterpretable diagrams and nothing more.

"Great," she muttered.

Chuck reached over her and found the lone tool, a wimpy little Allen wrench, and sighed. "Even better."

She realized, as they set about wrangling the parts as best they could while TJ called off countdown milestones with increasing fervor, that they had joined ranks with any high-stakes timed reality competition. Whether they were cooking an elaborate dish from a collection of pantry flotsam and jetsam, or solving a puzzle, or making a garment, or even learning choreography, there was always a countdown and something on the line. The handcuffs were an added obstacle. Like having to make soup from toothpicks and a packet of ketchup, or learn a dance blindfolded. She wondered as she handed Chuck screws to attach one of the couch's feet what other reality TV tropes the producers were going to subject them to.

Forty-eight minutes later, after what felt like the most bizarre game of Twister ever (Put your left hand *there*! No, use your *right* hand! Lift your leg! Your *other* leg!), and by some miracle, they had an assembled couch. They'd managed to do it without killing each other or with any injury—which was saying a lot on both counts, all things considered.

"Well, congrats!" TJ said, and unlocked their handcuffs. "I am duly impressed."

Olivia rubbed her wrist, where she'd surely have bruises from being yanked around for an hour. She couldn't help the proud grin on her lips. She noticed a similar one on Chuck's.

"One is better than none," Chuck said, and nodded at the two other pieces of furniture still in their boxes.

"Indeed, it is, Chuck. And in truth, we didn't even expect you to get one at all."

Chuck snorted. "Again, your faith is overwhelming."

"I call it like I see it." TJ clapped him on the back. "Well, go ahead and sit on it. Make sure it's sturdy."

Both Olivia and Chuck walked over and gingerly perched on the cushions. Olivia was less concerned about their handiwork than she was about the quality of the couch itself. Thankfully, it didn't collapse.

"Well well well," TJ said with a flashy grin. "Look at that. Nice teamwork! You're free to do whatever you want for the rest of the day now." He dropped his big game show grin and stepped off camera. He stretched out his mouth like it might have been sore from smiling so much.

Olivia was rubbing her wrist when Chuck turned to her.

"Is your arm okay?"

She noted that he too had a red ring around his wrist. "It will be fine. Good thing we aren't cuffed together the whole time we're in here."

He huffed a laugh and combed a hand through his mussed hair. "Good thing."

"How's your back?" she asked.

"Not great, but at least the past hour was a distraction. I think I'm going to go stretch in the gym and then lie down." He got up and left her there with their new couch and the camera crew and feeling guilty all over again.

●　●　●　●　●

WHILE CHUCK RESTED FOR MOST OF THE DAY, OLIVIA WATCHED a few movies, pined for the internet, and decided what to make for dinner. He found her in the kitchen around six p.m. flipping a pair of steaks in a cast-iron skillet.

"Is that what I think it is?"

She turned at the sound of his voice from her position in front of the stove. He was freshly showered, his hair wet and matted down, and wearing a black tee shirt that hit his arms in a way that made her take a big gulp of the wine in her hand. She took another sip for good measure because he'd already put on his glasses for the night.

Thoughts of asking him if he was intentionally making things difficult for her entered her mind, but she instead smiled and turned back to the slabs of meat hissing on the stove.

"Sure is. I made garlic potatoes and—"

"Roasted Brussels sprouts," he finished for her. She glanced over her shoulder to see him take a seat at the island and pluck one of the little roasted cabbages from the serving bowl where she'd left them. "My favorite meal," he said after he ate it. "Between this and the Pop-Tarts, I guess I should make you feel tremendously guilty more often."

Olivia used a pair of tongs to pull the steaks from the pan and then glared at him as she turned around and set the plate on the island. "How are you feeling, by the way?"

"Much better. I told you I just needed to rest and I'd be fine."

She scrunched up her nose. "I'm really sorry."

He shrugged and nodded at the plates. "I thought we had to agree on dinner. How did you manage this?"

She topped off her wineglass and then held the bottle over an empty one, silently asking if he wanted some.

He nodded and held up his fingers with about an inch between them.

She poured him an inch and a half, knowing that was what he really meant. "I managed by telling Tyler this is your favorite meal, and that I was *sure* you would agree to eating it tonight." She leaned over the island and conspiratorially lowered her voice. The camera crew had left early given that the day turned out exceptionally boring what with Chuck resting and her watching movies all afternoon, but there were still the cameras in the ceiling to mind. "Between you and me, Tyler is a pushover. It doesn't take much to convince him of anything."

"Or maybe you're just very compelling," he said with a crooked grin that felt like he was flirting.

Olivia quickly changed the subject. "The couch passed the rigorous movie marathon test I put it through today, so as long as we limit ourselves to gentle lounging, I think it should hold up."

Chuck sputtered into his wine, and the sound made her

realize he thought she was making a suggestive comment about other uses for the couch.

"Oh! I didn't mean—"

He shook his head with a shy flush in his cheeks. "The couch is for sitting or lying only, got it."

Olivia tucked her hair behind her ear and set about plating their dinner.

They sat at the barstools facing into the kitchen, which felt a little less intimidating than formally sitting at the dining table. A casual ease hung over the room, and Olivia found herself settling into a relaxed meal.

The wine might have had something to do with it.

Chuck cut into his steak and took a bite. A little groan escaped his throat that made Olivia sit up straighter. "You know, your cooking skills are underrated."

"Thank . . . you?" she said, and cast him a curious look.

He waved his fork over his plate. "I just mean we hardly ever eat anything home-cooked together, but when we do, it's amazing."

"Yeah, because we can't ever agree on anything." The words slipped from her lips like they were ready and waiting to go.

Chuck cast her side eyes and sipped his wine. She expected him to volley a snarky remark right back, but instead, he said, "You're right. I know I'd be considered a picky eater in some circles, and you're incredibly patient for putting up with it."

Olivia snorted. "I don't know if I'd consider giving up and ordering takeout for myself patient, but thanks."

"You did your best. I know I'm not that easy."

It took a willful effort to stop the next quip from slipping off her tongue. The habit was so ingrained, it was like unlearning how to ride a bike or write with her dominant hand. She suspiciously eyed him and took another gulp of wine. "Am I drunk or are you being weird? Why are you admitting to your faults right now?"

He laughed a warm, gravelly sound and nodded at the half-empty wine bottle. "Judging by how much wine is left in there, no, you are not drunk. You'd need at least another glass before your lips got tingly, and two more before you started getting philosophical and handsy."

Her mouth popped open to argue at the same time she blushed. She could not deny that either of those things was true. "Shut up," she said with a half smile. "You do not know my drink thresholds."

"Oh, but I absolutely do." He reached for the bottle and re-filled her half-empty glass. Then he leaned his elbow on the island and turned toward her. "I know all sorts of things about you, Olivia Grace Martin." He cocked his head like he was studying her. His eyes turned soft and sincere. Something daring flickered in them at the same time. "One glass of wine, you're relaxed, pliable. Two, your lips start to turn purple, and you kiss with your mouth open."

She felt herself flush again and swore he'd scooted closer. His eyes traced her mouth, and with the heat of his gaze, he might as well have been running his thumb over her bottom lip.

"Three," he continued, "and your hands find their way to my back pockets and the inside of my collar, and usually my hair, which I have to admit always made it hard to concentrate when you inevitably start talking about the finer points of human existence on a floating rock in the middle of nothing with drink four."

He really had moved closer. His knee was dangerously close to touching hers now.

"Five," he said in a low growl that she had to lean in to hear, "and I'm carrying you to bed, where things I will not describe in polite company tend to occur." His eyes flicked up to the camera in the corner. The soft grin on his face was positively wicked, and Olivia noticed she'd stopped breathing.

He stared at her for three more seconds, each one making her feel like her heart was going to beat out of her chest. She was the one to tear her gaze away and it was as if she'd severed a physical thing. When she regained the ability to breathe, she nodded at the bottle and stabbed a Brussels sprout. "Better put the cork back in, then, shouldn't we."

Chuck held still long enough to make it feel like the air between them might ignite and incinerate them both. Olivia wasn't sure what he was going to do, or what she wanted him to do. Half of her wanted him to pour the bottle down the drain and the other half wanted him to pour it in their glasses until they had to open another. He ended her game of daring him and damning him when he softly laughed and found the cork to wedge it back in.

Olivia exhaled in relief loud enough—louder than she'd meant—that he glanced at her. His lips lifted in an imperceptible twitch that no one else would have noticed except her, because she knew all sorts of things about Charles Michael Walsh too. Like how he tasted when she kissed him with her mouth open, and what his shampoo made his hair smell like. And how he lightly shivered when she ran her fingertip along his collarbone, and the sounds he made after he carried her to bed and polite company was gone.

At the risk of doing something she'd regret, she pulled away and focused on her food. "You never answered my question," she said.

"Which one?"

"The one about why you were listing your faults."

"Ah," he said as if her question was a buzzkill. And the buzz she was feeling definitely needed to be killed. "Dunno. I guess it seemed like a reasonable time to bring it up."

She snorted. "Why, because we're broken up and locked in a house together with nothing better to do than analyze where it all went wrong?"

He cast her a side glance and shrugged. "I mean, yeah."

Olivia couldn't help laughing. "You sure that's a good idea?"

"I don't see why not. Come on, you give it a try. It feels kind of good to admit after all this time. What's something you could have fixed?"

She frowned at him, not liking his implication that there was a list at the ready. But if she thought about it, he was right: there were several admissions she could make about herself that might have made their relationship a little smoother during its time.

She sighed and thought back to their argument on the day their relationship ended. She'd hated to admit it, but there was some truth to things he'd said. "Fine. I guess I can be a little stubbornly independent. I'm just used to being on my own, and I can see how that might be hard to deal with." The final words came out with the ease of a cat gagging up a hairball. A shudder shook her shoulders just as she reached for her glass of wine to wash down the icky feeling of self-reflection.

Chuck laughed. "See? That wasn't so bad."

"That was literally the worst thing you've ever made me do. I might never forgive you." She spoke into her glass, and her voice echoed back like it was a tiny amphitheater.

"Baby steps. I'll settle for one confession tonight, but we've got a long way to go in this house still."

"Ugh. Don't remind me."

"Oh please. It's not that bad. Look! We've survived almost forty-eight whole hours together." He pointed at the clock on the microwave.

"Yeah, well, we are about to encounter our first round of real dishes, and we both know our track record there."

A smirk bent his lips. "*I* will do the dishes tonight. It's only fair if you cooked."

She blankly stared at him, her expression one of utter shock. "Seriously?"

"Yes, seriously."

"Wow. If I'd known the threshold was a million dollars, I would have pooled my assets ages ago."

He rolled his eyes this time, and she couldn't help smiling.

The upturn in their compatibility encouraged her to ask a question she'd been thinking about all day.

"Earlier when we were working on the couch, what did you mean when you said there's nowhere to go this time?"

He paused chewing and looked over at her. "I thought it was obvious. We're locked in a house."

"Well, yes. I know. But you sounded kind of . . . happy about it?" Uncertainty colored her voice. After thinking about it all day, she did and didn't want to know what he'd meant.

Chuck took a sip of his wine and then cleared his throat. A cautious seriousness settled over him and made Olivia wonder if she shouldn't have asked. His voice came out careful and calm, as if he were tiptoeing through a minefield. "To be honest, I'm not entirely mad about it. You have the tendency to . . .

sidestep confrontation, and being stuck here together is a natural barrier to that."

She blinked at him in confusion. "Chuck, you and I fight like it's an Olympic sport. You think I *sidestep* confrontation?"

"Not in that sense, no. I mean you tend to never *finish* a fight. You walk away before it's over, and then I'm chasing after you for some kind of resolution. That I usually never get." He said the last part quietly and glanced at her.

She suddenly felt naked. Like she'd been stripped bare, and a spotlight shone on her right there on the kitchen barstool in front of all the cameras. Her reflex was to deny.

She folded her arms over her chest. "I don't think that's true."

"It is, though. You're like the sexy cat that's always trying to get away from Pepé Le Pew."

She snorted. "So, you're the problematic cartoon skunk in this analogy?"

"See, there it is again: deflection. If you aren't physically running, you're emotionally running."

"Thank you, Dr. Phil."

"You're doing it again! Stop it!"

"Stop comparing us to animated characters!"

"That was a bad example, sorry. But I'm only trying to make a point, and that is that we never really talk about anything because you're always avoiding it."

Olivia heaved a breath and held her forehead in her hand. She did, indeed, regret starting this conversation now, but since they were in it, they might as well continue. "Fine. You want to talk? Let's talk. As you've pointed out, there's nowhere to run."

A small, victorious, but hesitant smile twitched Chuck's mouth. "Great, let's talk."

"Let's."

They stared at each other, a million topics swimming like hungry sharks between them, and neither of them sure where to begin.

"Why'd we break up?" Chuck said.

Olivia sputtered much like he had done when she'd laid down *no sex* as their first rule that night in the diner. "*That's* where you want to start?"

"The end seems like a good beginning."

"Now who's getting philosophical?"

"Olivia! See, this is what I'm talking about! You're so predictable that we could turn this into a drinking game: *Take a drink every time Olivia avoids an emotional confrontation.* I'll have to call Tyler for a case of wine and then have my stomach pumped before I succumb to alcohol poisoning."

"Okay, drama queen. Calm down."

"You know what, forget it. I'm trying to have a conversation with you, and you're obviously not taking it seriously. I'm just going to do the dishes and go to bed." He stood from his stool, sending it scraping against the tile, and rounded the island.

Olivia watched his back as he started in at the sink. The urge to micromanage his dishwashing hit her like a sack of rocks, but she was too distracted by her body unpleasantly tingling all over. She didn't like being called out, especially on a topic that made her want to run faster and farther than any other. Whether it was conscious or not, she didn't finish fights because finishing would mean reaching an inevitable end point, and an end point might result in her being left alone. Abandoned. So it was better to run away before it ever got there. Do the leaving before anyone could leave her.

But she realized as she watched him squirt a truly inappropriate amount of soap into the filling sink, enough to surely result in a sudsy mess, that she hadn't been the only one to run that day they broke up. He'd called it quits too. The irrefutable proof was immortalized on the internet.

She stood from her stool and raised her voice to speak over the sound of the gushing sink. "You walked away that day too, Chuck."

He paused with the dishes and gripped the sink's edge. He didn't fully turn around but swiveled his head so that she could see his profile. His jaw was tight when he spoke in a resigned tone. "Only because you gave me no choice, Olivia."

The words walloped her right in the chest and left her feeling winded. She backed away before he could say anything else that would cut her off at the knees and scurried down the hall to the bedroom.

Now that they had a couch, she intended to give him the bed because she still felt bad about his back and wanted him to get a good night's rest. She brushed her teeth and removed her makeup, all while avoiding her reflection because she didn't want to see the truth of what he'd said staring back at her, and changed into pajamas.

He was still doing dishes by the time she returned to the living room to build a nest on the couch. He found her there watching *Finding Nemo* when he finished. He paused by the archway leading back into the entryway.

"So, I take it you're sleeping out here tonight?" A tinge of hope lingered in his voice. Perhaps he thought they might continue their conversation.

"Yep. Good night, Pepé."

He closed his eyes and shook his head with a sigh. "Good night." Then he flipped off the light and left her alone.

OLIVIA WOKE THE NEXT morning again confused about where she was. Less so because she was on a strange couch in a strange living room and more so because of the music blaring like she'd fallen asleep backstage at a show.

She sat up, and half her blanket nest fell to the floor. A slight ache pulsed in her temples thanks to the wine. She hadn't pulled the curtains the night before because she felt no need behind a privacy gate; there was no one to see inside. And they were on camera anyway, so the thought of hiding was moot. A hazy beam of light cut through the leafy trees outside the front window and spilled into the room. By the weak color of it, she knew the sun was hardly up.

What she didn't know was why the bass line of a heavy rock song was keeping time with the pulse of her headache and playing loudly enough to rattle the screws in their new furniture loose.

"Chuck?" she called to absolutely no avail. He could have been sitting right next to her and unable to hear in the racket.

Having a sneaking suspicion that she knew what was going on, she threw back the blankets and headed for the north wing of the house with her phone in her hand.

"Chuck!" she shouted. The music got louder as she headed into the hall. She swore the art on the walls was seconds from slipping off its hooks and hitting the floor. She wondered what kind of insurance *Name Your Price* had and what would happen if they broke something.

As she approached the door to the house's gym, she figured out what was going on. At six thirty a.m. on a Friday—she'd checked the time on her phone clutched in her hand—she knew right where he'd be. It was Arm Day. Or Leg Day. Or whatever Body Part Day required a grueling sunrise workout. The only thing he got up early for was a workout, and she knew she'd find him in the gym.

She nearly kicked down the door when she got there, but instead of screaming at him to *USE YOUR HEADPHONES*, she froze and was instantly stripped of all higher intelligence.

He was shirtless with his back to her and mid pull-up on the squat rack. It was one of those pull-ups with a wide grip that put enough muscles in his arms and back on display to count. (Eighteen. There were eighteen.) Just as slowly and deliberately as he'd pulled himself up, he lowered himself back down and then did it again. His ankles were crossed, and his feet in sneakers bent up behind him. His shorts clung to his hips, and other than that, he was just miles of skin. Sweaty, tanned skin rippled with muscles bulging and sliding against each other in a way that made her do an about-face and throw herself against the wall outside the room before he even noticed she was there.

Knowing what had to be done, she frantically thumbed her phone while her heart pounded. She'd begun to sweat and had to douse the flames before they burst into something uncontrollable.

Yellow bikini!!!!! she desperately texted Mansi.

Mansi's return text came almost immediately, and Olivia imagined her friend pausing her own early-morning workout to come to her aid.

Why? What's he doing?

> **Mansi! You said no questions asked! YELLOW BIKINI.**

Sorry! Stand by.

Olivia chewed her lip and fought for deep breaths as she waited. The music pounded on from the other side of the wall. She wondered if Chuck had even realized she'd opened the door.

Her phone vibrated in her clutched hands. She looked down to see a photo of a corgi puppy in a wagon with pumpkins.

All her speeding blood rerouted to her heart, and an *aww* escaped her mouth.

A second photo came in of a golden retriever puppy in a field of daisies.

Better? Mansi texted.

Olivia made an involuntary pouty face at the adorable dogs and quietly cooed.

> **Yes. Thank you. But now I want a puppy.**

She got a kiss emoji in return as a sign-off.

Her phone nearly slipped out of her hands when Chuck appeared in the doorway and startled her so much that she yelped in surprise. She hadn't heard him coming thanks to the music leaking out of the room at nightclub decibels.

"Liv? Are you out here?"

"*Jeez*, Chuck! You scared me!" she shouted over the noise.

He absolutely *towered* over her where she stood barefoot in her pajamas. His size would have been intimidating, especially given all the freshly pumped muscles, if the sight didn't make her want to climb him like a tree.

She took a deliberate and large step back.

"Sorry!" he called as his eyes went on a quick but conspicuous tour of her body. They lingered on her chest for a hot second before snapping up to her eyes.

At the sight of him, it was like their fight last night hadn't even happened. The urge to fling herself at him pulsed in her blood, despite the *yellow bikini* texts, and the air between them strained with a familiar angst that would soothe the immediate ache but only lead to more trouble.

Her tongue was thick and heavy and her heart was still beating hard, but she managed to wrangle both enough to form coherent speech. "Music is a little loud, don't you think?" she shouted with a hand on her hip.

Chuck seemed to notice the noise rattling the walls only then. "Huh. Yeah, sorry. I thought closing the door would help. I guess the sound system is really high quality here."

Olivia blankly stared at him, wondering at how oblivious he could be sometimes.

He flashed her a smile and made a show of stretching his arms in a way that flexed his bare chest right in her face. The sight of the toned grooves she'd once loved sliding her hands and lips over made something snap into place so sharply, she almost gasped.

It was payback.

He knew perfectly well that the music would wake her up and she'd come storming in to tell him to turn it down only to find him right in the middle of her favorite exercise to ogle.

He'd played her like a fiddle.

The stunt was retaliation for making him sleep outside, probably also for their fight last night, and not only did he wake her up early, but he also left her needing to dial *yellow bikini* for help.

Damn you, Charles Walsh.

She narrowed her eyes, and instead of letting him know she was on to him, she said, "I'm going for a morning swim," and padded off toward the bedroom.

She felt his gaze on her backside and smiled to herself, thinking two could certainly play this game.

●   ●   ●   ●   ●

FOR GOOD MEASURE BECAUSE SHE HAD IN FACT PACKED IT, SHE changed into the notorious yellow bikini. Once dressed, she made sure to slowly and completely needlessly walk back by the gym on her way to the pool. She could have left through the back bedroom door, but what would be the fun in that? Chuck had turned the music down to a reasonable enough volume that she could hear what sounded like a weight being accidentally dropped, perhaps slipping out of a distracted hand, when she passed the door. Her smile widened.

She had second thoughts when she stepped outside into the

brisk morning air, but she wasn't going to let a little chill ruin her retaliation plan. The sun had nearly reached the peak of the house and would soon spill over and warm the backyard, and much to her pleasant surprise, the pool was heated.

The clear, clean water welcomed her, and she found herself enjoying swimming a few laps. The pool was designed for floating and splashing, not exercise, but its rectangular form allowed her to get in several strokes before she flip-turned into another glide across its long center. Her heart rate was noticeably elevated when she came up for air to find Parker and Benny the cameraman standing on the pool deck.

"Morning!" Parker called with a wave. He held a to-go coffee cup in the other hand.

Olivia swam to the edge of the pool and gripped the wall. "Is the front door even locked?" she deadpanned in greeting.

Parker chuckled. "Yes, but we have keys. I'm here to see how things are going and to remind you that— Oh, good morning, Chuck." He cut off when Chuck emerged from the back door, still shirtless, still sweaty.

"Hey," Chuck greeted him, and swept his hand through his damp hair.

Even from down below in the water, Olivia could appreciate the intricate network of veins and muscles, the artwork, really, that he'd just further chiseled his body into.

She wasn't the only one suddenly unable to stop staring.

"Um, yes. Right," Parker said, seeming to have lost his train of thought.

Olivia took the cue to swim over to the ladder and hoist herself up out of the pool. Instead of reaching for the towel she'd draped over a lounge chair, she stayed soaking wet and walked over to join Chuck, Parker, and Benny, who'd lifted his camera. Her hair dripped down her back and her feet left little puddles with each step. She casually rested her hands on her hips and tried not to smile when she noticed Chuck bite his bottom lip. A small, strangled sound came from his throat.

"What were you saying, Parker?" Olivia innocently asked. "You wanted to remind us of something?" She made a point to squeeze out her hair and shake it so that it slapped against her back. Of course this made her chest bounce in a way that summoned another strangled sound from Chuck. Something close to a pained groan this time that almost made her smile.

Parker looked back and forth between them and grinned. "I don't know what's going on here, but I like it. You getting this, Benny?"

"Yep," the cameraman said.

A flush burned Olivia's cheeks at the thought of being on film dripping in her swimsuit, but it was nothing compared to the heat she felt from Chuck's gaze. Whatever game they'd been playing, she'd won. She knew it by the look on his face like he wanted to take her bikini off with his teeth.

She smugly grinned and kept her attention on Parker to spare them all from having to edit out explicit footage. "What's the reminder you have for us?" she asked him.

"Ah, right. TJ and the crew will be back this afternoon for another sit-down interview."

Olivia winced at the mention of another interview given how their last one had gone. She hoped TJ would behave himself.

"Is he not going to be an ass this time?" Chuck voiced her exact thought.

Parker made an exasperated snorting sound and half shrugged. "I rein him in as much as I can, but TJ will be TJ, unfortunately."

Olivia did not like his defeatist response, but she did like how Chuck, perhaps subconsciously, had taken a step toward her and angled his body like he was ready to step in as a shield. The memory of how he'd come to her defense when TJ crossed a line last time put a soft bubble of warmth in her chest.

"I'm happy to remind him where the line is," Chuck said with a cold grin that felt like a threat, especially given the way he was standing with his hands on his hips.

"That won't be necessary," Parker quickly said. He took a sharp breath and clapped his hands as if to reset the scene. "How about we keep this going for a little while this morning, hmm? The two of you could hang out by the pool for a little longer. I mean, Olivia needs to dry off, perhaps on a lounge chair, and Chuck, well, maybe you'd like to take a swim after what I can only assume was an intense workout." He grinned at them with the subtext of *Please stay half naked for the cameras*.

"Sure," Olivia said.

"That's fine," Chuck echoed.

"*Excellent!*" Parker cheered. "Benny!" He looped his finger in the air despite them already rolling. "I'll be back later for the interview. Have a good morning!" He left, guzzling his coffee and answering his phone, which had started ringing.

Olivia and Chuck stared at each other for a beat, Olivia still dripping, Chuck still sweating. The air seemed to thicken between them.

A wry smile tugged at one corner of Chuck's mouth. It popped out the secret dimple that he reserved only for Olivia. The rest of the world got the million-dollar dazzler, but she got the boyish grin. He shook his head with a quiet laugh. "You had to pack *that* swimsuit, didn't you."

She mirrored his smile but with her full mouth, silently

saying she knew exactly what he meant and exactly what she'd done. She turned on her bare foot and sent the strings tied at her hips swinging. The sun had come up over the house now and poured itself into an inviting golden pool directly atop the lounge chair where she'd left her towel and phone. Parker's suggestion for her to dry off outside seemed like a great idea. Especially with Chuck gazing after her as if she were a tempting morsel.

Chuck sat on the other lounge chair to take off his shoes. Olivia wrung her hair out with the towel, then laid it along the chair. When she grabbed her phone before she sat, she saw she had four new text messages from Mansi.

> I know you guys don't have internet, so you probably haven't seen this. I thought you should know. Let me know if you want me to do anything about it. Xo.

Olivia's heart took a swan dive to her toes as if it had leapt off the diving board in front of her. The other three messages were screenshots of an online tabloid web page.

> *Sources have confirmed that a recent viral video of a couple's breakup is serving as inspiration for a segment on the popular reality show* Name Your Price. *Even better, the couple in question includes actor Chuck Walsh, whose recent firing from* Safe Gamble *has left him without many allies in Hollywood. The other member of the duo is Olivia Martin, daughter of the late actress Rebecca Martin and Hollywood manager Bradley Harris, a couple whose tor-*

rid affair during the latter's marriage to Astrid Larsson launched one of the biggest scandals of the early '90s. To this day, beloved film star Astrid Larsson has famously never spoken publicly about the scandal, nor have the Martin or Harris families. While Olivia Martin has spent nearly her whole life out of the spotlight, the once-dubbed "love child that ruined Astrid Larsson's marriage" was recently seen out to dinner in L.A. with a friend and will now be appearing on a TV show. Like mother, like daughter? Perhaps the Martin women have a taste for Hollywood men with bad reputations. Either way, we will be tuning in for the drama when the show airs.

Olivia had trouble swallowing the thick lump in her throat as she read. Her struggle to function was made all the worse by her suddenly speeding heart. She swiped through the rest of the messages and saw the photos included with the piece: one of her from that night outside the restaurant with Mansi looking like a deer about to get mowed down by a semitruck—it was exactly as unflattering as she expected. Another of her and Chuck, a still from the sidewalk breakup scene, him with his arms out in a shrug, chest bare, and her pointing at him with a face angry enough to spit fire.

The third—one she'd seen before but that still managed to punch her in the gut with the force of a battering ram—the one the tabloids had favored when the scandal broke: her parents leaving a hotel together with infant Olivia bundled in her mother's arms. Her father, dark haired and handsome in a suit, had his arm out shielding her and her mother from the camera that caught the million-dollar image, while Rebecca held Olivia to her chest, her tiny head in her hand, and stared into the lens with a look of true fright. The bright flash had popped off their stunned faces and drowned everything else to inky black night behind them, as if they were insects trying to scurry from a flashlight. The harsh lighting only helped to serve the villain narrative. *Caught. Guilty. Secret Love Child Exposed.* The tabloids had had their pick of headlines to splash across the image back in the day. Her mother, served a disproportionate amount of the ridicule, had been called every derogatory term for a woman ever invented. Her father was demonized as an archetype of slimy Hollywood men given that he was fifteen years older and, in fact, Rebecca's manager. And she, a baby, was crowned the love child that ruined Astrid Larsson's marriage. At least now, none of the ugly words accompanied the infamous photo.

And, as always, to round out the plot lest anyone forget who the true victim was no matter how tangential the current story, the fourth photo attached to the article was one of Astrid Larsson. A red-carpet image with her looking like an elegantly aging goddess whose hands had remained clean in the whole matter.

Olivia had seen the latter photos before, but she did not expect to see them in a text from her friend while sitting poolside first thing in the morning. Nor did she expect to be pulled so wholly into the spotlight. The threat of being part of a scandal like her parents' filled her veins with an anxious urge to flee.

"Liv? What's wrong?" Chuck asked. She hadn't noticed that he'd turned to face her. They sat with their knees together between the lounge chairs.

She looked up at the sincere concern on his face and found herself struggling to speak. When a plump tear rolled down her cheek, she only then noticed she was crying. She wiped it away, and Chuck looked like he was ready to go to war with whatever had put it there.

"What happened?" he asked, his voice low and serious.

Olivia sniffled, not sure what to say, and held out her phone. "There's something about us online. Mansi sent me a few screenshots."

He took it, and she watched his eyes scan the tiny print. His brow furrowed in focus, and where she might have expected him to hurl the phone across the yard, he let out a resigned sigh. "That's really awful. I'm sorry. But you have to ignore things people say about you online; it's the only way to survive in this industry."

She flinched, not expecting a lecture. "But I'm not in this industry." Her voice came out soft and reedy.

Chuck cocked his head and then glanced at Benny. "Liv. Yes, you are."

An argument automatically formed on her tongue, but she swallowed it down, realizing he was right. She was actively filming a TV show, and even if her grandmother had shielded her from the spotlight, by heritage, Hollywood had a claim on her. And, obviously, people were still interested in poking their noses into her private life.

She looked up at Chuck with a vulnerable plea in her eyes. "So, what do I do?"

He shrugged. "Nothing. I stopped caring what people said about me online when everyone started calling me an asshole and spreading rumors. You'll drive yourself crazy if you let it in."

The defeat in his voice, the resignation, made her ache for him. It also sparked a tiny sense of admiration. She wasn't sure she'd be able to shake it off so easily, and he hardly looked fazed. She wondered if now was her chance to take advantage of his valor and ask what had gotten him fired.

"Are you ever going to tell me why those rumors started?"

He glanced at the camera and shook his head. "Not today," he said quietly.

She was used to his deflection on the subject, but she had never considered it might have been more than a pride thing. The way he'd looked at the camera made her wonder if the truth was something he didn't want to say, or something he didn't want to say on record. An odd feeling settled in her chest as he let out a big sigh.

"Why is Mansi sending you pictures of puppies?" he asked. She'd forgotten he was still holding her phone and saw him thumbing the screen.

"Hey!" she blurted, and snatched it out of his hand. "Why are you scrolling through my phone?"

"You said it was a few screenshots! I was making sure I read it all."

She scowled at him, knowing it was a flat lie. "No, you weren't. You were snooping."

He gave her his million-dollar grin that could get him out of jail anywhere. "But really, are you thinking of getting a dog?"

She hadn't been, but the pictures Mansi sent were admittedly enticing. "Maybe."

"You should. You'd make an excellent dog parent. You'd make an excellent human parent too." He sweetly smiled at her in a way that said he'd like to coparent either of those scenarios someday. Then he pushed up off the chair and bounded for the pool in two giant steps before launching himself into it. The resulting splash arced higher than the roof and spritzed Olivia with drops.

She stared at him when he surfaced and flipped his soaked mop of hair out of his face. How he could go from making her want to scream to making her ovaries burst in the same hour was truly a unique talent.

• • • • •

DESPITE WHAT CHUCK SAID ABOUT LETTING ONLINE GOSSIP GO, she couldn't. Throughout the rest of the morning, she found herself revisiting the screenshots. Of course, she couldn't click any of the links in the photos, and an internet search would end in no-signal failure anyway. Her only option was rereading the short article over and over until it left her feeling raw and exhausted.

The line about sharing her mother's taste for Hollywood men with bad reputations sank a particularly deep barb. Her father was, by all public accounts, not a good guy, a fact that Olivia had had to accept since public accounts were all she had to go off of. Chuck's reputation had plummeted thanks to getting fired, but she knew him—perhaps better than any other man she'd known—and she knew he wasn't *bad*. Sure, he had a way of finding her very last nerve and stomping it into oblivion, but that wasn't worthy of an industry-wide reputation. She hated to think he could join ranks with her father in the public eye.

When it came time for the interview that afternoon, Chuck found her sitting at the kitchen island staring at her phone. The house had become a hub of commotion and preparation as the crew set up for filming in the backyard. Tyler had dropped off a deli tray and a giant bowl of fruit salad. Olivia managed three cubes of cheese and a grape between her despair over the article and her pending nerves about another interview.

"Unless you're looking at more puppy pictures, you should put that down," Chuck said.

She glanced up to see him looking dapper in another dreamy button-down. He nodded at her phone clutched in her grip.

"Oh, I'm . . . looking at puppy pictures. Right," she said, and pressed it to her chest as a guilty flush filled her face.

He gave her an easy, crooked smile that popped out his dimple and simply said, "Liar."

How he managed to look so good while accusing her of dishonesty, she didn't know. She felt his eyes on her makeup and the green dress the stylists had picked out for her, and she swore she saw the ghost of a battle pass beneath the carefree look on his face. He swallowed and appeared like he might reach out to touch her but waved his arm in the air instead.

"I told you to let it go. I'll take your phone away if you need me to," he said.

She half smiled. "That won't be necessary. Cutting off my only access to the outside world might make me go full Jack Torrance on you."

"Better play it safe, then."

"Probably in everyone's best interest."

"Well, this banter is a little friendlier than the last time I saw you," TJ interrupted. He swanned into the kitchen and plucked a grape out of the fruit salad bowl.

"Yes, well, you don't have us handcuffed together trying to build furniture this time," Chuck said.

"I can always bring the cuffs back out to keep things interesting," TJ said with a wink. "Come on. They're ready for us out back."

Olivia slid off the barstool and straightened her skirt. She'd put on strappy heels for no real reason other than that they went with her dress. They wouldn't even be visible on camera. Either way, they made her a few inches taller and pinched her toes in a way that meant she'd only be wearing them to walk to the backyard and sit down before she took them off again.

When they entered the backyard, she saw that it had again been set up as a little studio with the patio chairs clustered around the table. An umbrella had been pulled over for shade, and the crew milled around in a jungle of tripods, monitors, cameras, and cords.

"What exactly are we talking about today?" Olivia asked as she sat in one of the chairs. She wasn't sure if they'd watched the footage from last night and at least wanted to be prepared if they were going to make them talk about their fight on camera.

"You will find out shortly," TJ said. Olivia lost sight of him while the mic tech stepped in front of her. The ever-present mischief in his voice had her on edge. She shook it off with a forced smile and once more silently repeated her refrain.

A million dollars a million dollars a million dollars.

"So! Let's get started," Parker boomed. Dan the director had returned and was positioning himself behind the camera. The afternoon had warmed into a sun-kissed L.A. day. Olivia was thankful for the umbrella providing shade and hoped her makeup didn't start to run.

"Same drill as last time, folks," Dan said. "TJ, take it away."

They were styled, mic'd, positioned, lit, and ready to roll. Olivia took a deep breath in the final second before Dan whispered *action*.

TJ turned on his megawatt game show host smile. "Olivia, Chuck, welcome back to another sit-down. You've been in the house now for two and a half days, and I have to say, after that explosive scene on the sidewalk that began all of this, it's longer than any of us thought you would last." He chuckled, and honestly, Olivia had to agree with him. "Since we've all seen where you ended up—that spectacular showdown and split—today we want to talk about where you started. What were your first impressions of each other? Olivia, let's start with you. What did you think the first time you met Chuck?" He turned his grin on her at the same time the camera pivoted to point at her like a laser.

Olivia took a deliberately slow inhale for one, because she was relieved they weren't diving into last night's argument, and two, thinking about meeting Chuck always winded her. She needed to brace herself because whether she wanted to admit it or not, that day changed her life. No matter that they were broken up, her days would always be divided between before and after Chuck Walsh.

"We met at a Westside coffee shop for the interview," she said, and felt the memory come back to her in vivid color. "We sat outside on the sidewalk, and I honestly wondered if he'd chosen the place to be seen."

There hadn't been any photos taken of them that day, but the image of him in a tight tee shirt and sunglasses with tousled hair lived permanently imprinted in her memory.

"He was very reserved at first. I thought he was going to keep his sunglasses on the whole time, but he took them off as soon as I sat down." She glanced sideways at him and felt his gaze pierce her now the same as it had that day.

"I'd done some research on him, but all I really knew was that he'd just landed his big-break role in *Safe Gamble*, that he was known for keeping distance in interviews, and that he was single."

"A status that changed that day, right?" TJ cut in, bursting the warm memory like a pin into a balloon.

"Um . . . yeah. I guess you could say that," she said with a flush.

Chuck had asked her out during that interview, but that memory, that rose-tinted exchange that still filled her chest with helium, felt too personal to share on TV.

She let herself privately sink into it.

They'd talked about where he grew up, moving to L.A., his early days in the industry. How his first manager suggested he go by Chuck and not Charlie as he always had, and it stuck. He told her about his big new role that would start filming in a few months. When she'd worked her way to asking him about his relationship status toward the end of their conversation because everyone was pining for that juicy tidbit, she'd expected one of the vague, dismissive answers he'd given in other interviews: *I'm focusing on my career. The timing isn't right.* But instead, he'd looked straight at her and said, "I haven't met the right person yet."

He'd been open and candid with her through the whole interview. Funny. Charming. As if she'd pried loose a lid that no one else had been able to budge. But even then, the sudden conviction threaded through his words, the vulnerability, stilled her breath. Her next question tangled on her tongue because she'd somehow known even after talking to him for only an hour how he was going to answer.

"How will you know when you've met the right person?" she'd asked.

"Because I'll have the feeling I'm having right now, talking to you."

They'd stared at each other, lost to the rest of the world and safe in their own little bubble, until Chuck had eventually smoothed a hand over his jaw.

"I'm sorry," he'd said. "That was wildly unprofessional of me. I'm not trying to hit on you. I'm just . . . being honest." The sincere, bashful flush that filled his face had made Olivia's heart flutter.

"That's okay," she'd said.

Hopeful light had flickered in his gaze. "Well, I guess if I'm this far in, I might as well go all the way. Do you want to go out sometime?"

Embarrassed laughter had pealed out of her, but it hadn't put him off.

He'd given her his movie star grin. "I'm so sorry. I'm ruining this completely. You're trying to do your job, and I'm being an asshole."

"You're not being an asshole. It's just—"

"You already have a boyfriend."

"I don't!" The words had leapt out of her and made her blush. "I mean, I'm not seeing anyone right now." He'd gazed at her in anticipation, hanging on what she'd say next. She'd carefully considered her words to make sure she was thinking her decision through. "I would very much like to go out with you too. But that is complicated."

He'd leaned closer over the table, excitement flashing in his eyes and his tee shirt straining against his biceps. "Then let's uncomplicate it. What do I have to do?"

She'd laughed again and wished that closing her notebook was all it would take for her to be able to reach out and touch him. To squeeze one of his corded forearms that he was so eagerly leaning forward on.

"How about this?" he'd said, and motioned for her to hand over her notebook.

When she did, he'd started scribbling his phone number on a blank page. "You think about it and call me if you want to. If I never hear from you again other than when this piece publishes, I'll live out my days finding a way to make peace with knowing I let The One get away."

She'd snorted a laugh, and he'd looked up at her with a crooked grin that popped out a dimple she didn't know he had until that moment.

She'd known she was going to call him before he even finished writing his number.

Now she shook herself to resurface from the memory and remembered they *were* in fact filming something that would be on TV, and she needed to answer TJ's question.

"I guess you could say my first impression of Chuck was surprising."

"How so?" TJ asked.

"Well, before we met that day, I'd only seen his most recent movie. I watched it to prepare for the assignment." From the corner of her eye, she didn't miss Chuck's slight wince at the fact that she hadn't opted to watch it on her own. "Surprisingly, I liked it."

Chuck straightened himself with a smug tilt of his chin. "You liked that one, huh?"

Her instinct was to roll her eyes at his self-indulgent question, but she couldn't deny a fact.

"I did, yes. And I liked the one that came after it."

He'd had supporting roles in both films. She really had

enjoyed them both, the second one perhaps slightly more because they'd been dating by the time of the premiere, and she got to attend a Hollywood party for a reason other than reporting on it.

"So you fell for his thespian skill," TJ said, reclaiming control. "What else?"

Olivia tried to stave off the heat curling into her face at the thought of Chuck's dynamic allure. The movies were just a 2D teaser. Seeing him in living color was an assault on all her senses. But she felt like that went without saying, and babbling about his good looks would reduce her to the ranks of an airhead reality TV contestant she'd decidedly determined she was above. So she reached for something deeper and just as honest.

"Well, when I finally met him in person, I thought he was charming, of course. Obviously ambitious. Self-assured. But what I found surprising was how remarkably vulnerable he was at the same time."

Chuck turned to her with a curious tilt of his head.

"Interesting," TJ said. "Tell us more."

Olivia all but tuned him out and turned to face Chuck. She found herself confessing a truth she hadn't really considered until that moment. "I think that's what I was most attracted to, honestly. His self-confidence is magnetic, but it's the tenderness beneath that really drew me in. I guess I was intrigued by why he felt he had to hide it in public."

A glimpse of the exact vulnerability she was referring to flashed across Chuck's face, the same as it had that day at the coffee shop. She knew she was one of the lucky few who ever got to see it. It sank a hook straight into her heart.

She cleared her throat and smoothed her palms over her thighs, turning back to TJ. "I was attracted to all that. And his arms. He was wearing this ridiculously tight tee shirt like he knew my weakness. What can I say."

TJ guffawed a loud laugh as Chuck stroked a bashful hand through his hair, showing off one of the arms in question.

"The heart knows what it wants, I guess," TJ said.

Olivia blushed and quietly laughed. "Or something."

"All right, Chuck. You're in the hot seat now. What was your first impression of Olivia?"

Chuck rounded his lips and blew out a big breath. He widened his eyes as if the encounter had been overwhelming.

Olivia gasped like she was scandalized. "What does *that* mean?"

He shot her a devastating grin that involved only half of his mouth but somehow squeezed her entire heart. "It means you stole the air right out of my lungs the first time I saw you."

She froze and wasn't sure she'd ever be able to move again.

Chuck's face softened into a wistful, hazy look. He spoke to her like no one else existed in the whole world. "You showed up to the coffee shop with your notebook and a pen like you'd come to study me. You were wearing that dress, the yellow one with the kind of ruffled skirt. You had your hair partway back, and you smelled like flowers when you walked by. I remember thinking, holy shit, I'll tell this woman anything she wants to know about me. I'm an open book; take it all. Your questions were so pointed and smart. I could tell you really cared about learning about me and writing a good piece. It took me two seconds to realize you're a very driven and passionate person."

Olivia gazed at the man sitting beside her and felt her heart swell like it had done the day they'd met. He hadn't said anything so perceptive and generous—so damn *sweet*—in a long time. She was at a loss for how to respond.

Chuck softly laughed. "I did question your judgment when you agreed to go on a date with me later that night, though."

Her face heated. "Yes, you asked me before we even finished the interview."

"And you only took about an hour to think about it before you said yes."

"It was at least two."

"If you say so."

They were smiling at each other when TJ's voice cut in. "So there were sparks from the start, as we've established. What do you think of each other now? I mean, obviously something went awry, right?"

His line of questions felt dangerously close to the ones that had led to their explosion during the last interview when he'd asked why they'd broken up. Not to mention, the same question had instigated last night's fight too. Olivia shifted in her chair and heard Chuck clear his throat.

"I still think she's driven. I still think she's passionate," Chuck said. "And I don't think anything necessarily went awry. We just got to know each other and realized some of our traits don't exactly align . . . peacefully."

An involuntary snort snuck out of Olivia's nose. She threw a hand to her mouth.

"Have something you want to share, Olivia?" TJ asked.

"That's just a polite way of saying it."

"How would you say it?" TJ said.

She considered and decided not to pander to TJ's quest for drama despite being able to list off a catalog of all the ways she'd describe their incompatibility. "The same, I guess."

A sly smile spread across TJ's face. "Well, maybe living together has taught the two of you some manners. A week ago, I can only imagine what choice words you would have used—some of which we all heard in that video from the street." He kicked a foot up onto his knee and pivoted.

"Speaking of lessons, what have you learned about each other living here these past few days? Any habits you can't stand?"

"That's a bit of a leading question, isn't it?" Chuck said flatly. "It hasn't been all bad."

"You tell me, Chuck. You were the one who spent the night locked outside that first night. How would you say things are going?" TJ turned a knowing, smug grin on him.

The embarrassed heat wave that consumed Olivia was not subtle. She felt everyone's eyes move to her, and she knew they'd all watched the footage from that night—from everything, surely. Confirmation of it made her want to hide.

Chuck folded his arms. "Well, sure. The first night was a little rough."

"Mm-hmm," TJ said. "Olivia? What are your thoughts about that night?"

She imagined her flushed face being turned into an internet meme. Or worse, the shot of her threatening to light his shirt on fire that night—even though she would never have actually done it—becoming a GIF.

Why had she signed up to be on TV?

A million dollars a million dollars a million dollars, she thought once more.

"I think things might have gotten a little carried away," she said quietly. "I'm still sorry."

Chuck shrugged. "I'm over it."

"So!" TJ said, loudly refocusing attention when they didn't

elaborate. "Back to my question. What have you learned about each other these past few days? Olivia? You go first."

She let out a breath and mentally sifted through everything that had happened. It had only been two and a half days, and she'd seen a new side of Chuck. Of course, she'd seen the side she knew well—the stubborn, brash, homing-missile-for-her-last-nerve side—and they'd gotten in a fight last night, which was par for the course. But she'd also seen the tender side of him that he kept hidden and only showed during his most vulnerable moments. Like when he'd tried to soothe her nerves over being on camera; when he'd intervened during the first interview; when he told her she'd make a good parent. And everything he'd said moments before about his first impression of her. And, however ill-fated it had been, he'd tried to have a real conversation with her last night about their problems.

She honestly wasn't sure she ever would have seen any of those things if they hadn't ended up locked in a house together.

Smoothing her hands over her lap, she turned back to TJ, to the camera, and said, "I've learned that he can surprise me still."

TJ gave her a look of sincere intrigue. "Interesting." But he didn't elaborate. He turned to Chuck. "And you? What have you learned?"

Chuck didn't look at TJ or the camera. He looked right at Olivia, again like she was the only person on the planet. "I've learned that she's capable of things I didn't know."

The statement was ambiguous, but the look on Chuck's face made her think it was more of a compliment than a dig.

"Well, that certainly is enticing, isn't it?" TJ said with another grin. Olivia wondered if his lips were capable of relaxing over his teeth or if they stayed peeled open even when he slept. "Surely that will keep things interesting until we meet again, assuming you can make it that far." He turned to Dan in a signal that the segment was over, and the backyard took a collective exhale.

Parker swooped in with his own eager grin. "That was great, you guys! The sentimentality will play nicely on screen."

Chuck had already stood up and began disentangling his microphone from his shirt. "Great. Excuse me." He seemed to be in a hurry to leave.

"What's his deal?" Parker asked when Chuck dumped his mic pack on the table and walked off.

"I don't know," Olivia said with a curious shrug.

Parker mirrored her shrug and then turned to her. "Olivia, I actually wanted to talk to you for a minute, if you don't mind." He held out an arm to direct her a few steps away.

"What is it?" she asked as she kept an eye on both Chuck retreating into the bedroom door and TJ doing a poor job of pretending not to eavesdrop on her and Parker's conversation.

Parker took off the sunglasses he'd been wearing the whole time and gave her a serious look. "I watched the playback from this morning, and I saw when you found out about the article online."

She hadn't expected this turn, nor had she been prepared for the topic to come back up so suddenly. A thick lump formed in her throat. She fought to swallow it down, fearing where he was headed. "Okay. And?"

"*And* I first wanted to say I'm sorry you found it upsetting. I can only imagine what it would be like to have your parents, rest their souls, talked about in the tabloids. And second, I'm wondering"—he paused and took a step closer before he lowered his voice—"I'm wondering if you'd reconsider doing a small segment on it for the show."

Olivia reeled back and gaped at him. "Are you serious? Parker, you just said in the same breath how upsetting it was, and now you're asking me to do an interview about it?"

"I know!" he blurted, and held up his hands. Her voice had risen, and a few heads turned to see why. "I only ask because the word is out now that you are on this show, and things will only continue to snowball. *Everyone* is interested in this story—they have been for decades! With you locked in here and inaccessible to the outside world for the next month, we can get a leg up on owning it."

She folded her arms and glared at him. "Did you hope that this would happen? Was this part of your plan all along, to *use* me just to get to a story about them?"

"Of course not, but I can't ignore an opportunity, Olivia."

Her anger only continued to multiply. "This is not an *opportunity*, Parker. Even if I weren't locked in here, I wouldn't talk to anyone about my parents. I never have before, and I am not going to start now." She turned on her heel and marched away fuming. She made it three steps before she turned back, unable to let the unjustness of it all go. The anger that had boiled up inside her threatened to push tears out her eyes. "If you're so interested in a story about them, why don't you go talk to people who actually knew them instead of preying on their daughter who never met them?"

The remorse she expected to see on Parker's face was not there. Instead, he looked inspired. Determined. "Because *that's* the story, Olivia! *That's* what people will want to know! How has this impacted you, their daughter, having grown up in the shadow of scandal and tragedy?"

She reeled again. "*In the shadow of*— Do you even hear yourself, Parker? My life's tragedy is not entertainment!" she shouted with her arms out, and all the turning heads from the crew present to literally film her life for entertainment made her feel like she'd lost her mind. She blinked and pivoted back toward the house. Before any of them could further invade her personal life, she slid open the back bedroom door and slammed it shut behind her.

Chuck was inside looking like he might have been in the middle of his own struggle. He stood between the bed and the closet staring at the ceiling while he unbuttoned his shirt like he was meditating or talking to a higher power.

The slice of his bare chest exposed by his undressing snared Olivia's eyes for a second before she sat on the bed's foot to remove her shoes, which had taken to feeling like bladed boa constrictors on her feet.

"What's wrong with you?" Chuck asked.

"Nothing," she spat, and lifted her right foot. She struggled with the buckle, which was disguised in part of the strap that wound up her ankle. Only a misogynist could have designed such torture devices and called them fashion.

"If you're going to lie, at least try to make it convincing."

When she finally got her shoe unbuckled, she hurled it at the closet. She missed and it hit the wall with a thud and fell to the floor.

Chuck quietly walked over and picked it up. He examined it as if it were an object from space before he bunched the straps dangling like noodles and carefully wound them around the sole. "I'm not going to press because I don't want to become the victim of flying footwear, but you can tell me if you want to."

She unbuckled her other shoe with much more ease and calmly dropped it to the floor. She took a deep breath and looked up at him. "They want me to talk about my parents.

Parker just pulled me aside and asked if I'd do a segment because he thinks since the news is out that I'm on this show, interest is going to snowball, and they want to get ahead of any story since they have me captive in here for an interview. It's all because of that damn article." Her voice wobbled, and he instantly stepped toward her, as if the sound of her distress pulled a string he was tied to the other end of.

He stopped just short of the bed like he'd hit an invisible wall. He bent down and picked up her other shoe, gently repeating his process of winding the straps, and set the pair beside her.

"Thanks," she said, doing her best not to sound weepy.

He sat on the bed next to her with the shoes between them as a small but meaningful barrier. And then he said something she didn't expect at all. "I mean, he's kind of right about it being an opportunity."

She turned to him in surprise. "What?"

He shrugged. "If I'm honest, I've never really understood why you're so reluctant when it's right there for the taking."

Olivia felt like her brain had melted and was oozing out her ears. She'd told him about her parents, of course she had. But other than a cursory overview that he could have googled on his own, they steered clear of the topic. They rarely even toed the line, and now he'd walked right up and kicked it. "Are you serious right now, Chuck?"

"Yes. You're like the first nepo baby in history who doesn't want the title."

She blinked at him, completely gobsmacked by what he was saying. "*No one* wants that title! It's insulting and reductive, and I honestly can't believe you just said that."

"Well, it's true. You have this industry at your fingertips, and you take it for granted—and I don't only mean the film industry. I know you don't want to be on camera. But you could use their story—*your* story too—to launch the career you actually want as an author."

She jolted up from the bed and clenched her fists, nearly shaking. "Why on *earth* would I want to welcome that attention?"

"The attention doesn't have to be negative. With the right team, you could spin it so that you're positioned in the best light."

She blinked at him in shock. "Chuck, my life story—*my parents' deaths*—is not something to be *spun* by Hollywood smoke and mirrors for consumption. Where is this even coming from? Why are you saying all this to me?"

He stood too and held out his arms. "I don't know, Liv. Maybe I've always wanted to say this, and now I can because for once, you can't run away, and you have to listen."

She sputtered and felt like she might explode. "Anything else you want to get off your chest while you're at it?"

"Yeah, actually. I think you're scared. You pretend you want nothing to do with this world, but deep down, you crave validation. Confirmation that you *matter* and will leave a mark. That you are bigger than your parents' legacy. But you're afraid to do anything about it, so you act like you're above all this and that none of it is important to you."

In true Olivia and Chuck fashion, they'd gone from zero to sixty in five seconds flat. The vein in his forehead throbbed, and she felt its mirror keeping time in her neck.

She sucked in a hard breath. "Okay, if we're trading honesty here, how about a few things I've always wanted to say to *you*?"

"Sure, I'd *love* to hear them." He scooped his arms toward

himself in a welcoming motion and then folded them over his chest.

"I think you care about this world *too* much. To the point that you lose sight of everything else because you're so obsessed with your career. You missed my grandma's birthday party to go to an audition, for example. And you live in an apartment that you can't afford for appearance's sake. Also, I think what you're saying about my parents is unfair. You have *no idea* what it's like for me because your parents think the sun shines out your ass! I think—"

"Do you know how much fucking pressure it is to have my parents think I'm perfect?" he shouted, and threw out his arms.

Olivia flinched, not realizing that particular button would be the hottest one.

Chuck took a breath and put his hands on his hips. "They don't even know I got fired—they don't even know we broke up! I couldn't bear the thought of telling them either thing because I didn't want to disappoint them." He sank to the bed and held his face in his hands.

This normally would have been the point where Olivia ran away. She'd spin on her heel and slam a door, leaving the unfinished emotional dregs trailing in her wake. The urge thrummed in her limbs, pumped in her pounding heart. But the sight of his distress, the memory of his accusation last night about her always running—and the fact that she had nowhere to go—made her stay.

She sat beside him on the bed and spoke softly. "How do they not know either of those things? They were both literally in the news."

Chuck popped up out of his hands, looking truly surprised

to see her still there. It took him a moment to speak. "They don't keep up with celebrity news; I told them not to. And I've never told them that we fight at all. They were so happy that I was in a serious relationship when we got together. I wanted them to think things were perfect. With them focusing on my dad's health, I didn't tell them when I got fired or we broke up because I didn't want to add to their stress on top of it all. I asked Chelsea not to say anything either." The pain threaded through his words made her chest ache. She almost reached out to touch him but remembered the rules.

"You're a good son, Chuck."

He huffed a strangled sound. "I try to be."

"No, you are. And I can't imagine Sam and Barb Walsh ever being disappointed in you. Like I said: sun out your ass."

A quiet chuckle bubbled from his mouth. "I can't tell if you're deflecting again or making an honest effort."

"Somewhere in the middle?"

He turned to her with a soft, warm look on his face. "I'll take it."

Her heart leapt with that familiar bungee-jump hiccup that only he could incite. It felt dangerously close to a feeling she was no longer supposed to have because they'd broken up.

She pushed up from the bed, ready to flee, but he reached out for her. His hand brushed her wrist without *really* touching her, but it was enough to make her turn around.

"Wait, before you go. Sorry I called you a nepo baby."

Olivia snorted. "Yeah, well, you're not wrong."

"I know, but it came out all wrong. What I meant was, sometimes it's hard to see your dismissive attitude toward the industry I'm killing myself to make it in. Call it a weird kind of envy, I don't know. Regardless, it's not fair of me to expect you to leverage your parents' story if you don't want to. I know I can't fully understand what it's like for you."

Olivia absorbed his words and blinked wide at him. "*That's* what you meant?"

"Yes."

"That's not at all what you said."

"I know. I'm bad at fighting. No one ever taught me how. Also, you never stick around long enough to let me figure out the right thing to say, so this is new for me too."

His confession softened her into staying even longer. "The one disservice Sam and Barb ever did for you, huh? Who knew never arguing in front of their kids would lead to this."

Chuck softly smiled and shook his head. "Still deflecting, I see. But you're right. They never fought, so I never learned how. And I can see I've got about thirty more seconds of your tolerance for this conversation before you run, so I want to say something else."

She lifted her brows in question, trying not to let on that he was right about her being ready to head for the door. All the disclosure had her itchy with discomfort.

"I'm sorry for how dismissive I was about the tabloid article earlier. I should have realized how that would impact you given your family history and been more sensitive."

"Oh," she said, surprised to learn he was still thinking about their interaction from that morning. "Thank you."

"Of course. And what I said out there in the interview about you being capable of things, I didn't mean that in a bad way," he said. "Well, you did make me sleep outside, and I didn't think you'd *actually* do it, but I more meant capable of things that scare you. Like being here. Doing this show. I know you didn't want to, but it's for someone you love, which is really admirable."

With the way he was giving her his only-girl-in-the-world eyes again and with the tender vulnerability she'd spoken of during the interview as plain as day on his face, it took her a heart-thudding moment to realize the person she loved whom he was talking about was Grandma Ruby.

"Right. Yeah. Thank you," she said awkwardly, thinking that her comment about him still surprising her was as true as ever.

"That's why I think that if you ever *wanted* to tell your parents' story—not saying you have to—I think you'd be able to do it. And I think you'd be good at it."

His faith in her gave her a non-negligible ounce of courage. She gave him a weak smile. "I'll keep that in mind. Thanks."

The air that had softened between them reshaped into something with a slight edge. Chuck stood up with another sigh.

"What were you doing in here?" she asked him. "When I walked in, you looked like you were doing self-affirmations with the ceiling."

He huffed a quiet laugh. "It was nothing."

"If you're going to lie, at least try to make it convincing."

He smiled down at her, and she thought they were going to continue with the intimate and uncomfortable self-disclosure, but he dodged the subject and continued unbuttoning his shirt instead. "I'm going to hit the gym again." He turned for the closet, and she was thankful he didn't strip down in front of her.

Left standing in the middle of the room, Olivia had two thoughts. One, hitting the gym sounded like a good idea because she could definitely use a run to burn off some steam. And two, Chuck had lied to her about being all right because he only did double workouts when he was training for a part or when something was bothering him.

● ● ● ● ●

AS OLIVIA POUNDED HER FEET ON THE TREADMILL'S BELT, SHE wondered what could be eating at Chuck. Perhaps it was simply the aftermath of all their arguing and the scene in the bedroom earlier; she was spent from it too. From her position on the treadmill, she could see him in the mirrored wall going hard enough on the rower to snap the cable. Sweat poured off him, and he'd probably put in enough meters to be halfway to Hawaii already. She was at least thankful he'd opted for cardio and wasn't putting on another show in the squat rack.

She further wondered about his mood when he easily agreed on having chicken Caesar salad for dinner without a fight. He even cleaned up the dishes again.

By the time they'd wound down for bed, his odd behavior was distracting her enough that she forgot they needed to decide who was sleeping where.

She ran into him in the hallway outside the bedroom on her way back from brushing her teeth in the kitchen. He'd already put on a cozy shirt and his glasses. He was barefoot and loose shorts clung to his hips. The distorted light coming from the pool cast rolling shadows through the back wall of windows and turned them both a dark shade of blue.

"Oh," Olivia said when they crossed paths. "I was just coming to ask where we're sleeping tonight."

He eyed her pajamas and the toothbrush in her hand. He didn't say anything, and Olivia wasn't sure what it meant.

She tried to break the odd tension. "If I sleep on the couch, you aren't going to wake me up in the morning with another stunt like you pulled today, are you?"

His lips twitched into a small smile. "What stunt?"

A full smile spread across her face. "Oh, you were *so* transparent, Chuck. Don't even pretend. Blasting music to wake me up and *conveniently* doing pull-ups right when I walk in? Please."

He looked like he might deny it for a second before he grinned. "Like you said: I know your weakness. And well-played with the swimsuit, by the way. I wasn't expecting such a swift and precise counterstrike."

She was glad to see him out of whatever sullen mood he'd been in. "I know your weakness too."

"Well, maybe we should agree to stop trying to sabotage each other and instead coexist for a few more weeks, because all things considered, I think we're doing pretty well."

"I agree."

"Shake on it?" He thrust out his hand, and she slipped hers into it.

"Deal."

Before the word was out of her mouth, and before she could remember they weren't supposed to touch each other, he yanked her forward. Their bodies slammed together like waves meeting in a storm and knocked all the wind out of her lungs. His hand caught the back of her head, cupping it like it was made for that sole purpose, and he pulled her mouth toward his. Olivia didn't even hesitate before closing the gap.

The kiss was so sudden, so shocking, and *so fucking perfect* that she couldn't do anything other than kiss him back.

It was a terrible idea.

It was an amazing idea.

It was . . . happening.

She opened her mouth and felt his tongue, hot and urgent against hers. He tasted like home, and she didn't realize until that moment that she'd missed him like a piece of her own body. A low moan escaped his throat, and he wrapped his other arm around her back. She pressed into him and felt her heart thudding hard enough to bruise the both of them. He began to lift her off the floor, crushing her body to his. The move brought on a floaty feeling due in equal parts to her toes skimming the tile and him greedily pulling her as close as possible. It was everything she wanted, and everything she knew she couldn't have. Something tight and coiled unwound in her chest, loosening freely, at the same time it seized in warning.

She put a hand on his chest and pushed him back.

He immediately broke away, setting her down, and dissolved into a flurry of apologizing. "I'm sorry. I didn't mean— I'm sorry. I just . . . Fuck." He spat the last word, made eye contact just long enough for her to see torment in his eyes, and pivoted for the bedroom. His footsteps echoed down the hall until the door shut with a firm snap.

Olivia was too stunned to process what had just happened. She saw her reflection, flushed and dazed, in the back windows. She felt like she'd been lit on fire. Her heart was still pounding when the bedroom door flew back open. Chuck came marching out, red-faced and still flustered.

"You know what? No. It's better this way," he said, and gripped her shoulders.

She thought (hoped?) he'd come back to finish what he'd started. Like Parker had said: if they were going to lose money by breaking rules, they'd better make it worth it. Her heart vaulted up into her throat when he directed her toward the bedroom with his hot hands on her skin. But as soon as she crossed the threshold, he let her go with a slight shove.

"You stay in here; I'll sleep on the couch." He reached around to the inside doorknob and twisted the little bar to lock it. Then he gave her another split second of anguished eye contact, before he said, "Good night," and shut the door, closing her in.

She had whiplash, certainly. She wasn't even sure she was breathing where she stood frozen with the hot imprint of his hands still on her arms, his lips on her mouth. Part of her brain—the majority of it, honestly—wanted to wrench the door open and charge out into the living room, where she would demand an explanation but, in all likelihood, tackle him and go back to kissing him before he could give one. And then they'd put that damned flat-box couch to the test and see if it could withstand what she was sure would be a furious and desperate reunion.

But the sliver of her brain not drowning in a hedonistic hormone soup commanded her to keep the door locked and her hands to herself. Chuck had had the sense to separate them before things got carried away, and opening the door would only be throwing a lit match on an already sparking tinderbox.

She took a very deep breath and sat on the foot of the bed. She pulled out her phone to stage an intervention on herself by texting Mansi.

Chuck just kissed me.

Mansi, bless her, immediately responded.

Is this a yellow bikini text,
or . . . ?

                      No. It's an I'm confused text.

What happened?

                      I don't know. One moment
                      we were standing in the hall
                      talking, and the next, he kissed
                      me. Then he locked me in the
                      bedroom and went to sleep on
                      the couch.

He locked you in the
bedroom?

                      Yes.

Isn't the lock on the inside?

                      Yes.

Liv, you horny sweet summer
child. He didn't lock you in.
He locked himself out.

The revelation hit her like a smack to the forehead. Mansi
was right: Chuck wasn't trying to stop her from doing anything; he was stopping himself with a physical barrier between
them.

Oh, she texted her friend.

Yeah. That's like oddly kind of
romantic?

Olivia thought about it and realized Mansi was right again. Locking the door was a bizarre and slightly chivalrous show of restraint. As if he knew he needed help to keep his hands off her—and to keep them from losing any more money than she was sure they'd already just lost.

But that indicated a much larger problem, money aside. The locked door meant he badly wanted to touch her, if not more. Based on the hunger in his kiss she could still feel lingering on her lips, she knew *exactly* what he wanted.

And did she want it too?

She chewed her lip and dug her toes into the plush carpet. It didn't take her long to realize what she needed to do.

Shit, Manse. Yellow bikini.

Mansi responded with a photo of a trio of penguin chicks huddled together on the ice like fuzzy gray bowling pins.

Olivia weakly smiled at it and flopped back on the bed, knowing it was going to be a long night.

CHUCK DID THIS THING with his tongue and teeth, kind of an erotic one-two combo punch, that always left Olivia gasping. She discovered on Saturday morning that the effect transferred to dreams almost as intensely as experiencing it in real life.

She woke gasping and damp with sweat in a tangle of sheets. With the way her blood was speeding through her veins, she half expected to find Chuck in bed beside her having just finished his torturous combo. But she was alone. And in need of a cold shower.

By a small miracle, the bedroom door had stayed closed all night. She left it that way as she entered the bathroom to shower off her dream and brace for inevitably having to interact with Chuck—and to face the music about how much they were going to be penalized for the kiss. She wouldn't have been surprised if he completely avoided her, but she was surprised when, after her shower, she found him in the kitchen flipping pancakes.

He stood shirtless at the stove with his back to her, and Olivia wondered if she was still sleeping and having some kind of food porn dream. White powder dusted the counters. A small stack of dirty mixing bowls teetered near the sink. Three eggshells oozed goo on a plate. The scene was a disaster, but she couldn't take her eyes off Chuck standing in the middle of it all with a towel over his shoulder and mumbling to himself.

"Come on, come on. *Yes!*" he quietly hissed when he successfully flipped a fresh pancake onto a plate. He turned around with a finger in his mouth, licking off whatever he'd stuck it into, and jumped at the sight of Olivia. "Oh! Liv, I didn't hear you come in."

He set the plate down and pulled the towel from his shoulder to wipe his hands. He was shirtless, his hair was a mess, he still wore his glasses, and he had a smudge of powder on his nose.

It was, quite possibly, the most attractive she'd ever seen him.

"Where's your shirt?" was the first thing that came out of her mouth.

"I got batter on it, so I took it off," he said like this was a perfectly rational explanation.

"Oh." She sat on a stool largely to keep her knees from wobbling. Her mind was off somewhere distant and feral.

He reached for a banana out of the fruit bowl and split its peel. He then picked up a knife and set about slicing the banana on top of the pancakes.

"What is this?" she asked, and nodded at the whole scene: the fresh coffee, the banana pancakes, the bottle of syrup. Clearly, he was making her favorite breakfast.

Chuck inhaled and let out a big breath. "It's . . . an apology for last night. Well, an attempt at one. I burned the first three rounds." He cocked his head to the end of the island, where a stack of charred pancakes sat waiting to be dumped into the trash.

The memory of their encounter in the hall would have swept her off her feet if she weren't already sitting down. She might have been the one to end it, but she hadn't done anything to stop him from starting it.

"Chuck, you don't have to—"

"Yes, I do," he said, and held up his hand to stop her. "That's what my mood was about yesterday. After the interview—before we fought, obviously—I got this intense urge to touch you after everything you'd said about your first impression of me, and knowing it was off-limits made me go a little wild. And then last night in the hallway, I couldn't take it anymore. I crossed the line, and I'm sorry. It won't happen again. Please accept this meager offering as my penance. And know that however they punish us financially, I'll take the hit." He slid the plate toward her along with the bottle of syrup.

She lifted the fork he'd set out for her and thought there was a joke to be made about swapping favorite meals for makeup sex when they'd wronged each other, but the situation would not have been helped by making it. Not to mention, she was flush with a stirring heat knowing that her recount of her first impression of him had driven him to break the rules. "Thank you, but you don't have to do that. It wasn't like I did anything to stop you. We are equally guilty."

"Fair enough." He watched her drizzle syrup on her pile of fruity cakes and take a bite. "And?" he asked with one eye impishly squeezed shut.

Pleasantly surprised, she swallowed and nodded. "Really good."

"Really?"

"Really."

He threw his arms up in victory and beamed. *"Yes!"*

Olivia smiled around another bite. "Pretty impressive for someone who doesn't eat carbs."

He smirked and threw the wadded-up towel at her. "I eat carbs. Watch me. Give me a bite." He gripped the edge of the island and leaned forward with his mouth open.

Laughing, she cut a square with her fork and stabbed a banana slice before feeding both to him. Syrup dribbled down his lip in a sticky little string. She caught it with her finger, and before either of them realized what was happening, he grabbed her wrist and wrapped his lips around her knuckle to suck it off.

Her finger came back out of his mouth with a slick pop that felt like a lightning bolt to all the most sensitive parts of her body and made them both freeze.

"Sorry, old habits," Chuck said, his face growing serious and his hand still wrapped around her wrist.

Time seemed to stop. The air stilled and took on a charge like it might explode.

He could have easily pulled her to him just like he had the night before. Up onto the island where they'd make a sticky, sweaty mess that left syrup in interesting places and maybe broke a few dishes and would certainly lose them more money. Olivia's heart pounded as she stared into his eyes, seeing the same fantasy play out alongside an intense battle to keep it at bay, and wondered what was going to happen. She knew, without a doubt, that after their encounter in the hall and her dream, she would follow his lead, even if it guaranteed disaster.

Before anything else could happen, the doorbell rang.

They snapped apart, both flustered.

"Are we expecting someone?" Chuck asked.

"Not that I know of. The crew usually just barges in too."

They abandoned breakfast and padded into the entryway. On the other side of the front door, they found TJ grinning like a fool and the usual camera crew. Tyler popped out and gave them a friendly wave.

"Morning, lovers!" TJ sang. "And I do mean that sincerely after last night," he added with a wink, and welcomed himself inside. He sniffed the air like a hound catching the scent of breakfast. "I only rang to make sure everyone was decent before we started rolling. I see we are halfway there." He eyed Chuck's bare chest with another grin. "Speaking of . . ." He pulled two envelopes from where they were tucked under his elbow. "Mail for you. Open this one first."

Olivia was still recovering from the whole early-morning circus, but her heart skipped at the red envelope he handed her. She knew before she opened it that it was their punishment for last night. It might as well have had *GUILTY* stamped on the front.

She chewed her lip and broke the seal. Chuck stood close behind her, reading over her shoulder.

"'Olivia and Chuck, the production team has found you in violation of the No Physical Contact rule for your indiscretion in the hallway last night, a kiss lasting approximately ten seconds. As punishment for this violation, the total prize money for each of you will be reduced by a sum of—'"

"Ten thousand dollars?" Chuck screeched. He reached over her shoulder and snatched the paper to read again.

Olivia's knees felt weak.

TJ chuckled. "Indeed. It was a good kiss. A-plus work, you two."

Olivia wanted to curl up and die for multiple reasons. One, they'd watched the tape at all. Two, they'd watched the tape closely enough to time their kiss, and three, TJ was grinning at them like he couldn't have been more delighted about the whole situation. And to top it off, she was suddenly ten grand poorer. It might have been a drop in the bucket compared to a million dollars, but it still felt like a gut punch.

"I think I'm going to be sick," she muttered.

TJ only laughed again. "Well, maybe you've learned your lesson. Or maybe not." He shrugged. "Still nine hundred and ninety thousand dollars to go, and plenty of time to lose it. So, on to the next envelope. Olivia, if you'll do the honors."

She was still reeling and noticed Chuck taking a half step away to put more space between them. She glared at TJ, a flush in her cheeks, as she slid her finger under the next envelope's seal.

"'Olivia and Chuck, your next challenge is a test of knowledge. You may be broken up, but every couple has history. We want to see how well you still know each other. Answer enough questions correctly, and you'll gain access to the dishwasher. Continue to answer questions correctly, and you'll gain access to the guest bathroom. Good luck.'"

"Well, that's some decent incentive," Chuck said.

"Yes. We take, we give. That's how this works," TJ said, and clapped his hands.

The Newlywed Game, Olivia thought. As far as game show challenges went, this didn't seem too bad. Her spirits took flight at the thought of what would be an easy challenge. She knew all sorts of things about Chuck, like his favorite color, food, movie. She only hoped he remembered the same about her. Before she could turn around to confirm, TJ grabbed both of them by the arm and started marching them toward the back of the house.

"Olivia, you wait in the kitchen. Chuck, go put on a shirt—actually..." He cut himself off and pinched his face in thought, eyeing Chuck's bare chest and abs like he might ask him to stay half naked for the cameras. "Yeah, go put on a shirt for this. And stay in the bedroom until we come get you."

"Wait, we're doing this *now*?" Olivia asked, and almost tripped when TJ pushed her back toward the kitchen.

"Yep. And you're staying separated until we're set up in the backyard. No chance to coach each other. *Go.*" He pushed them in opposite directions and looked all too pleased with himself. Chuck stumbled off toward the hall, throwing a desperate look back at Olivia as she tumbled through the kitchen entryway.

"Chuck! You should put on a *yellow* shirt while I finish my *banana pancakes*!" she called.

"Hey! None of that!" TJ protested. "You stay here and stay quiet. Tyler, keep an eye on her."

"Sure thing, Mr. Price," Tyler said, and hurried over to stand guard at the entryway.

Olivia glared at TJ but gave Tyler a friendly smile. TJ smirked back and then swept out the back doors with the crew to set up.

"I'll behave," she told Tyler with a little bow.

She returned to her stool and dove back into her pancakes. She wanted that dishwasher, and she wanted it bad—even more, she wanted her own bathroom. As if telekinesis were a real thing, she thought as hard as she could about the answer to everything that she thought they might ask, hoping Chuck could somehow read her mind from the other end of the house. *Please remember*, she thought equally as hard as *Please have paid attention during our relationship and know this stuff in the first place.*

Chuck had left his phone on the island amid the mess, and Olivia saw it light up with a text from someone named Maddy. She could not think of anyone Chuck knew named Maddy and was too distracted by mentally running through a list of everything she knew about him to think about it anyway.

Eventually, TJ returned and summoned her with Chuck already in tow. She was still wearing yoga pants and a tank and was thankful to see that Chuck had only put on a tee shirt and hadn't fully dressed for the cameras. He'd at least put in his contacts and smoothed his hair, but he was still rumpled and looking fresh from bed. Given that they didn't bring in hair and makeup, this obviously wasn't as formal as an interview, and likely because they'd wanted to catch them off guard with no time to prepare.

The crew had set up in the usual spot, except this time, they'd faced Olivia's and Chuck's chairs toward each other, and each had a little whiteboard and dry-erase marker sitting on it waiting.

"Contestants, please take your seats," TJ announced, and bowed with a stack of cards in his hands. His chair sat opposite theirs.

Olivia sat and looked dead ahead at Chuck. "We can do this," she said with a nod.

He nodded back, looking less confident than she'd hoped.

The mic tech swarmed them and wired everyone up. Soon the cameras were rolling, and everyone was on point.

"Ladies and gentlemen, welcome to the Chuck and Olivia Quiz Bowl! I'm your host, TJ Price. Today our contestants will test their knowledge of each other in an attempt to win a Shiny! New! *Dishwasher!*" he said in a booming voice as if there were a real audience in the yard and not just three cameramen, a sound tech, and a PA. "And a bathroom, if we get that far," he added with less enthusiasm.

"Oh, we're going to get that far," Olivia said. Her competitive streak was alive and well. They were going to *win*.

"I like the spirit, Olivia! Okay, so the way this works: I will pose a question to *one* of you about the other person, you will *both* have ten seconds to write the answer on your board, and every time your answers match, you get a point. Ten points gets you the dishwasher, twenty gets you the bathroom. You'll have twenty-five questions total. Make sense?"

"Got it," Chuck said, sounding more determined.

"Let's do it," Olivia said.

"Okay! Here! We! Go! Tyler, the clock, if you please."

Tyler came over with the same iPad from the furniture challenge, this time with *0:10* glaring in red, and propped it on the table.

"Olivia, the first question is for you," TJ opened. "What was Chuck's first childhood pet's name?"

Easy. She uncapped her pen and instantly scribbled. *A golden retriever named Biscuit.* He'd told her stories of growing up hiking and swimming with his beloved dog. Endless hours of fetch. She'd even seen pictures of the good old boy. Her heart trilled as she waited for the ten seconds to count down.

"Time!" TJ called, and they both flipped their boards around.

Olivia smiled at the sight of *Biscuit* scrawled on Chuck's board. She swore she saw his eyes lovingly gloss over at the sight of her board.

"Olivia going the extra mile by including the breed!" TJ cheered. "Unfortunately, that will not win you any extra credit. Chuck! Next question is for you. What is Olivia's favorite flower?"

Olivia flipped her board and swiped it clean before she

scribbled *tulips* and silently shouted the word over and over in her head. Chuck had given her flowers a handful of times during their relationship—her birthday, Valentine's Day, when one of her profiles hit it big online—but those had mostly been an assortment of whatever the florist picked out to qualify as *big* and *romantic*. She hoped he remembered that day they'd driven out east of L.A. to a botanical garden lush with tulip fields and she'd taken ten thousand pictures.

"Time!" TJ called.

They flipped their boards around, and Olivia smiled at the sight of *tulip* along with a cute little doodle of one.

"Wow, okay. Off to a strong start. Maybe we need to make these questions harder," TJ said, and shuffled his cards. "Ah, here's a good one. Olivia, what one thing would Chuck take with him to a deserted island?"

She bit her lip and didn't feel too bad about her visible grimace when she noticed Chuck tilting his head in consideration like he didn't immediately know the answer either. She eyed the ticking clock and thought. *Had they ever had this conversation before?* Not that she could recall. Instead of trying to remember, she took a practical approach to figuring it out. Chuck was strong, athletic. He'd be able to build shelter and hunt, so he wouldn't take any kind of tools or weapons with him. *Maybe a book for entertainment?* No. *Something logical like a phone or a boat to escape?* No. Those were universally off-limits on a deserted island; everyone knew that.

In the final two seconds of their time, a memory struck her like a flash of light—that trip to Mexico. He'd lost one of his contacts swimming in the ocean and said he was lucky he had his glasses as backup; otherwise he would have been screwed for the rest of the trip.

"Time!" TJ called just as she finished scribbling.

They flipped their boards around, and at the sight of *my glasses* on Chuck's board and *his glasses* on Olivia's, TJ frowned.

"Ha!" Chuck said. "Nice job."

Olivia proudly smiled at him.

"Okay, well, we didn't expect you guys to be *this* good at this . . ." TJ muttered, and shuffled his cards again. "Chuck, what is Olivia's biggest pet peeve?"

This time, Chuck grimaced. Olivia internally flinched too. The list was long. She could name a hundred peeves—they both probably could—but she had to pick the same one that he would pick. She thought hard about what they argued about most; what little thing *really* got them going.

In a pinch, she scribbled on her board.

"Time!"

They flipped and frowned. She'd written *dirty dishes* and he'd written *leaving the lights on.* Both were true, but they didn't match.

"Aw, womp womp *womp.*" TJ made a dramatic sad trombone sound. "Our first miss. Couldn't have you getting too cocky, could we. Olivia, over to you. If Chuck could have dinner with one famous person, alive or dead, who would it be?"

She reeled again. That was a great question, and she had no idea. She glanced at Chuck thoughtfully considering his board again and tried to read his mind. Alive or dead meant literally anyone. And Chuck's interests spanned beyond only Hollywood. A famous actor was an obvious answer, but he could as easily say an astronaut or author. Hell, maybe even the Crocodile Hunter, she didn't know. Running out of time, she opted for obvious. She knew he loved *The Godfather,* so she scribbled *Marlon Brando* and held her breath.

"Let's see!" TJ called.

They flipped their boards, and Olivia was disappointed to have been wrong but impressed to see *Barack Obama* written on his board.

"Brando is a close second," Chuck said with an encouraging nod.

"Close, but not good enough!" TJ sang. "Okay, let's spice things up a bit here. Olivia, staying with you, when is Chuck's favorite time of day to have sex?"

An embarrassed giggle burst from her mouth. She slapped her hand over her lips and deeply blushed. "Sorry. That's just, um . . . really personal."

"Well, you know him *personally* the best, don't you?" TJ said with a sly grin. "Or at least that's what we're trying to prove here. Clock's ticking!"

Her face burned as she buried it behind her board. She could see Chuck grinning over in his chair and fighting his own flush. Her breath grew jagged as she thought of the answer. Her blood spiraled. Chuck had no preferred time of day. First thing in the morning, midafternoon, midnight, three a.m. because she happened to roll over and bump into him in bed; he didn't discriminate. His enthusiasm equally spanned to all hours. The thought made her sit up straighter and cross her legs. Desperate, she scribbled an answer.

"Time!" TJ said. "Seems like this was a hard one to answer. Let's see what you said."

They turned their boards, and Olivia snorted a laugh.

Anytime, she'd written.

Always, he'd written.

She couldn't have been blushing any harder.

"Hmmm," TJ hummed thoughtfully. "Judges?" He turned and asked the camera crew behind them. Everyone was biting lips and grinning. Olivia wondered if any of them had watched the footage of their kiss and judged the cost of their violation. Benny gave a thumbs-up along with another cameraman Olivia didn't know by name. Tyler enthusiastically pointed both thumbs in the air.

"All right, we'll give it to you," TJ said. "Next question! Chuck, what is Olivia's bra size?"

"*Oh my god*," she muttered, and tried to melt between the cracks in her chair. She'd been wrong about not being able to blush any harder. She scribbled two numbers and the same letter twice on her board and couldn't believe she was about to reveal her measurements on a TV show. But then, everyone had just learned about Chuck's insatiable sexual appetite, so all bets were off.

"Time's up!" TJ called.

Olivia sputtered a laugh when Chuck turned his board around to show *perfect* scrawled across it.

She flipped hers to show the real answer, and everyone laughed.

"While that *is* charming," TJ said, "it is *not* correct. Sorry, Chuck."

They went back and forth for several more rounds of questions, getting most right (Olivia's dream vacation: Italy; Chuck's favorite superhero: Thor) and some wrong (Olivia's college major: journalism, not English; Chuck's favorite sport: soccer, not baseball) until they were down to the final two questions, and they needed them both to win the bathroom.

"Okay, Chuck," TJ said, deadly serious, "what is Olivia's favorite thing about *you*?"

Chuck let out a breath through rounded lips. "Saving the hardest question for last, I see."

"There's a lot on the line here," TJ said with his hands out.

Olivia thought about how to even answer that question. There were the superficial, obvious things like his body, his smile, his impossibly perfect hair. But those were complete strangers' favorite parts of Chuck Walsh. Anyone who knew him like she did knew he was so much more than appearance—though the appearance was inarguably damn fine. But as she sorted through possible deeper answers, she realized that ten seconds was not nearly long enough to come to a suitable one. He was complex and dynamic; fantastically frustrating at times and wildly tender at others. Through it all, she realized in a profound moment, that one thing remained constant. He was always trying. *Trying* to succeed. *Trying* to understand her. *Trying* to fix whatever problem they were having. And damn it if that wasn't what made her stick around when things got tough despite her reflex to run.

She scribbled on her board right as TJ called time.

"Big moment here!" he sang for dramatic effect. "Let's see what she said!"

They both flipped their boards around, and a hard lump instantly swelled inside her throat.

That I don't give up on anything, he'd written.

His tenacity, she'd written.

Olivia blinked away the moisture that blurred her eyes as she realized they were much more on the same page than she'd ever known. Chuck softly smiled at her with a flush in his cheeks.

TJ disrupted the moment with a low whistle. "Wow. Look at that! I mean, that's really just a matter of semantics, right? You guys *really* know each other. It's almost like you should still be a couple! I say we give it to them. Judges?"

The crew all nodded and murmured in agreement.

"Okay! Final question for all the glory here—and a bath-room along with a dishwasher! Olivia, your turn: What is Chuck's favorite thing about *you*?"

Her heart thudded, and she blinked away her still misty eyes. "If you say my boobs, I will murder you," she said thickly to a round of laughter, including her own.

Chuck playfully smirked at her and picked up his board to write.

In truth, she'd made the joke because she already knew the answer to this one and didn't need the full ten seconds. A dreamy memory floated back to her: them, naked, tangled up in her sheets and still tacky with drying sweat. She'd been flat on her back, arm over her head, with Chuck beside her tracing gentle patterns on her bare skin as she talked at the ceiling. It had been days after one of the more memorable and divisive political incidents in the past years, and she had a lot on her mind. Most of what she'd said had felt like rambling at the time, opinionated babble that would have gotten her har-pooned on social media, but Chuck intently listened to every word. When she finally paused to breathe, he stroked his finger down her nose and then hooked it under her chin to turn her face toward his.

"You know what my favorite thing about you is?" he'd said into the soft glow of afternoon light.

"My boobs?" she'd joked even then.

He'd shaken his head with a grin and then tapped his long finger on her forehead. "The way your mind works." And then he'd kissed her, deeply, and grabbed her thigh to hook her leg around his hip. They'd missed their dinner reservation that night and ended up eating cereal in front of a *Parks and Rec* re-run marathon instead.

She scribbled her answer on her board and looked up to see Chuck finished and waiting. A soft grin lifted his lips.

"All right, final chance here!" TJ sang. "Let's see those answers!"

They turned their boards, and Olivia let out a squeal of joy.

The way my mind works.

Her mind.

Chuck jumped out of his chair with a cheer. He flung his board aside and reached out to hug her.

Olivia was halfway out of her chair, reaching back, when she froze. "Wait!" she blurted. "No touching."

They both looked at TJ, who was watching them with bright, eager eyes.

"Can we hug?" Chuck asked.

"You can do whatever you want. It's your money," TJ said.

His message was clear, so they settled for a fist bump even though Olivia wanted to fling herself at him and dance in celebration.

She stepped out from between the chairs and did a small celebratory dance on her own. "We did it!" she squealed.

"Yeah, we did!" Chuck crowed. "Wild how much we know about each other, right? Also—" He leaned in and lowered his voice. "Well played with the boobs joke, but you didn't need to do that. I remembered," he said proudly.

Olivia flushed at the thought that he'd been thinking of that day in her bed too. The urge to fling her arms around him hit her again, and a realization hit her even harder.

"*Wait,*" she said, and glanced over at TJ and the crew breaking down the little set. "Oh, those sneaky bastards," she hissed.

"What?" Chuck asked, and followed her gaze.

The crew wasn't paying attention to them anymore; they

were too busy cleaning up and chatting. Olivia pinched Chuck's arm and dragged him away and back closer to the house.

"What are you doing?" he whispered.

She stopped under the eave outside the bedroom's back door. "I think they played us, Chuck!"

"What do you mean?"

"I mean I think that was on purpose—that game! They set it up to make us *feel* things. TJ even pointed out how well we know each other and said we should still be a couple. I think they wanted us to be in *this* position after." She pointed at the ground between their feet.

Chuck narrowed his eyes at her, trying to keep up. "What position?"

She punched her hands into her hips and looked up at him. "Do you want to kiss me right now?"

"Yes," he said plainly without a second's hesitation. And then realization dawned over his face.

"*See?*" She flung her arms out in exasperation. "I think they are trying to manipulate us."

"I get it now—wait. Does that mean you want to kiss *me*?"

She threw up her arms again and widened her eyes into an obvious *yes*.

"Oh," Chuck said with a smile. "Well, that's good."

"That is not *good*, Chuck! They are trying to sabotage us into losing more money! They know we made out last night, and now they just spoon-fed us a bunch of horny memories on purpose to get us to do it again!"

He was still looking at her with a dopey grin. "You really want to kiss me right now?"

She snapped her fingers in front of his face. "Chuck! Snap out of it! We've got a problem on our hands!"

He shook himself and scrubbed his face with a hand. "You're right. Sorry. What should we do?"

"We should stay the hell away from each other for the rest of the day, that's what."

"Right. Yes. Good idea. But, um . . . how?"

Olivia chewed her lip and thought. "Well, at least we have another bathroom now."

"*And* a dishwasher."

Olivia snapped her fingers again. "Yes! That's a good place to start. I'll go clean up the kitchen from breakfast, and you go move all your stuff into the new bathroom."

He nodded. "Wait. Why do *I* get the smaller bathroom?"

"Do you want to do the dishes instead?"

"Not particularly."

"That's what I thought. Now, *go*, and don't talk to me for the rest of the day."

His face pinched in angst. "That's going to be a very long day." He glanced over at the crew and then leaned toward her like he might try to steal a kiss while they weren't looking.

She held up her hand between their faces. "Ten thousand dollars, Chuck."

He grumbled in frustration and stomped off.

Olivia chewed away her smile, still buoyant from their trip down memory lane, and reminded herself that she needed to behave herself too.

CHAPTER 11

THEY MANAGED AS BEST they could to keep out of each other's orbit for the rest of the day. Olivia spent most of it sequestered in the office trying to distract herself with a book. She wasn't sure what Chuck was up to and decided not to ask when she ventured out into the kitchen for a snack and found him weirdly pacing off distances with measured strides and glancing up at the ceiling over and over. He gave her the bed that night, and she made sure to lock the door and shove a chair in front of it for everyone's benefit.

By the time Sunday rolled around and they were free of the camera crew, Olivia was looking forward to her phone call with Grandma Ruby as a break from the tension straining the house at the seams. She sat on the pool's edge with her feet in the water, smoothly kicking them back and forth in slow motion. She'd put her earbuds in so that she didn't have to hold anything while they talked.

"Olivia, my darling, how are you?" her grandmother answered.

"Hi, Grandma. I'm okay. How are you?"

"Oh, just fabulous, sweetheart. Vi and I have been taking walks before it gets too hot every day. I've almost finished the Sudoku book you gave me."

"I'll have to send you another," Olivia said with a warm smile.

"I would love that. How are things with Chuck? Are you enjoying your time with him?"

Olivia flushed, weighing how much to say. "Sure."

Despite the fact that we kissed the other night, got charged ten thousand dollars for it, are redeveloping problematic feelings, and have been avoiding each other since so that we don't lose any more money, she silently added in her head.

"Well, that's wonderful, sweetheart. Listen." Her tone shifted into something more serious, and Olivia took notice. "I saw something in a magazine about you, and about the show."

Cold dread seeped over Olivia like the sun had gone behind a cloud. "Grandma, please don't read tabloids."

"I don't! You know I don't, but Vi's granddaughter left one behind the other day, and I thought I'd pick it up and flip through it. I saw this little story about you and Chuck, and it said he'd been fired from a movie! You never told me that, Olivia."

Olivia flinched on reflex, feeling like she was in trouble. "I'm sorry, Grandma. It happened a while ago, and Chuck doesn't like to talk about it."

"Well, what happened? I can't imagine a boy that sweet doing anything worth getting fired over." She clucked her tongue in dismay.

Olivia gazed back toward the house, wondering if she'd catch a glimpse of Chuck through one of the windows. The burning daze she'd been living in since the night in the hallway cooled and sharpened back to reality at the reminder that the world existed outside the house. "I don't know what happened. He won't tell me."

"Hmm. Well, can't you search for it? *Google* it?" She said the last part like she was proud of herself for remembering the term. It made Olivia smile.

"I could, sure," she said, and decided not to go into detail over their lack of internet access. As she had the thought, she realized she had something better than Google, and she felt foolish for never having thought of it before.

She decided to finish her conversation with her grandmother before looking into the option she should have considered ages ago.

"Grandma," she said, moving on to a topic she was reluctant to broach but felt the article had granted a rare opportunity to speak openly about. She lifted her feet up out of the pool and turned to lie back on the warm concrete. She closed her eyes against the brilliant sun despite wearing her sunglasses. "When you saw the article in the magazine about me and Chuck, did it say anything about . . . my parents?" She held her breath and hoped her question wouldn't upset her grandmother.

Ruby paused long enough that Olivia worried she'd hung up. "It did, yes," she finally said. "I wish they'd let your mother rest in peace."

Olivia's heart ached at the sorrow in her voice. Whatever grief she felt over her mother, she knew her grandmother felt it a thousand times more. "I wish they would too. Actually, the producers of the show I'm on asked me to do an interview about it." Against her closed eyelids, a vision of the famed photo of her and her parents danced.

Ruby stayed quiet for a long moment. "Are you considering it?"

"Of course not!" Olivia at first blurted, but then she realized her grandmother hadn't asked to accuse her, but to simply ask her.

The memory of her conversation with Chuck came flooding back, how he'd told her that if she ever wanted to tell her parents' story, she'd be good at it. He'd also said that she was scared, and he was right.

"Do you think I should?" she asked her grandmother, utterly vulnerable and afraid of what she might say.

Ruby let out a long, slow breath. "I always knew this day would come. I did everything I could to protect you back then. They were so hideously mean to your mother—and you. The things they said about you, an innocent baby, I couldn't—" She cut off with an angry breath. "And then *she* kept her mouth shut about everything and let the world believe my Rebecca was a monster." Ruby had worked herself into a small fit, and Olivia was reeling.

"Grandma, what are you talking about? *She* who? Astrid Larsson?" She could hardly say the name aloud. She wasn't even sure she'd ever spoken it to her grandmother before. It felt forbidden.

Ruby tutted. "Of course that's who I mean. She's not as innocent in this as everyone thinks. In fact, she's complicit in your parents' name being dragged through the mud."

"Grandma, what—?"

"I'm sorry. You and I have never had the chance to talk about any of this because I wanted to keep you as far away from it as possible, but seeing it in print again has me riled up, and since you asked about it, I think it's time I finally tell you the truth."

Olivia thought perhaps she'd slipped and smacked her head

on the concrete, and this whole conversation was a wild hallucination. "Tell me the truth about *what*, Grandma?"

Ruby paused for a long moment that had Olivia ready to leap out of her skin with anticipation. When her voice came back, it nearly hissed with the relief of a valve being opened. Decades of pressure let go on an exhale. "Darling, your parents did not have an affair. Well, they did in the sense that your father *was* married to Astrid Larsson at the time, but what he had with your mother was more real than their marriage ever was."

Olivia blinked several times, still staring up at the sky. "What does that mean?"

"It means that there is a lot more to the story than the tabloids ever reported. You see, your father's marriage to Astrid was a business arrangement. She was a Swedish supermodel who they wanted to turn into an American movie star, so they had her marry an American man. I'm simplifying things, of course; there were immigration requirements and paperwork, but the primary reason they married was for appearances. A rising starlet and a successful Hollywood manager made for a wholesome pair, and having roots in this country helped her career take off. It was a lucrative partnership for them both, but that's all it was: business.

"It worked well until your father fell in love with your mother. I'm simplifying again." She paused with a warm, fond chuckle. "Their love was the kind movies are made of and songs are written about, but of course they couldn't do anything about it. A divorce would have hurt Astrid's career—things were a bit different back then than they are today—and in turn, Bradley's, so they kept it secret from the public, but *not* from Astrid."

Olivia was reeling under waves of revelation, but she managed to speak. "She knew? That they were together?"

"Oh yes. Not only that, but she *sanctioned* it. It was another arrangement—between the three of them. Your father stayed publicly married to Astrid while he had a relationship with your mother out of the spotlight. Everyone got what they wanted. But when your mother became pregnant with you, she was already famous enough for the attention and interest to be unavoidable, which left it only a matter of time before the truth came out—well, what people thought was the truth." She paused and harrumphed another breath. "And Astrid never corrected them. Not even after they—" She cut off, and Olivia filled in the heartbroken blank with *died*.

As she listened, an odd thing was happening inside Olivia's chest. Her heart seemed to be shattering and piecing back together at the same time. Holes that had been there her entire life were sealing shut while new shards were splintering off.

"Why didn't you ever tell me this?" she asked.

"I should have. I really should have. I'm so sorry that I never did. It was all so ugly and cruel that I wanted to shield you from every bit of it," Ruby said. "But I've done you no favors letting you grow up believing your parents are the villains of this story. They absolutely were not. Yes, they may have made some poor decisions, but they were guilty of nothing except loving each other."

Olivia sat up and felt blood try to refill her spinning head. She'd always feared her parents were a toxic fling, and she the product of a regrettable, cheap tryst that ruined lives, but hearing her grandmother's story made her brave enough to ask something she'd always been afraid to know. "So, they were . . . in love?"

"Oh yes, sweetheart. Tremendously."

Her instant and affirmative response lifted Olivia's heart as if she'd been scooped off the ground to float near the sun. "Really?" she asked, because the sense of relief spilling over her felt too good to be true.

A quiet, amused laugh bubbled from Ruby. "Yes. They were so smitten. He'd send her endless flowers and gifts. She'd tell me they were going away for the weekend, and then she would resurface a week later telling me they'd been to Paris and back. And they *loved* you, my darling. You were their absolute pride and joy. Your mother told me once—" She suddenly cut off with a tearful sniff. Her voice came back thick and strained though still filled with warmth. "She told me once that she was going to quit acting so you could have a normal life out of the spotlight. She wanted the world for you. That's part of the reason I shielded you from the spotlight after her death."

"She was going to quit? For me? But I thought she loved acting." Olivia's own voice had grown thick with emotion.

"Acting, yes. The spotlight, no. Your mother was a very private person, Olivia. She never wanted all the attention. The two of you are very similar in that way."

The revelation was almost too much to process. Olivia had spent her life believing her mother loved the glitz and glamour of the spotlight—that the two of them had nothing in common because she was an introvert who'd rather die than be on camera. And here she was, finding out her mother was so similar, she was going to give up her career to raise her daughter away from the public eye.

"Grandma . . ."

Ruby sniffled, and Olivia would have given anything to wrap her in a hug. "I'm sorry, sweetheart. You deserve to know everything you want about your parents—both of them."

It sounded like an open invitation, and Olivia wasn't sure she was prepared to go from a handful of biased facts to unlimited knowledge. It might drown her.

She tucked her knees to her chest. She felt like a child. "Was my dad—" She didn't know how to say it other than bluntly ask what she wanted to know. "Was he a good guy?"

"Darling, your father was a prince. He worshipped the ground your mother walked on and would have done anything for you."

A vision of the famed tabloid photo of her father with his arm out shielding her and her mother appeared in her mind, and for the first time ever, she saw it in a new light.

They were a family, not a scandal.

Her heart filled and ached at the same time.

"Too bad everyone thinks the opposite," she said with a bitterness that surprised herself. Astrid Larsson, the angelic victim, had suddenly been recast as the villain in this story.

"Yes," Ruby agreed without Olivia having to voice her thoughts. "Astrid knows the truth of it all, and only she has the power to clear their names like they deserve. Your mother confided the truth in me but told no one else. And with the way her name's been tarnished, no one is ever going to believe anything I say either. The silence has eaten me alive for decades. At least the public has stopped paying so much attention to it."

Olivia felt like her head had been unscrewed, had all its contents shaken up, and then been put back on. "Until now."

"Until now," Ruby said. "Interest ebbs and flows like with any scandal, but I don't think it's a coincidence that it has spiked again now that you are in the spotlight."

Olivia chewed her lip, feeling emotions that had her wanting to run away from the storm as much as she wanted to run straight into it. "This interview that the producers want me to do, what do you think my mother would think?"

Ruby paused and took a pensive breath. "I think your mother would be happy to have the truth told about her life and her love, but I also think she'd leave the decision of inviting the spotlight by sharing it up to you."

Olivia considered. "And my father? What would he think?"

"He'd think whatever your mother thought. Like I said: smitten." Olivia heard the smile in her grandmother's voice and couldn't help the small smile that curved her own lips.

"Thank you for telling me all this, Grandma."

"Of course, my dear. I'm sorry I kept it from you for so long."

She'd given Olivia plenty to think about. When they ended their call with promises to check in again next week, Olivia decided to make another call.

She wandered over to the back wall of the property near the pool house. The camera crew might not have been there that day, but the ceiling and outdoor cameras were still active. She now had two reasons to call her trusted resource, and she didn't want either of them getting caught on camera.

"Hey there," Mansi answered after a few rings.

"Hey," Olivia greeted her. "What are you up to?"

"Oh, you know. Out to brunch with myself because my best friend is imprisoned with her ex."

Sounds of chatter and clinking dishware leaked through the phone. Olivia assumed Mansi was dining outside both because she heard a car go by and because her friend was too classy to answer her phone in the middle of an indoor restaurant.

"Don't tell me you're at—"

"The sidewalk place in Santa Monica with the hot waiters? Sure am."

"*Ugh.* Have a mimosa for me."

"I've had three."

"I miss you so much."

"The feeling is mutual. So, what's up? Are we graduating to phone calls to ward off temptation? Don't tell me Chuck is skinny-dipping on a Sunday morning."

"Please don't put that image in my head."

"Sorry."

"And you should know that kiss from the other night cost us ten thousand dollars."

"*What?*"

"Yep. *No physical contact* is one of the house rules. They dock our prize money if we violate it."

"Yikes. No wonder he locked you in the bedroom to keep his hands off you. What do you expect him to do when you're walking around with that body-ody all day?"

"Manse, stop it. You're drunk."

"Hey, *you* called *me* at eleven a.m. on a Sunday, so."

Olivia smiled. "Fair."

Mansi sighed. "Well, if I can't provide my remote intervention services, what can I do for you?"

Olivia bit her lip, nervous again. "I just talked to my grandma, and—"

"Ruby!" Mansi lovingly sang. "How is she?"

"She's great, and now I'm wondering if you're sober enough to have this conversation."

"Uh-oh, this sounds serious. I'm here. What do you need?"

"Well, she brought up that tabloid article, which led to me

asking about my parents, and her dumping a truckload of family history on me."

"Oh?"

"Yeah. Turns out my mom hated the spotlight and was so in love with my dad, they'd fly off to Paris together without telling anyone, *and* my dad's marriage to Astrid Larsson was a business arrangement and totally fake."

"Come again?"

"I know. It sounds made up, but my dad married Astrid so she could put down roots in America and become a star here. And then when he met my mom, they fell in love and agreed with Astrid to keep it all a secret, and—"

"Wait, wait, *wait*." Mansi cut her off. "You're telling me that the root of this whole scandal was a lie?"

"Yes. And I want to talk to Astrid about it." The words were out of her mouth before she could stop them. The prospect of actually speaking to Astrid Larsson was deliriously daunting, but there was no chance for it to ever even happen if she didn't put the ball in motion.

"You— What?" Mansi asked. "You want to talk to Astrid Larsson? The beloved three-time Oscar winner whose storied career includes the earth-shattering scandal of your parents' affair that resulted in your birth? *That* Astrid Larsson?"

"*Yes*, Mansi. And I need your help. You're the only person I trust with this. The production crew here is already asking me for an interview about it, and I don't want word to get out that I'm even considering anything. I know you have all kinds of legal sleuthing resources. Is there a way you could *discreetly* figure out if she's willing to talk to me?"

Mansi paused for a few beats, probably still in shock and

running a list of her resources through her head. "Um, yes. I can do that for you."

"Thank you." Olivia let out a heavy exhale, dizzy at the thought of what she'd put in motion. "While we're on the topic of your sleuthing resources, my grandma also brought up that article mentioning Chuck getting fired, and it made me realize that all along I could have asked *you* to look into the reason why."

Mansi went silent again and stayed that way long enough for Olivia to overhear the full order of the person sitting at the table next to her (avocado toast with a poached egg and an Americano).

"Manse? You still there?"

"Okay, don't hate me," she blurted.

"What? What does that mean?"

Mansi's voice lowered and took on a serious tone that said she'd sobered up. "It means that I may have already looked into it and never told you."

"*What?*"

"Shhh! You're going to blow out my eardrum, Liv. Also, you are literally calling me right now to ask me to use my resources, so don't act so surprised."

She glanced over her shoulder at the house to see if her shouting had drawn Chuck's attention. No doors flung open, and no apparitions appeared near windows. She lowered her voice to a hiss. "Okay, you need to tell me *right now* what you are talking about, Mansi."

Mansi took a big breath and perhaps another gulp of mimosa before she spoke. "Look, Liv. Your relationship with Chuck has always been . . . volatile—"

"That's generous."

"—and when he got fired and all those rumors started, I thought it might be a good idea to do a little digging *just in case* you ever needed the information. At the time, you were so concerned about supporting him and keeping him happy that you seemed willing to let it all go when he said he didn't want to talk about it. And then it kind of blew over, so I didn't bring it up. But I have connections at my firm who work directly with studios, so I asked around—*discreetly*—to see what I could learn."

Olivia's mouth was hanging open. She couldn't believe the lengths Mansi had already gone to on her behalf. Not to mention, this bombshell boded well for her request regarding Astrid. "You are a terrifying and amazing friend."

"I know."

"So, what did you find?"

"Nothing."

"Manse, you don't have to protect me. Just tell me—"

"No, Liv. That's what we found. Nothing. My guy knows a guy who can get the most off-the-books information, and even he couldn't find anything. It's like the truth about whatever happened . . ." She paused again. "It's like it was covered up."

The capacity for thought left Olivia like thieves fleeing a robbery. At the same time, her fear of coming near a scandal trotted up her spine. She could hardly string two sentences together.

"So, what. You're saying Chuck is part of a conspiracy or something?"

"No! Yes? I don't know!" Mansi was flustered, which was rare, and by the edge in her voice, Olivia could tell she'd been dying to get this news off her chest for ages. "I don't know what happened but, Liv, people in Hollywood don't fuck around. When something happens that they don't want to get out, forms are signed, deals are made. Money is exchanged."

Olivia reflexively snorted at the last part. "Well, I know for sure Chuck wasn't bribed to keep quiet. He's too broke for that."

"Maybe not him, but someone else on that movie? I mean, there are a ton of big names on *Safe Gamble*. Who knows what it could have been."

It all seemed too impossible to be real. Olivia couldn't even believe they were having the conversation with any seriousness.

But maybe?

She remembered how Chuck had said *not today* and glanced at the camera the last time she'd asked him what happened. Perhaps there was some truth to what Mansi was suggesting.

"So, what does this mean? I keep prodding until he tells me?"

"Liv, that's what I'm saying: maybe he *can't* tell you. Maybe you have to let it go."

The thought that there was a secret between them, a *true* secret and not simply Chuck being stubborn, put a sour pit in her stomach. She hated that he might have been forced into the position, and she hated even more that he was choosing whoever had forced him over her.

"I always hoped he'd taken Richard Sykes's parking spot or drank his coffee and was too embarrassed to tell me about it," she said, half joking in an effort to lighten the mood.

"I mean, that's possible but it seems like it's something bigger than that."

Bigger than that. She let the words simmer in her mind, not really sure what to make of them.

Suddenly feeling overwhelmed by her two phone calls, Olivia decided she needed to head inside and lie down.

"I have to go, Manse."

"Have a good day, Liv. I'm toasting in your honor and will flirt with one of the waiters for you too."

Olivia quietly laughed, which she assumed was Mansi's intention.

● ● ● ● ●

OLIVIA REPAIRED TO THE BEDROOM, WHERE SHE STARED AT THE ceiling for an hour, thinking, before she fell into an uneasy sleep fraught with strange dreams about movie stars, fake marriages, and shadowy men with briefcases full of money. She woke at nearly four p.m., groggy, and noticed someone had pulled a blanket up over her. It cut the chill of the air conditioning and made her consider snuggling deeper and forsaking the whole day in bed.

It also made her smile that Chuck had obviously come looking for her and covered her up when he found her asleep. She wondered what he'd spent the day doing and wandered out to find him and say thanks for the blanket. When she found the gym and office empty, she padded into the kitchen and found him rummaging in the fridge.

"Oh! There you are," he said when he closed the door and turned to see her having sat on a stool at the island. He wore a pair of the loose athletic shorts he'd taken to wearing in the house and a black tee. He was her favorite combination of cuddly, soft clothing and all the planes and muscles she knew were underneath, like a mountain range in the clouds begging her to come explore.

"Hey," she said with a yawn. "Thanks for the blanket. I didn't mean to sleep for so long."

"You must have been tired."

She wasn't sure if she'd truly been tired or maybe just over-whelmed. But she was sure that Chuck was bending over to find something in a low cabinet, and the sight had her fully awake. The thought of what she'd been overwhelmed about vanished from her mind like mist. The shorts strained over his sculpted ass and clung to his strong thighs, which could have crushed her like a grape. Why were the backs of his knees sud-denly so hot? She wasn't usually a leg girl but, *holy shit*, every inch of his lower half had her blood spinning cartwheels in her veins.

Perhaps it was because she hadn't touched him in ages, and he was specifically off-limits now.

"What are you doing?" she asked for distraction.

He pulled a baking sheet from the cabinet and set it on the island like he wasn't exactly sure what it was. "Making, um . . . cookies."

"Cookies? You don't eat cookies."

He shot her a smirk. "Maybe I'm making them for you."

"Oh," she said, surprised. "Well, that's sweet of you. Do you even know how to make cookies?"

"Of course I do." He spun around to another cabinet and pulled out a mixing bowl. Then he paused and looked at her with a tilt of his head. "Actually, I was looking for the sugar in the pantry and couldn't find it. Could you help me?"

She arched a brow at him. "I'm sure it's in there."

"It probably is, but I could use your help." He nodded at the pantry door, which stood open next to the fridge. "Come here."

Olivia sighed, not wanting to get up. "Chuck, I trust in your ability to find sugar on your own. You can do it."

He disappeared inside the door, and his voice echoed back

into the room. "Sure, but it will be easier if you help me. I can't find it."

"It's probably right in front of you."

"Well . . . I don't . . . see . . . it . . ."

With a roll of her eyes, she slid off her stool and marched over to the door.

Inside, he was bent over again, looking on a low shelf. In half a second, her eyes went straight to the sack of sugar smack in the middle of the shelf directly inside the door.

"It's right here," she said as she stepped in and reached for it.

He immediately stood up and closed the door behind her. The small space instantly squeezed in around them. The air thickened. They were chest to chest with hardly six inches between them.

"What are you doing?" she said on a hot breath even though she knew. Her body was already deliciously tingling at such close proximity to his.

A wicked grin curved his mouth. "Not baking cookies."

"Clearly. Why did you just shut us in the pantry?"

"Because I want to talk to you. Privately."

His implication raced through her blood. She squeezed her thighs together to control herself and took a tiny step back. "And what exactly do you want to say?"

His grin grew, and he stepped toward her, eliminating the space she'd just put between them. "I think you know."

She was nearly trembling with want—no, *need*. The ache to touch him spread like fever, shooting out into her limbs and lighting her core on fire. "Chuck," she said, barely above a whisper. The air inside the pantry quickly grew hot, becoming more exhale than oxygen as they breathed each other in and out.

He moved even closer. As close as possible without actually

touching her. "*Please*, Liv. I'm losing my mind. I'm going to die if I can't touch you."

"I think you're being a little dramatic."

"Maybe, but tell me you don't feel it too."

Oh, she felt it. She felt every goddamned bit of it screaming through her blood. She wet her lips and backed up again, only to be met with a wall of shelves. She sucked in a sharp breath and steadied a can of beans she'd bumped with her elbow.

"Just once," Chuck said, his voice liquid hot and pouring over her. "To break this tension. Please."

Say yes, say yes, say yes, her body screamed at her. But her brain fought its way through the cloud of lust.

"Chuck, did you forget the rules? They docked us *ten thousand dollars* for that kiss. How much do you think they'll take away if we have sex?"

His eyes flashed with a blazing heat. "Whatever it is, it would be worth it. But anyway, they won't know."

"How? There are cameras everywhere."

"Why do you think we're in the pantry right now?"

"You can't be serious."

"I am. I scoped out every square foot of this house looking for blind spots for this exact reason."

She slowly blinked and remembered his odd behavior pacing out distances and looking up at the ceiling. *This* was what he'd been doing. Her lips were sluggish and heavy when she spoke, her voice hardly more than a breath. "Wh-where are they?"

A purely wicked grin lifted his mouth again. "It's either here, the bedroom closet, the bathrooms, or the laundry room, which would require some impressive flexibility, which I know from experience that you aren't capable of."

Olivia's mouth was hanging open. Her bearings were a scattered mess on the floor, so there was no sense in trying to gather them. He was obviously being serious, and despite herself, she humored him. "You mean to tell me the only places we can do it in this house are glorified closets or cold tile floors?"

He smiled again, and she wanted to lick his lips. "I would have sex with you literally anywhere, Olivia Martin."

She was suddenly a radiant, bursting star. The pinnacle of his desires, this man who stood a breath away from her and was ready to do anything she wanted. She felt like a goddess come to life. All she had to do was say the word, and they'd cross a point of no return.

"You are such a bad influence."

"Sorry, not sorry," he said, and put a hand on her hip. Her skin instantly ignited beneath his palm, even through her dress. To be in his presence and not touch him was truly torture; she'd never realized how much until right now. The urge to touch him back burned her from head to toe, crackling out into her fingertips and fuzzing her thoughts. Her will to resist was quickly waning, even with everything at stake.

"Chuck, we are *not* having sex in this pantry."

"Why not?" He put his other hand on her neck, curling his fingers around her nape.

"Because . . ." she tried, but the word came out feeble and half there.

He hungrily outlined her lips with his eyes, wetting his own, and moved closer. His breath spilled over her skin and sent a tingle all the way to her toes. By the look in his eye, she could tell he knew her resistance was only for show, and she wanted it as bad as he did. All he had to do was look at her like that, and she was a goner. This little waltz was simply a formality.

"Because . . ." she whispered again, and could not find an end to her sentence.

Chuck smiled in the remaining space between them, knowing he'd won.

"Oh *fuck*," Olivia said, and pressed her mouth to his in surrender.

Her body came alive with ten thousand volts of electricity. Her nipples pinched. She moaned into his mouth, finding painfully sweet relief. Her low belly grew hot and heavy with a delicious ache. Like he knew she needed it, he grabbed her hips to move his thigh between her legs.

"Hello there," she panted, and ground herself against the bulge already pressing into her hip.

"Hi. I've been dreaming of this for days. Actually, I never stop dreaming of this."

"You dream of having sex with me in a pantry?" she said, and grazed her teeth against his jaw, absolutely ravenous for him.

"Like I said, I dream of having sex with you literally anywhere." He scooped his hands under her thighs and lifted her up around his waist.

She hitched onto him with a gleeful squeal and fisted her hands in his hair. "Anytime too."

"Always."

Her body melted to his. She couldn't get close enough. She swept her hands over his broad shoulders, his arms flexed and holding her up, his chest. Every inch of him was divine, and she wanted to drown in him. At the same time, she felt like a rebellious teenager making out in a hidden closet.

"We're going to get in so much trouble if we get caught," she slurred against his lips with a laugh.

"They'll never find out," he mumbled, and moved his lips to her chest.

"I mean, we may not be on camera *in here*, but they'll know we came in here and didn't leave for a while."

"You're helping me find sugar, remember?" he said, and bit her nipple through her dress.

"*Yes!*" she cried out, and arched into him. Her head tilted back, and her eyes fluttered closed. She bumped up against a bag of rice. Chuck loosened his grip and let her slide down his body to stand again. Her legs were hardly functioning when he slid his hands under her dress and hooked his fingers into the waistband of her underwear.

"Liv, I haven't been with anyone since you," he said, and gave them a tug.

Somewhere in the depths of her drowning brain, she knew he was telling her he was healthy, and everything was safe. The same went for her, but instead of a simple affirmative on her part because she was too distracted by the feel of him peeling her underwear down her thighs, her chaotic mind offered up, "There's only you."

He looked up at her from his knees like a man before a shrine as she stepped out of her panties. "Everything else still in place?"

"Yes." Her voice was an impatient, ragged whisper. She appreciated his mind for safety and precaution, for confirming that her IUD was still positioned, and they could get as close as humanly possible without worry, but the fact that they were really going to do it right here in the fucking pantry had her ready to explode.

"Good," he said, and hooked her leg over his shoulder.

She flung out her arms to grab the shelf behind her and sent a box of macaroni and cheese tumbling. Unfazed, Chuck pressed a hot kiss into the inside of her knee and then worked his mouth higher and higher up her thigh, closer to an epicenter that would guaranteed undo her completely. She squeezed the shelf and breathed hard, absorbing the feel of his luscious mouth and wondering how she was going to survive this standing on one foot. He pushed her dress out of the way to grip her hips and tilt her toward him, nipping and kissing and scratching the soft skin inside her thigh with his stubble so exquisitely that she half whimpered, half moaned his name. Stars had already begun to prick her tunneling vision as his lips pressed into the aching apex of her legs, and—

The doorbell rang.

They both froze.

Olivia's heart thundered, and her legs were shaking, but the feeling that they'd been caught instantly refocused her attention. She scrambled to stand up straight, almost kneeing Chuck in the face in the process.

"Oh shit," she said, and smoothed her dress.

"Who's here?" Chuck said, and looked at the closed pantry door but stayed crouched on the floor.

"I have no idea. It's Sunday. Everyone is supposed to have the day off." Her mind was scrambling and fighting hard to come back from the lurid land of Chuck's hands and mouth all over her. "They couldn't possibly know already, right?"

"Know what?" Chuck said, still on the floor.

"About *this*," she hissed, and waved her hands around the small space.

He shook his head. "No. That's impossible. Even if it was on camera, there's no way someone could get here that fast."

Olivia wrung her hands, already embarrassed. "I don't

know. Tyler delivers pretty instantly when we need something. Maybe they have him on standby to dole out punishments too. I *knew* this was a bad idea!"

He looked up at her with a dark grin. "You seemed like you were enjoying yourself."

"Shut up." She scowled at him although it was completely true. "Come on, let's go see who it is." She moved for the door and cautiously pushed it open. At least no one had barged inside uninvited. She turned back and waved him along. "Are you coming?"

He was still crouched on the floor with one hand on his thigh and staring up at the ceiling. "I just need a minute. I'll catch up."

She understood his implication and left him there, realizing it would be best for all if he didn't answer the door with evidence of their tryst pitching a tent in his shorts.

On the way to the front door, she took several deep breaths and tried to get her head on straight. She had no idea who would be calling late afternoon on a Sunday: Parker, TJ, Tyler with another angry red envelope informing them they'd lost more money for breaking rules. Perhaps a solicitor selling solar panels who'd somehow made it past the security gate.

She reached for the front door's knob, and nothing could have prepared her for who was standing on the other side.

"Um . . . Chuck?" she called over her shoulder after she managed to close her gaping jaw. "Your parents are here!"

Barbara and Sam Walsh beamed at her like they'd shown up for Christmas dinner. Behind them stood the full camera crew, lenses lifted and pointed.

Olivia was too dumbstruck to do anything but stare. Mercifully, Chuck came jogging around the corner a few seconds later.

"What did you say?" he asked, and raked a hand through his hair, which she had thoroughly mussed.

"I said, your parents are here. Along with the camera crew."

Chuck came to stand beside her, thankfully back in presentable order, and blinked in shock. "Mom? Dad?" he said like he couldn't believe they were truly there.

Barb instantly stepped inside and threw her arms around her son. Petite and blond and fluttering her hands like little birds, she hugged him with her head hardly meeting his shoulder. She then reached for his face and yanked his cheek down to kiss it. "Oh, Charlie! It's so good to see you!"

Chuck stumbled in her grip before he gently hugged her back. His father used his cane to delicately step over the threshold into the entryway. He looked a lot like Chuck, only rounded at the edges, graying, and leaning slightly to the left. "Hiya, son," he said, and hugged him as soon as his mother released him.

Chuck was still reeling. "Hi. What are you guys doing here—?"

The sound of his mother's excited gasp cut him off. "Would you just *look* at this place, Sam?" she gushed, and spun a slow circle as she took in the entryway. "Oh! And Olivia, my darling!" She pulled Olivia into a warm, soft hug that smelled like flowers and minty chewing gum.

"Hi, Barbara," Olivia said, just as dazed as Chuck.

"Heck of a house you got here," Sam said with a chuckle. He clapped Chuck on the shoulder and pointed out the back doors. "Look at that! A pool and everything."

"Oh my *goodness*!" Barb cooed with another gasp. "And the cameras are right here! Sammy, we're on TV!"

"I don't think it's live, Barb," Sam muttered, but waved into the lens with a grin anyway.

His parents continued to fawn and gush while Olivia and Chuck exchanged a look of complete bafflement. Barb was all but skipping around taking in the sights. Sam leaned on his cane and nodded enthusiastically at everything she pointed out. They chattered like chipmunks.

"*Parents!*" Chuck eventually bellowed over them. "Why are you here?"

Barb hardly missed a beat as she fluttered back over to him and pinched his cheek. "Oh, Charlie, don't get excited."

"Mom, no one calls me that here," he said with a faint flush.

Barb clucked and swiped invisible fuzz off his shoulder. "Then what do you prefer I call you? My little gumdrop?" She squeezed his face again like she was about to eat him.

The Walsh family was very physical. Always touching each other; always smiling and kissing cheeks. It at once melted Olivia's heart and filled her with a lonely envy.

"*Mom*," Chuck quietly protested again.

Barb released him and flapped her hands. "Sorry, sweetie. I'm just so excited to see you. We're here because your *producer* called and invited us for dinner!" She said the word with starstruck glee. "I didn't think your dad was ready to travel, but when they said it was all paid for and they'd take care of any special accommodations, we couldn't miss the opportunity to come!"

"That's right," Sam said, and thumped his cane on the floor. "First time out and about since the surgery, and so far, so good! Though I have had a healthy dose of painkillers today." He wobbled a little with a dopey grin that popped the same dimple his son had.

Despite the buoyant charm of her ex-maybe-future-in-laws filling the room like bubbles, Olivia's insides roiled. This was another game show trope. A veritable *meet the family* like a hometown visit on a dating show. Throwing Chuck's adoring and adorable parents into the mix was sure to stir up drama one way or another. She could tell something was amiss already based on the nervous glances Chuck kept stealing at her.

Not to mention, they'd been seconds from screwing each other's brains out in the pantry when the doorbell rang, and she could tell by the flushed fluster on Chuck's face that neither of them had recovered yet.

"Sweetheart, will you help me with these?" Barb asked, and swanned back toward the open front door. She wore a pair of linen capris and a flowing blouse covered in a tasteful palm print that looked entirely like a Google search result for *What to wear to L.A. for a middle-aged woman*, and Olivia loved her all the more for it.

Chuck obediently trailed after her and stopped precisely at the door's threshold. Barb had stepped back outside and was now lifting grocery bags into Chuck's waiting arms.

"You went shopping?" he asked as she loaded him down.

"No. A very nice young man named Taylor—"

"Tyler," Sam cut in.

"Tyler," Barb corrected, "called when we landed at the airport and asked what we wanted for dinner. It caught me off guard, but then, we'd been flown first class, and had someone waiting for us with our names on a sign just like in the movies—what was his name, Sam?"

"Grayson."

"Yes, Grayson. Also a very nice young man. Anyway, the point is, they've rolled out the red carpet for us, so I shouldn't have been surprised when someone called and asked what we wanted for dinner too." She looped a bag over each of Chuck's arms and balanced one more in his hands. With the heft of it, Olivia wondered what kind of feast they were in for.

"Your father has been eating rather bland because the painkillers cause—well, we don't need to get into that," Barb went on, and lifted the final bag herself. "But this is a special occasion, so I made a special request, and Tyler—such a nice young man—had all this waiting at the gate when we got here."

"This looks like a lot, Mom," Chuck said, and turned back inside, careful not to smash into anything with his new load.

"Well, we only see you a few times a year, Charlie, so we're going to take advantage. Oh! And they also told us to give you this and asked that we tell you not to read it in front of us." She held up a finger at each word like she was reciting specific instructions and fished a familiar envelope out of the bag she held to hand to Chuck. "Where's the kitchen?" she asked, as if a mysterious sealed envelope wasn't an odd thing to hand over.

"It's this way, Barb. I see it through the doorway," Sam said, and pointed with his cane.

They walked off with the camera crew in tow, still chattering, and Chuck and Olivia knowingly looked at each other.

Chuck let out a sigh and handed the envelope to Olivia to open, since his arms were still loaded down with grocery bags.

She took it and slipped her finger under the seal. One of the cameras had followed Chuck's parents while the other stayed with them. She cleared her throat and read.

"'Olivia and Chuck, we hope you enjoy your surprise Sunday visit. There is nothing as special as family time. Barbara and Sam Walsh know nothing about the premise of this show aside from the fact that you are living in this house together on camera. We have confirmed that they are in the dark about other information as well. By the time they leave this house tonight, you must have told them the truth about either the end of your relationship or that Chuck was fired from *Safe Gamble*, or you will be docked fifty thousand dollars each. The choice is yours. Enjoy dinner!'"

Olivia finished reading with bitter disbelief stinging her tongue and looked up to see Chuck having gone ghostly pale. This was less a *meet the family* trope and more some warped version of Two Truths and a Lie. She glanced down at the letter as if the words would rearrange into something less downright cruel and looked back up at him, at a loss.

"This is really messed up. I'm sorry, Chuck. How do they even know you haven't told your parents these things?"

He was still blinking in shock. His mouth popped open, and his voice softly spilled out. "Because I said as much. On tape."

"You did?"

He nodded. "Remember that day we were arguing in the bedroom, and I called you a nepo baby?"

"Of course. How could I forget?" Her words came out bitterly, but she couldn't blame him for the unpleasant callback given he was in such shock.

"Well, I also confessed that my parents didn't know I'd gotten fired or that we'd broken up, remember?"

She thought back to that day, and the memory slid into place. He had in fact confessed on tape. "Shit," she said, and took a breath. "So, what do we do?"

"Charlie! Can you bring in those groceries, please?" Barb called, startling them both. "I need to get started on the peach cobbler so that it has time to bake and cool for dessert!"

Chuck blinked a few times as if he was trying to gather himself. Olivia could tell he was flailing.

She held out a hand to calm him without touching him. "Okay, let's take the easy one. We'll tell them we broke up."

He flinched. "I promise you, that is not the easy one, Liv."

A flush curled into her face at the angst with which he said it. Clearly, their relationship meant something to his parents, so much so that he was possibly willing to give up fifty grand to lie about it being over.

"Okay, then we'll tell them you got fired."

He shook his head. "That's not easy either."

She bit her lip, not wanting to voice the next option because of the loss to herself but also for the position the whole situation was putting him in. "Take the hit, then?"

Chuck shook his head once more. "I'm not losing you that much money."

Olivia let out a discreet breath of relief and then flopped her hands at her sides. "Well, we have to pick one of them."

"*Charlie!*" his mom lovingly sang from the other room, and they both tensed again.

A few strained beats of silence passed between them.

"Chuck, we have to pick one," Olivia repeated.

His eyes traced zigzags on the floor like he was trying to find a map back to safer territory. He shook his head once. "We will. Just . . . follow my lead for now." He started off toward the kitchen.

"What?" Olivia said, and hurried after him. "What are we going to do?"

"Improvise."

"Chuck! I can't improvise! You know I'm not a good actor!"

"Well, I'm a good director, so keep up."

She grumbled and silently stomped after him. She tried for a welcoming smile when they rounded the corner, but it landed somewhere closer to a nervous grimace.

Barb was already at home in the kitchen, fluttering around and placing groceries in the fridge. She'd pulled pots and pans from cabinets and had Sam set up on a stool with a glass of sparkling water. She was a little homemaking tornado. "Charlie, sweetheart, bring those groceries over here, would you?" she sweetly asked.

"Sure, Mom. But you don't have to cook for us."

"Oh, nonsense. I love cooking for my family." She flapped her hands and dumped a handful of whole peaches into a colander. "Where can I find a paring knife?"

Sharing a love for the kitchen and unable to resist Chuck's

mom's infectious spirit, Olivia found the knife for her and grabbed a bowl. "At least let us help," she said, and pulled the peaches over to begin slicing.

Barb sweetly smiled at her. "If you insist. But let Charlie do that; it's easy. You help me with the chicken."

Chuck scoffed. "Relegated to the simple tasks, I see," he said sourly, but smiled.

"Pull up a stool, son," Sam said, and patted the one next to him. They fell into conversation while Olivia and Barb unpacked the rest of the groceries.

"For dinner, we're doing roasted chicken with fingerling potatoes and vegetables and a kale salad—I know you love your kale out here in California." She leaned in and warmly bumped her elbow against Olivia's with a wink. "I want to get dessert in the oven first so that it's an edible temperature by the time we finish dinner." She pulled a tub of vanilla ice cream out of a bag and put it in the freezer. "Charlie, I do hope you'll indulge in a little treat; I know you keep so strict to your diet."

Chuck paused his conversation with his dad to sweetly gaze up at her. "I'll eat anything you make, Mom."

Olivia's heart swelled at the love in his voice. She suddenly hated the producers for putting them in the situation they had. With Barb and Sam looking at Chuck like their absolute pride and joy and one of their favorite people in the whole world, she ached for that connection she'd never felt and thought that fifty thousand dollars was well worth not doing anything to hurt them.

"Good," Barb said with a smile. "Don't slice them too thick." She nodded at Chuck's hands slicked with peach juice where he was peeling and slicing yellow wedges into a bowl.

Olivia met his eyes before he went back to talking to his

dad, and he gave no indication of which truth they were going to tell, so she kept helping his mom.

"Olivia, how is your grandmother?" Barb asked, and cracked an egg into a bowl. Olivia noticed that as she talked and moved around the kitchen, she was just as skilled as Chuck at ignoring the cameras. Sam's eyes kept drifting toward the lenses, and Chuck would gently nudge him to refocus.

"She's doing well," Olivia told Barb. "Her birthday was last week, and we had a little party."

"Oh, how nice. Excuse me. I need to grab some sugar." She rinsed her hands at the sink and glided off toward the pantry. She was halfway there when a horrifying realization struck Olivia like she'd stuck a fork in a light socket.

"Oh, wait—!" she said, and hurried after her. But she was too late. She bumped into Barb at the door with a pouch of sugar in one hand and a bundle of lacy blue fabric in the other.

"Olivia, sweetheart, I think you may have misplaced something personal in here," she said quietly, and pressed Olivia's wadded-up underwear into her palm.

Olivia wanted to die. Melt through the floor. Hide in a box of pasta. Bury herself under bags of beans. Luckily, they were still halfway in the pantry and off camera.

"Oh, thank you, Barb. I must have dropped them when I was, um, doing laundry." The lie burned her face. The laundry room was clear on the other side of the house and nowhere near the pantry. The only reason her panties would have been in the pantry was because Barb's very own son had peeled them off her trembling legs not twenty minutes before and she'd been too distracted by their sudden arrival to put them back on.

Barb gave her a sweet, innocent smile and swept back around her to continue making dessert.

Olivia almost opted to lock herself in the pantry for the rest of eternity. She couldn't bear the thought of turning around to face anyone. Her face was positively aflame.

She wadded her underwear in her fist and attempted a mad dash across the kitchen. Chuck had risen to wash his peachy hands at the sink and turned to stop her.

"Where are you going?" he asked with a curious tilt of his head.

Olivia glanced at the cameras, which had focused on Barb and Sam's conversation on the other side of the island. She leaned in close and hissed through her teeth. "To drown myself in the pool because *your mother* just found my *underwear* in the pantry where we were *having sex* right before they got here!"

Chuck's eyes popped wide. He flushed and looked like he was trying not to laugh.

"Shut up," she said with a mortified glare, and stepped around him. She hurried off to the bedroom, thankfully with no camera crew in tow, and headed to the closet for a fresh pair of underwear. Once she had it on, she stole into the bathroom to fix her hair and apply a little bit of makeup since before the surprise arrival, Chuck had tousled her hair into tangles, and before that, she'd been asleep.

What a whirlwind thirty minutes it had been.

When she returned to the kitchen, she caught Barb midsentence.

"—two of you should come visit this summer. I know you're busy with work, but we'd love to see you both at home."

Olivia stopped short, suddenly breathless and poised on the edge of both lies in the same sentence. She glanced at Chuck, who was now destemming kale, but he didn't give her any clue which way to turn. In fact, he completely pivoted.

"How's Chelsea doing at art camp?"

And then Barb was happily off in another direction. "Oh, she's doing great. She has a real knack for teaching, you know."

"Gets that from her mother," Sam said with a doting grin as he lifted his sparkling water in a toast.

"Olivia, sweetheart, can you please find me a roasting pan?" Barb asked, elbow deep in the sink with an entire raw chicken in her hands.

"Sure," she said as she went to search cabinets. As she passed Chuck at the island, she snared his gaze, silently asking him in which direction she was supposed to follow his lead, but he only shook his head. She quietly huffed in frustration. An unpleasant prickling of nerves had begun to sting her stomach. She passed the oven and smelled the peach cobbler already baking inside. Barb had commandeered the kitchen and begun conducting her own culinary orchestra in no time flat.

She found the pan deep in a low cabinet, and when she stood back up, she saw a bottle of wine sitting on the counter. "Here you go, Barb," she said, and set the pan on the island. "Chuck, will you help me open this, please?" she asked, and held up the bottle.

He looked up at her and knew from the stern tilt of her head that she wanted more than just his help. "Sure," he said like he was in trouble. He wiped his hands on a towel and circled the island to the corner where she stood.

Barb had started talking to Sam again, and Olivia noticed one of the cameras zoom in on her and Chuck. She fished a corkscrew out of a drawer and shoved it at Chuck.

He flinched when he took it along with the bottle.

She leaned in and hissed, "I don't like this."

"You think I do?" he whispered back, and hooked the

corkscrew into the cork. The corded muscles in his forearm flexed as he began to twist.

"Obviously not, but you need to *pick one*! This is making me so nervous. I feel like we're walking in a minefield."

He worked the cork out with a rubbery *pop* and reached for a glass. "I know. I'm sorry. Here. You just need to drink one point five glasses of this, and you'll relax."

"Do *not* be cute right now."

"I'm not being cute! I'm trying to help."

The buttery chardonnay glugged into the glass, and he handed it to her. Olivia took a sip and admittedly felt her frayed nerves start to dull already.

"What are you two whispering about over there?" Barb sang.

Olivia bulged her eyes out at Chuck and mouthed *pick one*.

He glared back at her and then smiled. "Nothing, Mom. Who wants a glass of wine?"

"Oh drats. I meant to put that in the fridge to chill," Barb said. "But I guess a little warm white never hurt anybody. I'll take one."

Chuck retrieved two more glasses and artfully held them with stems poking between his fingers and bowls in his palm as he poured. The sight reminded Olivia that he'd waited tables when he'd first moved to L.A., like many a hopeful young actor.

"None for me, son," Sam said, and sipped his sparkling water again. "Rumor has it booze and pills don't mix."

"I believe those are well-founded rumors, Dad," Chuck said. "Here you go, Mom."

Barb took it with an outstretched arm and lifted it toward the ceiling. "Thank you, sweetheart. A toast! To the happy life the two of you are building together."

"Hear, hear!" Sam cheered.

Olivia sputtered into her wine, which she'd been in the middle of sipping already.

Chuck patted her on the back and clinked his glass to Barb's. "Thanks, Mom."

"Cheers," Olivia managed to mutter as she wiped a dribble from her lips. She took another gulp for good measure.

Barb had wrangled the chicken into the pan and set about rubbing it with butter and sprinkling herbs on it.

Chuck returned to his kale station and softly cleared his throat. "So, um, what exactly do you know about the show?" His voice rose awkwardly high, and he nodded at the nearest camera. Olivia relaxed a fraction more, seeing that he was finally leading them in some direction, though she wasn't sure which.

"They told us it's a reality show about your life living together," Sam said. "I'll tell you, your mother almost did a backflip when she heard that the two of you had moved in together. She was *thrilled*." Sam leaned back on his stool with a chuckle and squeezed Chuck's shoulder.

"Well, I won't say I've been *waiting* for you two to take the next step, but I am rightly overjoyed to see you moving in that direction. It's interesting that you would choose to do it on TV, but what do I know about Hollywood!" Barb said with a boisterous laugh.

Barb Walsh's drink threshold for oversharing was apparently two sips of warm white wine.

Olivia's face burned hotter than the sun. She gulped at her wine until she almost needed a refill. Chuck had turned a shade of crimson.

"What direction?" he asked.

Barb tilted her head and gave him an adoring look that screamed *Oh my sweet, silly child*. "I think you know, sweetie."

Olivia suddenly understood, with an overwhelming sense of conflicting emotion, what he'd meant when he said confessing to their breakup was not the easy option. Barb was practically ringing wedding bells with her butter-coated hands.

Olivia twitched with a nervous urge to flee. To protect herself from falling in love with this family any further only to lose them because they weren't even hers to keep. But at the same time, she couldn't resist their pull. Barb's adoring gaze, Sam's lippy smile. The way both of them were looking at Chuck like they were thrilled for him to have found a partner, and for that partner to be her.

For a moment, she saw it too. Her and Chuck, a few years down the road. A house—no cameras. Maybe a dog to start. A couple of kids after that. Both of their careers taking off. Him becoming an A-lister while she wrote biographies that were hailed in the *New York Times Book Review* and adapted into screenplays. Maybe Chuck would even star in one as a truly full-circle moment. They'd spend white Christmases in Ohio and vacation on tropical islands. They would celebrate Grandma Ruby's birthday with her for years to come.

A small smile curved her lips. She looked up to see Chuck looking at her like he might have been painting the same picture in his mind.

The oven timer dinged and snapped them out of their reverie.

"Olivia, could you get that, please?" Barb asked. "It's the cobbler."

"Of course," she said thickly. Her voice had grown rough with emotion. Chuck noticed and got up to join her.

"Are you all right?" he whispered as she bent over to take the bubbling cobbler out of the oven. Heavenly wafts of cinnamon and peaches billowed out and filled the kitchen.

"Yes. This is just . . . a lot." She sniffled and used her oven mitts to set it on the stovetop.

"I know. And I'm sorry. My parents adore you, obviously. That's why I said this wasn't going to be easy."

"I know. I get it now. I think I just need a minute." She used her arm to wipe her sniffling nose and pulled the oven mitts off. When she tried to step around him to leave, he moved in front of her.

"No, Liv. Don't run. Please. I'm right here. We'll figure this out."

Every nerve in her body was primed to flee from all the feelings, but Chuck, knowing exactly how she'd react to something so overwhelming, had firmly planted himself in front of her like he intended to make her stay and feel them.

"Please," he said again.

Through a deep breath that she was sincerely trying to use to turn off her fight-or-flight response, she realized that he wasn't forcing her to feel anything negative. What he was trying to get her to stay for, to get her to feel in her heart and mind and every inch of her body the same way he felt it, was positive emotion in its purest form.

Love.

His parents' love. *His* love. Simply . . . love.

She took a shuddering breath and looked up at him. His eyes had melted into hazel pools. His mouth was soft. He looked like he wanted to give her another ten-thousand-dollar kiss, or maybe just wrap her in a hug.

"Okay," she quietly said.

"Okay," he said with a soft smile, then squeezed her hand where no one could see.

Her skin tingled where he'd touched her and gave her

enough of a boost to return to the island and help Barb trim green beans.

"Olivia, honey, tell us about work," Barb said. "Have you interviewed anyone exciting lately?"

She let Barb's genuine interest settle over her like a warm blanket and found that she liked the way it felt. She also liked the way everyone eagerly listened as she talked about her job. They continued talking while the food cooked and they set the dining table. Olivia was so caught up in it—plus she'd had two glasses of wine—that she almost forgot they had to break an unpleasant truth one way or another before the night was over. She didn't know how long the Walshes planned to stay, but at least TJ's iPad clock wasn't glaring angry red numbers at them and aggressively counting down the available minutes left. Based on the ease of their conversation, she wondered if Chuck planned to wait to the last second and blurt out whichever truth he chose as they shoved his parents out the door on their way.

When they eventually settled at the dining table—their first use of it since moving in—with their perfectly prepared meal laid out before them, conversation turned to Sam's recent medical journey.

No one could tell a story like Sam Walsh. They learned every detail about his surgery, his recovery, his physical therapy regimen, all the books he'd read while resting—plot summaries included. Chuck shone like the sun while listening to him talk, but Olivia could tell the indecision over which truth to spill was tearing him up inside. She saw it in his fidgeting, the tight lines around his smile, the large gulps of wine he was taking. And she couldn't blame him. There'd been no clear entry point into either topic. And the deeper they got into basking in the warm glow of one another's presence, the more Olivia felt like they were lying by omission.

As much as the truth was tearing Chuck up, it was *boiling* up inside her. Chuck might have been able to do it, but she couldn't lie to Sam and Barb Walsh. The best parents on the planet didn't deserve to be hurt, of course not, but letting them believe that their son was thriving and playing house with her as they snowballed toward a happily-ever-after left her feeling like a villain. A hoax when they deserved honesty and respect and someone worthy of their affection and not someone who'd sit there in charade as they wove plans for the future with her included as an important thread.

"One day, I was working on stair climbing," Sam said as he continued detailing the past several weeks. "My doctor recommended it as part of the recovery."

"Up with the bad, down with the good!" Barb tipsily recited and lifted her wineglass.

"Other way around, Barb," Sam said. "The saying goes 'Up with the *good*, down with the *bad*.' You're supposed to lead with your stronger leg on the way up the stairs to strengthen it, and your weaker leg on the way down."

"Are you sure?" Barb said with a scrunch of her face.

"Yes, darling. Up, good; down, bad. I wrote it down."

"Are you sure you didn't write it *up*?" Barb said with a giggle.

Sam gave her an adoring look that pulled the truth to the tip of Olivia's tongue. "Anyway, that day on the stairs, I was—"

"Chuck and I broke up!" she blurted, unable to take it any longer. The wine might have had something to do with it.

A stunned silence fell like a thick fog over the table, smothering all other sound. Barb's fork was halfway to her mouth. A green bean tumbled from it and landed on her plate. Olivia's heart pounded in her ears, and she felt Chuck's eyes boring into her. But she couldn't unring the bell.

Chuck's gaze slowly slid from her face and aimed down at his plate.

"Charlie, is that true?" Barb asked in a thick, concerned voice.

It took a while for Chuck to meet her eyes, and when he did, his voice came out strained and full of pain. "Yes." He glanced over at Olivia, and she subtly nodded in encouragement to continue. "We broke up a week ago, and that day, we had an argument outside my apartment building, and it ended up online—*don't* google it. Please. But it went viral, and the producers of this show saw it. Before we knew it, they were making us an offer to come on the show and try to win a million dollars by living here together for a month."

Sam sucked in a sharp breath, and Barb's mouth fell open.

Chuck looked at Olivia again. "Liv needs money to help pay for her grandmother's care, and I—" He cut off and swallowed hard, dodging the other truth. "I could use the cash, so we said yes. We've been here for five days so far."

His parents continued gaping at them as if he'd confessed that they were eloping and going to live on Mars.

"Why didn't you say anything before?" Barb eventually managed to ask.

Chuck guiltily shrugged. "I didn't want to stress you guys out while Dad was recovering. The timing was bad for sharing the news."

"Oh, honey," Barb said, and reached across the table for his hand.

Olivia's heart ached. She suddenly felt even more like the villain. "I'm sorry I brought it up so bluntly," she said. She glanced at Chuck. "But we thought you should know."

Silence settled back over them with an uncomfortable weight. Sam eventually cleared his throat.

"So, this—" He waved his hand at the cameras and spacious dining room. "All this is just . . . a game?"

"Yes," Chuck answered. "It's only temporary. We don't really live here. If we can make it a month here together without leaving the house, we win."

Barb still looked stunned. She lifted her napkin and dabbed her lips. "And then what?"

"What do you mean?" Chuck asked.

She nodded between them. "And then what happens to the two of you?" The hope in her voice speared Olivia in the heart.

The answer to the question had grown admittedly muddled what with the past few days pushing them closer together. But they still had three and a half weeks to go. Not to mention, the whole reason they were in the house at all was that they'd broken up for good.

"Oh, um . . ." Chuck said, and tapped his fingers on the table. "That's complicated."

"I don't see what's complicated about it. You two are obviously perfect for each other," Barb said.

Olivia felt her face warm and was glad when Chuck was the one to speak because her voice had disappeared inside her throat.

"Because that's what I wanted you to think, Mom." He turned to look at Olivia. "Liv and I . . . Well, we have our share of problems. Let's put it that way."

"Well, what couple doesn't?" Barb said with a flip of her wrist like the issue was trivial. "Your father and I—"

"Mom, we're not you and Dad, okay? *No one* is you and Dad," Chuck snapped. He took a tense breath and calmed himself. "Sorry. What I'm trying to tell you is that I haven't been honest about our relationship for a long time. I haven't been honest about . . . a lot of things."

The look of hurt on the Walshes' faces was too much to take. At the same time, Olivia felt like she was intruding on an intimate family moment. The combination triggered her urge to run like she was being chased.

She stood from her chair and placed her napkin on the table. "I'm going to give you all a chance to talk. Please excuse me. Barb, Sam, it was really great to see you. Thank you for dinner. I hope you have a safe trip home."

"Liv, wait—" Chuck tried as she headed from the room.

"I'm sorry," she said with a shake of her head, shame heating her face and tears threatening to fall. If she stayed one second longer, Barb might leap out of her chair and give her a hug she didn't deserve. "Good night."

●　●　●　●　●

AN HOUR LATER, CHUCK FOUND HER IN THE BACKYARD BUN-dled in a hoodie and sitting on a lounge chair surrounded by flickering citronella torches.

"Are we voting someone off the island tonight?" he joked, and sat on the lounge chair beside her. He wore his own hoodie and sweatpants. He held out a bowl with a spoon sticking out from it. "Mom's famous peach cobbler if you're up for it."

Olivia could smell the sweet, fruity dessert tinged with cinnamon and vanilla. There was no way she was turning it down, even if she felt like she didn't deserve it. She untucked her knees from her chest and sat cross-legged to accept it. "Thank you." The first bite melted over her tongue in the perfect blend of doughy crust and sweet, gooey fruit. "This is delicious."

"I know. I had two bowls already."

She scooped another bite. "Are they gone?"

"Yes."

"Are they mad?"

"At you? No. At me? A little. I told them the truth about getting fired too. They were more upset that I'd kept it from them than that it had happened." He sighed a heavy breath into the dark. With the house lights dim, it was only the glowing pool and the torches lighting the yard. The camera crew was long gone.

"I'm sorry, Chuck."

He shrugged with another sigh. "I mean, they were going to find out eventually when the movie comes out and I'm not in it."

She spooned another bite of dessert. "I'm sorry I left dinner. I'm trying to be better about running away, but it's overwhelming how much they love you sometimes. And I—" Her voice cracked with a watery sob that she couldn't control. She dashed tears from her eyes. "Sorry."

He turned to her with his face painted in sympathy. "Olivia, you don't have to apologize. My parents love you. They think you're a saint for going on a TV show to win money to pay for your grandmother's care, and they already thought highly of you before that. You didn't do anything wrong by telling them." He paused and swept a hand through his hair. His voice came back quieter. "And the only reason *I* didn't tell them sooner was because I didn't want them to know I let you get away."

The gravity of his words settled over her with a profound weight, and she sobbed again. While the reason for his omission was meaningful in complicated ways that she'd have to think about later, it wasn't the reason she was crying. "No, it's not that." She wiped her eyes once more and took a shuddering breath.

"Then what is it?"

She looked at him in the dark, his face carved into beautiful shadows, and confessed something she'd only just admitted to herself. "You know how you said you're envious of my parents? Well, their legacy? I think I'm envious of *your* parents. Of what you have with them. Because I never—" Her voice cracked with another hard sob. Her shoulders shook. She set her bowl down and wiped her eyes with both sleeves of her hoodie. "Sorry."

"Come here."

She heard his voice, low and firm, on the other side of the thick mask of her sleeves. At the same time, it ached with longing. She dropped her hands to see him sitting with his arms open, welcoming her. More than anything, she wanted to fold herself into them. To sink into his embrace and hold her face against his warm, steady heartbeat. She swiped at a stray tear and sniffled. "We can't, Chuck. It's going to lose us money."

"I don't care," he said with a resolute shake of his head. "I'll pay you back whatever it is. Come here."

Needing his touch like a balm for her aching heart, she climbed off her chair and onto his. She settled between his legs and curled into his chest. He wrapped his arms around her like a cage and kissed her head. At the warm tenderness of his touch, the feel of his heart beating so close, her tears returned.

He held her while she cried, softly stroking her hair and gently rocking. When her tears finally stopped flowing and turned into intermittent hiccups, she mumbled into his chest.

"You're so lucky. That they love you that much. Even when they are mad at you, they're still there for you."

He kissed her head again. "I know I am lucky. And I'm sure your parents loved you just the same."

Another shuddering sob punched out of her. "You know, you might be right. I talked to my grandma earlier, and she brought up the tabloid article and told me things I never knew. I always thought I was the product of a toxic affair, but apparently, they were madly in love."

"Really?" he asked in surprise.

"Yeah. And get this. They—" She stopped when she remembered they were close enough to the house to be on camera.

"They what?" Chuck asked.

She hesitated, wanting to tell him more but not wanting anyone to hear. She considered dragging him back to the pantry for privacy, but that would only lead to things they might regret. Getting interrupted earlier had been for the best.

"I'll tell you some other time," she said, and nodded at the nearest camera mounted on the patio ceiling.

Chuck nodded like he understood.

"But it did change things," she said, wanting to share at least some of her feelings.

"Oh yeah? What did it change?"

She tilted her head to look up at him. His jaw cut a dramatic silhouette against the night sky. Flickering flames danced across his face. "The truth. I know it now, and I think . . . I think I might be ready to talk about it."

He reeled back as far as he could go against the chair. His eyes popped and a small smile curved his lips. "Well, now I'm *really* intrigued."

Olivia quietly laughed and curled back into him. "Like I said: some other time."

He tightened his arms with a contented sigh. "I'll be ready when you are."

She settled against him and listened to his heartbeat. Steady. Strong. He was so warm and sturdy, she wanted to melt straight into him. "Can I stay here all night?" she half joked.

"You can stay here as long as you want."

She considered it. Being tangled up intimately with Chuck was one thing, but simply being near him like this, held in his arms, was another. The night had cooled; the stars had shyly popped out from the gauzy black sky. The moon lounged in a thick crescent. She could have easily fallen asleep, or perhaps simply stayed up all night enjoying his embrace.

"We better go inside," she eventually said. "If they charge us by the minute for touching, we just lost about fifteen grand."

He squeezed her like he didn't want to ever let go. "I don't think cuddling will count as being as intimate as kissing."

"You're right." She sat up and softly smiled at him. "Possibly more."

He let her climb off the chair and then followed her to the house. Inside, he let her have the bed, and when she woke in the morning, she found a piece of paper folded into a little tent on her nightstand with *Burn after reading* written on the front.

She opened it with a curious smile and found it scrawled with Chuck's hasty handwriting.

Liv,

They can't hear me if I say this on paper. I'm sorry about the pantry. Well, not entirely because it was the best three minutes since we've been here, but I am sorry if it loses us any money. The truth is, I don't know how I'm going to survive the rest of the month without touching you. And it's not just touching you. Being close to you; talking to you—really talking to you. I think being here is what we needed, but it's also creating a problem because I want more than I can have. I'm writing this as I watch you sleep right now like some creepy teenage vampire because it's either this or I climb into bed with you and lose everything. And you know what? I wouldn't even care. You're worth every penny. But I'm not going to do that to you. I will behave, I promise. Just know that if I turn into a cranky recluse for the rest of the month, it's only for the greater good, which, I guess that goes along with the brooding vampire motif.

Yours, Edward Cullen

P.S. You just mumbled something about "dry goods" in your sleep, and holy shit, if you're dreaming about the pantry right now, writing this letter about self-control will have been moot. I must leave. Sleep well, my gorgeous human.

Olivia laughed to herself and pressed the letter to her chest. She sat up to see that she was alone, but the armchair in the corner had been positioned to face the bed.

"Creep," she muttered with a smile, but didn't mean it in the slightest.

Another sunny day glittered outside the back door. The house was still quiet, but it was nearing eight a.m., which meant the production crew would show up any minute, surely excited to dole out punishment for last night and inform them of whatever curve ball they were going to throw at them next.

Olivia glanced down at Chuck's letter again, and instead of burning it, she decided to fold it up and stash it under her pillow. He was right: being in the house together was changing things between them, and she couldn't deny that the change felt good.

"Twenty-four more days."

CHAPTER

13

"G OOD MORNING, LOVERS!" TJ boomed as soon as he stepped in the front door some short twenty minutes later.

Before they answered the doorbell, Olivia had found Chuck sipping coffee in the kitchen, still wearing his glasses and barefoot in his pajamas. She'd brushed her teeth and pulled her hair into a ponytail but otherwise hadn't bothered to get dressed either. Based on the film crew and the makeup and styling team filing in the door behind TJ, it appeared they were in for a morning makeover anyway.

"Why do you keep calling us that?" Olivia sourly asked as she noted the familiar red envelope tucked under his elbow.

"Because, *clearly*, that is what you are." He winked at her and held out the envelope.

She took it with a scowl, at the same time fearing they were about to be docked half their prize money for the pantry encounter. "No, that is what you're *trying* to make us." She slid her finger under the seal as Chuck came to stand beside her.

Parker had shown up with a to-go coffee cup in one hand and his phone in the other. Tyler bobbled around shuttling cases of water and a carton of coffee.

"You can't fight chemistry," TJ said. "We're only creating situations *encouraged* to increase engagement. How you respond is entirely up to you."

"Spoken like a master manipulator," Chuck said. "That was a real jerk move having my parents show up unannounced last night, by the way."

TJ held up a hand. "Uh! Let's save that conversation for the cameras, shall we? Lots to discuss today. But first, Olivia, if you will." He flicked his hands at the red envelope.

She pulled out the sheet of paper with a sigh and read it out loud.

"'Olivia and Chuck, the production team has found you in violation of the No Physical Contact rule for your indiscretion in the backyard last night, a close-contact cuddling session lasting approximately fifteen minutes. As punishment for this violation, the total prize money for each of you will be reduced by a sum of fifteen thousand dollars.' Oh," she said, relieved. "That's not so bad."

"Should have been more," TJ said with a frown.

"It's an appropriate amount," Parker butted in. "That moment between the two of you was really beautiful." He gave them a warm, sincere smile that caught Olivia off guard.

TJ scoffed and stomped off, clearly indicating that they were at odds on the fact and had argued about it.

"Thanks, Parker," Chuck said, sounding as pleasantly surprised as Olivia.

"You bet," he said, and then took a breath to reset himself.

"Well, we'll be doing another sit-down interview in the back-yard today, so hair and makeup is ready when you are."

"Sure," Olivia said.

"Got it," Chuck echoed.

Parker gave them a nod and then shuffled off with the crew. Olivia and Chuck were suddenly alone in the entryway without any cameras in their faces.

"You were right about the fifteen grand," Chuck said, and nodded at the letter she was still holding. "I'll pay you back for it, like I said."

"You don't have to do that, Chuck," she said with a shake of her head. "I—" Her words lodged in her throat at the memory of the feel of his arms around her, his heart beating so close. "I, um . . . needed that last night, so it's fine."

He looked at her with a soft warmth that nearly melted her into a puddle. "Okay."

Suddenly drawn to him like a magnet, she leaned in and lowered her voice. "And thank you for the letter. I'm really glad we're not being punished for the *other* thing that happened yesterday."

The corners of his mouth twitched up. He leaned in close enough that his lips brushed her ear and his breath spilled over her like a warm bath. "I told you, there's a blind spot leading into the pantry. I didn't only mean there were no cameras *inside* it. They have no idea what we did."

His neck was an inch from her lips. She could nearly feel his pulse leaping under his skin. She wanted to kiss it. To bite it. To run her tongue against the vein keeping time with her own heartbeat.

"Are you guys *trying* to lose more money?" Parker called

from the back doors with a clap of his hands. "Come on! Hair and makeup, now!"

They snapped apart like rubber bands, fiercely blushing and flustered.

But Parker was smiling. He walked back inside and squeezed Chuck's shoulder. "I can only do so much here, kids. Stop self-sabotaging." He pulled Chuck away toward the guest bathroom and winked at Olivia over his shoulder.

"Are you rooting for us now?" she heard Chuck ask as their voices faded.

"What can I say. I'm a hopeless romantic . . ."

Olivia softly smiled and turned in the other direction for her own makeover.

Apparently on a tight schedule, the styling crew all but pounced on her. As they dressed her in a canary yellow jumpsuit, painted her lips flaming red, and twirled her hair into a classy low bun, she couldn't spare a minute to answer Mansi calling her not once but twice. She only managed to glance at a text that said Call me back as the crew guided her into the backyard. What all the rush was, Olivia didn't know, but she found the usual mini studio set up and Chuck looking less like he'd just rolled out of bed and more like he was ready for a date with a button-down and artfully tousled hair.

They sat next to each other, across from TJ, and let the mic tech wire them up.

"Is there a fire somewhere this morning?" Chuck asked with an awkward laugh as the tech shoved his hand up his shirt.

Olivia glanced at him and surmised he'd been sped through the same frenzied rush of preparation as she had.

"Just a lot to get to today," TJ said, and straightened his blazer. "Ready?"

Whether they were ready or not, they started rolling.

"Chuck. Olivia. We meet again," TJ said once Olivia was wired and the cameras were up. "So you've made it through your first weekend in the house. Congrats. There have only been a few . . . *hiccups*, let's call them, so far, and it seems like things are going better than anyone expected." He left a loaded energy lingering in the wake of his statement. Olivia wondered if they were going to pull a *gotcha* on them and announce they'd known about the pantry all along, but he didn't go there. Instead, he dove right into the topic Olivia was still recovering from. "Chuck, a surprise visit from your parents last night. Tell us how that went."

"You know how it went, TJ. You've seen the footage," Chuck said with a frown.

"Well, sure, but I'd like your take on it. Olivia, yours too, especially the reason you ran out on dinner."

"She didn't *run out*," Chuck said, defending her before Olivia could say anything. "That was an emotionally charged situation that you sprang on us out of nowhere."

TJ leaned his elbow on his knee and held his chin like they were heading in the exact direction he wanted. "Seems to be her MO, though, no? Running from such *situations*."

Olivia uncomfortably shifted in her seat at the reminder, again, that they'd watched all their interactions in the house, minus the pantry, including every one in which she and Chuck had discussed her reflex to flee emotional turmoil. A feeling of vulnerable exposure burned her face.

"Tell me more about last night," TJ said with a scheming note in his voice. "Why was it so emotional?"

Chuck folded his arms over his chest. "Because you forced us to tell my parents the truth."

"About your breakup."

"Yes."

"And why didn't they already know?"

Chuck sighed, seemingly annoyed that they were going to analyze everything that had happened. Olivia couldn't blame him. "Because I didn't want to disappoint them. They love Olivia and clearly have a lot invested in our relationship."

"So you lied to them."

"Yes."

"The same way you lied to them about losing your job?"

"Yes—and for the same reason, before you ask."

"Hmm," TJ hummed thoughtfully. "You're very protective of the people you care about, Chuck." He let a silence stretch. In it, Chuck straightened his posture and tugged on his collar. His sudden fidgeting put Olivia on edge.

"Yes," he said plainly. "I am."

TJ looked at him with a thoughtful if not sinister purse of his lips. "On that note, how much does Olivia know about the reason you got fired?"

Olivia's heart shot up into her throat. She hadn't been present when he'd told his parents last night, so she didn't know what he might have said on camera.

Chuck fidgeted more. He'd begun to sweat, Olivia saw when she glanced at him. "She knows enough," he said through tight lips.

TJ considered him again. "Hmm. I don't think that's exactly true, is it."

Olivia froze in fear, wondering if they were going to drop another challenge on them and force him to confess right there on camera or pay.

TJ reached for his iPad sitting on the table, and Olivia bristled. Nothing good ever came from the iPad. "Now, I know you're cut off from the world in here what with no internet or television, so I think it's safe to assume you haven't seen today's news, right?"

Olivia and Chuck swapped a nervous look.

"What news?" Chuck asked.

TJ grinned a sinister sneer and swiped the tablet. When he flipped it around to a screenshot of a tabloid headline and photo, Olivia's vision momentarily blurred out of focus from dread. *Secrets from the Set*, the headline read, and where she might have expected to see another unflattering photo of her and Chuck, she saw Chuck and . . . someone else.

"What is that?" Chuck asked, and all but lunged across the table to reach for it.

TJ yanked it out of his reach and instead handed it to Olivia. "Something I think Olivia needs to see."

He shoved it into her hands, and she could not rearrange the shock on her face as she read.

New photos from the set of Safe Gamble *emerge in the wake of Chuck Walsh's recent firing. The disgraced actor who is currently filming an episode of* Name Your Price *after a video of his breakup with now ex-girlfriend Olivia Martin—notably not the woman in these photos—went viral is seen here with a production assistant identified as Madison Bilton. The timeline of events tells us these photos were taken before the viral breakup video. What exactly was happening on that movie set?*

Olivia swiped to the next screen and found three photos that ripped her heart right in half.

The first showed Chuck and a pretty blond girl with silky mermaid hair sharing an embrace. His arm was hooked around her shoulders, and her face was partially hidden behind the swell of his biceps. Neither of them was smiling but rather looked like they were sharing a private, intimate, yet serious moment. The second could have been taken moments before or after the first. They stood in nearly the same position facing each other, except this time Chuck's hand cupped the crown of her shoulder, and her head tilted back in a laugh. Chuck was smiling, and the sight of it, his easy, gorgeous smile pointed at this stranger, flared a wicked, ugly insecurity inside Olivia.

The third photo was of her from that day on the sidewalk. A still from the fight that managed to capture her looking as betrayed and angry as she suddenly felt.

Her mind shot back to that morning with the banana pancakes, to the name she'd seen on Chuck's phone. Maddy. She'd thought nothing of it, and apparently, she should have. It had to be this same Madison. Chuck clearly knew her well enough to have her saved in his phone under a nickname.

Her breath had left her along with the ability to say more than three words.

"What is this?" she asked, and numbly handed the tablet to Chuck.

He grabbed it with a frown. She watched his eyes dart over the words and images. They grew wider by the second until a look of panicked guilt swallowed his whole face.

"This is not what it looks like," he said.

The hackneyed phrase bounced off her ears thanks in part to shock but more so to the fact that the fate she'd been running from her whole life had just sunk its teeth into her like an angry dog.

A scandal. And she was caught in its jaws just like her parents.

TJ leaned forward and plucked the iPad out of Chuck's hands like a card from a deck. "For the viewers keeping score at home, a piece ran online this morning that shows some *pretty compromising* photos of Chuck on the set of *Safe Gamble* looking rather friendly with a production assistant. Chuck, what can you tell us about this? Who is Madison Bilton, and does she have anything to do with the reason you got fired?"

Chuck flinched and dropped any sense of cordiality. "What is this? What are you doing?"

"I'm simply wondering if there's more to the story here. Those photos suggest that there was something going on between you on set, and—"

"There was nothing going on between us," he blurted, and turned to Olivia. "Liv, this is not what it looks like, I swear."

"Then what is it, Chuck?" TJ said. "You lied to your significant other about why you got fired, and now these photos show up."

"I didn't lie!" he cried. He reached for Olivia's hands resting in her lap, but she pulled them away. "Liv, please."

"If you didn't lie, then tell us the truth right now, Chuck," TJ taunted.

Chuck was all but panicking. He squeezed his hands with a pained grimace. "I can't—I literally can't! Liv, I swear, they are turning this into—"

"What's going on, Chuck?" Olivia asked, finally finding her voice but still reeling in shock.

He looked at her like he was being strangled. His brow knit; his lips twisted. Something sat on his tongue ready to explode, and keeping it in was nearly killing him.

"Looks like someone has been keeping secrets," TJ cut in.

"Stop!" Chuck said, and burst out of his chair. "You can't do this. Parker, this isn't—!"

Parker stepped in with a serious look on his face and holding up his hands like a referee. "TJ, this isn't the direction we agreed on."

"No, but it's an interesting one," TJ said with a mischievous sneer.

"Interesting or not, you know we can't go there," Parker said, his hands still raised.

Chuck was pacing and swearing, yanking his styled hair into a mess.

Olivia was completely numb and vibrating with fear at the same time.

Couldn't go where? Chuck literally *couldn't talk about it? Had Mansi been right that he'd been forced to keep quiet?* Most important, *who the hell was Madison Bilton?*

Her instinct to run, to protect herself from harm, kicked in hard. She popped out of her chair and dashed off toward the house.

"I think we're already there," TJ said with an ominous cackle.

"Liv, wait!" she heard Chuck call behind her. And then directed at TJ, "You asshole! Why are you doing this?"

She left it all behind and ran inside for the guest bathroom, remembering that Chuck had scoped it out for cameras. And at least this one had a door with a lock, unlike the other.

When she got there, she shut and locked the door behind her and found Chuck's stash of products lining the sink. A shower stall stood at one end on the other side of a toilet. Everything was shades of cream stone and green glass. She sat on the closed toilet to keep her legs from giving out and tried to take a deep breath.

Her hands shook as she pulled her phone from her pocket and dialed Mansi. She prayed she wasn't in the middle of a meeting.

"*There* you are!" Mansi greeted. "I've been trying to call you all morning. Liv, there's—"

"I've seen it," Olivia said, suddenly realizing why Mansi had been trying to reach her. It was to warn her. "They just showed me, on camera. I saw the whole thing. The photos, the article. Now I'm hiding in the bathroom and freaking the fuck out. Who is she, Mansi?" She heard the panic in her own voice.

Mansi didn't miss a beat, surely having already exhausted her resources digging up dirt on Madison Bilton. "She's an undergrad student at UCLA. Film major. She's listed as a production assistant on *Safe Gamble*, but it looks like she left the production at the same time Chuck did."

The earth fell out from beneath Olivia. As she tumbled, the rational part of her brain tried to tell her there was an explanation for everything, but the self-preserving part, the knee-jerking fight-or-flight part, told her to run from the ugly truth.

Her heart hammered in her chest right as someone knocked on the door.

"Liv? Are you in there?" Chuck called from the other side. He knocked and then tried the handle. "Olivia, please open the door."

"Are you okay?" Mansi asked.

"No," Olivia said on a shaky breath right as Chuck knocked on the door again.

"Liv, *please*. I need to talk to you."

Her breath grew shallower as the world narrowed to a hideous point. She didn't want to believe he would hurt her like this. Even more, she didn't want her pain splashed across the internet, and thanks to Chuck, both things were happening.

"I have to go," she told Mansi.

"Olivia!" Chuck called again, and pounded on the door.

"Liv, don't do anything you'll regret," Mansi said, clearly having heard him.

"Thanks, Manse," she said.

"Liv—!" Mansi tried, but she ended the call.

A familiar fire burned in her veins. One she knew talking to the man on the other side of the door would only fan into a full-fledged blaze, but she was going to do it anyway.

She wrenched open the door to find Chuck crowding the doorframe with the camera crew behind him.

"Liv—" he started to say, like he might have been about to step inside with her and lock the door, but she stood her ground.

"Who is she?"

He blinked at her sudden, furious appearance. "She's . . . no one."

She could feel her blood instantly start to boil. "Please don't insult either of us right now. She is not *no one*, Chuck."

He stared at her looking like he would have given up his million dollars if it meant he could not have this conversation with her. "Olivia, please. Just slow down here. They are manipulating us again by bringing this up. They want us to fight."

"Oh, *they're* manipulating us, Chuck?" She shoved her way around him into the hall, suddenly feeling suffocated in the narrow bathroom. The cameras followed on her heels. "You've been lying to me for weeks."

He followed, arguing back, as if it were a choreographed dance. "Olivia, I never lied to you."

They made their way back to the kitchen, her heels clicking angrily, where she whirled on him and clenched her fists at her sides. "Then you didn't tell me the whole truth!"

"I *couldn't*," he said, and flexed his arms and hands like he wanted to pick something up and snap it in half.

"What does that even mean?"

"It means—" He cut himself off with a tortured groan and clenched his jaw.

"Did you sleep with her?" she asked, seeking a truth she didn't truly want.

"Jesus Christ, Olivia. *No!*" he said, and flung out his arms.

The scene fit like an old glove, her glaring up at him and him glaring down while they were at each other's throats. She could see the vein in his forehead that ticked like a time bomb when they fought. She felt its mirror in the side of her neck.

"Olivia, please see this for what it is," he came back, trying to sound calmer. "They are preying on our problems by putting us in a position where I can't tell you the truth about something, which is only making you think it's way worse than it is. They sprang this on us on purpose. You have to trust me."

"Trust you? *Trust you.* After you've spent the past week in here making me fall for you all over again only to find out you've been *lying* to me? What's more, now it's *in the news* for everyone to see!" A tearful crack splintered her voice.

Chuck flinched at the sound, knowing how tender that particular wound was given her family's history. "Olivia, I'm so sorry about that. I will fix it, but you have to listen to me—"

"You can't fix this, Chuck!"

He reached for her when she turned again. They'd made it to the entryway now. "No, Liv. Don't run! *Don't run.* We can't let them win."

But it was too late. The urge to flee was too strong. She slipped out of his grip, tears blurring her eyes and heart hammering. She had to get away. Away from the lies. From the truth. From the same fate that had ruined her parents.

The front door was wide open, left that way by the production crew, and before she knew it, she'd passed through it to the other side. It wasn't until she heard Chuck shouting behind her that she realized what she'd done.

"Olivia, *no!*"

She turned and saw him on his knees inside the front door. Pure anguish mottled his face red. He squeezed his eyes shut and held both fists to his forehead like he might tear himself in half.

The production crew crowded the entryway behind him, catching the whole thing on camera. Tyler blinked in shock, Parker looked conflicted, and TJ full-on smiled.

It was the sight of the latter that made her fully realize what had just happened. What she'd done.

The wave that would drown her for the rest of time had only begun to swell when she too fell to her knees, breathless with regret.

Two days later, Olivia lay facedown on her couch while her grandmother sipped tea from her armchair and her best friend dripped nips of whiskey into everyone's mugs. When she'd finally changed out of the yellow jumpsuit that she'd fled the house wearing, she'd turned to a pair of sweats and a hoodie she'd called home for almost forty-eight straight hours. She'd refused to see anyone or take any calls until Mansi had shown up with Grandma Ruby and bags of Mexican food that evening and threatened to break down the door if she didn't let them in.

Now the three of them sat in her stuffy living room surrounded by half-eaten takeout containers and watched at least the fiftieth episode of *Friends* Olivia had left playing scroll by on her TV screen.

Grandma Ruby sat close enough to pet Olivia's hair, which was in dire need of a wash. "My sweet girl, you mustn't be so hard on yourself."

"Grandma," Olivia said into the throw pillow she'd reacquainted herself with after half a burrito, "*I gave up a million dollars.* Well, nine hundred thousand something and change after all the rules we broke."

She'd come clean about the premise of the show and her financial situation. She'd had to after everything, especially now that her grandmother's living situation was hanging in the balance again. She'd also told her the truth about what had sent her running from the house.

"Well, yes. That is true," Ruby said, and sipped her tea. "But it was just a game."

"If that were the case, it wouldn't be such a big deal that I lost it for us." She smashed her face back into the pillow.

"Look on the bright side, Liv," Mansi said.

Olivia lifted her head to see her sitting at her dining table still dressed in a slick skirt suit from work. At least she'd kicked off her red-bottomed heels. "You're not locked in that house anymore," Mansi said with a shrug before she blew on her tea and sipped it.

Olivia groaned and face-planted into the pillow again.

"Have you talked to Chuck yet, my dear?" Ruby said.

"No," Olivia said to the pillow.

Surprisingly, *he'd* called and texted. It was their modus operandi: she ran, he came to find her, but in this case, Olivia thought he'd never want to speak to her again. He'd even tried to get to her through his sister; she'd gotten an R U Ok? text from Chelsea begging for a response. Yesterday, Chuck had gone as far as coming by her apartment and knocking until a neighbor came out and told him Olivia obviously didn't want to talk to him. She'd huddled on the couch through the whole thing, hugging a pillow and crying over wanting to open the door and being too ashamed to face him.

"Well, then, how do you expect anything to get better?" Ruby said.

Olivia sat up and frowned at her grandmother. "There's nothing to get better, Grandma. I lost him a million dollars. Not to mention, he cheated on me."

"I don't believe that for a second," Ruby said with a cluck of her tongue. "You of all people should know how a tabloid photo can be manipulated, Olivia."

The conviction in her grandmother's words caught Olivia off guard, as did the reference to their family history. Through the potent fear of succumbing to her parents' fate, she'd only drawn parallels to the pain of being gossiped about in the press. Until this moment, she had not seen the similarity her grandmother had pointed out. That the infamous photo of her and her parents that initiated the scandal had been packaged in lies to fit the narrative. The truth behind it, she now knew, was something else entirely. The same could have been true about the photos of Chuck.

She didn't know what to say, so instead, she sat there with a complicated well of remorse roiling inside her.

Ruby reached for her hand and squeezed it. "Olivia, I don't mean to discount your feelings; the situation is upsetting for many reasons. But is it possible you are interpreting it as something it's not because it will build another wall around your tender heart?"

Olivia blinked and suddenly felt naked. She glanced at Mansi, who gave her a knowing nod like she agreed with Ruby. "What?" she asked in surprise.

Ruby took a deep breath and came back in a gentle tone. "Olivia, I did my absolute best to raise you with all the love and care that you deserved, but I knew from the start that I would never replace your parents. You were going to have a hole in your heart no matter what. I wish I could have filled it for you—and I hoped from the time you were a little girl that you would someday find a way to fill it yourself. But as I watched you grow up, I saw you learn to protect it, to shield it instead of trying to fill it. And I can't blame you for that; no one can. When you live with pain, you do everything you can to protect yourself from more pain, even if you don't realize you're doing it." Her voice pinched up with tears, and Olivia felt her own throat constrict. "You've been protecting yourself with Chuck. Preventing yourself from *truly* allowing yourself to have feelings for him because you don't want to get hurt. I've been around long enough to know that what couples argue over is never really what they are fighting about. Missing a dinner date? Not doing the dishes? Drinking the last of the coffee? Those are scabs to pick at because they are convenient and easy. You and Chuck use them as an excuse to keep your distance. With the way that boy looks at you, and the way you look at him—don't think I don't notice—I can guarantee you'll like what you find when you let each other all the way in."

Olivia was too stunned to respond. It was perhaps the most personal conversation she'd ever had with her grandmother, and Ruby was pulling no punches.

"These photos are another opportunity to push him away," Ruby said. "I struggle to believe he would ever betray you like this. There *must* be an explanation, and I think you owe it to him, and yourself, to hear it."

That reality weighed heavily. If there truly was more to the story, there was only one way to find out. She thought back to the desperate plea on Chuck's face the last time she'd seen him. In that anguished moment before she'd ruined everything when he'd given her a look pained in more ways than one. She knew him well enough to trust there was something beyond the situation's surface.

"I agree," Mansi said astutely. "I think you should hear him out. There are obviously things he hasn't told you, and Ruby's right that you have to actually talk to him to find out what they are." Mansi was never one to let emotion run over logic, so Olivia trusted her judgment that there was more worth considering. "Also," Mansi added, "I hate to tell you, but she's right on the other front too. Your track record with Chuck suggests that you want to fight *for* him more than with him."

"Of course she does," Ruby said. "Love is always worth fighting for."

Love. The word sent tingles prickling Olivia's skin and hollowed out her belly only to fill it with a floating feeling. It was something she and Chuck had never said to each other. In all their months of dating—all the lust, the passion, the fighting, the making up—the feeling that neither of them would name hummed at a frequency they chose not to hear. They'd come close but labeling it would have cracked open the superficial shell that allowed them to keep ignoring their problems and live from one tryst to the next. All along, they'd shielded themselves from the vulnerable pulse at the heart of their connection.

On some subconscious level, or perhaps a selectively ignorant one, Olivia had known it was there. And now she couldn't deny it given just how exquisitely her heart hurt at the thought that things might be irreparable between them.

She loved Chuck Walsh. Horribly. For better or worse.

"This is all my fault," she said, and buried her face in her hands. "I messed up so badly. I just . . . got scared. I don't want to end up like my parents with my life picked apart in the media. I panicked, so I ran." She looked up and took a shuddering breath. "You're right, Grandma. I do protect my heart. To my own detriment sometimes. And now I've ruined everything."

Ruby leaned forward to squeeze her hand. "You haven't ruined anything, sweetheart. There's still a chance to set things right."

"Speaking of setting things right, and while we're on the topic of tabloid photos," Mansi said. "Liv, I got that contact you asked for." She eyed Ruby and sipped her tea. "The, um, old movie star?"

It took a moment for Olivia to catch up. "Wait, Astrid Larsson? She's willing to talk to me?"

She heard her grandmother suck in a sharp breath.

"No, Grandma, don't worry. I only wanted to know if she'd be willing. I'm not going to—"

"She is willing," Mansi said. "Eager, actually. Well, that's what my guy who knows a guy who knows a guy said."

"Oh my god," Olivia blurted right as someone knocked on her door. She popped wide eyes at Mansi. "You didn't invite her over, did you?"

"No!" Mansi said with a laugh. "Are you kidding? I'm sure that woman has strict requirements for any face-to-faces. You'll probably have to get on a waiting list and pass a background check. I have no idea who is knocking at your door, but I hope it is a certain B-lister coming to win you back." She winked, and Olivia frowned as she climbed from under her pile of blankets. Her body had grown stiff from two days on the couch. Her joints popped in protest.

"*I* lost, remember? In multiple ways . . ." she muttered as she made her way to the door. For a fleeting second, she truly hoped it was Chuck. Rather than looking out the peephole to confirm and give herself an opportunity to hesitate, she threw the lock and swung open the door.

It was not Chuck, but rather, his sister. And a familiar-looking blond girl in jeans and a tee shirt standing behind her.

"Chelsea?" Olivia said, blinking in surprise. "What on earth are you doing here?"

"Hi, Olivia. We need to talk to you. Can we come in?" Chelsea stood shorter than her brother but was still lanky and fair. Her pale hair hung over her shoulder in a thick braid dyed pink at the bottom. She wore sage green overalls and combat boots and had gained a new nose piercing since the last time Olivia saw her. She stepped inside before Olivia answered her question and left the other girl awkwardly hesitating in the hall.

Although all the pieces were staring her in the face, Olivia could not connect why Chuck's younger sister had shown up on her doorstep and why Madison Bilton was standing in her hallway blinking at her like a terrified animal.

"This is Maddy," Chelsea said, and waved her in.

When Madison didn't move, Chelsea clucked her tongue and clomped back over to grab her and pull her inside. "Maddy, chill. She's not mad at you. Well, she won't be in a minute."

Madison still looked unsure as Chelsea hauled her over the threshold.

Olivia shut her front door and turned in a slow daze, still trying to make sense of things. "Chelsea, aren't you supposed to be at art camp?"

"Yes, but Chuck told me what happened at the house, and

you're not answering any of our texts, so I figured a face-to-face conversation was the best move here. Hello," she said, and awkwardly waved at Mansi and Grandma Ruby.

"Oh, um, this is my grandma Ruby and my best friend Mansi," Olivia said. "This is Chuck's sister, and um . . . Sorry, why are you here?"

"Nice to meet you both," Chelsea said, not deterred in the least and still in command. "Olivia, we should sit down." She directed Olivia to her own couch and pushed her down. She and Madison then stood in front of her on the other side of her coffee table like they were going to stage a living room skit.

"Chels, what's going on?" Olivia asked.

She wrung her hands and shot Maddy a look. Maddy looked back, biting her bottom lip, and nodded in some kind of final consent. "Okay, so, bit of a story, but here goes—and I have to be the one to tell you because Maddy and my brother had to sign NDAs. Fortunately, Maddy told me the whole story as it was happening and before there was any paperwork in place, so I don't think we're breaking any rules, but don't quote me on that."

Olivia flinched in surprise, shocked to learn there truly was a legal barrier withholding the truth. She glanced at Mansi, who shrugged with wide eyes. Olivia took it as permission to allow Chelsea to continue.

"Okay," Olivia said.

Chelsea took a big breath and dove in. "Maddy and I are roommates at school. She's my best friend. I'm an art major, she's a film major; we are kind of peanut butter and jelly. Anyway, she wanted experience in the film industry, and I was like, 'Hey, my brother is an actor. Let me help you out.' So I asked Chuck for a favor. He was working on *Safe Gamble* and was willing to lend a hand because he's awesome like that. So, he hooks her up with a PA job on set, and it was great, right, Maddy?"

Now that Olivia could see Madison in person and not a grainy tabloid photo, she could see how young she was. Both of them were. Mere girls living in a world that wanted them to be women. Maddy swallowed hard and looked like it took great strength to speak. "Yeah, it was great," she said, and tucked a strand of her silky mermaid hair behind her ear. Something brittle and fragile hovered over her surface. Cracks that exposed a faded light glowing underneath.

Chelsea nodded and reached out for her hand as if to infuse her with more strength. The power of their friendship was on full, shimmering display. Olivia could feel it in her bones. "It was great until it wasn't. Turns out Richard Sykes is an assface and started hitting on Maddy during the first week."

Maddy's face hardened, and Olivia felt her heart drop.

"Chuck became like a big brother to me," Maddy said quietly. "I don't have any siblings, and I've never really had anyone to . . ." Her voice trailed off in a pained pinch that Olivia knew well. She was almost certain her sentence ended with *look out for me*. Maddy sniffed.

Chelsea continued. "He noticed she was struggling on set. She was spending so much time avoiding Richard that she kept messing up. Forgetting things, missing meetings, making mistakes. She accidentally brought Duncan Miles a regular latte instead of a soy latte one day, and he almost had a stroke."

Olivia had heard rumors that Duncan Miles, Sexiest Man Alive three times over and costar of *Safe Gamble*, was a bit of a diva, so she could believe it.

"Chuck asked her what was wrong one day, and the truth

came spilling out," Chelsea went on. "She told him every-thing." She gave Maddy's hand another squeeze. "Things had escalated with Richard by then. He wasn't just hitting on her. He was following her, touching her, finding ways to be alone with her." Her voice took on a protective anger that pierced Olivia right in the heart. "She didn't know what to do—she didn't want to lose the job. It was the first opportunity she'd ever had in the industry, and, I mean, he was *Richard Sykes*. She couldn't be the girl who blew the whistle on him, not that any-one would have believed her anyway . . ." She bitterly trailed off, and Olivia could see where this story was going.

"You told Chuck all that?" She directed her question at Maddy.

Maddy nodded and gave her a knowing if not slightly guilty look.

"Yes, she did," Chelsea confirmed.

The pieces sliding into place made Olivia feel foolish for her previous thoughts: her suspicions that Chuck had ever been anything but unflinchingly faithful—to her and to everyone he cared about. She cleared her throat and realized the young woman in front of her had been through hell and didn't de-serve even an ounce of her anger.

"And I assume Chuck confronted Richard?" Olivia asked with a grimace.

Maddy pursed her lips and nodded again.

Chelsea let go of her grip and gestured with her hands out. "But not like what you think, Liv. I mean, that jerk totally de-serves to be punched in the face, let's be honest, but Chuck just tried to talk to him. He was only standing up for Maddy, and Richard went on a power trip and told him he couldn't work with someone trying to undermine him, and he fired him.

Chuck tried to say he'd go to the press, but Richard told him if he did that, he'd tell everyone Maddy had come on to him." She glanced over at her friend, who was tangling her fingers in knots.

Olivia's heart was in a knot.

Chelsea rounded the coffee table to sit on the couch beside her. "Liv, *that's* why Chuck got fired. He stood up for Maddy when it mattered, and Richard used his sway to cover it all up and make Chuck look like the bad guy. On top of that, he already felt awful for getting Maddy the job and exposing her to harassment—even though he had no idea it was going to happen—and he didn't want to make things worse. So he just rolled over and took it. Richard paid them both not to say anything and made them sign NDAs as part of it. That's why Chuck literally couldn't tell you, and of course he wasn't going to say it on camera at the house. Those asshole producers knew exactly what they were doing by showing you the photos and trying to make him talk about it, even if they didn't know the truth either."

Olivia gaped in shock, trying to wrap her mind around the key pieces. One piece jumped out at her. "Wait, Chuck was paid off? Then where's the money?"

Chelsea and Maddy swapped a loaded look. "My college tuition," Chelsea said.

Olivia reeled in awe of this man's selflessness. He'd given up a career-defining movie for Maddy by trying to do the right thing, and he'd used the hush money he'd been forced to take to pay for his sister's school when he himself was otherwise broke. How fortunate they all were to be in the small pocket of people he cared about.

Maddy came to sit on her other side. "I'm sorry it came out

the way it did. You must have thought the worst. Those photos *were* from the set, but he was just comforting me. It was the day I told him about Richard. I don't even know who took them, but they obviously sold them to start rumors."

Olivia was ashamed to admit that she had thought the worst—and that she'd fallen victim to the folly of believing what she saw in the tabloids. Images of the photos had been burned in her mind, and she suddenly saw them in a new light. *Of course* Chuck had been comforting Maddy. He was giving her a hug and trying to cheer her up like any loving big brother would. "I wish he would have told me the truth from the start," she said.

"He couldn't," Chelsea said. "He had to leave it at *artistic differences*, which is a load of crap. And Richard took advantage to ruin his reputation. But here's the thing, Liv. He's so in love with you. Like *embarrassingly* in love with you. That's the whole reason he went on that ridiculous show: he wanted a chance to get you back. To prove to you that he could do better. He doesn't care about the money. He did it for *you*. Everything is for you."

Olivia's breath was suddenly hard to catch. She was winded sitting down and felt like she'd been punched in the stomach at the same time her heart had lifted off to the heavens.

She knew Chuck loved her. She'd always known. But hearing Chelsea say it in such certain terms had her spinning.

She felt everyone in the room softly smiling at her.

"We have to go, but you should answer his calls, Liv." Chelsea squeezed her hand and stood up from the couch. "It was nice to meet you both." She waved at Mansi and Grandma Ruby.

Olivia stood up from the couch. She wasn't exactly sure yet

if she was ready to talk to Chuck or what she might say to him, but his sister's visit had changed everything. "Thanks for coming over, Chelsea." She turned to Maddy. "And I'm sorry for what happened to you. I hope that experience doesn't deter you from working in the industry if it's what you really want."

Maddy gave her a soft smile. "Thanks. I don't think it will. And I'm glad to know there are guys like Chuck around to make a difference. I just wish we could help him out somehow." As Maddy stood to leave with Chelsea, her words landed on Olivia with a stirring sense of urgency.

Chuck *had* made a difference for Maddy personally, but the truth had remained private. No one knew the real reason why he had been fired. The ripples of his actions would stay limited to the small pond of her life.

Unless Olivia did something about it.

A plan unfolded in her mind, and she quickly stood to catch the girls before they left. "Actually, Maddy, I think there might be something we can do to help Chuck."

Maddy turned back to her with a hopeful look in her eye, and she knew she could easily get her on board.

O N SUNDAY MORNING, OLIVIA found herself riding the elevator up to Chuck's apartment. It was the first time she'd returned to the scene of their breakup since it happened. This time, she wasn't coming over to give him a piece of her mind. More like a piece of her heart. And three thousand of the best, most terrifying words she'd ever written.

When she'd pitched her idea to her boss Stephanie, she'd gotten near immediate and emphatic approval. She'd memorized Stephanie's email and let the words bounce around her mind like a sugary little treat when she needed a boost of courage to remind herself that what she was doing was the right thing.

Yes. This *is the hard-hitting piece I've been waiting for. I knew you had it in you, Olivia.*

She ran the words through her mind once more as the elevator dinged and emptied her out into Chuck's hallway. She hadn't given him a heads-up that she was coming, but she knew he was home. Chelsea was still in town and had told her where to find him.

Olivia had worn a sundress and sandals and pulled her hair half back to contend with the warm day. She'd spritzed herself with perfume and painted her lips pink. Her heart nervously trilled as she stood at his door with her purse over her shoulder and an envelope in her hands. She knocked and held her breath.

A calm quiet hummed through the building. On a sunny weekend day, most residents were out at a farmer's market or hiking or dining al fresco. According to Chelsea, Chuck was at home in his pajamas bingeing strawberry Pop-Tarts and Netflix.

When he eventually opened his front door, Olivia found him looking freshly showered and startled. His hair was damp and mashed and a few water droplets dotted his collarbone above his tee shirt's neckline because he'd missed with the towel like he always did. Her knees wobbled and her heart walloped her ribs as if she needed a reminder how reflexive her desire for him was.

"Olivia. What are you doing here?"

"Hi. Can I come in?"

"Of course." He didn't hesitate for even one second.

She crossed into his living room and saw evidence of his despair. A small pile of dishes on the coffee table; empty bottles; a Pop-Tart box on its side, crumbs and wrappers leaking out; hoodies slung over the back of the couch. The tall windows on the opposite side of the room that normally let in a dazzling view of West Hollywood were at half-mast with their blinds pulled.

"Sorry," Chuck said, and hurried to clean up. "I didn't expect anyone to stop by." He scooped up the dishes and bottles and wedged the Pop-Tart box under his elbow and hauled it all to the kitchen. He gathered up the hoodies and threw them down the hall toward his bedroom. "What's up?" His embarrassment bled through his attempt to sound casual. He put his hands on his hips and gave her a cautious smile.

Olivia squeezed the flat envelope to her chest one last time, holding it close, before she extended it to him. "I have something for you—it's not a *challenge*, don't worry." She gently smiled.

He took it with a curious tilt of his head. "What is it?" He undid the tab at the top and slid out the small stack of pages.

"It's a profile on you. I finally wrote it." She watched his eyes scan over the title and first few lines. Her heart quickened as his face flushed. He looked truly shocked.

"How did you . . . ?" He sank down onto the couch like his legs might have been about to give out. He flipped the first page over.

"Your sister came to visit me," Olivia said. "With Maddy."

He sharply turned his head to look up at her. Worry bloomed over his face at the same time he went rigid with guilt.

"It's okay, Chuck. I know the tabloid photos were not what they looked like. They told me everything about what happened—without violating the NDA, don't worry. Mansi happened to be there for the whole thing, coincidentally. Turns out just because *you* can't talk about any of this doesn't mean that *I* can't. So that's what this is: the truth. Presented without any legal infractions."

His lips twitched at her word choice, and hope spread over his face.

"It wasn't fair to you, what Richard did. I got Maddy's consent to tell the story, of course, and the legal team at *Mix* is ready to talk with Richard Sykes's people about a statement, so all we really need is your buy-in." She bit her lip and looked at him with a mix of hope and nerves. "Everyone thinks it's a great piece, but I won't publish it if you say no. It's up to you."

He swallowed hard and gazed back down at the pages. "Liv . . ."

She saw him start reading again and stepped aside to give him space. She'd nearly memorized the words, she'd read it so many times. It had to be perfect. For him.

The Chuck Walsh You Don't Know

You probably know Chuck Walsh for the wrong reasons. The up-and-comer whose career derailed when he got fired midshoot from Richard Sykes's blockbuster Safe Gamble. *Or the guy from the viral breakup video seen arguing with his ex on the sidewalk who then ended up filming an episode of* Name Your Price. *What you don't know is the truth behind Chuck's reputation and the reasons why Hollywood wants to keep it that way . . .*

She wandered over to the windows and lifted the blinds to let in more light. The street moved with life ten stories below: pedestrians, cars, dogs on leashes. The sense of being removed from it all, high up on a cloud with only Chuck where no one could reach them, made her suddenly dizzy.

While he kept reading, she moved into his kitchen and set about cleaning it up. On any other day, the stack of dirty dishes would have made her scream, but she loaded them into the dishwasher and turned it on. And then she wiped down the counters and watered the succulent she'd bought at a farmer's market for him. The plump little spears stuck up from the green pot in a star shape. She was organizing a stack of mail on his granite island when she heard him clear his throat from behind her.

She turned with her heart stuttering, worried he might rip her piece in half and tell her to mind her own business, but she found him filling the kitchen doorway with the pages in one hand and a half smile on his face.

He bit his lip before he spoke. "Everyone is right: it's a great piece." His voice came out thick and gravelly. She noted a sheen to his eyes and felt something tight unfurl inside her chest.

"Yeah?" she asked, hopeful.

He joined her in the kitchen and set the pages on the island. Standing so close, she could smell his shampoo and the fresh, clean water still clinging to his skin like someone had bottled dewdrops on a spring day. He nodded. "Yeah. Thank you."

The warmth in her chest continued to unfurl. It shot out into her limbs and lifted her head into the clouds. She moved toward him, involuntarily, but her body around Chuck had a mind of its own. He was a magnet, and she couldn't resist.

He inched closer as well, and she felt the barriers they'd built between themselves tremble and threaten to fall. She felt his eyes outlining her lips as her pulse leapt in her neck, her wrists, between her legs. They had resisted for so long, and an uncertain future waited outside the door, but for now, they were together, just the two of them, above the clouds and existing in a moment that was, Olivia knew, inevitable.

"Chuck," she whispered on an exhale. It was a plea, a warning. An admission that she wanted him badly enough that the consequences didn't matter.

"Olivia," he said in the same breathy, desperate, aching tone, and that was all it took.

With a final step, the walls came tumbling down.

He reached out and gripped the nape of her neck and tangled his fingers in her hair. Their mouths were together in an instant. Olivia could already hardly breathe.

"I missed you so fucking much," he slurred against her lips as he swept his hands down to the backs of her thighs and scooped her off the floor.

"I missed you too." She threw her arms around his neck and linked her legs behind his back. He carried her—without looking because she refused to stop kissing him—to his bedroom. Her heart beat in a familiar rhythm, one that bruised her insides, and she gasped for air. She grabbed at him all over, taking handfuls of his back, his hair, his arms flexed and holding her greedy body against his. It was all so good, she equally wanted to speed to the end and make it last forever.

He stopped at the foot of his bed and pried his lips loose long enough to speak. "I still haven't been with anyone since you."

She smiled against his next kiss. "There will always only be you."

He dropped her onto the bed with a bounce and tore off his shirt. Finally, she could look *and* touch. With him no longer off-limits, she took advantage of smoothing her palms over the tight panel of his stomach. The hard muscles rippled under her hands, and touching them made them both suck in a sharp breath. Like she was painting a fantasy into real life, she traced her fingertips along the angled grooves pointing from his hip bones down into his jeans. Then she clawed at the button and yanked down the zipper. Because of the force with which she pulled down his pants, he nearly fell over on top of her.

"Someone's eager," he teased with a dark laugh, and caught himself as he kicked off his pants.

She softly bit the tanned swell of his shoulder when it landed in front of her face. The smell of his shower lingered on his skin in a fresh, breezy scent and drove her absolutely wild. She trailed kisses across his chest until she found the water droplets still clinging to his collarbone and licked them off. He shivered at the feel of her tongue in a way that made her tingle. When she slid her palm down his flat abdomen and slipped her hand into his underwear, he full-on shuddered.

"Yes, eagerness seems to be contagious," she purred, and wrapped her hand around the already hard length of him.

He swore under his breath and gripped the back of her neck to pull her into a hard kiss.

She continued to stroke him, feeling her low belly turn liquid hot at the soft moans escaping his throat while he consumed her mouth. He hadn't kissed her so deeply, so desperately, so absolutely, since before their breakup. The totality of it—his tongue sliding, lips sucking, thumbs stroking her jaw—narrowed the world to the points where they touched. And suddenly, a kiss was not enough. She ached for him in every cell of her body.

She broke loose with a gasp and pulled him closer with her hand still gripping the now *very* hard length of him. "If you're not inside me in the next ten seconds, I might die," she desperately panted.

The consumed lust on his flushed face parted ways for a wickedly pleased grin to curl his lips. "Now who's being dramatic?"

"I learned from the best."

He kneeled on the mattress between her legs and slid his hands up her thighs. He kept going, dragging his callused palms up over the swell of her hips and the indent of her waist, gathering her dress along the way until he peeled it over her head and tossed it aside. Then he stared at her with a heat in his eyes that turned her into liquid gold. He looked the way she had felt moments before when she'd been unable to tolerate not touching his bare skin, except that where she had thrown herself at him, he held back.

"You know you can touch me now," she said. "No more infractions."

One side of his mouth slightly curved up while the rest of his face stayed taut in focus like he was making a very difficult decision. "I know. I just can't decide where to start."

She nearly burst into flames. The thought that access to her body overwhelmed him left her feeling like a goddess again. She gave him a devilish grin and shoved her fingers into her bra cups to yank them down. "How about you start with your favorite part, then?"

His eyes grew wide at the sight of her breasts pushed up and together, her nipples hard peaks. He leaned forward like he was under a spell. "Every part of you is my favorite," he muttered into her neck before he kissed a trail to her chest. She arched into him with a gasp when he took one of her nipples into his mouth. Her hand fisted into his hair. His hands circled to her back to undo her bra's clasp, and when her chest tumbled free, he gently pushed her down onto her back.

He looked down at her sprawled on the bed, drinking her in. "You are . . ." he said in a reverent tone that made her feel radiant under his gaze. The way he left his thought unfinished said not that he didn't know the right word, but that there was no apt description.

"So are you," Olivia said, and sat up to reach for him.

He crawled over her, their lips locked again, as they moved up the bed and threw back the sheets. Olivia's head landed against the pillows, and he worked his mouth down her neck to her chest again. He buried his face between her breasts, kissing and sucking and moaning in appreciation.

Olivia quietly laughed and tangled her fingers in his hair. She tugged on it to pull his face up. "You sure they're not your favorite?"

He gave her a lopsided, drunk grin that was still white hot and completely disarming. Then he moved his lips to her belly and kissed his way down to her thighs. The soft scratch of his jaw sent her spiraling. It brought her back to the pantry, the last time she'd felt his mouth on her, when it hadn't lasted nearly long enough. Now the pressure between her legs, the ache, had her ready to burst.

"*Please*," she heard herself whimper.

Chuck paused what he was doing to look up at her with hooded eyes. "You make that word sound so goddamn hot," he said with a dark grin.

Olivia could barely stand the absence of his mouth, but the greedy spark in his eye had her begging for multiple reasons now. "*Please*," she breathed again, and watched his grin grow bigger. "*Please, please, please.*"

He obliged and slipped her underwear off. Then he spread her legs and pressed his lips to where her pulse furiously throbbed between her thighs. She gasped and fisted the sheets at her sides. Her hips canted into him, and she was gone. Lost to the haze of his skilled fingers circling and gliding, his tongue sinking in and stroking. It was perfect and relentless and made her feel like her body wasn't capable of absorbing anything more for a single second longer but then somehow kept going. She gasped out some unintelligible combination of his name and swear words over and over as she tugged at the sheets and his hair. In the seconds before she lost herself completely, she looked down and made eye contact with him, because she wanted him to know exactly what he was capable of. What he did to her. She saw a dark glint in his eye and a grin on his wet lips.

He knew, of course he did.

A hard cry ripped out of her mouth when she came. A pent-up need escaping in the hot rush of pounding waves. She exploded over and over, fizzling into oblivion all because of him.

She was a pile of bones afterward. Useless. And she knew just as well that it wasn't over. Not by a long shot. She could hardly open her eyes for all the dopamine flooding through her brain. She felt his weight shift and the warmth of his body move over her.

"I swear, the sounds you make could kill me," he whispered in her ear like he would enjoy the death.

A weak laugh burbled out of her mouth. She still hadn't opened her eyes.

"That one too," he purred, and she heard the smile in his voice.

He lay beside her and slowly smoothed his hand over all her curves, her peaks and valleys that had gone untouched by him for too long. She felt him hard and heavy pressing into her hip, but he knew the precise timing of every move. He knew how long to let her recover, to let her breathe, to let all the tight nerves in her body relax and prepare to swell up again and make the second act enjoyable for them both.

When she found the strength, she turned her head and softly smiled at him.

He smiled back, taking the cue. Then he rolled on top of her and sank his lips into her neck. He took her wrists and held her arms above her head as he tortured her with his mouth, kissing and nipping and grazing his teeth.

"You're so perfect, Olivia," he growled into her flushed skin. "Being in that house with you and unable to touch you was the worst kind of torture. I can't be near you if I can't touch you." He palmed one of her breasts and twirled his tongue around her nipple again. "Every part of you is so beautiful. So perfect."

Lost in his words, she found his hand in the pillows up above them and laced her fingers between his. Somehow that act felt more intimate than everywhere else they were touching. He moved his other hand between her legs and slipped a finger inside her. She sucked in a sharp breath and felt her body deliciously clench around him.

"Please," she breathed again.

"Please what?" he said, and pressed a hot kiss into the vein pulsing in her neck. He grazed his teeth over it and then traced it with his tongue.

"More," she said. It was the only word she could muster in the heady fog that had consumed her. The ledge she'd fallen over earlier was quickly reapproaching and preparing to pull her into the abyss again. She squeezed his hand that she held and felt his other hand still moving between her legs. His fingers dipped and glided; his thumb traced out delirious circles.

"More what?" he whispered, and bit her earlobe. Tingles

shot down her arm and turned the whole right side of her body to an icy fire.

"*Chuck!*" she whimpered, needy and fraught.

A soft chuckle puffed against her neck. He was getting off on teasing her, and if it weren't so fucking hot, she would have scolded him for it.

She used her free hand to grip his face and hold it in front of hers. "You know exactly what," she said sternly. "I'm going to die, remember?"

He looked down at her with a smug little grin. His pupils were blown out, his cheeks flushed, his hair a tumbling mess. *God.* He was the most beautiful thing she'd ever seen. She couldn't help smiling back at him despite the ferocious longing burning her alive. "Well, we wouldn't want that, would we," he said, and sat up to remove his underwear.

Olivia propped herself on her elbows to watch him fully undress. He was intentionally slow about it, knowing that her gaze was hungrily tracking his every move. How someone could make such a meal out of removing a single small piece of clothing was a true talent. Or perhaps she was simply starving for him. He hooked his thumbs into the elastic waistband of his boxer briefs and slid them down one painful centimeter at a time. The pronounced V of his lower abdomen slowly came into view like a rising sun, and when he fully exposed himself, Olivia reflexively wet her lips and had to make a conscious effort not to reach out and grab him.

"About time," she said with an arched brow once he pulled his underwear off his ankles and tossed them aside.

He moved back between her bent legs and placed his hands on her knees. "When did you get so impatient?" he said with a sly grin, and sat back on his heels.

She could hardly hear what he was saying. The need to feel him inside her was growing primal. Unable to stop herself, she reached out and took him in her hand again. "When someone locked me in a house with you and said I couldn't touch you. Please stop torturing me."

He fell forward onto one hand, his hips between her thighs, and stilled. He used his other hand to wrap hers and hold himself an unbearable inch from where her aching body eagerly waited for his. He grinned down at her. "I just wanted to hear you say it again."

She knew what he meant, and she knew that giving it to him would get her what she desperately needed. "Please," she said. "*Please, please, please.*"

He gave her the wicked version of his dimple-popping grin and rocked his hips forward. She let go of him and felt him sink in one thick, perfect inch. Her eyes fluttered closed, and her head tilted back. *Finally.* A guttural moan poured out of her as her body tightened around him. He sucked in a jagged breath and then pulled back out.

"No! *Please, please, please,*" she begged, and reached for him. The need was desperate. Frantic. Where she normally would have played along, savored his torturous game of slow, teasing inches, she couldn't take it after being forced to keep their hands off each other.

When he sank back in again, deeper this time, she took advantage. She swung her hands around to grip his ridiculously toned ass and shoved him all the way inside in one hot, firm stroke.

"*F-fuck,* Liv," he stuttered as he fell forward and caught himself on his forearms, sounding like he might have been about to come undone already. The smell of him, the heat and weight of his body fully on top of and inside hers, engulfed her in a swirl of perfection.

"Sorry, but we've been tortured enough. I need you now."

He looked down at her, messy hair tumbling forward and handsome face aglow, like he hadn't considered her point but agreed with it now. Whatever game he'd been planning to play dissolved, and he pushed his hips against hers, notching himself as deep as he could go and making her gasp. "You have me," he said with a soft bend of his lips.

It was the Olympics of makeup sex.

Chuck found angles Olivia didn't even know existed. They clawed at each other, caressed each other. Sped up and slowed down. Tangled all their limbs and slicked each other with sweat. Olivia couldn't get enough. It was equally new and exciting and like watching one of her favorite movies for the thousandth time. She responded to his every touch, rising and falling at his command, and he to hers. Their bodies belonged to each other. She was so consumed she couldn't tell where she ended and he began.

She eventually sensed him rapidly scaling toward a summit. She heard it in his hitched breath, felt it in the urgent speed of his strokes going deeper and deeper. All over again, she was climbing to the same peak. A burn had started in her toes and rose higher and higher until her thighs shook with want, with near painful need for relief.

When Chuck stilled against her with a hard shudder, groaning out an exquisite, jagged sound that made her heart swell, she tumbled over the edge with him as if he'd reached out to grab her as he fell. They crashed together, his arm hooked under her knee and his other wrapped underneath her, holding them chest-to-chest in an impossibly tight knot. They shattered to pieces because of and for each other, an infinite loop of giving and receiving that had her breathlessly gasping and him reciting a stuttered poem of her name and *perfect* and *so good* and *holy fuck* until they both collapsed in a blissed-out, exhausted heap.

● ● ● ● ●

THE USUAL COCKTAIL OF CONFUSION THAT SWIRLED THROUGH Olivia's blood after sleeping with Chuck was nowhere to be found as she lazed against his body. They were normally making up from a fight, their boiling blood temporarily setting a new course only to turn back to anger once they finished. But not this time. She felt nothing but peace. And it would have worried her if she'd allowed it to, given the uncertainty of their future. But she staved off thought of anything beyond the exact moment they were in. Only him; only her. His exhales becoming her inhales, the space between them nonexistent.

She lay halfway on top of him, facedown into the pillow with her head cradled between his shoulder and neck and his arm looped around her. The smell of him, the clean, heady scent of *him*, surrounded her: his pillowcase, his hair, his skin still damp from exertion pressed against her nose. She could feel his heart beating against hers where her chest pressed into his, a steady call-and-response as they drifted in a calm silence. Chuck used his thumbnail to trace a line up the back of her arm that broke her body out in tingling goose bumps. She shivered with a smile and snuggled herself closer to him.

Neither of them had spoken in ages, not wanting to burst the safe, perfect bubble. They'd taken to communicating by touch: her lips grazing his jaw, fingertips gliding over his chest;

his hand stroking her back and tangling in her tousled hair. Olivia could have existed in the moment forever.

"Liv," Chuck eventually said after what could have been the most perfect century of all time. His voice softly rumbled in his chest.

Olivia lifted her head to look at him and found a dreamy, warm haze in his eyes. His hair was a mess, his cheeks beautifully flushed. He looked plainly like a man possessed by feeling.

"Back in the house, when we were doing that interview about our first impressions of each other, you said you were intrigued by why I felt the need to hide my vulnerability in public." He paused, and she nodded, recalling the moment. "The truth is, I don't hide it. You just crack me open in a way that no one else can. In a way that honestly scares me, but I've known since the day we met that I wanted to be that open. With you. I love you."

All his guards were down, the walls utterly demolished. He was wide open and welcoming her in with no barriers. She remembered what he'd said that day, how he'd called her *The One* while he'd scribbled his number in her notebook. She saw on his face now that it hadn't been a cheeky joke, an attempt at ice-breaking, charming humor since they'd only just met. It had been the bone-deep certainty that would hold them together through all the ups and downs. Now he was finally giving voice to the steady current that had flowed beneath the surface of their relationship from the start. He'd leapt headfirst and was waiting for her to join him.

She scooted her body up along his and pressed her lips to his mouth for a slow, deep kiss. It burned all the way to her toes. Chuck let out a low, warm hum and rolled on his side to face her. She thought they were going to maybe go for a round two, but he pulled back and stroked her hair with a soft smile. His eyes melted into tender hazel pools and clearly said he was eagerly waiting for her to join him in the newly named territory.

But before she could join him, she had to say something else first.

"Chuck, I'm sorry about what happened at the house. Like *really* sorry."

He smoothed his thumb over her swollen lips while he shook his head. "Olivia, don't worry—"

"No, I need to say this." She pushed herself up against the pillows and pulled the sheet to her chest. She'd put almost as much work into figuring out what she was going to say to him as she had into writing her profile. She took a deep breath. "I . . . run. You're right. It took me running out on a million dollars to see how much of a problem it is—still very sorry, by the way. But I see it now. Not only do I run, but I also push you away. And it's because I'm scared. I'm scared of getting hurt, but most of all, I'm scared of ending up alone. Abandoned." Her voice hitched, and he reached out to tenderly stroke her cheek. "I probably need to spend a few years with a really good therapist to fully understand why, but I'm pretty sure it's because of my parents. I spent my whole life thinking they didn't care about me, that I was some unfortunate consequence of their affair and they'd rather have been out at parties than home with me—and I know that's not true now, but it left a mark. They *left* me. The people who were supposed to care for and protect me the most. They didn't do it on purpose, obviously, but it left this . . . *hole* in me, and a fear that it's going to happen again. That someone else who is supposed to care for and protect me is going to leave. That's why I run. Because if I leave first, no one can leave me." A tear pinched out her eye and rolled down her cheek. He swiped it with his thumb.

"But you—" Her voice cut off with a bumpy stutter. She dashed her eyes and wetly smiled. "Sorry. I'm not very good at this."

He sweetly smiled back and wiped her tears again. "You're doing great." His own voice was strained, thick with emotion.

"Thank you," she said with a sniffle. She took a steadying breath and felt her eyes grow wetter. "You make it all hurt less, Chuck. The truth is, I love you. Very much. So much that it scares me. Because I'm afraid—"

He scrambled to sit up when her words dissolved again. He held her face and kissed away her tears before he wrapped her in his arms. His heart thudded against her; his skin felt hot with emotion. When he pulled back to hold her face and look into her eyes, his swam with deep feeling. "I love you so much that it scares me too. Like *terrifies* me," he said. "Every time we fight, and you run, I'm afraid you're never going to come back, and I—"

"I don't want to run anymore," she said with a hard sob. "Not from you. Never from you."

He kissed her again and squeezed her whole body against his. She felt it in his touch: as much as she didn't want to run, he didn't want to ever let her go.

There was suddenly, resolutely, no more uncertainty about their future.

They pulled at each other, tugging their bodies as close as they could get. Inhaling the other like they needed it to survive. Their embrace slowly turned into something hungrier, more desperate. He pulled her over on top of him to straddle his lap, and she sank down onto him, taking every inch until they were fused together again. Soon she was gripping the headboard above him with both hands and trying not to black out as he squeezed her thighs and hit a spot inside her so intense that she could hardly breathe when she saw stars this time.

She collapsed on top of him afterward and nearly fell asleep to the feel of his fingertips lazily stroking her spine.

"So we're in love, but we're still broke," he said.

She chortled a laugh, still lifelessly draped over him like a jungle cat on a tree branch. "Yeah. That."

He inhaled a deep breath that inflated his chest and lifted her with it. When he let it out, she rolled off him but stayed cradled in the crook of his arm.

"I guess it's not too different than we were two weeks ago, we're just more aware now. You were right: being in that house was what we needed," she said with a lazy grin up at him.

He smoothed her wild hair and kissed her forehead. "Look at us. Growth."

She curled against his body and pressed a kiss into his chest. "And I'm glad we can touch each other now without losing any money or having to hide."

"Yes, definitely a perk of freedom," he growled, and pulled her back on top of him once more. He buried his lips in her neck, and she squealed with laughter as tingles shot down her arm.

When he let her go, she propped herself on her elbows and gazed down at him. His eyes were honey warm, his cheeks flushed. His lips beautifully swollen from kissing her. His hair, an even more hopeless nest. She pushed it back from his face and saw the tiny scar he had from falling off his bike as a kid. "Can I ask you something?"

"Anything."

She mulled her words, not wanting to burst the warm bubble they were floating inside. "When your sister told me about Maddy, she said it was fine because Maddy had told *her* the whole story while it was happening and before the NDA was in place. Why didn't you tell *me* at that same time while you were still able to?"

His glow dimmed a few notches. An invisible tension pulled his face taut. His brow knit. "Honestly, I was worried what you would think. I felt responsible for the whole thing. I mean, my kid sister's best friend, and I served her up on a platter to that jerk. And Maddy was so upset by it all—rightfully so. I didn't want to disappoint you. And then Richard paid me off, which made me feel like even more of a degenerate." He scrubbed his face with a hand. "And I'm so sorry about those photos. I don't know who took them, but I wouldn't be surprised if TJ himself got them to run the story so that they could spring it on us that morning with no warning. They knew I had an NDA and we'd agreed they wouldn't bring up my job. It was supposed to be off-limits, but TJ went rogue."

Olivia snorted. "Somehow not surprising."

"I know, but I still hate that it happened. Even if the photos aren't what they look like, I know that was a terrible situation for you given your history. But I couldn't tell you the truth, especially not on camera, because of the NDA. God, what a mess. Everything is my fault."

The remorse in his voice made Olivia's heart ache. She removed his hand that he'd placed back over his face and pressed her thumb to his brow to smooth out the deep crease. "Chuck, first of all, TJ is an asshole. And you weren't the one who ran out of the house. That was me, remember? And second, what happened with Maddy wasn't your fault. She is lucky you were there to intervene at all. You were put in a terrible position even though you tried to do the right thing—and you put that money to good use. Chelsea told me you're paying her tuition."

He flushed with a twist of his lips.

"Third, and most importantly," she went on, "I could never be disappointed in you. I think that's *your* toxic trait. I run, and you run around trying to keep everyone happy for fear you'll let them down."

He huffed a quiet laugh and turned his head away.

"No, I'm serious," she said, and hooked a finger under his chin to turn it back. "You lied to your parents because you didn't want to disappoint them. You lied to me for the same reason. You're always trying to fix everything. You hold yourself to this impossible standard like it's your job to keep everyone happy, and that's not fair."

A flush curled into his face. "I guess I just want to be . . . *good*."

"Chuck, you *are* good. You're an amazing son, an incredible big brother—to your sister *and* her friends. You're a talented actor, an inspiring coworker—do you want me to read the profile again? It's all in there . . ." She sat up as if she was looking for it.

He squeezed her ribs and tumbled over sideways with her. "All right. Point made."

"And, I might be biased, but you're a pretty decent boyfriend too."

"*Decent?* That's the best you could do?"

"Stellar? Stupendous? Worth a million dollars?" She jabbed him in the ribs, knowing he was teasing.

He flinched with a laugh. "*Oh*, too soon."

"Sorry. Bad joke. You're not going to hold that against me forever, are you?"

"What, that you lost me a million bucks? Nah. Why would

I care about that? I'm actually already over it," he said with a sarcastically casual eye roll and shrug.

She softly punched him in the ribs again. "Shut up."

He grinned a lopsided smile and then his face grew serious. "Speaking of the profile. That was very brave of you to write. That might be the nicest thing anyone's ever done for me."

"Does that mean you're okay with me publishing it?"

He stared up at the ceiling and took a long, slow breath. He exhaled it in a rush and turned to her with a light in his eyes. "I mean, might as well, right? I've already blown up the rest of my life. Seems only right to pull the pin in the last grenade."

She smiled at him, and he mussed her hair.

"And hey, it could end up working in my favor. A lot of people in this town hate Richard Sykes, including Isabel Ramírez, whose new movie I happen to have an audition for." He dropped the news casually, and Olivia's reaction was clearly what he'd been hoping for given the grin on his face.

She gasped a sincerely ecstatic sound. "*You have an audition with Izzy Ramírez?*" A glee as genuine as what she'd felt when he'd gotten the part for *Safe Gamble* filled her full enough to burst.

Izzy Ramírez was a current It director in Hollywood. An indie darling who'd broken out big last year with a dark comedy box office smash. Studios took interest and started hurling money at her. She had her pick of projects and teams to work with. Olivia knew all this because she'd stepped in to finish a *Mix* piece on it when her coworker went on maternity leave.

"Mm-hmm," Chuck confirmed with a proud hum. "Cameron set it up for me as soon as we got out of the house."

Olivia gasped again and excitedly punched him in the chest. "Chuck! This is amazing!"

"Ow!" he said with a laugh, and clutched her fist. "Don't get your hopes up. It's a long shot, but if that profile manages to come out at the right time, things might go my way and I could be starring in next summer's dark comedy hit."

"I will hit publish tomorrow if that's what you want," Olivia said with a thrilled grin.

Another chuckle bounced his chest. "You have my permission. But really, the part would be a huge payday. Like 'leave *Name Your Price* in the dust' payday."

Her jaw dropped and she genuinely could not stop smiling. "I am so happy for you. Seriously."

"Thank you. And I want to take a moment to say that I am sorry for all the times I got a little too obsessed with my career. I know I've made some insensitive decisions in the past, and I promise to be more aware of that going forward."

Olivia gave him an impressed nod. "Much appreciated."

He sighed a dreamy sound and stroked his fingers through her hair again. It sent her body tingling. "So, what have you been up to since you're no longer under twenty-four-hour surveillance? I mean, other than writing hit pieces on sleazy industry men."

It was her turn for the big disclosure. "Well. Believe it or not. I have a meeting." He looked at her with lifted brows when she paused. "With Astrid Larsson."

At this, he jerked to sit up. A dozen questions zipped across his face like he couldn't decide which to ask first. "How? Why? Where?"

"Because Mansi knows someone who knows someone who knows someone; because I want to talk to her; and at her house, which is obscenely intimidating, and I have no idea what to wear."

He blankly gaped at her, from shock at what she was saying or from shock that she was saying it at all, she couldn't tell. He rubbed his face with a hand. "Okay, I feel like I missed something here. You're willingly going to talk to Astrid Larsson, the woman who very famously was married to your dad when—?"

"I know who she is, Chuck," Olivia said with a soft smile. "And yes, you missed something. I didn't want to tell you on camera at the house because I'm not ready for anyone to know yet. That's why I had Mansi set it up. Discreetly. The truth is, that day your parents came over, I'd had a long conversation with my grandma, and she told me things I didn't know—that no one knows. Other than her, Astrid, my parents, and now me and Mansi."

His eyes had grown wide with expectant wonder. An eager but not intrusive hope that she was going to let him into the circle too.

She knew staring back at him that she could trust him not only with the truth, but also with her whole heart.

She told him everything.

Chuck's eyes had grown wider as he listened to her, taking in the shocking truth, until they were nearly filling his whole face. Then his brow suddenly bent into a jagged furrow, and he jumped out of the bed.

"*What?*" he shouted. His anger on her behalf ballooned into the room and made her tingle in a very specific and pleasant way. He began to pace at the bedside, swearing and fuming in indignation. His whole reaction was slightly undercut by the fact that he was naked. "Olivia, this is huge! *Astrid Larsson* has been lying for thirty years? I can't even—" He swiped his hair and huffed. "No. This is too much. You have to—" He couldn't seem to keep up with his own thoughts. "This is— *Wow*. For-get the profile on me. *This* is your bombshell!"

"What are you doing?" Olivia asked when he reached for his phone on the nightstand.

"Calling—I don't know. *Someone*. This is—! I can't—! I'm going to—!"

"Okay. *Easy*, cowboy," she said, and sat up to remove his phone from his grip. "I don't need you to run to my rescue on this."

He paused, chest heaving, and stared at her. "But, Olivia, this is . . . *wrong*." The word burst from his mouth like something he coughed up. A foul, bitter thing that he could not stand to have inside his body.

An endearing laugh warmly bubbled from Olivia's chest. "Chuck, while I appreciate your enthusiasm on my behalf, this kind of reaction is what got you fired from a movie, re-member?"

The realization visibly settled over him. The tension dissolved from his brow, and he blinked a few times. "You're right. Sorry."

"You don't have to apologize. It's honestly really hot that you care so much. But I don't want you to do anything to get yourself in trouble again. Come here." She waved him over and pulled back the sheets he'd thrown aside.

He gave her a sly grin and spoke in a low growl. "You think this is hot?"

"Yes. And it doesn't hurt that you're standing there naked. Now, get back over here before I totally lose my train of thought."

He climbed back in the bed and looped his arm around her looking all too pleased with himself.

"Don't look so smug. You can't even form a sentence when I wear leggings."

He grabbed her arm and pressed a trail of kisses up the inside of her wrist. "I would have killed a man to see your ankles in the Victorian era."

"Good thing it's not the nineteenth century."

"Indeed." He continued his kiss trail up her shoulder and to her neck, where he sank his lips into the crook below her jaw that positively melted her.

"Are we going to continue this conversation?"

"What conversation?"

"Chuck."

"No, I've seriously forgotten. What were we talking about?" He unsuctioned his face from her neck and looked at her with a drunken grin.

"Your lack of self-control."

He kissed her lips. "Sorry. Making up for lost time."

"I have no intention of leaving this bed for the rest of the day, so we have plenty of time."

His drunken grin returned, and he leaned in. She stopped him with a raised finger against his already puckered lips. "But we were talking about my meeting with Astrid Larsson."

He suddenly sobered and sat back against the pillows. "Right. Sorry." He let out a big breath. "What do you hope to get from her?"

Olivia matched his sigh. "I don't really know. Confirmation of the truth. An apology, maybe."

He gently ran his fingers against the crown of her shoulder, making her tingle again. "Well, you deserve all of that, but remember she's basically been committing slander by omission for thirty years, so don't be surprised if it doesn't go how you hope. Do you want me to come?"

She'd honestly considered it. Maybe not inviting him specifically, because she hadn't been sure how this reunion was going to go, but she had thought of bringing someone for support. But the more she thought of it, the more she realized she needed to go alone. If she was going to set her parents' legacy right, she needed to do it herself, as their actual living legacy.

"No," she said. "But thank you for offering."

He took her hand and threaded his fingers between hers. "I'm proud of you, Olivia. That's a really brave thing of you to do."

His faith infused her with warmth. She curled against his chest. "Thank you. I will let you burn me some banana pancakes after, though."

"*Excuse me*, my pancake skills have greatly improved."

"Yes, I guess we learned a few things in that house, didn't we."

Chuck paused and then cleared his throat. "Speaking of the house. Are you, um . . . okay? With money, I mean?"

Olivia groaned and burrowed deeper into his chest. "Please, can we talk about literally anything else."

He wrapped his other arm around her and kissed her head. "Yes, but I just want to make sure first."

She freed her head, sending her hair messily flying. "Why, it's not like you can do anything to help me out. You're broke too."

He gave her a knowing shrug of agreement.

They both sighed.

"At least I still have the advance from the show," she said. "That will cover Willow Grove while I figure out what to do."

He squeezed her. "At least I have you. Because that's all that really matters."

She looked up at him, and instead of saying how she wished that were true, she smiled. Because for right now, inside his warm bed up in the clouds, that was all that did matter. Only him; only her. And the fact that they'd found their way back to each other.

AFTER CALLING IN HELP from Mansi because she simply could not determine what was appropriate to wear for a midmorning Monday meeting with her late father's ex-wife, Olivia ended up in a classy dress and a pair of heeled sandals. *Power red*, Mansi had called it. Something modest and tasteful but also unmistakably present. Olivia nervously tugged at its sleeve after she reached out her car window to buzz at Astrid's front gate.

It had been two weeks since that fated day at the *Name Your Price* house, and Olivia now found herself back in Pacific Palisades. But unlike the house where she and Chuck had been imprisoned, Astrid's house did indeed have towering privacy hedges, and given its location, very likely an ocean view. When the gate swept open and she followed the rosebush-studded driveway to what was essentially a small parking lot with a fountain, she found that the house also had three stories, marble columns, and more sparkling glass windows than she could count. It screamed wealth but with the tasteful elegance of a soprano hitting the highest notes unreachable by most humans. Which, considering one of the most revered and accomplished actors in history lived inside it, felt fitting.

All that was to say, it was wildly intimidating.

Olivia took a very deep and nervous breath as she climbed out of Mansi's car. Not only did her friend dress her, but she also let her borrow her Mercedes so that she didn't have to pull up to a movie star's house in a car that was in desperate need of a tune-up and still mysteriously whistled like a tea kettle.

Feeling insignificant in many ways, she made her way to the front steps. The shallow stone scallops rippled out toward her like a wave that was at once welcoming and imposing. When she planted her foot on the first step, she felt like she might slip inside it and disappear. She also felt the urge to turn around and run and momentarily wished she'd taken Chuck up on his offer to come so that he could at least hold out his arm like a guardrail and prevent her from bailing at the last second, but he was busy dealing with the aftermath of the profile having been published that morning anyway.

Olivia had basically dropped a bomb and run away. The profile went live at nine a.m., and she silenced her notifications at 9:05 a.m. in order to prepare for her meeting with Astrid. The only people who could get through to her were Chuck, Mansi, and Willow Grove in case of emergency. And so far, silence on all those important fronts.

Given that she'd already buzzed at the gate and her presence was known, the front door swung open before she could ring the doorbell. One half of the towering gateway peeled back to view of an airy entryway and a smiling face. Not Astrid Larsson, but someone of similar Nordic heritage, surely.

"Good morning, Ms. Martin," the woman said with a

cheerful smile and Swedish accent. She wore her blond hair twisted into a braid and had sparkly blue eyes. Olivia guessed she was a housekeeper or caretaker of some sort, what with her plain and utilitarian outfit of blue blouse and black pants. She looked to be in her midforties. "I'm Hanna. Ms. Larsson welcomes you to her home. Please, come in."

As welcoming as the housekeeper was, Olivia found the two wagging hounds at her hips more inviting. Tall and lean with black coats and cream tips, they were either the world's worst guard dogs or simply friendly to strangers.

"Hi," Olivia said, and stuck out her hand to one of the dogs, who promptly licked it with a warm tongue.

"I do hope you like dogs. Ms. Larsson has many. This way, please," Hanna said, and waved her in.

Olivia followed her through a cavernous entryway with a chandelier the size of a Volkswagen Beetle and a split staircase curving each wall and joining at the top. The dogs excitedly sniffed her as she walked, poking their noses from her ankles to her hips.

"What are their names?" she asked.

Hanna glanced over her shoulder as if to check which dogs she was asking about. "This is Nico and Sebastian. Yes, like the crab."

Olivia grinned and scrubbed Sebastian's ears, finding it somehow endearing to know that Astrid Larsson had a dog named after a Disney character.

"Ms. Larsson is waiting for you on the patio. The morning is so nice, she thought outside would be a lovely place to meet," Hanna said as she led Olivia through a stately sitting room full of daylight thanks to the entire back wall being glass.

A sweeping view of the Pacific Ocean stole Olivia's breath

for a beat. She'd grown up next to it and seen it countless times, but seeing it from above, a sheet of blue silk stretching to the horizon, never failed to impress. Only so many people could afford to frame that view inside their home like their own personal painting, and that was part of the allure. Astrid Larsson's home displayed it like a crown jewel.

The rest of the room held large furniture pieces with long, clean lines that looked intentional to keep it from disappearing against the view's grand scale. A glint of gold caught Olivia's eye from the marble mantel, and she counted all three of Astrid's Oscars on display.

Her red dress suddenly felt like an embarrassingly inferior power move. Hanna had probably been instructed to walk Olivia through the room with the Oscars to remind her who exactly she was coming over to meet. The reminder served its purpose because Olivia felt foolish for thinking any good could come out of this conversation. Surely Astrid only planned to remind her of her status and shove her back out the door.

When Hanna led her through a pocket of the glass wall that had been slid open, Olivia entered a picturesque backyard that looked fit to be a diving platform into the ocean. Of course, a rocky hillside separated it and them, but the appearance of needing only a single step to slip into the sea left the house feeling like it was floating in the sky. A prim lawn and row of palms filled one side of the yard, and a crystalline blue swimming pool lined with lounge chairs and a covered bar filled the other. Between the pool and the house, and in the direction in which Hanna was leading her, sat a pergola climbing with morning glories and bougainvillea in shades of indigo and fuchsia almost too brilliant to look at. Beneath the volcano of color sat a scene equally stunning.

Astrid Larsson.

Olivia's heart stopped at the sight of her. A screen goddess come to life, but also a woman at home in her backyard. The clash of the untouchable ethereal beauty she'd seen from a distance her whole life and Astrid's Birkenstocks, linen pants, and simple blouse threw her for a loop.

She was stunning, and yet . . . normal.

She sat at a table spread with coffee, pastries, fresh fruit, and a glass jug of orange juice beside a bottle of champagne in a bucket. A fluffy white Samoyed sat next to her panting on the patio deck.

Olivia's first instinct was that she'd interrupted something, someone else's fancy brunch, because this couldn't *possibly* have been for her. But then Astrid popped out of her chair and removed the sunglasses she'd been wearing to gape at her. Her famous ice blue eyes pierced her like hooks.

"My god. You're the spitting image of your mother."

Hearing her voice in person was even more of a mind trip than seeing her. She stood tall and slender, still possessing the supermodel figure that had made her famous. Her grayed hair was pulled halfway back and otherwise tumbling over her shoulders. Her skin creamy pale with rosed cheeks. She was impeccably preserved for someone in her seventies. It took Olivia several seconds to register that Astrid Larsson, *the* Astrid Larsson, was speaking to her.

"Hello," she said nervously. Somewhere in the depths of her brain, she was trying to remember that she was supposed to feel anger toward this woman, but she should have known that feeling starstruck would snatch at least some of that away. "Um, thank you for meeting with me."

Astrid kept staring at her, looking almost as if she'd seen a ghost. She eventually cleared her throat and motioned for her to sit down. "Of course. Thank you for coming." On the way back into her own seat, she bumped her coffee mug and sent it sloshing. "Oh dear," she muttered, flustered, and looked for a napkin among the decadent spread.

Olivia realized then that she was just as nervous, if not more so. The fact that she could make Astrid Larsson nervous filled her with a surprised sense of powerful confidence.

"Here," Olivia said when she found a cloth napkin folded beside a strawberry tart. She extended it to Astrid, who took it with a surprised look.

"Thank you," she said, and dabbed up the spill.

The Samoyed stood to lick the dribbles on the concrete.

"What's that one's name?" Olivia asked, and pointed at the dog.

Astrid sat in her chair and buried her fingers in the dog's thick and shockingly white coat. He looked like a sterile cotton ball roaming the colorful backyard. "This is Jax," she said, and reached over to the chair beside her to lift a little stuffed sausage of a French bulldog that Olivia hadn't even known was sitting there. "And *this*," Astrid said like lifting her was no small feat, "is Minnie. Who you can see is in a delicate condition." Her voice squeaked as she cradled the dog like a baby and gently rubbed her rotund belly. Astrid looked up at Olivia with a smile. "Let me know if you're in the market for a puppy."

Olivia noted then that the pudgy dog wasn't simply pudgy, but pregnant. Astrid set her on the ground, where she waddled off to lie in the sun. At the sight of it—the cute dog, the breakfast spread, the stunning view—a befuddled laugh popped out of Olivia. The sound of it startled even her and made Astrid look over.

"Is something wrong?" she asked.

Olivia couldn't exactly put a finger on it. "I'm sorry. This is all just very strange. I didn't really know what to expect, but it certainly wasn't a champagne brunch and a puppy. Kind of feels like a trick." An embarrassed flush immediately curled into Olivia's face for insulting her host, but it was true. She felt like a kid being lured off the street.

Astrid kept quiet long enough to make Olivia look up. A small smile played at her mouth. "You sound just like your father."

Olivia reeled as if she'd reached out and slapped her. She had never, not once, been compared to her father. She didn't even know the first thing about him to know if they had anything in common.

Astrid softly, and sadly, smiled again. "I can tell that's surprising to you, but it's true. I was married to him for ten years, so I would know. You may look like your mother, but your mannerisms, the way you talk, your natural skepticism, that flush in your cheeks right now, that's all your father. It's so plain to see."

The revelation left Olivia breathless. It struck her that Astrid was likely the only person alive with any intimate knowledge of her father, and she'd just dipped a ladle into the well that she possessed. Both of these facts had Olivia wanting to swan-dive into that well and swim to the bottom to gather up everything she knew.

She found herself unable to speak.

"Look," Astrid said to fill the silence. She traced her manicured fingertip around her coffee mug's rim. "I know you must know the truth by now, otherwise you wouldn't be here, and I know you have no reason to trust me, but I hope that you will believe me when I say, I'm sorry."

The apology pierced through Olivia and did not feel the way she thought it would. Where she wanted to feel restored, vindicated, made whole again, the simple sorry felt cheap. Easy. Inadequate.

"For what?" she said coldly, unable to keep the edge out of her voice.

Astrid's eyes shot up to her. She was well versed in faking emotion—she'd literally won awards for it—but Olivia could not mistake the expression spreading under the mask she tried to hold.

Shame.

Olivia sat up straighter, empowered by the sight of the imposing woman wilting before her. She didn't care if this was difficult for Astrid. She wanted to hear her say it. "Sorry for the way they were treated? Sorry for how I grew up thinking my parents were terrible people? Sorry for the way *I* was treated? Sorry for staying silent for thirty years?" Her voice rose with each question, and Astrid further wilted. All her life, Olivia had never had anyone to direct her anger at, and now with the person she hadn't even known was the source of it sitting in front of her, a fire hose had been turned on.

"Do you know what it's like to only know your parents from tabloids? To see them called every terrible thing possible for something they didn't even do? And to find out *thirty years later* that the person who could have cleared their names kept quiet the whole time?"

"Olivia, I—"

"I thought they didn't want me," Olivia said. Tears had found their way into her voice, and she did not hold them back. She was not ashamed to cry in front of Astrid Larsson. She *wanted* to cry. She wanted her to see the damage her choices had inflicted. "I thought I was a mistake. An unwanted accident from a toxic affair that turned *you* into a victim and left *me* alone. You could have fixed all that, and you didn't. So don't tell me you're *sorry*, because it's not good enough." She used one of the heavy cloth napkins to wipe her eyes and didn't care that she was staining Astrid Larsson's linens with makeup.

A thick silence expanded between them. In it, the only sounds were birds chirping and Jax lapping at the pool water. Olivia's outburst had lifted a weight off her. One that she hadn't realized she'd been carrying until it was gone. Astrid, on the other hand, looked as if it had settled firmly on top of her and might have been limiting her ability to breathe. When she finally spoke, her voice came out soft and sounding nothing like the woman Olivia had seen command the screen for decades.

"No, I can't imagine what that was like at all. I admit, when your grandmother decided to keep you out of the spotlight, I felt like I dodged a bullet. And I'd be lying if I didn't say I've been holding my breath for thirty years, waiting for this to come, for you to show up wanting answers. I've thought of reaching out to you over the years. I thought that seeing Brad and Becky's daughter would be like seeing an old friend—two old friends. But then I'd remember how everything happened, the choices we made, and it was simply easier to let it all go. To keep it all quiet."

As Olivia digested her words, three of them rang like chimes she couldn't unhear: *Brad and Becky.* She'd never heard anyone refer to her parents like that. She didn't even know there was anyone who *would* refer to her parents like that. The casual nicknames implied a level of intimacy reserved for friendship.

Her own voice came out thick and strained with pain. "If

you considered them friends, why would you do this to them? Why wouldn't you tell the truth?"

Astrid sighed. "That is complex, and I don't think my answer will satisfy you."

"I think I deserve to hear it, regardless."

She gave her a stiff nod like she agreed but was still reluctant. "Your father and I married as a business arrangement. I was on the cusp of stardom, and being an American citizen would have helped my career in multiple ways. Your father was a businessman who knew what levers to pull to make things happen. Neither of us was interested in a family life. I wanted the biggest career I could have, and he wanted to get me there. It was settled with a trip to the courthouse and a few months of immigration paperwork. No one questioned that it wasn't sincere, and it worked for years. We lived together, married on paper but married to our careers in reality. It worked until he met your mother."

Where Olivia might have expected to hear bitterness, a sour resentment toward the woman who threw a wrench into her golden plan, she instead heard fondness. Perhaps even a hint of envy.

Astrid continued with a small smile on her lips. "You know those stories where someone is set in their ways until one person comes along and turns their world upside down? Well, that was your mother for your father. I'd never seen him like that before. He was like a teenager in love, and his whole worldview from before ceased to matter. When he told me he wanted a life with her, there was no way I could stand in their way. You see, Olivia, I was never *in* love with your father, but I loved him dearly as a friend. And I could not deny him the true love of his life when he found her." She let out another long breath and tapped her fingers on the table. "But we'd also been building my career for most of a decade and didn't want to undo all that work. So, we made an arrangement. Among the three of us."

She paused as if to remind Olivia that her parents had been complicit in the plan too.

"That also worked for a few years," she continued, sounding like she was fondly remembering again. "I was off traveling for films most of the time, either shooting them or promoting them, and Rebecca all but moved into our house. She was . . ." She paused again and looked down with a smile. "She was really lovely, your mother." Again, another skim of a deep well that Olivia wanted to dive into, but Astrid looked up with a grim expression. "When she got pregnant, we knew things were going to get difficult. And then after their accident . . . It was just easier not to correct the assumptions everyone made."

The faint joy that had been brimming Olivia's heart faded into an ache. She stared down at a lemon Danish pastry that had begun to melt and looked too fancy to eat anyway. "How could you do that to them?"

"Honestly, at the time, I wasn't thinking of them. Or you," Astrid said, and Olivia's eyes bounced up. "I was only thinking of myself. I was thinking of what *I* would lose if word got out that I'd knowingly let my husband have an affair for two years. That I'd let the other woman live in my house, and to top it all off, that it wasn't even truly an affair because my marriage wasn't real to begin with. Everything I'd worked for—that your father had worked for too—would have been lost. So I didn't say anything at all."

A new breed of anger burned inside Olivia. It wasn't the explosive kind she felt when she argued with Chuck. The kind that burst and then faded into an afterglow that eventually healed like a sunburn. This anger was core-deep and powerful. Dangerous.

"Was it worth it?" she said hardly above a whisper.

Astrid considered her with a steady gaze. "I don't think you want me to answer that question."

The answer was clear enough, what with their presence in the backyard of a fifty-million-dollar home with purebred dogs at their feet and champagne at their fingertips.

Olivia reached for the champagne and pulled out the cork without permission. She crudely poured a glassful and sipped it before the bubbles even stopped fizzing. "So I guess this is the part where you beg *me* not to say anything in order to preserve your legacy." She took another gulp.

"No."

Olivia paused with the glass halfway from her mouth and almost choked. "It's not?"

"No," Astrid said. She gazed out at her yard. "I've lived the life I wanted." She turned her piercing blue eyes back to Olivia. "You haven't had that chance, at least not to the extent that you deserve, because I took it from you. I owe it to your parents, my friends, to give it back."

Olivia blinked at her in confusion and wondered if the champagne had been spiked with a hallucinogen. "You're not like dying, are you?" she blurted, suddenly realizing there could be an alternate explanation for her strange response.

Astrid gently laughed. "No, dear. Not yet, at least." She sighed, sounding resigned and relieved at the same time. "What I'm saying is, I won't stop you if you want to share their story, because it's your story too, and you deserve to be able to tell the truth."

The anger Olivia had felt dialed back a few notches. The tension in her jaw dissolved. She couldn't fully believe what she'd heard.

"Really?"

"Yes. I don't deserve your forgiveness, so I won't ask for it, but instead, I'll give you the truth. It's yours to do with whatever you please."

As little as Olivia had expected to show up to brunch and be offered a puppy, she expected even less for Astrid to give her permission to talk. If anything, she'd expected to have her silence bought.

"Um, wow," she said, overwhelmed. "Thank you."

"You're welcome. I only ask that you please give me a heads-up before you share anything so that my team can prepare for the backlash." She folded her hands in her lap as if bracing herself for a battle.

Olivia had thought about it, honestly. She was in her right to slaughter Astrid Larsson in the press the same way her parents had been thirty years ago. But what would that achieve? An eye for an eye might feel good in the short term, but what about after the initial stab? When the dust settled, and millions of fans learned that their beloved favorite actress was a liar? What good would tarnishing Astrid's name do for anyone but Olivia? None. And hadn't she gotten into journalism to prevent the types of headlines that marred her childhood? Unlike her takedown of Richard Sykes, there was nuance to Astrid's story; it wasn't a black-and-white crime. Yes, she'd thrown her husband and friend under the bus for her own advancement, but it hadn't started as malicious intent. Staring at the elegant, elderly woman sitting across from her, Olivia decided that people deserved to hear her side of the story too.

"What if we tell it together?" she said.

Astrid perked up in surprise. "What do you mean?"

She took another sip of champagne for courage. "I mean that people have wanted to know what happened for thirty years—from *you*. Yes, I'm part of it too, but I don't remember any of it, not the way you can, at least. I don't think it has to be a one-sided takedown of anyone. It can simply be . . . the truth."

The look on Astrid's face turned to one of wonder. Her eyes glossed over, and she blinked a few times. Then she softly smiled. "That right there, that kindness, is your mother."

Olivia instantly choked up. She felt a tear pinch out of her eye. She dashed it away and tried to cover with another sip of champagne. "Sorry."

"Don't apologize, dear. But please, help me eat all this." She leaned forward and lifted a knife to cut into the strawberry tart. "And don't hog the champagne. I love a good mimosa in the morning."

Olivia snorted a laugh that sent bubbles tingling her nose. Never in a million years did she think she'd be sharing a champagne brunch with Astrid Larsson, and yet here she was.

Astrid slid a slice of tart onto a plate and handed it to her.

"Thank you. Did you make all this?"

"Of course not," Astrid said with a smile. "Hanna is an excellent chef."

The bite Olivia took was a perfect combination of flaky crust, custard, and berry. "Yes, she is."

Astrid gave her a knowing smile and settled into her own slice. The tension that had been present between them eased into something still there but softer. It had Olivia feeling brave. That might have also partly been due to the champagne.

"Astrid, will you tell me more about my parents?"

Astrid poured her own glass of bubbles and topped it with a splash of orange juice. "I'll tell you anything you want to know, dear."

●　●　●　●　●

OLIVIA SPENT THREE HOURS AT ASTRID'S. TWO OF THEM LISTEN-ing to stories about her mom and dad and one of them sobering up from the mimosas so that she could drive home. In that last hour, they'd also discussed what telling the story together might look like, and the prospect had Olivia positively buzzing with anxious excitement.

Before she left, she turned her phone notifications back on and was met with a crash of alerts. Texts, missed calls, dozens of emails. She didn't even dare open her social media accounts. The profile on Chuck was alive and well.

She smiled at an email from Stephanie that held the entire message in the subject line: AMAZING JOB.

She had two texts from Chuck: the kissy face emoji blowing a heart with **THANK YOU** that she took to mean he was pleased with the reception of the piece, and another that said **How'd it go?**

He'd told her that no one could have written the piece like her, and she had to agree. Because she knew him better than anyone, she'd thoughtfully cracked him open for the public in a way that only she could and finally exposed Chuck Walsh as he deserved to be seen. Based on the public response, the world had been waiting for a deep dive into his story, and now they would only want more.

She quickly texted him back. **It went well. Heading home.**

I can't wait to hear about it.

I love you.

She smiled that he'd responded so quickly given he too was surely drowning in messages and had sifted hers to the top.

I love you too, she wrote back, and climbed into her borrowed car.

Halfway back to her apartment, her phone rang. She didn't have it synced to Mansi's car, so she had to look down to see who was calling. **Parker Stone** flashed on the screen, and pure curiosity made her answer it and put him on speakerphone.

"Hello?"

"Olivia!" he sang. "Good to hear your voice. How are you doing?"

"You know, Parker, all things considered, I'm doing pretty well. Please don't ruin it with whatever reason you are calling."

He chortled a laugh. "You know me well. But that's not why I called."

"No?"

"No. I'm calling for two reasons. First, I wanted to apologize for how things ended in the house. TJ wasn't supposed to bring up Chuck's job like that. The photos, yes; his job, no. We'd discussed it beforehand, and given the legal situation, he knew it was off-limits."

Olivia's grip on her steering wheel tightened. She hadn't been expecting a sudden callback to one of her worst moments. She'd thought back to that whole scene a lot in the past weeks, and she agreed with Chuck that they'd been trying to manipulate them into fighting. And now Parker had confirmed their suspicion. The fact that it worked so easily left the memory even more shameful. Her voice came out thick. "Okay."

"Okay," Parker repeated. "And the second reason I'm calling is to thank you."

"Thank me?"

"Yes. See, because of what TJ did and with the way the show ended, we were in a bit of a bind over what we'd be able to air. We've been going back and forth with Legal over if we'd have to edit out anything related to Chuck's NDA, but thanks to your piece that dropped this morning—which is a great piece, by the way—the situation is public knowledge now, and we can air everything. You solved the problem for us!"

She did not exactly match his cheer that the whole messy ending of their time at the house would end up on TV—she'd honestly hoped the whole episode would get canned—but she did her best to sound positive.

"That's great, Parker."

"It is! And what's better is Chuck told me you two are back together now, which, honestly, that's all I was hoping for."

She flinched in surprise. "You were?"

"Well, that and the massive ratings this is going to haul in. But like I said, I'm a hopeless romantic." She could hear the smile in his voice. "Speaking of Chuck, how do you feel about a follow-up episode after this one airs? Kind of a *Where Are They Now* thing."

"Oh my god, Parker. *No.* I didn't want to be on TV in the first place. I'm certainly not signing up for it again."

"Come on, Olivia. People would *love* to see your happy ending!"

"No, they wouldn't. People want to see drama. And that's what we gave you: six days of drama."

"It wasn't *all* drama. There are some really tender moments in here too. I've watched all the footage."

"*Ugh.* Don't remind me."

Parker laughed. "But listen, if you ever change your mind, you know where to find me. Also, the offer still stands on doing an interview about your parents."

"Ever the opportunist," she said with a roll of her eyes, but she stopped halfway. Her heart suddenly trilled in her throat. Her hands grew tacky with nerves, but a thrilling anticipation thrummed through her like an electric current. "Actually, I might have an opportunity for *you*. Can I swing by the studio office?"

CHAPTER

17

TWO DAYS LATER, OLIVIA was returning home midday when she happened upon a scene that looked straight from a movie—partly because there was an actual camera there filming it.

Chuck stood on the sidewalk outside her apartment's living room window throwing pebbles at it two stories up and shouting her name.

"Olivia!" he called a second time.

The first time, she'd thought she was imagining things and her boyfriend couldn't possibly have been hurling pebbles at her window like a lovesick teenager in an eighties film while Benny the cameraman stood by and Tyler the PA kept the sidewalk clear. But alas, that was exactly what was happening.

"Liv! Open up! I have to tell you something!" Chuck shouted again as she climbed out of her rideshare and he threw another pebble. Where he was even getting the pebbles, she had no idea because the only bits of nature around her apartment were stray leaves and the occasional empty Starbucks cup that the wind nipped from a trash can.

"What are you doing?" she asked when she approached.

He stopped and turned to her in surprise. "Oh! Hey. No wonder you aren't answering." He gave her his dimple-popping grin and eyed her outfit. She wore a businessy skirt and blouse with heels that had him eyeing her legs and looking like it was difficult to speak. "Did you have a meeting this morning?"

"Yes. But again, what are you doing?" She nodded at the camera and up at her window, which thankfully wasn't chipped.

He eyed the camera and then pinched her elbow to lean in and mutter, "I'm *grand gesturing*. Parker thought it would play well for the end of the show."

She narrowed her eyes and gazed around for the EP in question, wondering if he'd somehow beat her home. "I just talked to Parker, and he didn't mention anything about filming a new ending."

"Yes, well, it's supposed to be a surprise. We've got Benny and Tyler here," he said with a smile.

"Yes, I see that. But again, why?"

He threw out his arms and half squatted in excitement. "Because I have something to tell you!"

"Then tell me."

"I will! But can you go upstairs and *pretend* you heard me down here calling you instead of finding me out here?" He looked at her like an eager puppy.

She arched a brow at him. "No."

"Liv, come on. Play along."

"I'd rather not."

"Do it for Tyler!"

"For Tyler?"

"Okay, do it for me, then."

She paused. "We've already done plenty for the cameras, Chuck."

"True, but this is one last hurrah." He made jazz hands and moved his hips side to side. That, along with his doughy little dimple still popped, *almost* got her, but not quite.

"You can hurrah me here in the street."

"*Ugh*. Fine! You have to act surprised, though."

"If it's surprising I will be surprised on my own."

"It is. *Trust* me."

"Oh god," she muttered in dread right as Chuck turned to Benny and twirled his finger in the air like Parker even though he was already filming. Olivia took it to signal *this is it*.

Chuck cleared his throat and turned back to her with a huge grin. "I got the part!" he shouted, and threw out his arms.

Sheer shock—and then joy—crashed into Olivia. Her mouth fell open. "Wait, seriously?"

"Seriously! I told you the timing of your profile could change everything, and it *did*. Izzy Ramírez gave me a callback and hired me on the spot."

Olivia happily punched him in the shoulder. "Chuck! This is incredible! I'm so happy for you!"

He scooped her up off the ground in a bear hug, and she wrapped her arms around him. "Thank you! It wouldn't have happened without you, and I mean that, so thank you for the profile, again."

She cupped his face in her hands and kissed his lips. "I'm so proud of you."

"And the best part is," he blurted like he'd never stopped

talking, "I can pay for everything now—my rent, *your* rent, unless you want to move in with me—also, please move in with me? *And* I can take care of Willow Grove too, so Grandma Ruby doesn't have to go anywhere. And I—"

"Wait, wait, wait. Slow down," she said, and loosened her grip so that she slid down his body back onto her feet.

He paused to catch his breath. "Sorry. I know that was a lot really fast. I just want to fix everything so that we can be together, and so you don't have to worry about anything, and—"

"I'm not worried," she said.

"And I— What? You're not?" He finally stopped talking enough to let her get a word in.

"No, I'm not," she said with a soft smile. "Not anymore."

He picked up on her smile and slyly smiled back. "Okay, what did I miss this time?"

She placed her hand over his heart, which she could feel thumping hard. "Well, while you were out landing your big part, I was out selling the rights to my parents' story."

This time his mouth fell open in shock. "Seriously?"

"Yes. Turns out, they're just as hot of a commodity as we always suspected. I got Astrid on board to tell the story with me, which obviously drove up the price substantially, and Parker wants to turn it into a documentary. *And* we already have four publishers interested in a book deal. That's where I was this morning. With Parker and Astrid."

Chuck's mouth continued to pop open and closed as if he couldn't figure out which words to form.

"You look like a really sexy fish right now," Olivia said, and squeezed his face.

"I'm a really *impressed* fish right now. Holy shit, Liv. This is incredible. How much—? I mean, what kind of payday—?" He cut off and cleared his throat, obviously wanting to know but not wanting to ask.

She smiled at him, still unable to believe the number herself. "Enough."

He impishly squinted at her. "Like *cover your basic needs* enough? Or like *let's buy a yacht* enough?"

She laughed and leaned into him as he wrapped his arms around her. "*Enough* enough, Chuck. But a yacht isn't out of the question." She quickly muttered the last part and buried her lips in his neck. He smelled so perfectly like *him* that she could have gotten drunk off it.

"So, what does this mean for us?" he asked, pulling back with an excited grin.

She pushed her hand through his tousled hair. "It means that money isn't an issue anymore." She looked over at the camera to make it clear that she was calling back to her declaration in the viral clip that instigated this whole journey and winked. Then she looked back at Chuck, the love of her life, and smiled. "And it means that I'll be with you, always, for free."

EPILOGUE

ONE BRIGHT, SUNNY L.A. day in September—the obnoxiously gorgeous kind that people pay through the nose to live in California for—the time had come for Olivia Martin to do something she'd been running from her whole life. Give an interview about her parents.

She sat out on her back patio, a sweeping terrace with a swimming pool that edged up to a lawn that then gave way to a hillside tumbling over into the basin below. Her and Chuck's house nestled like a jewel in the Hollywood Hills and had a view of the L.A. skyline, a distant, pointed tiara, from every room. A giant oak tree shaded half their yard. Olivia listened to its leaves rustle in the breeze, the birds chirping from its branches. As she gazed out at the spectacular, perfect day, she couldn't help thinking that the city was nodding on in approval—that her parents were nodding on in approval.

She took a steadying breath, a rare quiet moment to herself that she'd learned to steal whenever she could, and smoothed her hands over her skirt. Her life had done a one-eighty over the past two years, and although it still sometimes made her dizzy, she had a profound sense, a knowing deep in her heart, of being right where she belonged.

Thanks to the bombshell profile she'd written, the Izzy Ramírez film being a smash hit, and the endless offers that followed, Chuck had become a certified A-lister. A got-recognized-everywhere, paparazzi-followed-him-to-the-grocery-store, had-to-book-reservations-under-a-fake-name A-lister. He relished it. He ate up every moment of it and left no crumbs. But through it all, he always, *always* put Olivia first. Making sure she was comfortable with any public appearance, shielding her from any attention she didn't want, hiring her a bodyguard so people would leave her alone in public. When his name blew up and fans started camping out outside their apartment, which they'd identified from the viral breakup video, they bought a house in the hills behind a gate.

Olivia woke up in that house every morning now feeling at once like she was in a dream and like she was fulfilling a destiny buried in her heritage.

Chuck wasn't the only one who got recognized these days, though. Word was out that a documentary on Rebecca Martin, Bradley Harris, and Astrid Larsson's torrid love triangle was in the works. Not to mention, Olivia's book deal chronicling the same events had made news when it sold for seven figures. The book and the documentary would release in tandem the next spring, and the world would finally learn the truth about her parents.

Parker was helming the documentary, and the paycheck was obscene, of course. The likes of people who Parker and Astrid got to agree to participate kept driving up the production value. A-listers from the eighties and nineties who'd known Olivia's parents jumped on board once they knew Astrid was part of the deal and would finally be opening up. Olivia had had starry-eyed dinner dates with actors so famous, their only choice was to host them privately, and she'd left every one of them over-flowing with love and joy for learning more about her parents. She'd been given photos she'd never seen before and been told stories she'd never heard—things Grandma Ruby didn't even know. The whole experience unlocked a door she'd spent her life reluctant to approach, let alone consider opening. Because of it all, she knew more about the people who'd brought her into the world than she ever thought possible.

Now it was finally her turn to sit down in front of the camera.

The production crew had overrun the house, but Olivia had grown used to cameras and cords and assistants buzzing around. The chaos didn't make her as nervous as it used to, and that was largely due to Chuck purposely showing up to insert himself like a tonic every time things got hectic.

"Hey," he said from behind her now in the soft, warm tone that immediately dulled her nerves. Like honey in a strong tea.

She turned to see him crossing into the backyard from the living room doors flung wide open to the day. Like many houses in the hills, the entire back wall of their home was mostly glass doors and windows that provided an unobstructed view. The living room doors had become the throughway for the crew. They'd set up cameras and lighting panels under the pergola laced with wisteria. Olivia waited perched on a cushy patio chair for the filming to start. Gina the makeup artist had just finished dusting her nose and glossing her lips.

Even after years of seeing Chuck every day, Olivia's heart still did the bungee-jump hiccup at the sight of him. While she was trussed up in ready-to-wear runway and full makeup, he was at-home casual in a green tee shirt, loose shorts, and a pair of sandals that scraped the pool deck in a scratchy hiss when he walked. He was so stunningly perfect, it often overwhelmed her.

They'd spent the past two years fighting *for* each other instead of with each other. With counseling and hard work and learning to communicate, together they'd both become better versions of themselves and the partner the other person deserved. She didn't run anymore, and he didn't have to chase her. He'd also stopped trying to keep everyone happy all the time.

"Hey," she said back when he rounded in front of her chair. Francis, their French bulldog adopted from Astrid, skipped at his feet like a little heartbeat. Olivia felt him weave in and out of her ankles, his way of saying hello, before he trotted off to lounge in the shade.

Chuck gripped the chair's arms and leaned in. The scent of him, fresh, clean, spicy, hit her in a rush and forced her to straighten her posture. "You look amazing," he said after a hungry sweep of her appearance.

"Thank you. This dress is actually comfortable for once," she said, and gently tugged at the loose sleeves fluttering at her shoulders. To keep up with Chuck's exploding career, she'd attended many red-carpet events and forced her body into countless outfits that looked gorgeous on camera but really had no utility beyond standing still and having photos taken. Having Chuck remove them from her after any given event—in a hotel room, sometimes the back of a limo, or in their own bedroom—was always the highlight of the night in many ways.

"Always a bonus," he said with a grin before his face grew serious but tender. "How are you feeling? Are you ready?"

Olivia inhaled another deep breath, feeling sure of herself. "Yes. I am ready and I'm feeling good about this."

Chuck's mouth pulled up into the crooked smile he saved only for her. The one that popped the hidden dimple in his cheek and left her falling in love with him all over again.

Despite her freshly painted lips, she couldn't resist kissing him.

He kissed her back, still leaning over her, and smiled. And then he kissed her again, deeper and harder. He slipped his hand around her nape and parted his lips. The heat of his mouth moving against hers, the glide of his tongue, the nip of his teeth, made her forget that someone had just spent an hour making up her face and hair, and that there were dozens of people milling about their house.

She pressed a gentle hand to his chest and pushed him back. "Chuck, you're going to mess up my lips."

Her protest did not deter him in the slightest.

"Well, you shouldn't"—he paused to peck her lips again—"have made them so juicy, then."

She pushed him back with a laugh. Then she reached up and swiped her thumb over the pink smudges clinging to his mouth. "*Ugh*, now *yours* are juicy and mine are just smeared. I'm going to have to call makeup back in."

Right then, Maddy appeared with the bottle of water Olivia had requested. "We're almost ready to start shooting, Olivia. Here's your water. Hey, Chuck," she said pleasantly. Maddy and Chelsea had recently graduated from UCLA. They'd remained best friends and roommates, and Maddy was getting her feet wet in the industry again while Chelsea was starting in a local MFA program. They were both regular dinner guests at their house.

"Maddy, could you please tell Gina I need a touch-up because my husband can't keep his hands to himself?" Olivia said.

Chuck playfully smirked at her. "Be sure to tell her it's my wife's fault because she kissed me first," he said to Maddy.

The labels still sent her swooning. In true Olivia and Chuck fashion, their wedding had been an impulsive explosion but in the best way possible. Chuck had asked her to marry him the night the Izzy Ramírez movie premiered. She'd said yes, and two months later, they'd flown their loved ones to Maui for an intimate beachside ceremony. They'd exchanged vows with their toes in the sand, Chuck in a linen suit and Olivia in a fluttering gown with flowers in her hair. They'd honeymooned on the islands, and over a year later, Olivia was still adrift in the tropical glow of newlywed bliss.

"Sure thing," Maddy said, unfazed. "Oh, and Ms. Patel and Mr. Smith just arrived. They said they'll be in the kitchen when you've got a break."

"Thanks, Maddy," Olivia said.

In retrospect, it wasn't *too* surprising when Mansi brought Chuck's agent to their wedding as her plus-one. The two of them had been sneaking around together since that day way back in the *Name Your Price* office. When the show abruptly ended, Mansi hadn't shared the news of the new man in her life given that Olivia's world was in complete upheaval. Once things had settled, Mansi casually mentioned *this guy* she was casually seeing but failed to mention that it was Cameron. Turned out two quick-witted, sharp-tongued career warriors made an excellent pair.

"Oh, Maddy?" Olivia called after her. "Where's my grandma?"

"She's inside with hair and makeup. She'll be out soon," Maddy reported just as the phone in her hand rang. She answered it and headed back into the house, on a mission, like a seasoned PA.

Of course Ruby was going to be in the documentary too. Her daughter was the primary subject. She'd been hesitant at first, but Olivia's encouragement that she had the most unique and intimate perspective to share, along with Chuck's persuasive charm, ultimately won her over.

"Could you go check on her?" Olivia asked Chuck with a squeeze of his arm as the film crew spilled out from the house.

"Of course," Chuck said. He kissed the top of her head and smiled down at her. "You're going to be great."

She gave him a smile back, feeling a surge of confidence at his faith in her.

"Okay, gang, let's get rolling while the light is good," Parker said with a clap of his hands as he marched out onto the pool deck. Gina the makeup artist reappeared to touch up Olivia's lips with a knowing grin.

"Sorry," Olivia guiltily muttered to her with a flush.

"It's fine. I'd kiss him too if he were mine," Gina said with a wink.

And then the space cleared out around her, and it was just Olivia, a camera pointed at her, and the crew standing behind it.

But it wasn't just her. She wasn't alone. She was with her friends, her family, the spirit of her parents being brought back to life by those who knew and cared for them. And Chuck. The love of her life looking on like he was the luckiest man alive.

He shot her a smile, and she shot him one back. Her heart bungee-jump hiccupped once more, and she took a breath, ready.

"Quiet, please!" Parker called. He circled behind the camera with their director and gave Olivia a nod. "Okay, here we go. In three . . . two . . . one . . ."

ACKNOWLEDGMENTS

What a journey this book has been. The hook had been in my head for years, but the execution was another question. Of all the stories I've written, this one saw the most change. It's no exaggeration to say that the copy you're holding in your hands is the fourth major reimagining of it. The journey from the first draft to now would not have been possible without the guidance and thoughtful input (and patience!) of many people.

My agent Melissa Edwards, thank you for initially encouraging me to shape this book from a tangle of scenes into a coherent plot. Chuck and Olivia never would have made it off that sidewalk if it weren't for you! Thank you for sticking by me through it all and for your willingness to humor my wild ideas. My career would not be what it is without you.

My editor Cassidy Sachs, your thoughtful guidance pushed me to find the true heart of this story. I didn't know what I was trying to say until you helped me figure it out. I can't thank you enough for your patience, enthusiasm, and ability to make sense of imaginary worlds.

The team at Dutton: Christine Ball, John Parsley, Isabel DaSilva, Hannah Poole, Erika Semprun, Tiffany Estreicher, Daniel Brount, Vi-An Nguyen, Melissa Solis, Janice Barral, and Madeline Hopkins, thank you for giving my third book a home and helping make it shine.

My agent siblings, eternal thanks for the continued support, cheering, commiserating, and sharing of knowledge.

The group of fellow romance writers I've been lucky enough to meet in person, in particular, Fallon Ballard, Courtney Kae, Elissa Sussman, Ava Wilder, and Susan Lee, who've managed to make me feel like I belong not only on this wild journey but in this genre too. Thank you!

The entire romance writer community. Telling love stories is hard! I'm so grateful for the guidance, friendship, and unconditional excitement over each other's books.

The Bookstagram community. My favorite corner of the internet. Thank you for hyping, sharing, shouting, and loving all the books.

My local romance indies, Meet Cute Bookshop and The Ripped Bodice, thank you for giving authors and readers a place to come together and celebrate all things romance.

Donnoban Orozco, thank you for that day in the lab when I asked how much I would have to pay you to drink a tube of saliva (I WAS KIDDING), and you actually considered it. That moment planted the seed for this book about doing something truly undesirable for the right price, long before I ever had thought of writing it. Thanks for being the best lab manager ever, letting me listen to my Hannibal Lecter music while we ran samples, and keeping me from totally losing it during those days. You're one of the GOATs, friend. I can't wait to watch where you go in life.

Mansi Joshi, thank you for being one of the coolest boss girls I met in college and inspiring Mansi's namesake.

My friends and family fan club, thank you for preordering, traveling to events, selling my books to strangers, and for all the intangible support. It means the world to me.

The ride-or-dies, Natalie Bell and Nathan Grebil, thanks for letting me text you updates with news before I can share with anyone else, for always showing up, for cheering, for finding the most thoughtful and unique book swag/gifts, and for being amazing, truly priceless friends.

Natalie Bell, thanks for answering my medical questions.

My dad, thanks for answering my medical questions, and for inspiring Sam Walsh's love for a good yarn.

Both my parents, thanks for being excited over this whole publishing journey, no matter what.

My husband, thank you for offering me the sage advice of "just write a book that you love" when I was seriously struggling with this one. I probably wouldn't have finished it without you, and I do love it now. Thank you for the continued support, willingness to act out scenes with me so that I can correctly describe the blocking, and for being a steady hand as we ride this roller coaster together.

To all the readers, thank you for coming along with me on another journey.

Holly James holds a PhD in psychology and has worked in both academia and the tech industry. She loves telling stories with big hearts and a touch of magic. She currently lives in Southern California with her husband and dog.